DESTROYER

THE SHATTERED CITY
BOOK ONE

MEG SMITHERMAN

ROSE & MOTH BOOKS

Content warning: Death, violence, scenes depicting PTSD.

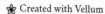 Created with Vellum

For my sister Rose

PROLOGUE

This is how the story went:

It was early morning in Ordellun-by-the-Sea in the Kingdom of Navenie. King Alaric II was wide awake. He had been awake for hours, unable to sleep. He paced about the city's central keep, stopping every once in a while to gaze out at the still-foggy waters of the sea. And always following in his wake was Taryel Aharis, royal advisor, sooth-sayer of a sort. In some stories he was called a mage, a sorcerer, a wielder of power. Some called him a healer.

Whatever his title, Taryel stayed a step behind the king, clinging to the shadows.

The two men stood in one of the keep's many chilly hallways. Cold bit at Taryel's fingers and nose. He followed as the king descended stairways, wound through corridors, until they were outside in the gray, fish-smelling cold of early morning Ordellun-by-the-Sea.

King Alaric proceeded to the city's central square, a short distance from the keep. It was quiet, the shouts of distant fishmongers drifting toward them from the port. And Taryel followed obediently in his king's wake.

A thick, fishy breeze wafted in from the water. A beggar woman, stifling a cough, dropped a curtsey to her sovereign, leaning so far forward in her deference that she nearly touched the damp cobbles with her lank hair.

The king's lip curled.

They came then to the center of the square; Taryel and the king stood now side by side, as if carrying out the steps of a dance.

King Alaric spoke then. His eyes were wide, rimmed in fire, the rising sun reflected in his gaze. "Festra wills it."

Taryel, the wind in his dark hair, remained silent.

Here is where the story gets murky. Academics have argued for centuries over what exactly happened next. Was it a feat of powerful engineering and chemical work? A combustion, far ahead of its time? But this isn't a story for academics — it exists outside of history, impossible to quantify, the bones of a memory, a suggestion of something that might have happened once, long ago.

According to most versions of the tale, it went something like this:

Taryel knelt on the dew-wet cobblestones, dark robes spreading around him like ink. He planted his hands, palm down, firmly on the ground. He chanted something unintelligible, and a great blackness exploded from his hunched form, as if night were gleaming outward from him, a reverse sunlight.

And then there was silence.

And then everything, everything — Taryel, King Alaric II, the beggar woman, the square, the keep, the city of Ordellun-by-the-Sea... all engulfed in complete darkness. There came a wave of impossible destruction, a rupture from the nucleus of Taryel.

And when the sun was finally able to break through that thick dark, days later — it was gone. The city of Ordellun-by-the-Sea had been demolished. Completely eradicated. Some called it the lost city, but it wasn't really lost.

It was shattered.

Taryel Aharis is known as many things — sorcerer, traitor, villain... genocidal maniac. But more often than not, he is called simply the Destroyer.

CHAPTER 1

A hot midday sun hung in the sky. Ruellian Delara squinted, pulling her brimmed hat lower on her head. The stiffly woven brim was so wide that it impeded her vision, but it didn't matter. She was focused on what lay at her feet.

Dig Site 33 was one of the Cornelian Tower's smaller sites. It was certainly the smallest that Ru had worked on — a cluster of dwellings, probably once a farmstead; it was a manageable expanse of building-shaped holes in the dirt, bits of wall protruding from the ground here and there.

Ru was crouched over an item she had just unearthed from the "ancient soils," as Professor Thorne loved to call it. One of several professors at the Tower, he looked at the Tower's archaeological digs as a source of amusement rather than serious scientific discovery. To him, and many other academics who studied at the Cornelian Tower, true learning came in the form of books and experiments. History had its uses, but progress... *that* was the future of science.

Ru, meanwhile, had always loved getting her hands dirty. She relished the grime under her fingernails, the hot sun on her back, the way soil fell away from curved vases, bowls, and plates, all shapes in the earth. Almost as if they were waiting for her — vessels that told stories, held memories long forgotten.

To Ru, there was a magic to the discovery of ancient lives. There was power in the souls that had come before. Connections were everywhere — energy flowed through every living being, the electric buzz of a nervous system, its billions of neurons firing. The beat of a heart. The clench and stretch of muscles.

But her love of history, of the ancient denizens of Navenie, went deeper than the notes she scribbled with charcoal, the sketches she made in her notebooks.

Ru now held her latest discovery, a large squat vase, and turned it slowly in dirt-caked hands. Even after centuries in the ground, it was in shockingly good shape. She couldn't begin to tell its original color. She would need to clean it first, gently and with purpose. But the vase was mostly whole, only a few shards were missing, a rarity among ancient artifacts.

This was Ru's fifth vase of Dig Site 33. She strongly believed that she'd been assigned to excavate a cellar of some kind. Perhaps herbs and spices had been stored here, in these vases. Or maybe, whoever had lived here in this farmstead was also a potter.

Maybe, Ru imagined, with the fervor only a true academic could feel with such a thought, every room in the house would contain similar items. A house of vases.

She would know soon enough. After she finished excavating what she thought was the cellar, she would move on to the next room. The thought of that centuries-old dirt waiting for her, concealing stories and histories, filled her with a low hum of excitement.

Discovery. Uncovering the unknown and the unknowable; that was what Ru lived for.

The breeze rose up, scattering debris up under Ru's hat and into her face. She coughed and sneezed in quick succession, rubbing her nose. Her oil lamp, unlit and perched precariously on a nearby rock, fell with a clatter.

A wind was coming in from the south, and would only grow as the day marched on.

"Water?"

Ru started, turning toward the voice.

She hadn't seen anyone approach, her hat's brim blocking her peripherals. She lifted the edge of the brim and saw the dirt-smudged face of Archie Hill, her friend and fellow academic.

Archie had come to study at the Tower the same year Ru had when they were nineteen. Most academics at the Tower were in their late teens or twenties, pursuing education and specialized research that couldn't be accomplished in the colleges of the capital city, Mirith.

And Archie, educated by a private tutor since childhood, had tired of the wealthy lifestyle and gone to the Tower for two reasons: First, the pursuit of higher education. And second, to get away from his family. Even so, from his speech to the way he carried himself, Archie's entire being simply screamed *aristocrat*.

But beyond that, something about his jovial nature, his inability to take anything seriously, had drawn Ru to him. She was, in many ways, the exact opposite of Archie. Where he was easygoing, she was uptight. Where he was happy to let things happen as they may, she was unable to operate without a plan. They worked in concert, then, balancing one another. Although they were constantly disagreeing about things.

The two had met in one of the Tower's libraries, both searching for books on ancient knives. Ru had been looking for sources to help her determine whether a knife she had found at Dig Site 15 was made for slicing bread or meat. Archie, meanwhile, had been hoping to determine what kind of knife would have been used by coastal merchants to skin fish in the 600s.

Archie and Ru had knocked hands when they reached for the same book at the same moment. Bursting into laughter, they had been friends ever since.

In their second year at the Tower, they brought a third into the group: Gwyneth Tenoria. She was a young woman from a noble family in Mirith, and like most of the noble families, she was very distantly related to the Regent of Navenie. But unlike most nobles, who oozed upper class with every breath, Gwyneth did a far better job of hiding her upbringing. She was far more interested in discussing her various hypotheses surrounding the domestication of livestock in the western coastal city of Solmaria.

Ru almost wished Gwyneth could be here, looking at vases with her in the sunlight. But Gwyneth had her own research to work on, and experiments to conduct in the labs of the Tower.

Archie grinned brilliantly. His own wide-brimmed hat was pushed back to hang behind him from his neck, his lightly curling hair blowing across his forehead. He had the pale green eyes of his family, and while his jaw could have cut glass, his lips were conversely full and soft. A dash of freckles fell across his nose.

He was handsome, and Ru had conducted her own experiments on those lips in the past. But they were short-lived, mainly for fun, and ultimately fizzled out. The only experiments between the two now were purely academic.

"You look absolutely parched," he said, waggling his water canteen, its leather marred from years of careless use.

Ru grabbed the canteen from his long fingers and took a deep, almost desperate swig. She hadn't realized how thirsty she was, how much time had passed while she'd been delicately brushing at dirt-caked ceramics with a tiny brush.

When she'd drunk her fill, she returned the canteen, wiping her lips with a dusty sleeve.

"You've guzzled all my water," said Archie, performing anger.

Ru only laughed. "Should have thought of that before you offered."

Archie wouldn't mind. In fact, Ru suspected he never truly minded anything she did. On the contrary, she knew he liked her. More than liked her. They had long since ceased falling into bed together, but she saw him; the way his eyes lit up for her, the way his smiles curved when she was near.

But he never made any attempt to rekindle the dalliance, which was a relief to Ru. He was one of her closest friends; she hated the idea of that changing. And anyway, he would move on soon enough. There were plenty of other girls at the Tower, most of them far prettier than Ru.

Ru knew that her looks were outstandingly average. Her brown hair was long and unruly, curling in the rain and going brittle in dry heat. She wasn't tall and elegant, nor was she petite and delicate like Gwyneth, who had no shortage of suitors. Her eyes were brown like her hair, her skin sun-tanned, and she rarely wore makeup. Her nose was slightly longer than she would have liked, her ears slightly larger. And her mouth, though her lips were full enough, seemed always to be curved downward in a slight frown.

None of it made much of a difference to Ru, though. Love and romance were very low on her list of priorities. She was wholly devoted to the life of academia for the time being, and that was how she liked it. She felt that she would never get bored of studying the lives of past civilizations, of the different ways in which people lived, lifetimes and lifetimes ago.

Even the thought of it, the secrets and stories she had yet to uncover, lit joy in her heart. Though the joy was never as bright now as it had been once — when she had allowed herself to study the subject that truly spoke to her soul.

"Hey," said Archie, indicating Ru's newly unearthed vase. Its mouth was wide enough for a hand to fit through, its belly even wider. He knelt to touch the thing gingerly, fingers brushing away a patch of dust. "What is this, your fourth this dig?"

"Fifth."

Hot wind ruffled Archie's hair, almost the same light tan color as the vessel in Ru's hands. "You think it's a potter's house?"

Ru shrugged. "Or a fancy cellar, maybe. Last year we found a house where someone had been storing food in what we thought were ceremonial urns."

Archie studied the vase, reaching out to run his finger along its rim. "I wish we could see them, you know. Just have a little glimpse. Go back in time and peek through the window."

Ru smiled. They always talked about what it would be like, to spy on the people who had lived in these homes. She thought it might be like peering into the house of a good friend, if said friend had no idea they were involved in the friendship. Immoral, impossible, silly... but she still wished she could do it.

Just then, a clamor arose from the square white tents that were posted at the edge of the site. Past the tents was the road, which wound eventually back to the Cornelian Tower.

The road had been quiet since Ru had arrived at Dig Site 33 weeks ago, but now was anything but. There was a muffled sound of hoofbeats on packed dirt, a jangling of metal, and a chorus of muffled voices.

Curious, Ru lifted the edge of her hat again, craning her neck to see the tents. She and Archie were crouched nearly all the way across the site from camp, and the sun was so glaring that it was difficult to see what was happening.

All Ru could see was the tents and their colorful flags, bright in the noonday sun. And then something else glinted, catching her eye. Squinting, she saw horses and armor, plumed hats, bright weapons.

"Odd," said Archie, setting down the vase. "What do you suppose the king's riders want from this dirt hole?"

"Maybe they're looking for a deal on vases," said Ru.

Archie laughed, seemingly purely by reflex.

Despite her joking, Ru wondered the same. The riders were an elite force, seldom coming to the Tower, let alone Tower-sanctioned dig sites. They were simply unneeded in the realm of academia.

It was possible that they wanted something from the professors who ran the site, some sort of historical task. Summons from the regency seldom cropped up, but when they did, the professors would always argue about who would have the honor of wearing the ceremonial Cornelian robes.

Whatever the riders wanted, it had nothing to do

with Ru. And she was far more interested in her vase. She picked it up, along with her smallest brush. It would take a while to clear the dirt from it completely, and the sun was already beginning its descent from the apex of midday.

"Ru!" Archie hissed, leaning closer. "They're coming."

She sighed, setting down her vase. She once again lifted her hat brim, and squinted out toward the tents.

Sunlight bounced painfully off the planes of the polished chest plates affixed to the fronts of two king's riders who made their way on foot toward Ru and Archie. Ru turned, looking behind her, thinking there must be a professor or someone important nearby. But the nearest academic was Buford Hennes, whose back was to them, clearly deeply engrossed in the ancient toilets he was unearthing.

Ru didn't understand. She and Archie crouched silently in the dirt, blinking, until the riders stood over them.

The riders were dressed in military attire, their trousers and jackets midnight blue, with black leather boots that went up to the knee. Tasseled silver epaulets perched on their shoulders, and white plumes burst from black felt hats. Over their uniforms, they wore plates of armor, strapped with leather across their chests, legs, and forearms. They towered over Ru and Archie like metallic trees, shining in the sun.

"Excuse me," said one of them. "Are you Miss Delara?"

Ru's breath caught. What could the king's riders want with her? Fear looped through her chest, dredging up old terrors and anxiety. Her father, a traveling merchant — had something happened? Her brother, placed precariously in the ranks of Mirith nobility, dealing in secrets and information — had an assassin's blade finally found its home in his neck?

Archie's hand found her shoulder, and with his touch, she breathed more freely.

Ru knew she had done nothing wrong. And if a member of her family had come to harm, if something tragic had occurred, the riders' faces would reflect it. She saw no lines of sympathy, no shining eyes to give her pause.

She stood, brushing dust from her worn trousers, acutely aware of how unkempt she looked, how unlady-like. She pushed her hat back until it fell down her back, dangling from her neck. Her hair was hopeless, a mess of dark waves, not worth smoothing or trying to contain just now.

Without her hat in the way, Ru could see the riders' faces more easily. They were a man and a woman, both dark-haired with solemn eyes. The woman was tall and formidable, with skin as dark as her hair. The man was pale, his oversized nose burnt red in the sun. Their hands rested casually on sword pommels, great long things with gold-trimmed scabbards that caught the sun's glare. Nowadays swords were outdated, the latest weapons being flint guns, horrible loud things that spewed smoke. But the regent preferred the elegance and accuracy of a blade, outfitting her men accordingly.

"I'm Ru Delara." The words felt heavy on her tongue, tinged with anticipation, with the remains of fear.

"Don't be alarmed," said the woman, clearly noting a waver in Ru's voice. "I'm Sybeth, and this is Lyr. We've come at the behest of Her Ladyship Sigrun."

Archie stood then, brushing dirt from his long-fingered hands. "The Regent?" he said, incredulous.

Ru reached for him, her hand tightening around his arm. "Are you sure I'm the right Miss Delara?"

"Yes," said Lyr, his eyebrows so thick and heavy they threatened to obscure his eyes altogether. "Ruellian Delara?"

The ground seemed to warp under Ru very slightly. This was an entirely new experience, a series of events she'd never foreseen or imagined. A contingent of King's Riders, sent by the Regent Sigrun herself. The reason was immaterial — Ru's body and mind would behave the same.

She was grateful for Archie's support, his steady

presence. He seemed far less affected by this turn of events. Eager, even.

"I'm Ruellian Delara, yes."

Lyr nodded briskly. "As I said. We've been sent to bring you to the Sh—" He stopped short as Sybeth elbowed him. He coughed, his brows lowering as he pulled himself together. "We're under orders to take you to another dig site. Your experience is needed there. You've been requested by name."

Ru and Archie turned to stare at one another. Their expressions were of mirrored disbelief. There were dozens of renowned scientists, philosophers, and artists whose work first came to light at the Cornelian Tower. Ru was not one of them.

"Sorry," said Archie, cutting through Ru's silence, "but I'm convinced you've got the wrong Ruellian Delara. Unless you need an expert on vases and vessels, which I can't imagine isn't readily available among the palace scholars."

Ru pursed her lips. Normally, she hated when Archie spoke for her. But now, so caught off guard and plunged into reticence, Ru was grateful for him.

Sybeth and Lyr glanced at one another.

"You are Ruellian Delara," said Sybeth, slowly, as if explaining to a child. "Daughter of Laurelian Delara."

"Yes," admitted Ru. Her unease expanded, filling her.

At Ru's admission of her identity, Sybeth nodded once. "Good. Then you're the one we need."

"Better confirm the paper," said Lyr, watching Ru with steady dark eyes.

That was it, then. The paper. Ru felt equal parts sick and embarrassed, almost on the verge of bolting. Not here, not now, not like *this*.

"Fine," said Sybeth. She reached into a pocket and pulled out a slip of paper, peering at it. Then she said, "Miss Delara, please confirm that you're the author of the academic text entitled 'From Sorcery to Science: A Study Of Particle Matter Dilation, The Transformation Of One Substance To Another, And The Transfer of Energy Between Invisible Lines, An Argument In Favor Of The Existence Of Magic.'"

For a brief moment, Ru closed her eyes. If she thought about her room in the Tower very desperately, the softness of her bed and the music of birds outside her window, maybe by some miracle she would open her eyes and appear there. Safe. Far away from the gazes of Sybeth and Lyr, from Archie's tensed shoulders and the leering academics in the distance.

Lyr raised an impatient eyebrow.

Something occurred to Ru then, a cruel thought. She spun, facing Archie. Anger welled up in her. "Is this a joke? Are you making a fool of me?"

It wasn't beyond the realm of possibility. Their friendship was lighthearted, full of mutual jabs and taunts. But neither of them had ever gone to lengths like this. Still, she couldn't wrap her head around another explanation. What else could this be but a joke?

Archie, though, gazed back with clear wide eyes. He shook his head. He, too, had gone slightly pale.

This wasn't a joke. Not one set up by Archie, anyway.

Ru, consumed by equal parts embarrassment and anger, turned her attention back to the riders. "Yes," she said, working to keep her tone steady. "I wrote that paper. But if this is some kind of prank set up by my brother Simon Delara, then please go back to Mirith and tell him I'm going to kill him."

The attempt at ironic hyperbole fell flat. The riders glanced at each other.

"Are we missing something?" asked Sybeth.

They were missing plenty. But Ru didn't want to go into it. She didn't want to go into the academic work she was most proud of, the work she'd put so much of her heart and mind into writing and researching. The work which, upon publication, was promptly maligned and dragged through the mud by what felt like every academic and intellectual in Navenie.

Because what sane scientific mind could possibly believe in *magic*?

Ru would never live that paper down. Its subject had

been the fire that lit her life, her passion project, and now... well. She had been a laughing stock for six months. And in that time, she'd done her best to fade into the background of academia. She'd turned her attention to archaeology and found a love for vases, old pottery, the lives of those who came before. She was happy, and even, sometimes, fulfilled.

And yet she hadn't entirely given up — she was quietly determined to write a follow-up to her paper one day, a hypothesis that she could *prove*. Something indisputable. She felt in her bones, in the quietest part of her soul, that magic, or something like it, had to exist. It didn't matter that she had never seen it. It didn't matter that no one had, that she had no reason to be so adamant. But this, the age of science and discovery... this couldn't be all there was. There had to be more.

Yet after all that, the humiliation and the crushing failure, here stood the King's Riders. Sent by the regent, who had sought her out by name.

"Why would you reference that particular paper?" Ru asked, ignoring Sybeth's question. "I've written half a dozen since. They were far better received."

"We were told to find the author of *that* paper," said Lyr, as if he couldn't understand why Ru was being so difficult.

"I'm a joke," she managed to say, despite the tightness in her throat as she said it. "My hypothesis was never proven. I failed."

"Sigrun seems to have taken the paper seriously," said Sybeth, her words tight with impatience. "Seriously enough that she requested your professional assistance. Will you come with us willingly?"

"Or do we have to carry you?" added Lyr.

Sybeth's lips pressed together in obvious annoyance.

"Can't you tell us what's at the other dig site?" asked Archie, speaking Ru's thoughts.

"Short answer?" said Lyr. "No."

"Long answer, we don't know," said Sybeth, clearly eager to leave. "Miss Delara, you will receive a full explanation upon arrival at the other site. I can promise you that."

"You'd be useless without one," said Lyr.

"Thanks," said Ru, voicing the word like a curse. She was hungry and tired from being in the sun all morning, and a strain threatened at the edges of her eye sockets. Bending over pottery, staring at small things up close, did a number on the eyes.

Yet despite her embarrassment, her anger, and everything else, she couldn't help but wonder why she had been summoned. What was at the other dig site? A flare of possibility was kindled in her momentarily. If the Regent sent for her based on *that* paper...

But no, she shouldn't hope. It was impossible. Magic, if it did exist, wasn't so easily spotted. If it was, she would have been able to show it to the world, write it down in ink. Surely, if something clearly magic had been uncovered, they wouldn't have sent for a single academic from the Tower.

No. It was too much to hope, even to consider.

"We need to hurry," said Sybeth, her hand flexing at the pommel of her sword. "We have a full day of riding ahead of us."

"Where's the site?" asked Ru, grasping at threads of reality. Anything to keep her grounded. Could she really just... up and leave? With no planning or notice at all?

"It's new," said Lyr.

"It's new," said Sybeth, "And we can't tell you. You'll have to come with us."

Ru felt like arguing out of stubbornness, but there would be no point. This was a summons from the regent. The King's Riders themselves had come to collect her. There was no arguing, no refusing. She would go.

"Fine," she conceded. "I'll come with you, but this had better not be an extremely elaborate trick to make me look stupid."

Archie walked with them to the tents. Most of the academics had gathered there to watch as Ru was escorted between the pair of shining riders. Even the professors were clustered together where four horses stood tethered. A third rider stood with the horses, looking harried as the professors plied her with questions. It was obvious to Ru from the glints in her peers' eyes, the frowns on the lips of her professors, that they had been told the reason for the riders' arrival.

When they heard Ru and the other riders coming, the professors all spun around as one.

"Delara!" cried Professor Obralle, shoving her way to the front. Short in stature but no less intimidating, she glared at anyone foolish enough to be in her line of sight. Pale pink hair was piled artfully on her head, vaguely resembling a pudgy swan, and her eyes sparked with accusation. "Are these people mad? Have they told you where they're taking you?"

Lyr and Sybeth bristled at this.

"Now, let's all take a breath," said Professor Cadwick. In contrast to Obralle, he was tall and spindly with a shock of white hair puffing up from his skull, a pair of tiny pince-nez perched on his arched nose. "There's no need to imply that Lady Sigrun's riders are taken by madness. We know the regent has nothing but respect for our work at the Tower."

"True," said Lyr, his hat's plume ruffling in the wind. Everyone ignored him.

In that moment, her peers chattering around her, the professors exclaiming incredulously, Ru wanted nothing more than to disappear into the earth. To be engulfed, like one of her vases, buried and hidden.

"Wait," said Grey Adler, dark-haired and sneering. Ru would have called him her nemesis if she was a more dramatic person. He, too, had come in from his excavation to witness the commotion. Like the rest of the gathered academics, he was windswept and covered in dirt, his expressive mouth curved in a self-righteous smirk. "Delara, are they being *serious*?"

Scattered laughter erupted from the gathered academics. The professors attempted to shush them with no success. Ru picked up a few choice words and phrases amongst the cacophony: … *magic… can't believe… foolish… they'd pick her?*

"I don't even know what I'm being picked *for*," snapped Ru, at nobody in particular. Avoiding the gaze of everyone around her, she felt her cheeks reddening and hated herself for it. She shoved her hands in her trouser pockets, fists clenched, and stared at her feet.

"Oh shut up everyone," said Archie, his clipped upper-class accent cutting through the laughter and confusion. "Aren't we supposed to be adults? Consider behaving accordingly."

Ru shot Archie a look. He shrugged as if to say, *you weren't going to do it, so...*

She wished he wouldn't stick up for her, not like that. It made her look weak, and it made him look even weaker. Academia was a lions' den of competition and animosity, everyone vying for an upper hand in any possible situation.

"He said if you can't say something nice," snickered Grey.

"Don't say a thing at all," finished Buford Hennes, who had come away from his ancient toilets to join in the fray. "I guess we're bound by nursery rhymes now."

Archie snapped back, his words cutting.

But Ru was done listening.

Her mind had moved on to what was yet to come, the vibrating unknown. If everyone wanted to bicker about her paper on magic, then fine. They could go right ahead. Even the professors were joining in now, attempting to quell the tide of sharp laughter and general animosity, a feat which they were used to attempting and seldom achieving. Academics could be exceedingly antagonistic if they put their minds to it.

"Excuse me," said Ru, sidling closer to Lyr.

The tall dark-haired rider looked like he was getting ready to draw his sword, so aggressive were the academics' antics. He turned at the sound of Ru's voice, relaxing slightly.

"Do you have water?" she asked. "I'm indescribably thirsty."

He nodded. "With the horses."

Ru thought about what would happen next. She

would wait for the academics' aggressive ire to die out, wait for their attention to sway back to her. And then she would say goodbye, awkwardly, avoiding direct eye contact, avoiding hugs, staring at the ground. She would say something pointless, like "goodbye for now," or "see you later." She would bite back tears, flaming with self-consciousness as everyone looked on, before turning to go.

Would it all be worth it? The hugs, the goodbyes, the stilted niceties… she decided with a sigh that she would rather avoid it altogether.

She nodded, too, matching Lyr's. "Right. Let's go."

She was glad that she had already been wearing her satchel of tools, otherwise, she would have had to make an embarrassing trek through the tents to gather her belongings.

It was the work of a moment — struggling into the saddle, watching the other riders leap onto their horses, the hot sun glinting on their armor. She willed Archie to look at her, to catch her eye. At last he did, first glancing around for her in the small crowd of academics and professors, then away toward the riders, until at last their eyes met. His brows raised slightly, his lips parting in shock.

She lifted a hand, a quick wave, her smile apologetic. *I'll see you soon*, she tried to say through expression alone. And while chaos reigned around him, Archie stood stock still, watching her, and finally he smiled as if to say, *Good luck then, Ru.*

He understood.

And then with a quick sharp cry, Sybeth marked their departure. In a flurry of hoofbeats and dust and the waning cries of surprise from the academics and professors, Ru and the King's Riders were off.

CHAPTER 2

R u hardly registered most of the journey to the mysterious new dig site, she was so deep in thought. It was now clear that something in the realm of perceived magic must have been discovered. Why else would they send for her?

The more she thought about it, the more it all seemed so silly. The last several decades had seen a great emergence of advanced, progressive thought in Navenie. Mirith, the capital city, led the charge in popularizing scientific discovery. While the Tower had been the center of scholarship and discovery for centuries and was widely considered Navenie's beating heart of education and progressive thought, it wasn't the only center of learning in the kingdom. Only in the last hundred years had science become fashionable to the upper crust of society.

Naturally, the regent's palace was host to countless intellectuals, inventors, authors, and all the brightest minds of a generation. She even had a contingency of her own royal scholars, collected from graduates of the Cornelian Tower, and more distant universities.

Yet the popular focus was always on hard facts, proven hypotheses. Even the study of astrology, a metaphysical science, was based on the celestial bodies. The concept of magic had no basis. Simply intuition, theory, and — in Ru's case — persistent, stubborn passion.

She had been given a horse to ride, a chestnut gelding named Sky. She wasn't overly fond of riding, but Sky was docile and patient.

The saddlebags housed a canteen of water and a generous amount of food, basic traveling gear, and even a change of clothes, which was a small luxury in the field. Ru was used to washing her own clothes while on site.

As they rode, despite the flurry of thoughts of magic and wonder that kept her distracted, Ru felt… not relieved… but free in some way. Ahead of her lay a great unknown, something that could be exciting, maybe even wonderful, if she allowed herself to hope.

They rode south, which was vaguely baffling to Ru. While there were bits of ancient civilization all over Navenie, ready to be dug up and studied, the direction in which they traveled was proven to be barren. Everything even close to the Shattered City had been completely vaporized in the Destruction.

But that was not worth thinking about. Not now. Thinking about the Shattered City, that strange stretch of land marked by a massive crater that was said to have once been a grand, beautiful city, always made Ru feel slightly nauseated.

When night began to fall, Sybeth stopped their small company for supper. The third rider, Rosylla, made a fire while the others brushed the horses.

"Can I help?" asked Ru, hovering by the fire while Rosylla set out the dinner things. She suddenly felt useless, pathetic. These were trained riders, accustomed to travel, to eating on the road. Ru was used to plush feather beds at best, and soft camp cots at the very worst. She had never learned to start a fire, and that fact — for the first time — filled her with shame.

Rosylla looked up, blinking in surprise. She had dark, kind eyes, a round face, and curling brown hair. She seemed younger than the other two riders, or perhaps it was just that her expression was so open. Friendly. "Oh no," she said, waving a calloused hand. "I can tell you're not used to riding. You need rest."

Ru, so out of her element she felt almost like a child,

settled herself on a log near the fire. She watched in silence as Rosylla tended to the fire before pulling packets of food from her pack. The rider's movements were efficient, clipped, confident. Ru wondered if she looked like that while uncovering her vases as if she knew what she was doing.

She doubted it. Even though she loved archaeology, and felt so much fondness for past lives, there was something forced in it. Magic was her first love, the reason she had gone to the Tower to study. She imagined herself as Rosylla might see her, crouched in the sun, dirt-caked and sweating, her skin tanned and peeling in places.

But would her fingers move without thought? Would her dark eyes reveal a surety that she didn't always feel?

"Hungry?" said Rosylla, drawing Ru from her thoughts.

The rider had spread out a modest but surprisingly varied selection of cured meats, flatbread, and four oranges. Lyr and Sybeth came to join them by the fire, and tucked in without preamble.

Ru reached for her dinner with awkward reluctance. She had never dined with King's Riders before. Were there rules? Expectations? But the riders seemed completely unconcerned with formalities, so Ru followed their lead.

"You really have no idea why they've sent for me," said Ru, more a statement to confirm than a question. "Me, a scholar of magic and ancient pottery."

The riders shared a glance. "We weren't informed of it," said Sybeth, firelight dancing on her dark skin. "We're not paid to make conjectures."

Ru frowned. She hadn't expected an explanation, but the question wouldn't leave her alone.

"You said this new dig site is a day's ride away?" Ru asked.

"Correct," said Sybeth. "And we need to keep moving."

With breathtaking efficiency, the riders put out the fire, gathered up the remains of dinner, and packed it all away within a matter of moments. Ru stood watching on the sidelines, feeling like a dead weight. She was relieved when it was time to ride out. Sky was a comfort now, and expected nothing of Ru but occasional neck pats.

As they rode through the dark, stars winked down between the trees, and Ru found herself feeling strangely lonely. She was used to being away from family, but in the years since she'd come to the Cornelia Tower, her life had been crowded, full of academics and professors. Even with three riders in her company, she felt alone.

The road wound ever southward, toward the southern coast of Navenie, where Ordellun-by-the-Sea, the lost city, had once been.

After a while, Ru found herself riding alongside Rosylla. She liked the curly-haired rider with her unaffected smiles and open nature. Rosylla was very unlike the other riders: Sybeth, whose tall figure radiated confidence and power, and then ever-frowning Lyr, whose stern jaw spoke of quiet competence.

Rosylla brought a packet of sweets out of her pocket and began tossing them to Ru as they rode, the two of them giggling as the sweets bounced off Ru's nose. It was a welcome distraction from what felt like a growing weight on Ru's shoulders, a gradually heightening dread of the unknown and possible humiliation.

But as the night wore on, everyone became quieter as they rode, and Ru found it extremely difficult to stay awake. She caught herself nearly falling out of Sky's saddle twice, the second time only avoiding a painful tumble by getting her foot caught up in its stirrup.

"You academics don't get out much," said Lyr, after Ru had finally managed to right herself in the saddle.

"It has nothing to do with that," said Ru, annoyed. "I'm half-asleep."

Wordless, Lyr handed her a small flask full of liquid that smelled horribly pungent.

"What is that, rotten coffee?" Ru grimaced as he brandished it under her nose.

"You're not far off," he replied. "Better though."

She downed a great swig with a cough, and even though it burned her throat and made her heart feel like it was just shy of exploding within her, it kept her awake enough to avoid a fall from her horse.

~

MORNING BROKE OVER A DESOLATE LANDSCAPE. The earth all around them was black and mostly flat as if a massive burning fist had flattened the land for miles around them. Ru turned to see the distant gold-streaked peaks of mountains, kissed gently by first sunlight. There was a blueish blur that had been trees and forest, to the north and stretching east.

The road had, at some point in the night, narrowed from a well-traveled packed dirt thoroughfare to a winding track that disappeared and reappeared at random. Ru could already feel the sea air, its humidity causing her hair to curl as a damp breeze washed over them.

Ru peered ahead into the purpling gloom, watching as it lightened to blue and then pink, their shadows reaching out like dusky fingers on the black land. As the sun rose, as they plodded forward, their destination became clear. In fact, it was impossible not to notice. Ru had never been this way, had never seen anything in person, but she had read so many texts and seen so many artistic and scientific depictions that there was no doubt in her mind.

They were approaching the Shattered City.

"Don't see that every day," said Lyr, indicating the same thing Ru had just seen: far ahead of them, so far it was difficult to gauge the size, a jagged chunk of rock jutted out from the earth, angling toward them like a finger, pointed forever away from the sea. It marked the edge of the crater, the site of the Destruction. Once, the city of Ordellun-by-the-Sea had stood there, shining and vivid. Now it was gone, the land barren, only the odd remains of its walls and buildings left jutting from the land as hints of a horrific explosion.

Everyone remained silent. Ru pulled a stale cinnamon bun and an apple from the depths of her saddlebag. She held out the apple for Sky and ate the cinnamon bun with slow precision. If she focused her mind on this, the consumption of her breakfast from start to finish, she could avoid the other thoughts, the worries that clamored for attention.

Ru's pulse thrummed; her breaths rose shallow in her chest.

When the cinnamon bun was gone, she set about mentally solving a math problem. The orderly calm of math, of logic, steadied her. She thought she might be able to calculate how many steps Sky had taken since they left Dig Site 33. She counted the number of steps he took in the space of a minute, multiplied by sixty to make an hour. She had to round down slightly, as she was sure they'd been trotting for a stretch of road, and—

"Hey," said Rosylla.

Ru started. She hadn't noticed the woman come up beside her as they rode.

"I came to check on you," said the rider, holding out a canteen, its strap flapping in the breeze. "You look catatonic. Coffee? It's cold, but it'll do the job."

Ru shook her head. Her heart didn't need another reason to speed against her ribs. "I'm fine."

"You look... a little peaky."

"I'm fine," repeated Ru, knowing full well that she wasn't. She didn't like being here. She wanted to turn around and flee. Whatever they were doing here, whatever this dig site uncovered, Ru wanted nothing to do with it. The Shattered City was a graveyard. Cursed. A memory of nightmares.

Rosylla's face softened. "Is this your first time at the crater?"

They were passing another piece of rock that seemed to burst outward from the earth, its shadow falling alongside them. She stared uneasily at it, at its obvious nature — man-made, probably a chunk of wall, with some lines between bricks of stone still visible. The elements had smoothed it over countless centuries, lessening its brutality.

But Ru was no less struck by it, her gut no less sickened.

"Yes," Ru replied belatedly, the words thick on a dry tongue. Of course she had never been here. Travel to the Shattered City was forbidden by law unless you had special dispensation from the regency. Had Rosylla been here? The rider seemed so light, so calm, as if she watched the sun rise over enormous fingers of stone every day.

She glanced at Ru. "It can be a bit... off-putting. I got a stomach ache the first time I saw one of those rocks up close."

Ru swallowed roughly. "They're... the remains of the city. Fragments, blown outward. I've seen illustrations, but... none of them really capture it." Her skin crawled as more of the massive stones came into view, their shadows reaching for her across dark terrain. Ru felt the telltale wash of blood leaving her face, and her vision swam.

And even though she dreaded seeing the crater, she felt equally drawn to it. Her heart quickened as if she had been waiting to come here, the hairs on the back of her neck prickling with fear, and... what felt like anticipation. And as she rode, gazing toward a destination she couldn't see, she felt as if something inside her was just now waking up.

The feeling terrified her. Not because it felt wrong — on the contrary, in fact. She felt a pull toward the crater, a touch that was somehow strange yet familiar.

"Do you want to talk about something else?" asked Rosylla. The wind picked up and the rider lifted a hand to her hat, its plume fluttering wildly.

Ru nodded, swallowing thickly. "Yes please."

"Right," said the other woman. "I heard you believe in magic. Is that true?"

The cinnamon bun roiled in Ru's stomach. That touch in her mind, the strange pulling sensation, grew stronger as they rode. She gripped the reins until her knuckles whitened. Her horse jostled beneath her with every step.

Ignore it, she thought. *You're imagining it.* A sweat broke out on her neck, her upper lip.

If she were to round down for the times when Sky trotted, calculating roughly three trots throughout the trip, possibly one canter, and then an hour for supper—

"I've said the wrong thing, haven't I?" said Rosylla, when Ru didn't reply. "It's all right. Never mind. Let's see... Do you like croquet? It's all the rage at the palace."

Ru wished with every fiber of her being that she was in a tended garden right this moment, held within the structural confines of a flouncy, corseted gown, chasing little wooden balls through decorative topiary. Instead, she was here, with this... this compulsion taking hold of her like a finger pulling at her consciousness, drawing her forward with an urgency she couldn't understand.

Nausea rose in her gut with every step. Blood roared in her ears. The sky pressed down on her like a weight.

Come to me, a voice seemed to say. No, not a voice... a thought, a feeling. Calling out for her.

Swallowing bile that rose in her throat, Ru glanced at Rosylla. Did the rider feel it too?

But Rosylla only smiled, her brows drawing together in slight concern as she took in the sight of Ru.

Understandably, Ru thought — she must look ghastly, the sweaty sheen of her sickly pale face, hunched over the neck of her horse as if her life depended on staying in the saddle, resisting the call.

"Ru?" Rosylla said, but her voice sounded as if it was coming from miles away.

Then Ru heard the rider call something to the others, heard her own name amidst a jumble of muffled nonsense. The roaring in her ears was doubling, trebling, and as they all slowed to a snail's pace, everything reached a fever pitch. Darkness filled Ru's vision. Her balance wavered. Stars flickered at the edges of her sight.

"Forward," she managed to say. She kicked feebly at Sky. She had to keep going. She didn't know why. She didn't know what was happening to her beyond a deep, desperate need to go toward the crater. Every particle of her body felt the pull, felt instinctively that she needed to hurry toward the Shattered City.

"Have to go," she gasped, eyes closed against the confusing pain, the compulsion. "Faster."

Ru heard hoofbeats and muffled voices. Sybeth's voice, close by, asked a question, and Rosylla replied. She couldn't parse their words over the roaring in her ears.

Come to me, said the voice. Was it her own, or something external?

I have to keep going, she thought. *I'm needed.*

These thoughts were meaningless, overbearing in their insistence. Yet something kept pulling at the core of her, pleading with her, beckoning.

And more than anything, deep down, she wanted to obey.

"Faster," she mumbled. She was conscious enough, cognizant enough to follow the pull, the heat of it like wildfire, rushing forward.

With all her strength, she kicked at Sky with her heels. Instantly, as if waiting for the command, he shot forward at a gallop.

There was a flurry of voices and hoofbeats as the riders set off after her, but Ru didn't care. All she knew was that she was going in exactly the right direction. She was heeding the call.

As she sped toward the Shattered City, the wind in her dark hair, the voice in her mind, the compulsion... it gradually began to fade.

CHAPTER 3

The Shattered City waited by the sea. The name was misleading — there was no city here, only a miles-wide crater lined with jutting fingers of ruin that seemed to erupt from the ground. The stories said the stones had been flung aloft with the force of the Destruction, the explosion that decimated Ordellun-by-the-Sea ages ago. And when they plunged back to earth, some were large enough to stay intact, to avoid vaporization, all flung outward from a central point.

These were the gravestones of thousands of lives cut short, of a city lost to memory.

The center of the crater itself was mostly flat, but as they galloped toward its edge, Ru could see a cluster of white shapes near its center.

The weight on her shoulders, the rising nausea, and the intense pull... it was nearly gone now. It had faded almost immediately as their pace sped. Now she slowed, concerned for Sky, the strange call in her mind nothing but a distant whisper.

The riders pulled up beside her in a rush, their horses' hooves kicking up clouds of black dust. As they did, she saw them shooting each other meaningful looks. Ru could guess their meaning: *This girl is mad.*

She would have explained everything to them as they rode, laid out a logical explanation if she had understood it herself. Was it magic, the pull she'd felt? And if so, could magic affect the nervous system, the mind, or the workings of the body? Ru wanted to delve deeper into the possibilities, but part of her didn't want to think about it at all. Most of her, in fact, was afraid. Her reaction, this inner voice calling her toward the crater... she had never felt anything like it.

And if she told anyone, admitted to what she'd felt, what she'd heard in her mind, they'd call her mad. She would lose the last shreds of credibility tied to her name, and her academic career would be over.

She would keep this to herself, then, until absolutely necessary.

When they finally descended the crater's edge into the Shattered City, overwhelming in its devastation, she was overcome with relief. There remained an itch in her head, an echo of the feeling that had been telling her to keep going, keep moving. But now that she was here, riding through a forest of wall fragments and broken turrets, that itch had gradually lessened until it was gone.

No one spoke as they rode. As if this was a graveyard; out of respect for the dead. Ru reached out to touch one of the stones as they passed, worn by harsh winds, and shivered as her finger brushed against the rough, hot stone.

The sun was high in the sky now, and despite a steady breeze from the ocean, the day was already sweltering.

Eventually, it became clear that the cluster of shapes Ru had seen in the center of the crater was actually made up of tents. Similar to the ones at Dig Site 33.

"Is this dig sanctioned by the Cornelian Tower?" she asked, grateful to be distracted with solid things. Real things.

The riders all turned to her, eyebrows raised. This was the first Ru had spoken since nearly passing out, since leading their pell-mell gallop to the Shattered City.

"Is what?" said Lyr.

"Are you taking me to a Tower-enforced research site?" clarified Ru. As far as she was aware, the Tower oversaw every archaeological dig in Navenie, at least technically. The regent's scholars kept their research to the laboratories and libraries of the palace, where they could be easily overseen and directed.

"No," said Sybeth. "This dig is sponsored wholly by the regency. Not many know it exists."

Ru wasn't shocked, but the truth of it made her uneasy. Why would the regency fund their own dig, forgoing the Tower's resources? Only a need for secrecy explained something like this, and secrets put her teeth on edge. She twisted the reins more tightly around her fingers, involuntarily shivering as she gazed out over the expanse of ruined earth. Now that the strange prickling in her head, that inexplicable call, had faded to background noise, she allowed awe to take over.

She was quickly overtaken by the truth of the situation: she was *here*. At the Shattered City. The site of the lost Ordellun-by-the-Sea, the shining city. She'd never imagined she would see it, let alone ride through the legendary crater toward a secret dig site.

"I've been wanting to study this place for ages, you know." Her words came unbidden, an exhale of truth.

Sybeth and Lyr continued riding in silence, their stern countenances silhouetted against a clear blue sky.

"Did you think such a thing impossible?" asked Rosylla, expression earnest.

"Nothing's impossible," said Ru.

～

THEIR SMALL COMPANY approached the dig site just past midday. They had made good time, according to Sybeth. No one mentioned it was due to Ru's mad gallop to the crater — the strangeness of her reaction had everyone on edge, not least of all Ru. She thrummed with the remnants of that need to hurry, to be near whatever had called to her.

Had she imagined it?

Maybe she had simply felt an urge to move forward, to move through the frozen graveyard of an old city.

Fear, panic, anxiety, her own inner voice... they could have worked together to send her over the edge, to believe something that simply *wasn't*.

Whatever the truth, Ru wanted to forget it. Pretend it never happened. Believing in magic was embarrassing enough, but to fall into madness as well? She would simply have to disappear altogether. The humiliation would be unbearable.

Then a commotion arose as they rode up to the dig site, dismounting at the edge of the tents. Shouts came from beyond the tents, and Ru craned her neck to see what lay beyond. She saw nothing but dirt, tents, the usual archaeological accoutrements.

A circle of armed King's Guards stood around the perimeter of the dig, their armor shining bright. "Who goes there?" said the nearest guard. His tone was friendly and open; he clearly recognized members of the King's Riders.

Sybeth strode forward, saluting him. Then she removed her black felt hat, its plume whipping against her shining chest piece. "Sybeth, charged with escorting Miss Ruellian Delara, as ordered by the Lady Regent Sigrun."

The guard peered at Ru, who stood partially obscured by the riders. The wind chafed her cheeks, her hair whipping across a cold nose. She was here, now. Finally. She wanted desperately to see the dig site, to get her hands dirty, to find out what she was meant to see here. To find out why they'd sent for her.

"Right," said the guard, eyeing Ru.

She was suddenly aware of her appearance, which was anything but presentable. She still wore her usual field clothes — utilitarian trousers, shirt, boots, and waistcoat. Her satchel of digging supplies was slung across her chest, and her hair, loose and flowing, was also tangled beyond belief. Self-conscious, she pushed her hair behind her ears and brushed her palms across her waistcoat. She coughed as a cloud of dust rose from her as she did.

While the guard eyed Ru, unconvinced, a woman

came striding from around the corner of the nearest tent. She was sun-browned like Ru, coated in a fine layer of dirt, and her black hair was pulled back in a tight bun. A satchel of clanking tools hung from one shoulder. She looked every bit the field researcher, much like Ru, except that she carried herself with the confidence of an aristocrat. Her thick dark brows arched in a way that said she had everything under control.

"Well?" she said to the guard, words clipped. "Are you going to let them in, or are you planning to make them stand out here all day?"

"Apologies, Lady Maryn," said the guard. "Only, I wasn't informed—"

"You've been informed as of now." Lady Maryn turned to Ru, meeting her gaze despite the glare of the sun. "Miss Delara. I'm pleased you managed to come. Your expertise may be exactly what we need. We seem to have unearthed something that... well. You'll want to see it for yourself."

Ru's thoughts seemed to freeze in time for a split second. *Unearthed something.* The reality struck her like lightning. Something buried beneath the Shattered City, in what should have been a completely barren wasteland. Something strange enough to warrant outside help, help from a woman who believed in magic.

She swallowed, her mouth suddenly dry with anticipation.

"What did you find?" Ru asked. She gripped the strap of her satchel with both hands, trying to ground herself.

Maryn's lips thinned. "An artifact. You'll see momentarily. Sybeth, help her with her things, please."

Ru's head spun. In a day, she had gone from one dig site to another, her world tilting ever so slightly on its axis, as if it would never be the same again.

She gathered her things from the saddlebags — her hat, and some leftovers from supper. Then she patted Sky on the nose and whispered a thank you to the horse.

She turned to the riders, who stood by their horses as if waiting for an order. "Will you stay for the night?" Ru asked. She was suddenly afraid to be separated from them. Brief though their time together had been, the riders were a source of stolid reassurance, a reminder of everything rational and regimented.

"The King's Riders will depart immediately," said Lady Maryn, overhearing. "They have not been cleared to enter the site."

"But they rode for an entire day," said Ru, stopping short. "Surely they—"

Lady Maryn interrupted. "They will be fed, horses watered, and sent on their way. They are free to set up camp wherever they desire, outside of the crater."

Sybeth nodded curtly, clearly expecting this. Ru frowned, watching as Sybeth motioned her colleagues to take care of their business quickly.

Then Ru turned to Rosylla, who held out her hand for a shake. Ru pulled her in for a hug instead, her heart seizing slightly.

"Be safe," she said in the other woman's ear.

"Always am," said the rider. "Good luck, Ruellian."

Too quickly, Ru was ushered away from the three riders. She had come to consider them, in so short a time, almost friends. Her heart ached. She missed the Tower, the familiarity of its corridors and stairways, the ever-present smell of leather-bound books. The Shattered City was so vast, so unwelcoming, and none of these guards or researchers — bustling though the site may be — were familiar to Ru.

Lady Maryn either had no interest in Ru's discomfort or didn't notice it. She was all business, taking Ru's shoulder with one hand and leading her past the guard, past the circle of tents and into the dig site at last.

As they made their way into the site, a slight caress of emotion pulsed against the deepest recesses of Ru's mind. A reminder, a confirmation that the internal pull toward the crater had been real — not just a flare of panic. She bit her lip, focusing on Lady Maryn's confident gait, the packed earth at her feet, the murmur of voices, the ocean's breeze in her hair. Tangible things.

They approached a small group of researchers, dressed much like Ru and Lady Maryn, standing in a cluster at the center of the dig site. A few of them hurried forward to greet them with handshakes and nods. They all seemed excited, on edge, or both. Their eyes were wide, their bodies practically vibrating with… *was* it excitement? Or contained dread?

Ru shook their hands, introducing herself to each of them. She wondered if they felt like she did, frightened but eager. Their restless movements and bright expressions said they did. She was grateful that no one seemed to mind that she was a joke in the academic world, the woman who had set out to convince everyone of the existence of magic, only to fail completely.

"There's no time to waste," said Lady Maryn, putting a curt stop to the handshaking and empty pleasantries. Her sharp gaze alone settled everyone into an anticipatory silence.

When all was quiet, the wind in the tents the only sound, Lady Maryn spoke again. "Show her."

An excited murmuring rose immediately, the researchers glancing at one another, sharing wan smiles or apprehensive looks. As they did so, they parted, leaving space for Ru to walk between them. To what, Ru had no idea. Her chest felt tight as if she might cry or take off running.

She felt, ridiculously, that whatever lay beyond them had been waiting for her. That *it* was the voice that had called to her.

Lady Maryn held out a hand, encouraging Ru to step forward.

"Don't touch it," she warned, as Ru started forward, heart in throat. "We'll set you up with equipment later, everything you'll need. But I want you to see it first."

Ru hardly registered these words. The murmur of the researchers faded to a low hum. Her eyes landed on a dark earthen hole beyond them, deep as a grave but circular, shadowed in its depth. Her feet moved of their own volition, and she continued forward as if in a trance.

That strange feeling again took hold of her, pulling, encouraging.

When she came to the edge of the hole, heart pounding, she paused. She was breathless, aching with anticipation, like a lover on the edge of climax. She felt as if she should jump bodily into the hole. She believed that she might have actually done it if Lady Maryn's warning wasn't still ringing in her ears.

And yet, despite the pull she felt in her core, Ru was afraid to look. Terrified to peer down into the strange gloom where the sun — even so high in the sky — didn't seem to reach. As if she might see an ultimate truth there, an answer to a question she didn't want to ask.

"Well?" said Lady Maryn.

Ru, startled, turned away from the hole. She saw the gathered researchers, watching tensely, their expressions mirroring her own. Lady Maryn stood in front of them, arms crossed over her chest.

"What?" Ru said, feeling stupid, her brain working wine-slow, as if intoxicated.

"The artifact," said Lady Maryn. She was frowning, worrying at her lower lip. "Take a look. We'd like to know, based on your professional opinion, whether or not it's magic."

CHAPTER 4

What is fate? What cords that run through time and space, through souls and living matter, draw us together or apart? What alchemy guides us through our lives from birth to death? Is it random? Or is it guided by an unseen force?

Ru had asked these questions before, but never deeply or intensely. Rather, she asked in passing, wondering as she fell asleep, in boredom, or when she woke in the night and felt alone. Maybe that was what drew her to the concept of magic, the peeling back of the known to reveal an unplumbed depth. So much of the world was a mystery. So much of science was obscure, an equation yet to be solved.

Even the Destruction, the cause of it, King Alaric and Taryel Aharis, figures more of myth than history. Yet, here she stood, where a city had once been. How did the pieces fit together? What science, what mathematical formula, explained a city's total destruction, countless generations ago?

Perhaps Ru had always been asking, seeking an answer to those questions. What lay behind the meaning? Did unseen forces push and pull us as we stumbled through existence?

Something snapped in her, then, when she knelt at the lip of the hole, knees in the dirt. A brief wonder. Clarity of thought. For a split second she knew, more clearly than she had ever known anything, that she was meant to be here.

A pull on her mind, her heart, whatever it was, told her she was right. A pull that came from the darkness, from whatever lay in that excavation of the earth.

There were no lights to illuminate the cavity. Whatever they'd dug up had been left exactly where they found it. She wondered if it had been touched at all, aside from with brushes. With gentle gloved fingers. They were afraid of it, whatever it was. Afraid and excited, in the way someone would be after seeing a ghost, or magic.

Ru felt neither excited nor afraid. She felt... right. Correct. As if there were no alternatives; everything converged on this moment.

"Well?" said Lady Maryn. "What do you think?"

Ru squinted, lifting a hand to block the sun's glare. Eventually, her eyes adjusted, cutting through the shadows, and she saw it.

"I think it's a fossilized head," came another voice.

"Shush," said a third.

But she ignored them, gazing silently at the thing. It lay quietly, almost the exact color of the earth around it: a black rock. As her eyes adjusted further, she saw that it wasn't quite the same. It was darker, more pure. A rich, smooth black, like obsidian. It was slightly misshapen, quite small, maybe the size of a man's fist, with no sharp edges. Obviously not a fossilized head.

It called to her and she wanted to answer. She yearned to jump into the hole and touch it. To hold it to her chest, run her fingers along its curves. Some unknown part of her understood now that her distance from the object had been causing her nausea, the pain in her head. As if it needed her to meet it at just the right moment, to gaze upon it at some pre-arranged time.

Now that she was here, there was only a gentle touch against her thoughts. And while it seemed tethered to her in some way, anchored to the base of her consciousness, the pull was no longer sharp and needy. It was unsettlingly... comforting.

I found it, she thought. *At last*. But there was no further realization, nothing to explain what it was, or where these feelings came from.

Ru shook her head, squeezing her eyes shut as if to dislodge an unwelcome thought. This thing had to be magic. It had to be. These thoughts, as if fate had drawn her here, as if a rock were speaking to her? It didn't make sense. Nothing had made sense since that morning when the Shattered City came into view.

"Well?" Lady Maryn said for the third time, her tone impatient. She came forward to crouch beside Ru, fixing her with a stern gaze. "You've been peering at the thing for five minutes without speaking a word."

"Sorry," muttered Ru. In fits and starts, she became more clearly aware of where she was, and pulled her attention away from the stone to focus on her surroundings. But five *minutes*? It had felt like five seconds. A brief moment of connection with an inanimate artifact. "I've never seen anything like it, Lady Maryn."

She wanted to call it beautiful, but bit her tongue. It should be terrifying. A strange artifact uncovered in the Shattered City, a stone that seemed to reach into Ru's thoughts and feelings, affecting her psyche with disturbing ease. It *should* be terror incarnate.

Then why couldn't she tear her gaze from it?

"We've all read your paper on magic," said Lady Maryn, matter-of-fact. "Made a point of it. We have a theory about the air around this thing. The particles, you might say. It made our technology go haywire." She paused, pulling a watch from her waistcoat pocket and flipping it open with a metallic *ping*. "Only... it seems to have stopped, now you're here."

Ru didn't want to delve into what that might mean. Not now, anyway. Turning to face Lady Maryn head-on, she blinked at the change in brightness. "Have you noticed any other properties that might suggest magic? An inexplicable pull, for instance. Or an inner voice."

Lady Maryn shook her head, a wrinkle forming on her brow. "Nothing like that. Why?"

"Trying to narrow it down," Ru said vaguely. Then

she was the only one who felt so intensely when she was near the artifact, the only one who felt… drawn to it. Her stomach tightened. She glanced over her shoulder at the gathered researchers, watching and listening intently. Tents shuddered in the breeze. "The artifact could have been emitting a kind of frequency," she said, low enough so that only Lady Maryn could hear. She sat back on her heels and wiped her hands on her trousers. "That could explain any clockwork mechanisms acting strange."

Lady Maryn nodded, listening, brows drawn together. "I've never seen or heard of anything like it before," she said at last. "And my people don't like it. Other than its effect on our devices, there's definitely something about it. Something beyond our experience, something…"

"Magic?" Ru finished, raising a dark eyebrow.

Lady Maryn nodded, a dip of the chin. "So we asked for an expert."

Ru gnawed at the inside of her lip. "And the Lady Regent," she said, "she agreed to this? She read my paper?" It was difficult to stay focused on the conversation. The stone was so near, and even though she did her best to ignore it, she could feel its pull against the edges of her mind, as if waiting for something. As if she were tethered to it, from mind to stone.

"Apparently so," Lady Maryn replied, pushing a loose piece of hair behind her ear with distracted impatience. "Although I'm told the regent's advisor brought it to her attention. He's a man of science. Everyone is these days. Beyond that, we're all in the dark."

She coughed suddenly and stood, offering a hand to Ru. "Well, you've seen the thing now. We'll set it up for a proper inspection, if you don't believe it will cause us any harm to do so. And in the meantime, you and I will lunch."

Ru allowed the other woman to help her to her feet, stumbling slightly, her legs partially numb after crouching for so long. The researchers were beginning to peel away in small groups now, seeing that Ru was finished with her initial assessment. Yet they hovered outside their tents, eyes still catching on Ru, making her uneasy.

She didn't like being the expert. She wasn't used to being the center of attention. The strangeness of it rankled. Despite everything the riders and Lady Maryn had said, the reassurances, the summons from the regent herself, it all felt precarious, unreal. As if a stiff wind could come and blow it all away, revealing Ru to be the laughingstock she truly was.

Yet the feeling she'd had at the edge of the darkness, gazing down at that smooth black stone... had it been real? A touch against her mind told her that it had.

A pair of researchers approached carrying tongs, digging tools, a rolled-up blanket, and a small woven basket.

"Ah," said Lady Maryn, "good. Get the artifact out of its hole and safely inside. Miss Delara will conduct her inspection after she's fed and rested. If it's safe to do so, that is."

"I don't think moving it will harm anything," said Ru. "It doesn't appear volatile. But use caution."

The researchers nodded their assent, moving toward the artifact. They were clearly reluctant to conduct this specific task, but even so, Ru noticed a strange excitement about them. The artifact had everyone buzzing, whether they wanted to be or not.

"It may not be physically volatile," said Lady Maryn, "but I think you're correct — it was emitting something... a frequency, as you said." She turned, taking Ru's dusty arm in hers, guiding her away from the artifact.

Ru's belly tightened as the artifact reached out to her across an unseen thread, wanting her closer. Goosebumps formed on her arms; how long would this go on? How could she get it to stop?

"We didn't dig here at random," said Lady Maryn, her voice low. "There were orders."

Ru looked at the woman sharply. "How?"

Lady Maryn shrugged, veering toward the largest tent. "The regency sends patrols here on a regular basis.

Not very often, once a year at most. My theory — based on only conjecture, you must know — is that someone, one of the riders on patrol, must have sensed it, just as our pocket watches sense it." She smiled ruefully, shaking her head. "And the fact of its location... Strange things are coming, Miss Delara."

"Its location?" Ru said, her attention split between Lady Maryn and the artifact. "You mean the Shattered City."

But Lady Maryn shook her head, her eyebrows raised suggestively. "Yes, but... *look.*"

Ru looked. They stood on black packed earth, scorched since the Destruction. On every side were the massive remnants of stone, large and irregular, reaching upward. All around them, equidistant.

And then Ru saw. It was silly that she hadn't noticed until now, hadn't seen the truth of it. The artifact had been uncovered at the very epicenter of the crater.

~

IT BECAME QUICKLY apparent that life at the dig site was strictly regimented. Ru was allowed an hour to lunch with Lady Maryn, and another hour to rest in a well-shaded tent before she was expected to come out again to inspect the artifact.

She spent most of lunch trying to wheedle every droplet of information she could from the other woman, but Lady Maryn was tight-lipped when it came to the politics surrounding this dig and the strange black stone it had uncovered. She only smiled conspiratorially when Ru asked why the Cornelian Tower hadn't been informed, which Ru found deeply frustrating. If anyone ought to be aware of a dig at the crater, the first sanctioned dig since the Destruction, it would be the Tower.

The food, at least, was far better than what Ru was used to in the field. They were served cold fruit, tea sandwiches, scones with cream and jam, and even hot tea. It was almost good enough to make Ru forget the artifact for a moment, the incessant thrum at the back of her thoughts, its inexplicable presence.

A liveried servant whisked back and forth with their lunch items. Ru was acutely aware of just how different a regency-funded dig site was to the rough-and-tumble Tower sites. At Dig Site 33, she and the other academics had brought in their own food, preserved meat, and soon-stale bread. Ru thought she could get used to this, the drip of peach juice on her lips, fresh cream on soft scones.

When they finished eating, Lady Maryn stood abruptly, all business. "Now for rest, Miss Delara. The artifact waits for none, and I don't want you to be sleep-deprived when you inspect it."

Despite her initial desire to see the artifact again, to touch it, Ru's exhaustion decided otherwise. A heavy tiredness settled over her, eyelids hanging low, her stomach full of sandwiches and tea.

She was shown to a little tent with a rug and a small bed inside. There was a miniature stove and, to Ru's surprise and delight, a basin of water. Lady Maryn explained that this tent would be her home for a while, until they decided what the stone was and what to do with it, and whether there might be more of them in the crater to dig up.

After washing her face and pulling her hair into a loose braid, Ru fell into bed, grateful for even its firm mattress and thin pillow. It was luxurious compared to what she'd had at Dig Site 33.

Yet even in the haze of exhaustion, despite the softness of the bed, sleep refused to come. No matter how hard Ru tried to succumb to sleep, her mind raced. The soft murmurs of the researchers outside, the plunk of metal tools on dirt, the breeze flapping the tents... it would have lulled her to sleep at any other time. These were her comfort sounds, evidence that she was home.

But nothing could wrench her thoughts from the artifact. It was as if she had bonded with it. As if it needed her. She felt, inexplicably, that it wouldn't be safe without her. That she should go and soothe it, or carry it back to bed with her. Make sure that it was comfortable and protected.

And not just that — there was an urge, deep down, to simply hold it. She wanted so badly to know what it felt like against her skin. Would it be smooth or rough? Cool or warm?

The more she thought about it, the more restless she became. How was she supposed to sleep when the artifact was just outside? She could hear the researchers out there, extracting it from the hole. She vibrated with tension. What if they dropped it?

She sat up suddenly, ready to bolt out of the tent.

Ru took a long, slow breath and laid down again, feeling foolish, undone. Nothing felt right, and she sought desperately for something solid to cling to in that moment. After that day-long ride, the hot sun, the touch of something foreign in her mind, her certainty that she had been called here by the artifact... she was overwhelmed. Confused. A stone, talking to her? Nothing about it made sense. What if she was going mad?

Wind buffeted the tent.

She needed sleep. Exhaustion had taken hold of her mind and made her delirious. Ru lay back on the pillow, certain now that everything was due to lack of sleep and too much sun. She would wake, and all would be well. She owed Lady Maryn, Regent Sigrun... she owed them her sharpest mind.

With these thoughts, her mind was finally able to rest. And by the time Lady Maryn came bustling in, calling her to action, Ru was more than ready to see the artifact up close.

CHAPTER 5

The artifact seemed far less mysterious bathed in the late afternoon sunlight. It sat on a delicate wooden table that was out of place in that desolate, dirt-strewn landscape. Ru recalled now that it was the same table that the tea had been served on.

On either side of the artifact lay various tools and implements, ready to be used in the inspection. There was even a brass microscope, such a new piece of technology that only three were housed at the Tower and there was a waiting list a mile long to use one.

Ru noticed with relief that instead of a bevy of researchers looking on, only Lady Maryn was present this time. Ru suspected that Lady Maryn had banished the researchers to their tents, possibly for safety reasons, but more likely to free Ru from distraction. And while she truly felt that the artifact was not volatile, Ru's shoulders relaxed in the knowledge that if anything went awry, she and Lady Maryn would be the only ones in immediate danger.

Pulling her mess of hair into a loose braid down her back, Ru approached the table. Lady Maryn stood a few feet away, arms crossed over her chest, watching with arched brows. Lady Maryn expected results and answers, but Ru was desperate for clarity.

As she came to the table, Ru bent over slightly to see the artifact more closely. It appeared, as she had earlier thought, to be made of some kind of obsidian. Like a bubble of ancient magma, belched from the earth's core. And now that she was close to it, with a sense of relief, she found that she no longer felt the obsessive desire to hold it.

Yet its touch remained, an invisible tether from it to her, soft against her thoughts. So it hadn't been exhaustion, then, or delirium.

She would need to lift it, to allow her fingers to move over it, to study it with every one of the five senses. If she was expected to determine if it was, indeed, magic, she should feel it on her skin.

And if Ru was being honest with herself, she had no idea where to start. How were any of these tools meant to determine the artifact's nature? The thoughts and feelings this particular artifact had been communicating to Ru were not normal, but how could she prove something that was taking place only in her mind?

She breathed slowly, trying to calm her nerves. The hum of anxiety had leaped up in her, making her doubt.

But Lady Maryn had shown confidence. The regent herself, her advisor, they believed what she'd written — called her here because no one else would do. Surety moved through her like sinking into a warm bath, returning to a place of understanding. This was where she belonged; these were the questions she had been born to answer.

The artifact sat in the sun, still and dark. And even though Ru knew it couldn't, she almost thought that she saw it moving, or a shadow of a memory of movement. The projection of something living, breathing... and then it seemed to tug at its tether, pulling suddenly taut against her mind, urging her.

Encouraging her.

She knew what it wanted. She blinked hard, feeling at once full of knowing and completely off-kilter; a drunkenness of thought.

"Please take a note," she said, surprised at the steady confidence of her voice. "I am going to begin the inspection now. Item one: physical touch."

"With bare skin?" asked Lady Maryn, scratching at a leather-bound notebook with a small pencil.

"Yes," said Ru. "It's safe."

She had no proof that it was. There was no logic behind her statement, no rationale. But she wanted to. She needed to press the whorls of her fingers to its surface to understand what it was.

"This thing was buried at the epicenter of the Destruction," said Lady Maryn. "Possibly since the event itself. It could be a weapon. An explosive. If it's magic, it could be some kind of conjuring stone."

Lady Maryn's words faded to a distant wordless hum in Ru's ears as she went on and on with her overly cautious rhetoric. Of course it wasn't a weapon or a conjuring stone. It was only at the epicenter of the crater because it… well, it didn't matter. Somehow, it felt imperative to Ru that she touch it. The weight of it on her mind was too much, her need too strong.

She was meant to be here. She was meant to find it.

From far away, as if someone were knocking on her door while she slept, the sound entering her dreams but failing to wake her completely, Ru heard Lady Maryn's protests. She took them into consideration. And then dismissed them.

"It's safe," she said again, reaching for the artifact.

"Wait—" Lady Maryn's voice was harsh, frightened. She rushed toward Ru, an arm outstretched.

There were other voices, suddenly, emerging from the tents behind them. As if they saw something Ru didn't.

But it was all background noise, muffled, easily ignored, like the buzz of a fly. Ru reached out and pressed both palms to the artifact.

Silence rang in her ears.

It was cold, just as she had predicted. Smooth. Perfect. A burst of white joy exploded in her, radiating outward like sunlight.

She was meant to be here.

And in that instant, wanting to share the moment with Lady Maryn, she glanced over her shoulder.

Horror was etched across the other woman's face, her mouth twisted in a scream, only inches from Ru.

Then everything went black.

Ru saw nothing. Heard nothing. Felt nothing. She hung suspended in it. And then the burst of light drew inward, imploding, a rupture. Ru was crushed by an impossible weight.

She fell to her knees, eyes squeezed shut, her body curled around the artifact like a shield, before her thoughts, too, went dark.

CHAPTER 6

Breath did not come easily. Ru felt as though she might never breathe again. Fear exploding in her, she wrestled with her lungs, desperate, panicked, until oxygen finally filled her empty chest. She gasped, choking. The air was thick with dirt and dust, filling her throat. She blinked, tears leaking from the corners of her eyes, and saw only darkness.

What happened?

How long had she been lying here? Had night fallen? Had she passed out when she touched the artifact? The artifact. Where — but there it was. Pressed to her stomach, her arms still wrapped around it, her body curved inward like a child. The stone was cold against her belly, and with horror and confusion, she realized that she was naked. Her clothes, her satchel — everything was gone.

All except for the artifact.

She blinked again, trying not to panic, waiting for her eyes to adjust. But there was only darkness. She felt around her, thinking she must have been carried to her tent, that she must be confused. Surely it was the small hours of the night after the moon had set. Just before sunrise.

But her shaking fingers brushed hard-packed dirt instead of her cot.

She sat up slowly, trying to make sense of where she

was, and a cold wind pulled at her hair. She let the breeze wash over her, slowing her frenzied thoughts. Then it occurred to her — the wind should be moving the tents. It should be shifting any loose tools, it should be making sounds. Shaking, she listened, tried to understand... and heard nothing. No rustling tents, no researchers snoring, no soft clanking as the guards made their rounds at the edge of the dig site.

All she could hear was the fast, wheezing rhythm of her own breath.

"Hello?" she rasped.

She sounded awful, as if gravel lined her throat. Had they packed up and left her then, for some unknowable reason? Left her to waste away in the crater? Maybe they had confirmed that she was mad, that the artifact was nothing but a normal stone, that she was better served by abandonment. Better this than return to the Cornelian Tower for another round of humiliation.

With great effort, Ru struggled to her feet, clutching the artifact to her. She was so stiff. Every joint ached.

"Lady Maryn?" she said, so quietly it was almost a whisper.

The wind pressed at her and whipped her hair across her face. She stumbled, shuffling in short, awkward steps through the dirt.

"Lady Maryn?" she said again, louder this time.

Only silence.

The possibility of a nightmare flitted across her mind, but she knew reality when she was in it. Shivering in the dark, she tried to think of an explanation. But her thoughts were moving at half speed, maybe slower, and everything that occurred to her was so improbable it verged on nonsensical.

A total eclipse could have explained the darkness, but there would be no solar eclipses in Southern Navenie for the next several decades, let alone a complete blackout of the sun. This couldn't have been a prank or a setup. It was too intricate, too cruel. Even Grey Adler would never go this far.

She stood for what felt like an eternity in complete

silence and darkness, clutching the artifact to her naked skin. There was no answer, no conclusion. Only terror and bewilderment. She desperately needed to find light, clothes, and water.

Horror-stricken but determined to use her intellectual brain, she took off walking in a random direction. Standing in one place, feeling sorry for herself, would do nothing.

She tripped and fell almost immediately, sprawling in the darkness. Tiny pebbles ground at her palms and her knees smarted. The artifact rolled, and she nearly broke down crying, scrabbling in the dirt, searching. But it hadn't gone far. Her fingertips brushed it within moments, and she tucked it to her bare chest once again.

A sense of sudden comfort blossomed in her, unbidden and unexpected. She was sure the artifact was reaching out to her, trying to lessen her pain. She pushed its touch away, fear choking her as she did.

The moment she had touched the artifact, everything had gone dark.

"What am I supposed to do?" she said, her voice a whimper. She lay curled around the stone, helpless, tears clinging to the corners of her eyes.

"You could try asking for help."

Ru jolted and sat upright in the vast blackness, her heart pounding. She hadn't heard anyone approach. She had been too busy panicking, trying not to cry.

"Who are you?" she asked, voice tight in her throat. "How can you see me?"

There was a rustling and crunching of pebbles under boots as someone approached. The voice was much closer now, deep and accented. "I can see you because you're the only living thing within miles, completely naked, in the middle of the Shattered City."

Ru went cold, the hair raising on the backs of her arms and neck. A million wild questions wrestled for purchase, and at last, the least important one came out: "But you can see?"

"You can't?"

There was a long silence. Ru sat in the dark, unwilling and unable to accept it. She was dreaming. Or she really was being pranked. It was a very dark night and this strange person only happened to have better eyesight than she did.

She wasn't blind. She refused to be.

Something soft and comfortingly heavy settled over her shoulders without warning. A cloak. Her breath caught as she greedily pulled it over her body, relieved at the warmth. She realized now that she'd been shivering.

"Thank you," she said. She felt herself blushing, despite everything.

Her nakedness was last on the list of things to worry about, and yet she was painfully aware of it. The feel of dirt crusted to her skin, her sticky skinned knees; she felt like a lost child. And now a stranger had come across her in this most vulnerable state, offering up the very clothes from his back. She felt she should say something, but she couldn't begin to fathom what.

So she held the cloak tightly around herself, silent, crouching in the dirt.

"You're welcome." The voice was oddly soothing, vowels curved in a way that Mirithans' were clipped. Ru had never heard an accent like it. "Although," said the stranger, "I would recommend wearing clothes next time you visit the Shattered City. What's your name?"

"Ruellian," she said, automatically. "Academic... Cornelian Tower. I was..." she closed her eyes, willing the tears to go away, willing herself to stay strong. She managed to bite out words in quick bursts, holding back the sobs she knew would come eventually. "I was here with a party of researchers. There were guards... Lady Maryn. Tents, a dig site. Did you see them? Are we near?"

The pause was a bit too long before the answer came. "There are no tents."

Ru swallowed, and it felt like knives in her throat. "But they were just here. A moment ago. Maybe there are tracks, or... I think I passed out. Maybe they forgot me, and left..."

A hand, gentle yet steady, settled on her shoulder.

Time stopped for a split second. In that moment, Ru felt again the snap of a piece falling into place within her, a light blooming from a dark depth, the surety that she was exactly where she ought to be.

She breathed in, slow. Somehow, inexplicably, she felt she could trust him.

"You're safe," he said. "I won't hurt you. But you can't stay here. Will you allow me to guide you to my horse? We can ride away from here together, and while we ride, I'll tell you what I know."

Ru clutched at the artifact, as comforted by it as she was terrified. She felt its soothing hum in return, warm in her chest. She wished it would stop, leave her alone. She wished she *was* mad.

"What do you know?" she asked, teeth chattering slightly. "Did you see—"

"I saw a very strange thing from a great distance," he said. "I'll tell you everything, I promise. As soon as we're away from this cursed place."

Ru frowned, ready to argue, when two strong hands took firm hold under her arms and lifted her. The cloak was large enough to cover her completely, and she clutched it close around her with one arm, her other hand holding the artifact. Then she was set gently on her feet and steadied by the stranger's warm grip.

"Who are you?" she asked again. Her thoughts were gradually clearing, and she wondered if she shouldn't feel more frightened, more cautious in the presence of a strange man. Where had he come from, and why was he here at the Shattered City? Travel here was forbidden except to the King's Riders, or by order of the regency. But he was no rider. If he had come from the palace, he would have said so.

"Call me Fen," said the deep voice, closer now. She felt the warmth of his body and heard the creak of leather when he moved. He smelled like a winter forest. She still couldn't place his accent, but something about it made her think of snow and jagged mountains.

"Stay here," he said. "Don't move."

Ru had no intention of moving; she would only embarrass herself, or injure herself further, or both. She heard him move away, the step of his boots on loose dirt. And then a muffled clunking, a murmured curse. When he returned, he pressed a bundle of cloth against her chest.

"Put these on," he said. "They're mine, but they'll cover you at least. I won't look."

"You've already seen everything," said Ru. Not that it mattered.

"I tried not to."

She glared into the darkness and felt she almost caught a glimpse of a dark shadow against shadow, but then it was gone. "And were you successful?"

At least he sounded apologetic when he said, "Mostly."

Ru turned away from his voice, hoping that her back was to him. She set the artifact gingerly on the ground, doing her best to keep one toe against its cool surface as she dressed. Whatever Fen had given her was far too large — trousers and a shirt, a pair of thick socks. He was tall, then, and broad-shouldered.

Fully dressed, the cloak once again fastened over her shoulders and the artifact clutched tightly in one hand, she called for Fen. His boots hurried across the earth, and he appeared at her side once more. She was struck again by the unearned trust she placed in him, an odd sensation that she knew him somehow. Something at the core of her responded to him, and it wasn't just his deep voice, his gentle strength.

She needed a plan now. Direction. Answers. This blindness and whatever had caused it, her nakedness, the disappearance of the dig site. She wanted to be home, surrounded by those who were safest to her. Gwyneth, Archie, her books. There, things would make sense. There, she could rest.

"May I take your hand?"

The words caught Ru off guard. "Why?"

"So I can lead you to the horse without you falling again."

She held out a hand in acquiescence.

His fingers were rough but gentle, warm to the touch. She thought he might take her fingers lightly in his, but his grip was strong, his hand engulfing hers. He led her slowly, carefully forward. There were no obstacles, nothing for her to trip over, but his care was obvious. She felt herself relaxing slightly, his very presence putting her at ease.

"I need you to bring me to the Cornelian Tower," she said, her hand still clasped tightly in his. She had to get home, somewhere safe, so she could think. She was still frightened. When she tried to wrack her brain, to remember what had happened after she touched the artifact, it was like an imaginary wall stood in her way. No thoughts could penetrate.

"Stand here," said Fen, stopping suddenly, and dropping her hand. "We'll discuss plans later."

"Fine," she said. "As if I have a choice."

A puff of air left Fen's nose; it sounded like laughter. There was a jangle and the squeak of leather against metal, and Ru guessed that Fen was astride the horse. A hand tapped her shoulder from above.

"Come closer," he said, "and hold tight."

Ru inched toward his voice, apprehensive. Then his strong arm wrapped around her, and almost as if she were weightless, he swept her up and settled her on the saddle. The breath left her lungs for a moment. And then she was relaxing into firm leather, the steady warmth of the horse beneath her, and Fen's broad chest at her back. His thighs pressed against hers. His breath was close to her ear, and his arms encircled her as he pulled on the reins, urging the horse forward.

She tamped down a restless heat, a thrill at Fen's proximity. Ru wasn't a prude. She had tumbled into the beds of other academics at the Tower, not just Archie's. But Fen was a stranger, unseen, unknown. The mystery of it set Ru's heart racing. She was glad for the distraction.

"Comfortable?" asked Fen, flicking the reins. They sped to an easy amble.

"Comfortable might be an overstatement," Ru said,

reaching blindly for the edge of the saddle to steady her-self. "I'm not used to riding."

Fen's hand found hers, guiding it to the saddle's pommel. "Hold this," he said. "The blindness will pass and your balance will improve."

How could he know that Ru's sight would return? He sounded so sure. His reassurance gave her a small com-fort; it was enough to settle her nerves.

They rode in silence at first. And while Ru was eager to learn more about this man, to discover who he was and where he had come from, why he was at the Shat-tered City of all places, she wasn't sure what to say. Her mind was still mostly a haze of confusion, of recent memories she'd rather ignore.

"You *will* take me to the Tower, though," Ru said after a while. "I need to get back. To make sense of..." she trailed off.

"You need answers," said Fen. "I understand. A strange man sees you wandering naked in the desert, carrying a shiny rock, and sweeps you away on his horse. Not a normal day for anyone."

Ru stiffened at the mention of the artifact. But Fen's tone was unconcerned, lacking interest. If he wanted the stone, he would have taken it and left her for dead. But curiosity pulled at her, goaded her.

"Why are you here?" she asked. "At the Shattered City. You said you'd explain once we were safe."

"We're not safe yet, not in this place."

"Can't you explain while we ride?" Ru said, impa-tient. This man, who had so cavalierly ridden into for-bidden territory, could be taking her anywhere. And despite her inexplicable trust in him, she couldn't help but imagine all the things a strange man could do to a young woman, alone in the wilds, blind and helpless. If she was going to trust Fen, then she deserved answers.

"I told you," he said, voice low and rough. "Not yet. This place is cursed. What happened to you..."

Ru gripped the saddle, fighting back a wave of nau-sea. There was a sharpness to his words, edged in regret. Her worst, darkest fears... Lady Maryn's cry of horror.

The artifact... the darkness... Ru shoved the memory into a dark corner of her mind, gritting her teeth.

"You think it could happen again."

"I can't rule it out," he said. "I'd like to put as many miles between us and that crater as possible before we stop; before I explain. We won't stop to camp until we reach the main road. This place... feels wrong."

Perhaps under normal circumstances, Ru would have dismissed the statement as superstition. But the events of the past two days had painted a new perspective; changed the categories. Belief in magic was one thing, but coming face to face with the unexplainable... it was a different thing altogether.

And though she was doing her best to pretend otherwise, to ignore it, the artifact agreed with Fen. She felt that it wanted to leave, it wanted to get away from the place where it had waited under the soil. It was an urgency, an insistence at her core, the same insistence that had called to her before.

As they rode, as time slid by in unguessable increments, Ru began to relax. The artifact mirrored her, its rankling insistence muted by distance from the crater's epicenter. And as its insistence faded, she felt a new sensation coiling up within her — comfort, reassurance.

She knew she should be afraid, wary. She should say something to Fen, to warn him. The last time the strange black stone "spoke" to her with such urgency, she woke up naked and blind.

But now it soothed her, and this was what frightened her.

CHAPTER 7

Time passed.

Ru had little concept of how long they had been riding, or in which direction they traveled. But there was plenty to keep her distracted as they went, even with her still-foggy mind and unseeing eyes. She made a point of noticing small details along the way, taking stock of everything she could smell, touch, and hear.

She knew that Fen's horse was very large, a well-muscled mare. She knew that the mare's saddle was made of the best quality leather, and her mane was brushed and braided, smooth to Ru's touch. It was clear that Fen took great care of his horse and spared no expense on her upkeep. But there was no sound of bells or tassels on the saddle or bridle, so Ru knew that Fen was also practical.

As they rode, she became increasingly aware of Fen himself. Every once in a while as they rode, the inside of his arm would press against her, holding her steady when he made a sudden turn. And while she was still in a state of what felt like prolonged shock and disbelief, she found her body responding to Fen. His touch was a comfort, a reassurance that was far more solid and acceptable to Ru than the inner voice of the artifact. She allowed herself to relish Fen's competence, his unassuming strength, his deep voice.

Eventually, Ru's sight began to return.

The change was so gradual that she hadn't noticed it at first; she thought she was imagining things. Where before there had been nothing but darkness, she now saw spots of light amongst the shadows. Tiny specks at first, and then they grew larger, seemingly by the minute.

"Fen," she said. Her voice was faint, almost a croak. They hadn't spoken much since the beginning of their journey, beyond the odd word here and there. She hadn't wanted to, and Fen didn't push. But now... "I can see something. Little clouds of light."

A slight chuckle rumbled in his chest. "What did I say? Temporary. And perfect timing. We're nearly to the main road."

By the time Fen found a perfect spot to camp, built a fire, and helped Ru settle in by the warm flames, she had begun to see complete shapes. Everything was still a blur, but differentiable. She would be able to find her way around on her own in a pinch, but not without a lot of stumbling.

While Ru sat staring at the blur of flames, Fen went in search of more firewood. She was alone then, her thoughts and the artifact her only companions. The stone made her uneasy; it chilled her despite the cloak around her shoulders and the crackling fire. She felt oddly empty, detached. As if the events in the Shattered City had cut her off from the world, isolating her in a bubble of regret.

She cradled the artifact, moved her fingers over its smooth, uneven surface. Her gut roiled and tied itself in knots.

Her thoughts spiraled into darkness as she sat, twisting down shadowed pathways. What mania had brought her to touch it in the first place? The voice of a stone... impossible. Ridiculous. She must be mad, deluded. The strange energies at the crater had warped her mind.

But even as the thought entered her mind, the artifact's pull reminded her of its reality. Bile rose in her throat, and she closed her eyes tightly.

What had truly happened at the dig site? Where had all the tents gone? The researchers? Lady Maryn?

An expression of horror, a cry cut short.

Lady Maryn's hand, reaching for her. Fear shining in the woman's eyes.

The last thing she remembered, the last action she'd taken — her skin against the stone.

No. Ru didn't want to remember, didn't want to know.

She doubled over where she sat, jaw clenched. *Breathe*, she told herself. *Breathe*. But the breaths came too fast, quick, and shallow. As she tried to relax, tried to calm herself, the panic only grew. She felt light-headed, dizzy. Her fingers against the artifact began to stiffen, curling inward like claws.

She felt the artifact in her mind, its comforting voice, but it was useless in the face of her panic.

She had lost control.

Her body wouldn't listen, her hands were now completely numb, separate from her. White splotches filled her already blurred vision, and she knew she was about to pass out.

Then strong hands grasped her arms, and a voice spoke. His words were soft, steady. "You're safe. Listen to me, Ruellian. Breathe in. Good. Now breathe out. Very slowly, like this."

Hot tears fell from her eyes, sudden and with no warning. They wouldn't stop, and she coughed choking sobs, her breaths coming faster and faster.

"Listen to me," said Fen. He took her face in his hands, gentle yet firm. "Ruellian, you're safe. Your sight is returning. I won't let anything hurt you. Breathe slowly in. There. Now slowly out."

She breathed in, breathed out again. Her body was shaking violently. But as she listened to Fen's voice, in tandem with the artifact's soothing presence at the edges of her thoughts, she felt herself relax from the inside out.

"Again," said Fen.

In again, and out. Her shaking lessened; her tears slowed. The calm from within her spread until she was breathing normally, shoulders slumping in relief. Her cramped, numb fingers began to relax, to move again.

And all the while, Fen never moved away, never let go. He was an anchor, holding her to the earth when all she wanted to do was float away.

She opened her eyes, still wet with hot tears. And with a wave of relief, she found that her vision had finally returned in full. Blinking and wiping her eyes, she looked up and saw Fen for the first time.

Somehow, inexplicably, Fen looked exactly as she had imagined.

The first thing she noticed was his eyes. They were dark gray, like a winter sky before snow, and framed with dark lashes. Unruly black hair fell over his forehead, curling just below his ears. And his features were refined and elegant, yet rough around the edges. A regal nose arched gracefully down to a pair of well-shaped lips, curved in a slight smile. Stubble peppered his angular jaw.

The man that had been living in Ru's mind's eye, a made-up version of Fen... it matched him perfectly.

Still collecting herself, distracted and unsettled, Ru's gaze roved over the man. From cracked, suntanned knuckles to his thick, dark brows. He was dressed in all black, his high shirt collar hung slightly open revealing a hint of finely curling chest hairs.

When her eyes finally caught his gaze, watching her with an expression of bemused interest, she looked away quickly.

"Sorry," she said. She wiped drying tears from her cheeks, sniffing loudly. Her nose was clogged, and she felt embarrassed to be caught staring. "It's just that you look exactly the way I thought you would."

Fen's smile widened slightly. "I hope that's not why you're crying."

The joke surprised Ru, and she let out a strangled

laugh. "Thank you," she said, pulling herself together. "For..."

He reached out a hand as if to touch her face again, then let it drop. "You were panicking. I'm no stranger to that feeling."

Ru bit her lip, smiling faintly. Who was this man? Nothing about him was logical, none of him made sense. Only a madman or a criminal would travel through the Shattered City without permission from the regent. Yet he had done it. And he'd come across a naked woman, stumbling and alone, and taken her under his wing, kept her safe, and treated her with respect. And he was no stranger to unfettered fear and panic sweeping the body.

"Are you hungry?" he said, standing abruptly. Not waiting for an answer, he went to where the horse was tethered and began digging around in the saddlebag. The horse, Ru saw, was a dappled gray. Almost like Fen's eyes.

"I suppose," Ru replied. She was hungry, but her stomach was churning, and the idea of eating made her feel sick. She turned back to the fire, a heaviness settling over her. Flames licked the air, clean and bright. The wood was bone-dry, and hardly any smoke rose into the clear morning sky as she watched. A hawk wheeled far above.

Woodland rose around them, clusters of aspen and stately birch and poplar. Ferns burst up in rich greens, foxgloves appearing at random intervals in pink and pale purple. This was a relatively new forest, grown from the ashen remains of the trees that had stood here centuries earlier. Further from the epicenter of the Shattered City, old-growth forests stood for millennia, since before recorded history.

Beyond the obvious decimation of surrounding woodlands, there was little proof of anything that had existed near the Shattered City before the Destruction.

The trees above Ru, thin morning sun drifting down through their green-gold leaves, were evidence of rebirth after a far-reaching death. They were a reminder that nature would behave in its mysterious way, no matter how many numbers or algorithms were applied.

Fen sat down across from her, the fire between them, jolting her from her thoughts. He pulled a packet out of his leather doublet. "Sandwich?"

She nodded, knowing it would be rude to refuse, knowing she needed the sustenance.

He tossed the packet to her and pulled another out for himself. "Luckily, I had the foresight to pack multiple sandwiches."

"Thank you," said Ru, taking a hesitant nibble. The bread was slightly stale, but the thick slices of bacon and cheese tucked between it were lovely and salty, setting off Ru's appetite. "And thank you for the clothes," she said between bites. "Even though they're huge on me. I feel like a little boy in his father's clothes."

"Trust me," said Fen, catching her eye. "You don't look like a little boy."

The fire felt too hot all of a sudden, and as Ru crossed her legs tightly, she felt the artifact's pull — a gentle encouragement. She pushed the feeling back, trying to ignore it.

"That thing you did earlier, with the breathing," she said, eager to change the subject. "Thank you. I don't know what happened. I still don't know what…" she trailed off, terrified that she'd cry again, lose herself to terror if she said anything else. She had never been good with emotions; had always felt off-balance when overcome with strong feelings. Unable to calculate, to process.

Fen glanced down at his sandwich thoughtfully. "It's something I've learned over the years. A little technique that calms the mind and body."

Ru took a bite of sandwich to avoid speaking for a moment. She was frightened. She had been afraid since the moment she woke up in the crater, blind. And she didn't want to let it out, to feel the full effects of terror and everything that came with the fractured memory of what had happened. Whenever she thought about that moment, just before the darkness came, just before she touched the artifact... her mind threatened to break down on her.

But she had to know.

"Fen," she said, her words wavering. "What exactly happened at the crater?"

He caught her gaze, his gray eyes steady. "Are you sure you want to know?"

"I need to," she said, setting down her sandwich, her appetite suddenly gone.

Fen leaned forward, then, elbows on knees. "Where would you like me to begin?"

"With you," she said, the answer coming easily. She instinctively felt that he was somehow meant to be there, just as she was. "Who are you, really?"

Fen seemed unsurprised by the question. He frowned slightly, and Ru noticed a fleeting darkness pass across his eyes, but it could have been a shadow cast by a cloud, or the waving trees.

"I'm Fen," he said at last. "You can probably guess it's not my full name. And before you ask what *that* is, a man is entitled to his past."

Ru could read people better than most — it was all a calculation, just the common sum of countless little movements or hints of the body — but he was a closed book, somehow. An unknown.

"Are you in disguise," she said, "or trying to forget?"

He smiled sardonically. "Trying to forget."

"You're not much older than I am, surely. What past could you possibly need to forget?"

"You're steering the conversation away from what scares you," Fen said, hitting the mark so perfectly that Ru almost flinched. "Who I am doesn't matter. I study things. I have an interest in history, the occult, the strange and misunderstood. I've always been drawn to the Shattered City. At first academically, and then the urge became too great. I had to see it myself."

"If you're a historian, then you must have visited the Cornelian Tower," said Ru.

He shook his head. "Never."

"But how else would you study the Destruction?"

Fen gave her a look of incredulity. "Do you really think all the knowledge in the world resides in that pretty little palace you call the Tower?"

"It's not little—"

"My apologies. That *large* palace you call the Tower."

He was obviously joking, but Ru wasn't in the mood. "So you're a historian, a scholar who's never been to Navenie's center of learning. Is that all?"

"You know," he said, "plenty of people read books and study outside of the Cornelian Tower. There are libraries in Mirith, Solmaria, even in my own home. Which is, for the purpose of continuing my story, where I typically read things."

"Where do you live, then?" asked Ru. "Are you an aristocrat? You must be if you own so many books." She knew she was being difficult, prying into irrelevant details. Who cared where he lived? Where he studied? She pressed a knuckle to one eye. The artifact's touch was uneasy, unsettled. "It doesn't matter."

Fen huffed a grim laugh. "You're right, it doesn't. But you deserve to know who I am, the man who came upon you at your most vulnerable. Shouldn't I reveal myself equally?"

The response surprised Ru. "All right, Fen. Reveal yourself."

"You're right. I *am* from a noble family," he said, without preamble. "My father was a marquis. I'm the third son of three. I was raised on books. My family home had a beautiful library in the east wing. I spent most of my time there, curled up on chairs by windows, reading about any strange topics that I could get my hands on. And I never really grew out of it. That's what brought me to the crater yesterday. My unwavering sense of curiosity."

"But weren't you afraid of, I don't know, being arrested?" wondered Ru.

"It hadn't crossed my mind," he admitted, running a hand through his hair. He seemed agitated, as though recounting this tale was setting him on edge. "In fact, I had never dreamed of going to see the site of the Destruction in person. But something in me..." He looked up at her, his face softened by the fall of hair over his forehead, the dappled sunlight on his skin. "Do you believe that some things are meant to happen?"

Ru hadn't expected a question like that. "You mean fate?"

"Destiny, fate, whatever you want to call it."

"I think so." She was surprised at her own answer. A day ago, she would have said no. She would have listed all the reasons why those who believe in such a force are misunderstanding the inherent chaos of the universe. But everything was different now. When she had first seen the artifact... how else could she describe the sense of knowing, of a missing piece falling into place?

Fen seemed to relax at this, the muscles of his jaw loosening, and he sighed. "I woke up one morning, and my only thought was of the Shattered City. I couldn't have explained why, and I still can't. But I knew somehow that I had to see it, that I'd been waiting my whole life, and now was the moment."

Ru watched the fire, her fingers playing thoughtlessly along the edge of the artifact, pressing against its uneven curves until they were almost warm from her touch. Fen glanced at the artifact for a moment, and Ru worried suddenly that he would ask her about it. But almost immediately he looked away again.

"You think I'm mad," he said.

"No," she said at last. "It's just that what you said... I understand. I feel silly saying it, but I do."

Fen let out a long breath, one corner of his mouth curving upward in a half-smile. "One can't ignore the call of destiny."

"So you went? For no reason other than a feeling?"

He nodded. "That very morning. I packed up my things and traveled south until I reached the Shattered City."

Ru knew what came next.

Whatever he had seen, whatever had happened that was unknown to her, was about to be revealed. Despite her insistence, her determination to know, she wasn't sure she was ready. Would anyone in her place? She wondered what would happen if she went on forever without knowing, without understanding. Would the memories surface eventually? Or would she live with it like the constant itch of an open sore?

She looked up and saw that Fen was watching her intensely.

"Have you read about the Destruction?" he asked.

This caught her off guard. "Yes, of course."

Who hadn't? While nobody knew *exactly* what had occurred inside the epicenter, it was now a matter of common knowledge that long ago, there was some kind of explosion, some destructive force in the city of Ordellun-by-the-Sea. The stories say the city was drenched in darkness for days, maybe weeks. And most stories mentioned a figure in the center of the explosion, burning bright white, arms spread wide as if all that destructive energy had poured directly from his body, tissues, muscle, and skin. They called him the Destroyer.

"When I came to the edge of the Shattered City," continued Fen, his gaze never leaving hers, "I saw something... like that."

Ru tried to react emotionally to this news, but she couldn't. She reached inside and found that she was empty, a void. "What do you mean?"

"I mean I saw an explosion of darkness erupting outward from the epicenter, like a burst bubble, flowing away from a glowing figure. I..." he trailed off.

Ru was a woman of science. She understood, logically, the sequence of events: the obvious trajectory of physical force combined with immense explosive power, the inciting device itself despite its unknown nature, a chemical interaction between active particles of skin meeting stone, an inevitable calculation so smoothly falling into place that it must have been there, in the darkness of her mind, all the while.

"I see," she said.

Fen's expression was pained. "You should know that the explosion... it wasn't nearly as great as the Destruction. Much smaller in diameter and scope. You—"

"I vaporized the entire dig site," Ru finished for him. "Lady Maryn, the guards, all the researchers. Gone."

She fixed an unfocused gaze on the fire, and calmly contemplated throwing the artifact, or herself, or both, into the flames.

CHAPTER 8

Fen was quiet while Ru processed. She knew that he watched her with concern, leaned slightly forward as if ready to jump into action should she do something unwise. But he was only on the periphery; most of her thoughts were jumbled, confused.

Most of all, she felt a trickle of horror, bleeding in from somewhere unknown, filling her slowly. And yet, somehow, there was also a bizarre sense of relief in the knowing — every piece of the puzzle was in place.

"I vaporized my clothes," she said tonelessly. "The force of the explosion affected my vision, but only temporarily. Intense waves of pressure against the cornea, or an interaction from…" she had meant to say the artifact but stopped. Wary. What would Fen say if he knew she was carrying around a potential bomb? Even though it had sat quietly since then, never hinting at another explosion, he would no doubt demand that she get rid of it. And she should. She wanted to. Ru wanted nothing more than to be rid of it, to destroy the cursed thing. But at the same time, all she wanted was to be near it, to protect it, to make sure it never left her side.

Only its voice, its unending press against the back of her mind, let her know that it was more than it seemed.

"We don't have to talk about this anymore." Fen's voice came from far away, cutting through the thick fog of Ru's thoughts.

She took a long, shaking breath. "No. It's fine. I understand now. This was my fault."

"Was it?" said Fen, voice low. "What I saw... I don't know. I saw a glowing figure, yes. I think that figure was you. But—"

"You don't have to describe it so clearly," Ru snapped, feeling too-hot by the fire in that heavy cloak. Angry, terrified, wanting to feel nothing at all. "I can imagine it myself. They uncovered some kind of... they shouldn't have called for me. You didn't see what I did. You saw the aftermath. There are only so many paths from a specific action to a specific outcome, and I am at fault." Her words became choked, hot tears coming unbidden. "What I don't understand is why I couldn't have been granted the mercy of being destroyed along with everyone else!"

"Ru—"

But she didn't want to hear it. She wanted to be away. She wanted to disappear. She stood abruptly, cloak sweeping around her as she spun. Without a word or a glance at Fen, she strode into the trees, aimless, her vision blurred with tears.

She crashed through the underbrush and nearly slammed into trees as she went, now half-blinded by tears that wouldn't stop coming. The artifact was cool in her hand as she careened forward, a source of both comfort and incalculable pain. The worst of it was, even in her mad rush through the trees, *knowing* that the artifact was to blame, her own skin against it was to blame, she still felt unable to rid herself of it.

Overwhelmed by misery and tears, Ru stumbled directionless through the forest until it became so thick and dark that the sky was no longer visible, the sun glancing through in tiny bars of gold. The air was thick and hot. The shadows were deep.

It must have been attracted by her choked sobs, by the trashing of her progress through the woods. She wasn't used to this. She was a city girl. She had never been fully alone in the wilderness, wandering a forest with no path.

She didn't see the danger until it was upon her.

Ru was mid-sob when a hulking gray shape flew out from a cluster of ferns to her left, knocking her off her feet and sending her sprawling sideways.

Her ribs collided with the artifact, punching the air from her lungs.

She tried to scream, if only to startle whatever had attacked her. But breath wouldn't come. She choked, gasping, pulling herself to her knees.

But the creature fell upon her again, slamming her back to the ground. Snapping teeth missed her throat by an inch as she wriggled sideways, kicking at it wildly, missing by a mile.

It was a wolf. A scraggly, starved thing, it wasn't much bigger than a racing hound, ribs visible through its fur. The wolf's desperate snarl and rolling eyes told Ru that it was hungry, had been for a while, and would do anything for a meal.

She wondered hysterically when the rest of its pack would come, whether this one would draw out her life until they could all enjoy her entrails together. She wondered whether it wouldn't be a relief letting them.

But still, she struggled, her instincts taking over. She kicked out at it again, her boot connecting with its gut, drawing a yelp from the oversized thing.

And when it snarled, baring its fangs, she was hit with the sudden knowledge that she was desperate to live, to see her friends again, to walk the sunny cobbled streets of Mirith, to curl up in an armchair by a fire with a book.

The revelation lit her from within.

With renewed energy she struck out, yelling, smacking the wolf on the side of the head with the artifact. The wolf swung its toothy snout, knocking the artifact from her hand. It rolled and disappeared into the underbrush.

I don't want to die, thought Ru.

But here she was, in the jaws of certain demise. And she had brought it on herself, running into the woods like a fool, hoping to lose herself in the trees.

She half-screamed, half-sobbed, trying to scramble away from the wolf.

But she was far too slow. It leaped upon her, heavy paws pressing down on her. It slavered, its drool landing on her neck. Then it bared its teeth with a greedy snarl, ready to kill. She could smell its foul, rotten breath.

She squeezed her eyes shut. She didn't want to see it come for her, watch it latch its jaws around her neck.

And then there was a sudden noise as something came charging out of the brush. All at once, the wolf's heavy weight was gone from Ru's chest. There was a growl, a scrambling flurry of grunts and wet sounds. A sickening yelp, and then stillness.

Ru opened her eyes and sat up shaking, her heart racing. There lay the wolf, bloodied and limp, only feet from where she sat. And standing over it, chest heaving, a red-slick dagger in his hand, was Fen.

He turned to her, pale. The dagger fell from his fingers, and he rushed forward, kneeling at her side. He took her shoulders in his hands, fingers gripping tightly, almost painfully.

"Are you safe?" he said. His voice was hoarse, almost desperate. "Are you hurt? Did it harm you? Are you bleeding?"

She was taken aback by this overwhelming show of concern, the slight crack in his voice. What did Fen care? She was a stranger. A murderer.

"I'm fine," she lied.

Fen was clearly unconvinced. He began gently inspecting her for wounds, his fingers lightly brushing hair away from her neck, pressing his hands to her limbs, studying her with a determined gaze.

"I told you, I'm fine," she said, wishing he would stop. She felt that she didn't deserve his care. "It only knocked me down."

"Don't do that again," said Fen, still breathing hard.

"I didn't mean to be attacked by a wolf." She made to stand but was lifted to her feet by Fen, his hands under her arms.

"I mean running off alone," he said.

"I'm not a child," she snapped, letting obstinacy mask the residual terror that coursed through her, the sense that she shouldn't be alive. She stepped back and brushed herself off. She glanced at the wolf, its gray shape still in the underbrush. That could have been her. Should have been.

"Exactly," Fen said. "You're old enough to know not to barge into a strange wood without a guide or a weapon."

"What do you care?" said Ru. The instinct to live, to fight off the wolf, it was fading now, replaced by a burning self-loathing that Fen couldn't possibly understand. "You don't know me. It's not as if you'd be implicated if I was eaten by a wolf."

His eyes darkened. "It's basic human decency. I couldn't let you just… disappear."

"*Let* me? I suppose because you found me helpless in a crater, you think you're responsible for me. Well, you're not. If I want to disappear into the woods, then I'll damn well disappear."

Fen glared at her. She glared back. Then, wordlessly, he knelt. Ru thought for one hysterical second that he was about to propose until he reached into the underbrush and pulled out the artifact.

"You dropped this."

Ru snatched it out of his hands, cold fear washing over her all of a sudden. She could have lost it, or broken it. What would have happened if she had? Would it be safe there, lost forever in the ferns? Or would it come back to her somehow?

Still shaking, sweat beading on her forehead, Ru tucked the artifact into a pocket. "I'm going back to camp," she said. Not waiting for Fen's response, she turned on her heel.

"Camp's the other way," said Fen, pointing.

She pressed her lips together. "Just take us there."

As soon as they arrived at the makeshift camp, Fen went to where his saddlebags lay against a tree, and started looking for something inside.

"Get that thing wrapped up," he said, not turning as

he crouched, broad shoulders flexing as he dug through one of the leather bags.

Ru, hovering near the now-dead fire, froze. "What thing?"

"That cursed rock you've been carrying around. I have a bad feeling about it."

She reached for it involuntarily, touching it with the tip of a finger. He couldn't know; he couldn't possibly know that it spoke to her. "It's just a rock."

Fen turned, one eyebrow raised, and tossed her the woolen blanket he had pulled from the depths of his saddlebags. "Swaddle it in this. We'll put it in with the other things."

She caught the blanket, her senses now on full alert. Did Fen know more than he was saying? Did he believe that the artifact was a weapon, a bomb? She *should* wrap it up. They didn't know what it could do. But she didn't *want* to. She wanted to have it close.

"Ruellian." Her name on Fen's tongue was a warning. "I promise you, I will not let any harm come to you, *or* your little rock. I would die first."

"That's a little dramatic."

"I'm serious."

His tone was clear and unaffected in the same way he'd spoken of fate. Ru's inclination was to believe him, to trust him. As it had been from the moment she'd felt his touch on her shoulder.

And now, after the run-in with the wolf, Fen had proven to be true in his word to protect not only her, but also the artifact. He was the one who had lifted it from the forest floor and handed it back to her. If he wanted it for himself, or if he wanted to destroy it, he could have done so easily.

Ru sighed, wrapped the artifact in the blanket as tightly as she could, and handed it grudgingly to Fen. He took it and tucked it gently into a saddlebag.

"There," he said. "Now sit down and let me have a look at your knees."

"My knees?"

He came back toward her, a small box in his hands. "They're torn up. You tripped when you were blind."

As if realizing her knees existed for the first time, Ru looked down at them. They were skinned, raw, and red. Dirt and bits of forest debris were stuck to them. And they did sting, now that she thought about it. With everything else, that small pain had been the last thing on her mind.

"Oh," was all she said.

Fen raised a dark eyebrow. "Sit."

Ru remained standing. "We don't have time. I need to get back to the Tower. My knees are fine."

"You will get to the Tower eventually," Fen said, moving toward her. His expression was gentle but stern, unyielding. "Sit, please."

She knew that if she didn't clean the wounds, they might get infected. The infection could spread. And they really did sting. Giving in, she went to the nearest log and sat.

Appeased, he knelt in front of her, inspecting the wounds. They weren't deep, just bits of skin scraped raw by that strange black earth in the Shattered City. Blood was crusted at the edges, a dried trail of red-brown leading down from her left knee.

Fen made a soft grumbling sound, his long fingers tracing the air about her knees, inspecting, careful not to touch. Then he stood and went to the saddlebags again, pulling out a canteen of water and a cloth.

Ru watched him with grudging interest. His movements were practical yet fluid, almost like an efficient sort of dance. When he turned back, he caught her watching and smiled almost imperceptibly. Embarrassed, she turned away quickly, avoiding his eye until he was kneeling at her feet again.

Rolling up his sleeves to the elbow, Fen set about cleaning her wounds. He dabbed at her knees with the damp cloth, removing any foreign debris. When he reached a particularly sore spot, Ru hissed, a sudden intake of pained breath.

"Sorry," Fen said, glancing up at her.

She was struck by how odd it was, this familiarity she felt toward him. While she still didn't know his motives, knew she shouldn't trust him unequivocally, *knew* he was an unknown entity... her gut told her otherwise. Every nerve in her body seemed eager to relax in his presence.

"It's fine." She could handle a little sting. It was everything else that made her feel like the world was spinning off its axis. And Fen, somehow, a look of pure concentration on his face as he tended to her wounds... he felt like an anchor.

"Have we met before?" she said. The words were unplanned, unexpected even to Ru, but as she spoke she felt as if they would have come eventually, inevitably. The way she felt when she looked at him, when his gray eyes caught hers, it was familiar. Comfortable, in a strange and inexplicable way.

Pausing in his ministrations, one hand holding her leg steady, the other holding a damp rag, he frowned up at her. "Why?"

She shrugged. "There's something familiar about you. What did you say your family name was?"

"I didn't," he said. "We haven't met before."

"Oh." There was no reason for her to slump in disappointment, to feel oddly dejected by his response.

"But I know what you mean."

She brightened a little. "You do?"

"I do," he said, a distant haze drifting across his eyes. And then he was in the moment again, dabbing with the cloth, his thick eyebrows pulled together as he focused his attention wholly on her. Caring for her, even for as small a thing as a knee scrape.

Fen quickly finished clearing away the debris from her knees. He set aside the water, reaching into his doublet and removing a silver flask.

"I'm sorry," he said, apologetic, "but this is going to hurt."

Ru knew what came next. She watched him pour a bit of spirit onto the cloth, enough to soak it through.

Alcohol would clean the wound and lower the chance of infection.

"Ready?" he said.

She nodded, then flinched as he pressed the cloth to her knee, the stinging liquid dripping into her flesh, smarting horribly.

"Shit," she swore through gritted teeth.

He chuckled. "Very. Just one more."

The second knee hurt worse somehow, but the sharp sting meant a clean wound, a quick recovery.

Ru was still catching her breath after the burst of pain as Fen pulled a roll of bandages out of the box. With deft hands, he trimmed bits of bandage from the roll and wrapped Ru's knees — tight, but not uncomfortable.

"Thank you," she said.

This moment felt intimate, and it made Ru want to stand up and move away, to seek normalcy, an interaction between near strangers that made sense. But her knees were still smarting, and Fen's sharp gaze caught at her.

"You're welcome." He stood, gathering his things and returning them to the saddlebag. "I think we'll stay here for the night and set out for the Tower in the morning."

Ru frowned, standing shakily. "Why not leave now? It's not even midday."

"Because you need rest."

This was true, but Ru could rest on the road. She wanted to be home, surrounded by comforts, and to put her thoughts on hold until then. Out here in the forest, with Fen... everything was turned on its head. At the Tower, things would make sense. She could study the artifact. Determine what it was. How it was able to caress her at her very core. And maybe answers would bring a sort of peace.

"I'd rather go now," she said. She didn't want to give those memories of the dig site, of Lady Maryn's face before the darkness, any more time to fester. Somehow, she thought she could purge them if she could only get home.

Fen ignored her, returning to where she sat near the fire. He settled himself nearby, perched on a lichen-riddled boulder. "Ruellian," he said as if tasting the word. Rolling it on his tongue. "Family name?"

It was as if he hadn't heard her at all. "If you don't take me to the Tower now," she said, impatient, "I'll simply go on my own."

He regarded her coolly. "And what, steal my horse?"

"No," she said, "you'll let me borrow her. If you were a gentleman—"

"I'm not a gentleman," he said, cutting her off. "I may be the son of a marquis, but I've never set foot in the palace at Mirith. I don't know the first thing about courtly pleasantries. And yet, somehow, I would wager that a woman's safety should be prioritized above all else. Or would a gentleman disagree?"

Ru thought of her brother, who she considered to be the perfect gentleman. His mannerisms, his behavior, from the way he walked to the way he spoke — it was all a product of the court, a practiced dance. Was that what she looked for in a male companion, what she expected? Grudgingly, she had to admit it wasn't. It was pretty, sugar-spun, but mostly nonsense that playacted politeness and care.

Fen was rough around the edges, cutting straight to the point. But it felt real, genuine in a way that palace politics had never seemed. Even academics often let competition and clever turns of phrase lead the way instead of openness. Instead of genuine emotion, expression.

Ru hated to admit that Fen was far more attentive and gentle than any man she had met in her youth, when she had spent time at court with her brother. Before she departed for the Tower.

"Fine," she agreed, at last, the acquiescence taking a great deal of effort. "We'll leave in the morning. But in exchange, I want to know more about you. If we're going to spend the night together, I feel entitled to at least one of your secrets."

"One of my secrets?" Fen said, laughingly. "I still know nothing about you, other than your name."

"You know I'm an academic."

"I could have guessed that from the start." A smile crept across his handsome features.

She frowned. "How?"

"The way you speak. Your mannerisms."

"I'm not sure if that's a compliment," she said, annoyed. She knew she didn't have the refined bearing of a highborn woman or the fast-talking confidence of a city-dweller. But to be so transparently an academic felt strange, as if her true self was on full display for everyone to see, no matter how she felt about it.

"It is," said Fen, and the warmth in his expression told Ru it was the truth. "You're confident. You think before you speak. And you don't talk just for the sake of it."

The accuracy of the statement set Ru off-balance. "That's quite a conclusion to come to after only knowing me for a matter of hours."

"And now you're deflecting," he said, grinning, "because you know it's true."

Ru sulked slightly, pushing her hair behind her ear, fidgeting in the face of his perception. It was true, but that didn't mean she had to admit it. That she had to like it.

"You're uncomfortable," said Fen, his smile fading. "Tell me something, then. On your own terms."

She had no reason to protest that. No desire to, either. *On your own terms.* She wanted to hold the words like a gift.

"Ru," she said at last, letting out a long-held breath. "Call me Ru, if you want. All my friends do. I'm twenty-three. My father's a textile merchant whom I rarely see, and my mother passed when I was young. My older brother, Simon, lives and works in Mirith. He has rooms at the palace, but we're not nobility. And I live at the Tower, as you've obviously surmised."

Fen blinked. "That's it?"

"It's everything relevant."

"You've just told me about your family. I asked about you."

The way he sat there, so calmly leaning forward and fixing Ru with that steady gaze. It set her on edge, but not in the way she would have expected. His eyes on her made her blood thrum, made her want to be nearer to him.

"Don't you owe me a secret?" she asked, glancing down at her hands. His gaze was too piercing. As if he would uncover all of her, see straight to the crux of her, without even trying.

"What do you study at the Tower, Ru?"

"You're very good at that," she said, crossing her arms over her chest, catching Fen's eye as he smiled. "Deflecting."

He raised his eyebrows slightly, one disappearing under the shock of thick black hair that always hung over his forehead. "Should I be flattered, or issue an apology?"

She snorted. "I study archaeology, specializing in ancient pottery. Very dry, both literally and figuratively."

"And what drew you to that?" he asked, resting one elbow on his knee, chin on hand. He looked every bit enthralled, eager to hear the dreary details of Ru's studies.

She sat in silence for a moment, thinking. What *had* drawn her to pottery? She smiled to herself, thinking of the wide-mouthed vase she had uncovered at Dig Site 33. Back when things were simple, when the worst thing that could happen to her on any given day was having to interact with Grey Adler.

"The stories," she said at last. "Every piece I uncover from the earth, every curve, every imperfection, tells a story. Ancient things hold memories. Not just history, or facts, but... emotions. Lived experience."

Ru's cheeks colored a little at speaking so honestly, and she hoped Fen wouldn't notice. She loved learning, loved to put together the pieces of a scientific question, answering it with meticulous work and regimented steps of study. But at the core of it all, she loved the humanity behind the artifacts. The things that couldn't be measured or calculated.

Fen listened intently. "Objects reflect the events around them," he said, a faraway look in his gray eyes. Then his gaze flicked up to hers, and his expression softened. "You love what's in the background. The unseen."

"You could put it that way," said Ru. In fact, he had worded the feeling exactly. And there was no judgment in him, only solemn interest. "You know," she said, chewing her lip, not knowing why she said it and yet pushing on anyway, "I used to study magic."

"At the Tower?" he asked, sitting up a bit straighter. But he didn't laugh or smirk, as she thought he might.

She nodded, her thoughts flickering to the artifact. It responded, a pull at her consciousness, sharper than usual, as if she and it had thought of each other in the same instant.

"I wrote a paper on it," she went on, trying to ignore the artifact's louder presence in her mind. "That's why I was summoned to the Shattered City. The regent had read my paper and thought it might somehow relate to..." she trailed off, angling her head toward the saddlebag where the artifact was swaddled.

"But you gave up on it?" Fen asked, leaning forward a bit, his brow furrowed. "Studying magic, I mean."

"My paper wasn't received well by the academic community. To put it mildly."

"How odd," he said. "I would have thought... Well, I suppose I don't know what's generally accepted in the academic circles of Navenie. I would have found your paper fascinating."

"I doubt that," said Ru, old feelings of shame rising up in her, dulled with time but still sharp enough to hurt. "It was ultimately pointless. And even after all that studying, all that preparation, I was useless at the Shattered City. I provided no help. All I did was..." she trailed off, biting the inside of her mouth to distract herself enough not to cry.

"Ru," said Fen, starting to get to his feet.

"Don't," she said, shaking her head. "I'm fine. I'm just tired."

"You need rest," he said, sitting down again. "I've pushed you too hard. Wait there."

He stood and went to the saddlebag, pulling a bedroll from within. In a few long-legged strides, he crossed the small clearing, settling the bedroll in a patch of shaded grass. When it was laid out, its wrinkles smoothed, he turned to Ru.

"Get some sleep," he said. "I'll be here if you need anything."

With the offer of sleep came the realization that she was tired, so bone-tired that her eyelids hung heavy like weights.

"Thank you," she said, stumbling over to the bedroll and crawling inside. The ground was hard and uneven, but the blankets were soft, and she was so… so tired.

"Sleep tight," said Fen, his voice low as he settled himself by the fire once more. "And here's my secret. I believe in magic, too."

She wanted to respond, to ask him how, and why, but her thoughts pulled her into darkness and she slept, the trees waving above her in the afternoon sun.

CHAPTER 9

Ru woke once in the small hours of the morning, confused and damp with dew. Sitting up in a panic, her eyes roving, she wondered where she was, how she got there. And then she saw Fen, curled up not far from where she lay. He was using his cloak as a blanket, and beads of dew clung to his hair. In sleep, he looked so peaceful. Younger than he had initially seemed.

Ru felt her heartbeat slow, her breaths coming in an even tempo.

She didn't wake again until morning.

THEY RODE AT A COMFORTABLE PACE. They took the main road northeast, knowing it would branch after half a day's ride. One way continued east to the capital city of Mirith, while the other turned northward, toward more wilderness and eventually the Cornelian Tower.

The entire journey to the Tower would take days, a fact that made Ru uneasy. So many days alone with Fen and the artifact, knowing what she had done at the dig site, wondering if it might happen again... The thought of it was like an itch on the inside of her skin.

But she had no other choice.

After a few hours of riding in relative silence — Ru

wasn't fond of early mornings, and Fen's attempts at conversation had been immediately rebuffed or completely ignored — she finally asked the question that had been bothering her since they set out that morning. She felt awkward voicing it, as she was settled firmly between Fen's thighs, her back to his chest. But she had to know.

"Why are you staying with me?" she asked. "Why take me all the way to the Tower?"

Fen huffed a laugh, and his breath ruffled her hair. "Aside from the fact that you asked me to?"

"That's not what I mean," she said. "You didn't *have* to take me anywhere. You could have left me." Even to her, the words sounded harsh. But nothing bound him to her. Why should he help her?

"You're not at your sharpest in the morning, are you?"

"What's that supposed to mean?"

He laughed, truly laughed, for the first time since she'd met him. It was a deep, musical sound, reverberating through his chest. "Do you really believe that anyone with half a heart would abandon you, just like that? I'm not a monster, Ru."

"I know that *now*," she grumbled, staring out at the road ahead, wide and lined with sparse trees.

"A good point," he said, hands adjusting the reins, one arm brushing against Ru's shoulder. "Strange men, until proven otherwise, should always be considered monsters."

The morning continued on, the sun rising ahead of them until another hot summer day reached its zenith. Ru found herself relaxing into the horse's gait, the sound of hooves on packed dirt, the way the breeze lifted her hair off her ears.

Fen kept her entertained with stories about his travels over the years. They were all harmless, silly tales that revealed little about who he truly was. But the more stories he told, the more Ru wondered how old he actually was; how he'd had time for all of these adventures.

For a relatively young man, he claimed to have done a lot of things in quite a lot of places.

As Fen finished his latest tale, Ru found herself only half-listening. The sun was now falling behind them, their shadows lengthening along the road. It was only when he feigned a cough that she realized she had failed to react to an exciting moment in his story.

"Sorry," she said quickly, "my mind wandered."

He was quiet for a moment. Then he asked, almost cautiously, "How are you feeling?"

Ru wasn't sure how to respond. If she was honest with herself, she didn't know. But she wasn't fine, she wasn't all right. So instead of answering directly, she asked a question of her own. "You've studied the Destruction. Do you know anything about the Destroyer? Beyond what's commonly known, I mean."

Fen's gloved hands flexed on the reins. "An open-ended question, but I might."

"I keep wondering whether he was a catalyst or a weapon of sorts. The Destroyer, I mean. Taryel. Could he have been an explosive device? Or did he use a focus, a magical object, something he might have activated in order to create such a massive reaction? Something that could vaporize an entire city."

She was glad that her words came out so calmly, matter-of-fact. Her insides were the opposite, her gut in knots as she thought of the Destroyer, and the blackness that had — as the stories said — burst outward from him.

Fen leaned forward, his cheek nearly touching hers. She could feel him smile. "You're talking about that infernal rock," he whispered, and the hairs on her neck stood on end.

"I am not," she lied. "I'm asking a scientific question. Trying to make sense of things."

"If I wanted to take that thing from you and leave you dead on the roadside," he said, voice low in her ear, "I would have done so already. You can speak openly."

Ru shivered. "I don't even know if I *am* talking about the artifact," she admitted, exhausted, wanting to be honest. Wanting to open up. She was tired of evading, tired of feeling as if she had something to hide. And then she remembered Fen's voice from the night before, just as she had drifted off to sleep. She'd thought it was a dream, but she was certain he had said it.

I believe in magic, too.

Then why not share her fears, her worries about the stone? If he believed, maybe he could help her find answers. Help her come to understand it. "That's why I want to bring it to the Tower," she said. "I need to know what it is, how it ticks. Whether or not it's magic. To find out what happened, to determine if it's my fault."

She carefully refrained from mentioning the fact that the artifact seemed to be speaking to her, calling to her in the subtlest of ways. That, too, spurred her academic curiosity — if it was magic, and it had to be, was its communication with her a remnant of a spell? Was it sentient in some way?

The possibilities, the unknowns, made her spine tingle.

"Your motivations are understandable," said Fen, straightening so that his face was no longer inches from hers. "I did suspect that your pretty stone might be... more than just a stone."

"Do you think it's a magical weapon?" she asked softly. The evidence was there. Found at the epicenter of the Shattered City, exploding in raw power the moment Ru touched it, an echo of what had occurred ages ago in that very spot. "Could it have belonged to the Destroyer?"

Ru felt Fen shift behind her in the saddle. "It's as solid a guess as any," he said. "But if that's the case, then I have to know. Why carry it around with you? Shouldn't you be afraid of it? Why not just... leave it there?"

She balked at the question, grasping for an explanation that would make sense. That he would believe. She knew precisely why she kept it near, why she felt as much connected to it as she was terrified.

Because it spoke to her even now, as if it were attached to her sternum by a taut thread. What kind of witch would he think she was if she admitted the truth of it, that she felt drawn to the stone in a way she couldn't understand or explain? That she somehow knew she was always meant to find it? He would dump her by the side of the road and probably destroy the artifact. Or destroy them both. He was taking a big enough risk transporting her as it was, knowing the stone could be dangerous.

"I don't know," she said at last. Another lie. "I haven't exactly been thinking straight. First, I was blind. Then a strange man found me naked in the dirt. That stone was the only thing I had."

Fen made a low sound in his throat, a hum of understanding. "As good a reason as any to carry around a deadly artifact."

"It's not funny," said Ru, noting his sarcasm.

"I know," he said, a smile in his voice. "It's just that you're very resilient."

"And *that's* funny?"

"No. It's endearing. Surprising."

Ru opened her mouth to respond but lost herself in thoughts of what he meant by that. Surprising? How could she surprise Fen, a man who didn't know her? Why would he, a stranger by all accounts, find her supposed resilience endearing? He confused her and kept her on her toes. He was an unknown, a stranger, but the way he made her feel was almost like the missing piece of one of her vases falling into place, a shattered vessel finding its shape again. How could he foster such tenderness, such trust? It made no sense; it set her off balance. But she was glad he had found her.

She didn't know if she would have made it on her own.

THE SUN WAS ALMOST FULLY behind the horizon now, lengthening shadows fading into a dusky purple road. She and Fen had been riding all day, stopping only for brief meals and for the horse to rest and drink. Every muscle in Ru's body was sore, her legs now almost numb from the strain of riding.

Soon they would come to the crossroads, their journey veering northward, away from the sea, toward the Tower.

Out of the gloom ahead, above the rising song of evening crickets, Ru heard the pounding of hoofbeats. She stared into the growing dusk and was able to make out approaching riders on horseback. A flag rose from the cluster, flapping red and gold, the colors barely visible from such a distance.

"King's Riders," said Fen. "We'd better make ourselves known before they raise an alarm."

Ru half-turned, giving Fen a sideways look. "It's not illegal to ride on the main road."

"Maybe not," he said, sounding unconvinced. "But they've no doubt heard about the dig site. They'll be looking for us."

She hadn't considered that possibility. She bit at her lip, anxiety winding its way along her nerves. Could the palace have received word so quickly? It had been less than two days. Reality tasted bitter on her tongue — there would be questions, inquiries. And she would be at the center of everything.

But there was little time to fret, to guess what might happen. The riders appeared before them in moments, in a clatter of hooves and armor. There were three in total, and Ru saw with a rush of relief that they were Sybeth, Lyr, and Rosylla. Had they come back to see how she was doing at the site?

She waved, calling out.

Sybeth recognized her first in the low light. "If it isn't our academic," she said, pulling her horse up close to Fen's.

Rosylla gasped, holding out a hand as if to clasp Ru's with it, and Lyr gave a polite nod.

"It's such a relief to see you," said Rosylla, her face pink with exertion, her hair a curling mess around her face. They had been riding at full tilt, their horses' hides shining with sweat. "The regent received a dove calling for aid — a fisherman offshore saw something strange at the dig site, and sent word to the regent should she wish to investigate. We were sent straight back from Mirith after a day's hard ride. But... where are the rest of the academics?" Her eyes darted back and forth between Fen and Ru.

"Who's this fellow?" asked Lyr, studying Fen with narrowed eyes.

"All will be answered in time," said Sybeth, all business. "Are you safe, Miss Delara? You've not been kidnapped by this man?"

Ru almost wanted to laugh. If anyone was traveling under duress with a stranger who harbored an unknown danger, it was Fen. "I'm perfectly safe. This is my... friend, Fen."

She placed her hand on his thigh in what she meant to be a friendly gesture, to make a show of their platonic intimacy. But his muscled thigh flexed as she did so, and he exhaled sharply, hot breath puffing against the back of her neck.

She removed her hand from his leg as if burnt by hot coal. "He's a historian."

Sybeth frowned. "I see. Were either of you involved in, or witness to, a strange occurrence at the dig site where we left you, Miss Delara?"

Ru opened her mouth to speak, but Fen's voice carried over hers. "Unfortunately, yes," he said. "We're the sole survivors of a tragedy. We were on our way to Mirith to inform the regent."

Lyr tossed Sybeth a look. "Should we continue to the dig site, per our orders?"

Sybeth shook her head, her dark eyes sharp in the twilight. "I want a first-hand account. Sole survivors, you say? So there *was* an event of some kind. The letter said there was an explosion."

Ru, practically vibrating with a heightened agitation, refused to let Fen guide the conversation. These riders were her friends. She knew best which version of the story to tell them. "Sybeth," she said, "he's telling the truth. There was a... an explosion. We still don't understand what happened. When I arrived at the dig site, I was asked to examine something they found in the crater. An artifact. And when I began to inspect it, the thing… well, it…" her voice stuck in her throat. Her eyes stung. She clutched at Fen's leg. Breathed in, breathed out.

The artifact, always present, called to Ru gently then. A warmth spread from her chest outward, as if the stone were sending comfort through the tether between them, as if it understood she was upset.

"It vaporized the dig site," Fen finished roughly. "I saw the whole thing."

"Oh Ru," Rosylla said, her expression crumpling as tears shone in her eyes. "What a terrible thing. How did you survive?"

"Never mind that," said Sybeth, always the professional. Though Ru noticed the line between her brows deepening, her shoulders tensing. "So, they found a weapon in the ground? We need to inform the regent immediately."

"Wait," said Ru, as Sybeth made to turn around and lead them all back the way the riders had come. "Wouldn't it make sense, academically, to bring the artifact to the Cornelian Tower for study? I feel it's imperative that we understand it. How it functions, what it's made of, how to… destroy it, if need be."

"You still have the blasted thing?" asked Lyr, his expression changing from vague annoyance to a mix of horror and disgust.

Sybeth and Rosylla shared a look of shock and dismay, and Ru realized she'd made a thoughtless blunder.

"You'd better come with us," said Sybeth.

Ru half-turned in the saddle, enough to meet Fen's gaze. He held it for a second, then frowned almost imperceptibly. He disagreed with Sybeth.

Ru shouldn't be surprised; he was a loner, a traveler. And he had agreed expressly to take Ru to the Tower, not Mirith. But surely, she thought, after Mirith, they could still go to the Tower with the stone. They would need to take safety precautions, but… Was there any real reason to hide the artifact? As a scientist, Ru felt, rationally, that it should be studied, understood, and categorized. The only thing she wanted to conceal was its unseen connection to her.

That was her secret to keep, and hers alone.

"We'll go to Mirith, then," she said at last, nodding at Sybeth. There was no reason to argue, and without the regent's blessing, there was only so much she could accomplish in studying the artifact. "It's the only sensible destination."

Fen sighed, only loud enough for her to hear.

The small company rode out together, then, following the main road until it forked to the southeast, toward Mirith.

Fen remained silent but threatening, like a roiling storm cloud at Ru's back. The King's Riders were unusually taciturn. Ru tried to think of pleasant things, like prime numbers and intact pottery and the ivy that grew on the Tower like a green blanket. But her mind was always pulled back to the artifact, its voice without words, and the inevitable feeling that it would not leave her in peace for long.

CHAPTER 10

Mirith was as loud as it was colorful, as filthy as it was beautiful. It had not always been the capital of Navenie. Centuries ago, it was only a mid-sized port town, known for its sea trade routes to the neighboring kingdom of Mekya to the east, and the city of Solmaria on the far western edge of Navenie. But after the Destruction of Ordellun-by-the-Sea, Navenie's then capitol, the title was bestowed upon Mirith.

When Mirith was given what should have been a great honor, it floundered. Many of those who had been displaced by the Destruction — rural farmers who relied on trade within Ordellun-by-the-Sea, travelers whose permanent homes were now gone, and anyone who survived the horrible event by simply being away from the city at the time — came flooding to Mirith, until its gates had to be closed to visitors. There simply wasn't enough room, enough resources to go around.

The gate remained closed for centuries, and only those with permits were allowed to enter the city walls. Gradually, outside Mirith's walls grew another city made of the hovels and dwellings of Ordellun-by-the-Sea's refugees who had nowhere else to go, or who had remained out of sheer stubbornness.

Now, the original walls of the old Mirith were gone, the two cities had merged into one. But the city never stopped being dirty, overcrowded, and filled with the ever-present sense that it was on the verge of some kind of collapse.

Even so, warm breezes and sea rains kept its gardens lush, and the sun shone year-round. It was also the only place, other than the Tower, that Ru considered to be home.

She was used to the city's brightly painted buildings and plazas, its sparkling fountains, its hanging gardens and uneven cobbles, and green, well-tended parks. She was used to the press of bodies on the road, which began well before one reached the city. And she was familiar with the shouts, the smell of sewage, the random snippets of cries, or laughter, or singing that emanated from every window or door or shop front.

And while Mirith was familiar as an old friend, Ru never became bored of the city. She gazed about in the early dawn light as they rode through the city's main gates, the guards standing aside and saluting as the riders escorted them through. The market crowds made way — albeit slowly and with complaint — for the small procession, but nobody bothered to look up for more than a moment's glance. King's Riders were coming and going from the city constantly and were no more interesting than a farmer's pig cart on its way to the market.

Despite all her heaviness and the incessant weight of the artifact, Ru felt lighter as they rode into the city, the sights and smells of Mirith energizing her after a mostly sleepless night.

She found herself turning this way and that in the saddle to catch sight of a cathedral's steeple gleaming in the sun, to watch a young man dart nimbly across the road with an armful of bread loaves, to gaze down a colorful side street lined in bright shop awnings.

"You love it here," said Fen.

She turned, smiling. She had almost forgotten he was there, she was so swept up in the city. "It's where I grew up. I haven't been back in nearly a year."

"The way you look at the city... like you're seeing it for the first time." His words were low, thoughtful. Almost as if he was talking to himself.

Ru turned to look at him, or as much of him as she could see so close to him in the saddle. "What about you?"

"What about me?"

"Where's home? And I don't mean where you grew up. What place makes you feel safe every time you return?" She felt a bit silly asking, but the relief of being home was so immense and a bit surprising that it practically oozed from her pores.

Maybe here, home, with her family nearby and under the Lady Regent's authority, they could sort everything out at last. The artifact would be identified, it would stop talking to her forever, and somehow everything that occurred at the dig site would make sense.

"I don't have a place like that," said Fen. Though his tone was nonchalant, the words cut across Ru's thoughts like a cold wind. "Not anymore."

She turned away, not knowing how to respond. The idea of not having a home, not feeling safe and happy in any place… she couldn't imagine it. "I'm sorry."

"Don't be," he said. "I'm not the kind of person who deserves a lovely home to return to."

"What's that supposed to mean?" asked Ru. "Everyone deserves comfort, relief, a place to feel cared for." Especially Fen, who had been nothing but patient and kind and who had saved her life twice.

Fen chuckled. "I suppose I'm just a miserable old man."

Ru made a noise of incredulity. "Old man? You're not much older than I am."

"If you say so."

As he spoke, the group turned left onto a wide promenade. Just as they did, a cart piled with hay bales came barreling toward them. The riders maneuvered their horses out of the way easily, and Fen did the same. Ru, however, wasn't prepared for the sudden turn and started losing her balance in the saddle, knowing she was about to tumble humiliatingly onto the cobbles below.

But before she could, Fen dropped the reins with one

hand and wrapped his free arm around her waist, steadying her firmly against his chest.

"Careful," he said, his voice rumbling against her ear. She found — heart hammering in her chest at the shock of nearly falling and the further surprise of Fen's closeness — that she had completely forgotten what they were talking about.

THE PALACE WAS LOCATED near the edge of Mirith, on the white coastal cliffs that afforded a sweeping view of both the city spreading out below and the bay and its colorful ships that came and went. Everything, from the manicured lawns to the palace walls to the sea beyond, caught the morning sun and seemed to glow.

The palace itself was a sprawling system of buildings, some red brick with white trim, others white stone, all connected to the oldest central building, which was dark gray and aged. Mismatched towers and parapets arose from the palace, belying the patchwork way in which it had been built. It had begun as an ancient keep, and, over time, several of the city's rulers had added their own wings or towers to the building. The royal family of Navenie's blood had thinned over the years since Mirith became the capitol, but the family's defining characteristic was its eccentricity. The mismatched palace was a testament to that.

Ru found the palace intimidating. She had been there many times as a child; her father had been the king's primary textile supplier before the regent had taken over as Navenie's ruler. She and her brother had been allowed to wander the gardens, playing hide and seek in the topiary. Once, they had been given a tour of the courtiers' wing of the palace, a footman pausing to point out each of his favorite paintings along the corridors, noting the noble families who had rooms there. Simon had loved those days so deeply that they had been the impetus for his career. He never grew out of the palace, the opulence and pomp of it all.

As Ru, Fen, and the King's Riders neared the palace entrance, the riders stopped momentarily, palace guards questioning them in low voices.

While they waited, Ru allowed herself to be transported by the morning rays on towering stone, by the hustle and bustle of courtiers and various dignitaries, and even by the food and drink vendors who set up shop along the grand thoroughfare that led up to the palace's main doors, hawking fried sausages and fried potatoes and fried breads.

Ru's mouth watered at the smell, sweet and salty and warm. She briefly considered asking Fen to buy her a bag of fried sugar bread, but her thought was interrupted by Sybeth's bold voice, which carried easily over the general din.

"Miss Delara, Fen, come with me." She waved one arm to indicate that they would enter the palace.

"I'll see you again soon," said Rosylla with a smile, departing with Lyr toward the stables and riders' quarters.

Sybeth led Ru and Fen to a cluster of footmen and stable boys hovering near the palace entrance, waiting to be useful. Sybeth dismounted and said something to one of the young stablehands who ran up to take her horse's reins. He nodded and chirped something to a colleague, who came running to Ru and Fen. He held out a hand. "Need help, Miss?"

Before Ru could respond, Fen vaulted out of the saddle and landed next to the boy, who started.

"I've got her," said Fen. Then he turned to look up at her, winking and giving a little bow. "Miss," he said, holding out one gloved hand.

"Ridiculous," she muttered, willing her cheeks not to redden. She tried to dismount as gracefully as she could, but she still wasn't used to riding, and her foot caught on the stirrup as she half-stepped, half-fell into Fen's arms.

He laughed, catching her easily, and set her on her feet to face him. Morning light shone in his eyes, his hair lifted off his forehead by a light breeze. She had to look away or risk blushing even deeper. Fen's effect on her was undeniable, but she pushed it aside, impatient with herself. It was only because he had saved her life, been there for her in a traumatic moment. Surely he didn't see her in that way.

"All sorted?" said the stable boy, taking the horse's reins.

With a shock, Ru realized she had been about to let the boy walk off with the artifact, still wrapped in its blanket in the saddlebag. What if someone had found it, had touched it?

"Just a moment," she said in a rush, reaching into the saddlebag and pulling the blanket bundle from within. "There."

With a tip of his hat, the stable boy led Wind away while Fen stared after. "He'd better treat her well," he said.

"These are the king's stables," said Sybeth, frowning deeply. "Your horse has never known such luxury, nor will she again. Follow me."

Fen raised his eyebrows but said nothing. Ru, arms wrapped tightly around the swaddled artifact, wondered if her brother might be in the palace. He had rooms there, but he was often called into the city for his services. She tried not to get her hopes up, but seeing Simon, with his easy laugh and terrible jokes, would be a comfort.

They approached the grand entrance to the palace, up a flight of carpeted steps and between two lines of ornamental guards in bright golden armor, and were finally stopped just before the doors by a pair of functional guards. Sybeth explained her errand in low tones, and the guard listened with a frown and finally nodded, summoning a footman from within the palace.

Even with the hope of seeing her brother, Ru found her thoughts straying to darker things. Holding the artifact so close, even through layers of blanket, was draining on her emotions. At the moment, it seemed to be amplifying her anxieties, feeding them back to her in a spiral of insecurity. What *was* it? And why wouldn't it comfort her when she needed it most?

Fen's hand pressed her shoulder for a moment and

she let the warmth of him calm her, a solid reminder of where she was, allowing her to breathe easier. Even the artifact seemed to respond, its touch on her mind growing softer, soothed.

But she didn't have time to wonder why, or how, the stone responded to her emotions. Sybeth turned back to them, a footman just behind her. "As I'm sure you are aware," Sybeth said, "you will not be allowed an audience with the Lady Regent in your current state. Mr. Goodfellow will show you to your temporary rooms, where you will bathe. I will collect you in an hour. Don't do anything foolish." She caught Ru's gaze with this last order.

As if Ru hadn't already learned her lesson. Yet Ru only felt warmth for the rider, gratitude for her matter-of-fact way.

Without further ado, Mr. Goodfellow led them into the palace.

～

RU WAS RELIEVED to find that her and Fen's rooms were across the hall from one another. It wasn't that she felt unsafe in the palace, but the circumstances were vastly different now than any other time she had visited.

Everything made logical sense — the regent would want to know everything about the horrific event that occurred at the dig site she had funded from her own coffers. She would want to question everyone involved. But Ru couldn't help wondering what the regent would think of Ru herself, whether she would be accused or demonized.

And what would happen to the artifact? The uncertainty made her uneasy to the point of nausea. She voiced her physical pains to the lady's maid, who had been assigned to her for the duration of her stay.

"You'll want a bath, Miss," the maid had advised. "A bath cures everything."

Ru lay now in a vast brass tub, lavender petals drifting across the surface of water that had been infused with oils and perfumes. Her temporary room was a thing of dreams, a fantasy of filigree and velvet and silk. The ceiling was painted to resemble a summer sky, pale blue with soft clouds drifting across it, and she could even see tiny cherubs dotting the clouds if she squinted. The bed was practically boat-sized, and she hoped fervently that they would stay the night in Mirith if only for the opportunity to sleep in it.

Any other time, she might have drifted off to sleep. But instead of allowing the beauty of the room to lull her into a peaceful doze, Ru's brain refused to stop ticking. It reached ever backward to memories of dirt and gravel scraping against her naked body in the darkness... Fen holding a bloodied knife... Lady Maryn, her fingers reaching for Ru... and always, the horror in Lady Maryn's eyes.

Ru realized that tears were running down her cheeks and into the now tepid bathwater. Sniffing loudly, and slightly embarrassed by this display of unchecked emotion, she dragged herself out of the bath and stood dripping on the thick rug.

The lady's maid heard this and came running from whatever nook she'd been waiting in. She held a fluffy towel at the ready, and dried Ru with incredible speed, before helping Ru into a pair of slippers and draping a soft robe over her shoulders. These small ministrations were a balm for Ru's soul, drying her tears along with her body.

"There we are, Miss," said the maid. "We haven't much time now. Would you allow me to do your hair?"

Ru couldn't remember the last time she had "done" her hair in any way beyond brushing it or braiding it hastily down her back. She nodded, not trusting her voice to be steady yet. Her throat still stung with unshed tears.

The maid instructed Ru to sit on a cushioned little chair in front of a vanity, facing a circular mirror framed in gold filigree. The sudden appearance of her reflection almost made Ru bolt. She hardly recognized the creature staring back at her. Her skin, usually so tan from the sun, was now wan and sickly. Heavy purple-blue shadows hung under bloodshot eyes. She looked like a ghoul or something that should live under a bridge.

Unbidden shame rose in her when she realized that Fen had seen her like this. She bit down on the feeling, pushing it away. Why should she care? It shouldn't matter whether she looked like a drowned rat or a beautiful maiden; he was only here to help her travel to the Tower. After that, they would go their separate ways.

Yet, while she had only known him for a few days, the thought made her unexpectedly sad.

Unperturbed by Ru's haggard appearance and tear-stained face, the lady's maid began her work. She was a magician — that was the only way Ru could describe the transformation. First, the maid brushed and powdered Ru's hair until it was shiny and smooth, no longer tangled and greasy. Then she wrapped it up effortlessly and pinned it into an elegant coil at the back of Ru's head. It was painfully simple compared to the intricate, grandiose hairstyles worn by ladies of the court, but Ru felt like a new woman.

Then, spinning Ru around in her chair without preamble, fully in her element, the maid began her work on Ru's face. Ru had never seen so many creams, powders, and tinctures — all for the purpose of making a face look presentable. By the time the maid was finished, and Ru was brave enough to look in the mirror once again, she was amazed. She actually looked human again. *Better* than human in fact, with only her bloodshot eyes a reminder that she had been through her own version of hell in the past few days.

"You're incredible," Ru breathed, admiring herself in the mirror from every angle. She looked like a proper courtier, no longer a rough and tumble academic. "What's your name?"

The maid blushed. "Pearl," she said softly.

"Pearl, you are a wonder."

The lady's maid continued to amaze when she left the room for a moment and came back toting a selection of fine gowns. She instructed Ru to choose one as quickly as she could, or Sybeth, she warned, would come bursting in while Ru was in a state of dishabille.

So Ru chose the dress that reminded her most of the Tower: a deep green silk affair with long sleeves that puffed at the shoulders, a low-cut square collar, and a row of gold buttons leading down the front of the bodice.

It wasn't anything special, not quite fit for a ball, but it was perfectly adequate for an academic. And after being so long in the field wearing a shirt and trousers, the feeling of being in a gown again, her back held straight by a firmly boned corset, gave Ru a much-needed boost in confidence.

Moments after Pearl finished picking the last bits of lint from Ru's dress and making sure her hair was perfectly in place, Sybeth knocked thunderingly at the door and burst in before Pearl or Ru could open it, the tassels on her epaulets swinging.

"Miss Delara, are you ready?"

Ru knew it was a rhetorical question, but nodded anyway.

"Bring the artifact," Sybeth ordered. Her demeanor had become rock-hard since they arrived at the palace, and now that Ru thought about it, the riders had all been more distant on the ride back to Mirith.

She supposed she would have distanced herself from Ruellian Delara too if she could.

Swept up in a sudden rush of loneliness, Ru gathered the artifact in her arms and followed Sybeth out into the hall.

She wasn't at all prepared for what she saw there.

Fen stood waiting, arms casually folded across his chest. She almost didn't recognize him at first. He was no longer the scruffy wanderer who had come across her in the wilds. He still wore his leather doublet and boots, now wiped clean and polished. His slightly worn black shirt had been replaced by a soft cream one, its collar brushing against his stubbled jaw, open to the throat. His black hair was still unruly, apparently its only state, but had been washed and shone like a raven's wings in the corridor's many lamps and chandeliers.

He looked so regal he might have been a lord about to go hunting, or an aristocrat's first son visiting the palace in search of a wife. But even with clean clothes and hair, something about him still seemed wild, unfettered. As if he didn't quite belong. The sight of him stopped Ru in her tracks.

When he saw her staring, his eyebrows raised slightly, and a smile lit his face.

Ru, immediately self-conscious of her gawking, smiled shyly back before catching herself. She shouldn't allow herself to feel anything for Fen, least of all attraction. He wouldn't be around for long, and there were bigger things that required her full attention.

"Stop dawdling," said Sybeth, waving them along. "You can stare at each other later. The Lady Regent awaits."

CHAPTER 11

Audiences with Regent Sigrun were usually more commotion than substance, affairs with too much pomp and not very much purpose. At least, that was what Ru's brother had told her once, deep in his wine. But as Ru and Fen were led into the throne room, she quickly became overwhelmed by the grandeur of it all and found it impossible not to be impressed.

The room itself was cavernous, hung with red and gold banners, its ceiling so high Ru would have had to tilt her head back to see it. Tall windows on either side let in the summer sun, painting the marble floors with stripes of bright light. Columns lined the length of the room, partially concealing shadowed alcoves, areas where courtiers could stand and converse without attracting eavesdroppers.

Except that now, every eye in the room roved toward their small party, toward her.

The throne room was packed to the brim with people of all sorts. Courtiers, guards, footmen and servants, aristocrats, scientists, musicians, artists, and anyone to whom the regency took a liking. It was important to the Lady Regent to keep the palace lively, to ensure that it was a place of art and science, a cultural touchpoint for the kingdom.

Ever since the neighboring kingdom of Mekya's great boom of technological and cultural advancement

over a century ago, Mirith had followed closely behind. And while she only held the throne in lieu of a
blood heir to the monarchy, Regent Sigrun had
stepped eagerly into the shoes of Navenie's ruler, ensuring that the kingdom's advancement continued to
grow.

Ru glanced around, hoping for a glimpse of her
brother, but knew it would be hard to recognize him in
the throng. As she scanned the crowd, she noticed several oddly dressed men and women in small clusters
about the room. They were dressed all in white with
gold chain belts, their only adornments. They wore
white caps over close-shorn hair, and seemed to whisper
and mutter animatedly to one another without inter-
acting with anyone else in the room.

She wondered who they could be. There was an air
of religion about them, but they didn't belong to any
church she recognized. As far as she knew, religious
leaders and groups weren't usually invited to the palace
anyway; they generally preferred to hold their own sov-
ereignty at their places of worship, and had little interest
in the political affairs of Navenie.

But there wasn't time to ruminate over it. As Sybeth
led them forward, those gathered in the throne room
began to quiet gradually. Raucous conversation and
laughter faded to discreet murmurs as they watched the
procession of three.

Word must have spread quickly through the palace,
maybe the whole of Mirith, of what had happened at the
Shattered City. Even if the details weren't known, it was
obvious to Ru that she and Fen were an intriguing arrival, and that everyone gathered in the throne room
was eager to hear what they had to say.

"Welcome," said Regent Sigrun, her voice carrying
through the room. She motioned for the group to approach her.

She was seated in a large chair to one side of the
throne. As the kingdom's regent, it was her right to sit
on the throne if she wished. But there had been love between the late king and the regent, so she honored his

memory by leaving the throne empty for a blood heir — if one ever turned up.

Sybeth led Ru and Fen most of the way to the dais, but when they came to the foot of it, she moved to one side and bowed, facing the regent. Fen and Ru stepped forward alone, facing their leader side by side. Fen bowed deeply, and Ru curtsied. She stumbled slightly, cheeks heating immediately as she did. Her legs were exhausted from riding, even after soaking in a hot bath.

"Are you well, Miss Delara?" asked Sigrun by way of greeting.

If Ru hadn't known she was the regent, she might not have guessed this woman held the most powerful seat in the kingdom. Sigrun looked more like a general dressed in military attire with cream, skin-tight breeches, knee-high calfskin boots, a jacket of deep red, practically bursting with gold buttons and tassels, and a large feathered hat perched on her graying hair.

The woman herself was tall, her long legs crossed at the ankle, one long, large-knuckled finger tapping the arm of her chair. Her features were elegant and slightly masculine, and her nose reminded Ru of marble statues.

"Apologies, Lady Regent," said Ru. "I'm well, thank you."

"You must be exhausted from your travels," said Sigrun, leaning forward. "Your story isn't a pleasant one, as I surmise from the reports of my riders."

Ru wasn't sure if this was a statement or a question. She nodded slightly, her fingers curling tightly against the blanketed artifact.

Sigrun's eyes narrowed in thoughtful observation. "And who are you?" she asked, inclining her head toward Fen.

"Fen, my lady," he replied. "A traveling historian."

She raised an eyebrow. "And your family name?"

He glanced at Ru. "Verrill," he said.

"Fen Verrill, I would say it's a pleasure to meet you, but unfortunately you arrive here under less than happy circumstances." The regent shifted, and with the movement, her medals and tassels jangled softly, metal against cloth. "I have no desire to draw out this encounter. I am sure that you're both in need of rest. I wish only to hear a first-hand account of what occurred at the dig site, Miss Delara. While the memory is fresh. I understand you were at the very center of this horrific event."

Ru nodded. "I was."

Another soft metallic clinking as the regent leaned forward, her stern chin resting on curled fingers. "How did you survive?"

The regent's words were like ice in Ru's veins. She felt Fen stiffen beside her, the rush of inhaled breath. She was beginning to develop a headache on top of her already roiling gut. "You want me to tell you now, Lady Regent?" she said, keenly aware of the countless eyes fixed upon her. "Here?"

"Yes." Tap, tap, went her finger against the arm of her chair.

Ru had no choice.

Unsteady, frightened in the face of the regent's attention, the crowd, Ru reached inside herself for a source of peace. She found the artifact there, its presence less disturbing each time she looked for it, and yet she nearly recoiled when it reached out to meet her, soothing her in the dark of her thoughts.

The throne room was silent but for the low murmur of scattered whispers, the rustle of skirts and frock coats.

She began her story at Dig Site 33. She explained how she had been summoned by the King's Riders and escorted to the Shattered City. How, once there, she had been informed of the nature of the thing she was meant to be inspecting: an artifact that might be magic.

When she came to the moment she was about to examine the stone, she paused in her recounting. A coil of remembered terror tightened around her throat. How was she supposed to explain what happened then? The inexorable pull on her, the desperate need to touch the artifact, her skin's desire to trace the smooth edges of it as if it were the only thing that mattered.

The regent cleared her throat, and Ru realized that

she had been silent for too long. She tried to breathe like
Fen had taught her. In. Out. And then his hand was on
her back, a light, reassuring touch. She looked up at him,
and he tossed her an encouraging half-smile.

"Then," she said, her breathing finally steady. "I began
to examine the artifact. But the moment I touched
it, I—"

"You touched the stone?" asked Sigrun, raising her
head slightly, the plume on her hat fluttering.

"Yes," said Ru. She willed confidence to imbue the
timbre of her voice, knowing that any hesitation could
raise doubt or questions about her methods. "Due to my
expertise in ancient artifacts, my extensive studies in the
nature of magic objects, I determined that it was safe.
There were no signs of volatility. I sensed no charged
particles and no unusual interactions with air or mois-
ture. The artifact, as far as I could see, lay dormant. And
I needed to interact with it on a physical plane. How else
could I make further deductions about its molecular
properties?"

The white lie came to her lips almost too easily, and
with it a wave of suppressed emotion — Lady Maryn's
face, darkness bursting outward from the stone, a spark
of pain behind her eyes.

"I see." The regent appeared grimly thoughtful. "I understand that some kind of explosion occurred shortly
after you inspected the artifact."

Ru squeezed her eyes shut, just for a second. "Yes."

"Do you recall the nature of the explosion? How
were you not destroyed along with everything else at the
dig site?"

Fen shifted at Ru's side. Tension radiated from him
like heat from a stove, even though he wasn't the one
being questioned.

"I'm..." Ru stammered, fighting to stay upright.
How had she not been destroyed? There was no answer. No explanation. Only the memory, again and
again, looping in her mind's eye. She felt the blood
drain from her face. Her corset was so tight; sweat
beaded on her brow. She knew the signs of a faint

coming on, but she refused to do it, not here. Not in front of everyone.

"You can see this line of questioning is distressing Miss Delara," Fen said then, his voice low and shadowed with warning.

The regent raised her eyebrows, eyes flashing. "You will forgive me, Mr. Verrill, for attempting to learn why over a dozen innocent Navenians were vaporized in one fell swoop. Ruellian Delara is strong enough. She will answer my questions."

Ru glanced at Fen, both with gratitude and to say, silently — *I'm okay.* But he continued to watch the regent, jaw clenched.

"Apologies, Lady Regent," Ru said, remaining upright, remaining conscious, with only pure strength of will. To remember the moment was unspeakably painful. But to repeat it aloud to the court of Navenie... She swallowed thickly. "I recall the nature of the explosion. It was darkness. Complete darkness, swelling out from the artifact." She breathed in once, then out. "That's all I remember. I woke up alone, afterward. Everything at the dig site was... was gone."

There was a lengthy silence as the regent contemplated this. Gone were the hushed murmurs; all eyes were fixed on Sigrun. Anticipation hung in the room, tense, like a storm cloud just before a lightning strike.

Ru's hand found Fen's, his cracked knuckles, and he held her there. Steady.

Finally, the regent spoke. "Miss Delara, you have no idea what could have set it off, made this artifact explode into darkness?"

"No," said Ru.

"Nor do you understand why you survived it. You alone."

"No, Lady Regent." Ru was grateful that her words were clear and firm. Her hands shook; the garrote of that memory pulled tighter and tighter around her.

"You see how this is a great difficulty for me," said Sigrun, leaning back in her chair. "My duty requires me to find answers. You seem to be my only method of doing so."

This was Ru's opportunity. Her chance to ask permission to take it to the Tower, to ask the questions she desperately needed to answer: Was it magic? How could it speak to her? Why had she been the only survivor? Sigrun wanted those answers too.

Ru was bound to the stone. As much as she wished she could leave the thing in the regent's care, left to be studied by scholars in some dimly lit wing of the palace, she knew she couldn't. Her fingers, wrapped so tightly around the swaddled stone they almost shook, betrayed her.

Deep down, in the farthest reaches of herself, Ru knew that she would never willingly leave the artifact behind. But she couldn't stay in Mirith — there would only be questions if she stayed, suffocating oversight, deadlines, and all the regulations that went with life in the palace. So there was only one solution left.

"Lady Regent, let me take the artifact to the Cornelian Tower," said Ru. A low hum of voices swept across the room as all those gathered reacted to this request. "I'd like to study it. I believe I can discern its nature and answer all of our questions."

The regent frowned, thoughtful. "There are plenty of scholars here in the palace, the latest tools and technologies. And I would like to oversee the process personally."

Ru stood firm, gripping Fen's hand with whitened knuckles. "Forgive me, Lady Regent, but even the King's Scholars are no match for the Cornelian professors. The palace's library is grand but pales in comparison to the Tower's halls of books. Every possible precaution is already in place at the Tower. And I fear I could not live with myself knowing that I brought a dangerous object into the palace, should it... well, there's no knowing what it can do."

There was another rumble from the gathered onlookers, this one much louder and a bit frightened. A few gasps arose from the crowd.

The regent still appeared unconvinced. She leaned

on her hand again, brow furrowed. "You must know that I dislike this idea."

Then a figure moved out of the shadows behind the throne, approaching the regent's chair. Ru hadn't noticed him there — one of the white-clad people, standing silently and statuesque all this time. He was pale and almost ethereal, with a shock of long golden hair falling around his shoulders.

As she watched, the man in white leaned over the regent's shoulder and whispered something in her ear. She cocked her head as he spoke, a thoughtful look crossing her face. Then she waved a finger, and he retreated back to the shadows.

"Very well," said Sigrun, sounding resigned. "Perhaps the Tower is the most logical place to uncover the mysteries of this artifact."

Ru curtsied, trying not to show the fervent relief that washed over her. "Thank you, Lady Regent."

"You will depart tomorrow morning," said Sigrun. "And tonight, you will attend dinner with me as my personal guests. Sybeth, see that they do not leave the palace grounds." With that, she waved a hand and sat back in her chair, her epaulets and medals clanking as she did.

It was as if a spell had broken. The clusters of courtiers about the room slowly returned to their usual chatter and delicate laughter. Women flicked their fans, footmen came in with trays of finger food, and somewhere a lutist began playing a lively tune.

Ru turned to Fen, her hand still clasped in his. She let go of him in a rush, suddenly aware that she'd been clinging to him. They shared a silent look of mutual surprise and relief. She let out a long exhale.

"You did well," Fen said. He stood out like a sore thumb from the surrounding courtiers, their pastel silks and dainty mannerisms so at odds with him. He was formidable, all in black, and somehow he radiated competence and power. Ru knew he was only the third son of a marquis, but if she had only just met him, she might have guessed he was a foreign prince. Or a king's general.

Fen raised an eyebrow, a smile lighting his features and Ru glanced away quickly. She'd been staring.

Just then, saving Ru from further embarrassment, Mr. Goodfellow appeared at Fen's elbow.

"Mr. Verrill," he said, "Miss Delara, come with me if you would."

They trailed after him in silence, Ru holding the artifact close to her with a stubborn fierceness, ignoring the stares of everyone as they passed. Fen strode behind her, so quickly becoming a comforting presence. Sybeth met them outside in the hall, her eyes glinting under the light of glass chandeliers. She gave Ru a small nod, which was as much a show of respect as Ru could hope for from the rider. Together, Sybeth and Mr. Goodfellow escorted them to their separate rooms.

It wasn't until Ru collapsed onto her bed, not caring whether she wrinkled her lovely dress, that she began to wonder who the man in white had been, and how he'd managed to change the regent's mind. And, most intriguing of all, *why* he had done so.

HOURS after the audience with Sigrun, her mind still reeling in the aftermath, Ru found herself unable to stop thinking about the strange people in white, particularly the one who had spoken in the regent's ear.

Who were they? What kind of influence did they have over the regent? And why would they have any interest in, or opinion about, the artifact? This last question hung heaviest on her mind.

As she gazed up through her bed's gauzy canopy at the pale blue ceiling, an idea came to her. Simon. If he was working in the palace, he would know every detail of even the seemingly innocuous goings-on at court.

With his job came innate danger, the kind that lurked in the shadows and attacked from behind, but that danger was balanced by a rich supply of information.

He was a minstrel, one of the most culturally revered and sought-after people in the court, and also one of the most endangered.

Centuries ago, minstrels had been pure entertainers, singers and musicians who traveled the kingdom sharing stories and songs for coin. But their ability to blend into the background of any tavern, to be invited into the home of any noble, set them up as the perfect vessel for information. And these days, while there were many musicians whose only purpose was to perform, true minstrels were a thing unto themselves. They worked in the shadows, neither sanctioned by any ruling body nor condemned by the same. Everyone at court needed information at some time or another, and minstrels would always be there to sell it to them. No group of people was assassinated or mysteriously disappeared without a trace more than minstrels.

Simon sometimes jokingly called himself a courtesan of conversation, but Ru knew how seriously he took his work. He was a performer, a charmer, and he would tell you any secret for a price.

Leaping up from the bed, Ru went to the panel of little tasseled rope pulls that indicated various services she could call for. She yanked on the second tassel, calling for her lady's maid.

She paced the room until Pearl appeared at the door.

"Pearl," said Ru, pulling the maid into the room and closing the door gently behind her. "Would you do me a favor?"

The maid's eyes widened. "A favor, Miss?"

"I mean, I suppose it's within the purview of your job," she said. Ru wasn't used to servants. At the Tower, everyone dressed, washed, did everything for themselves except cook. Growing up in their cramped house in Mirith had been much the same, with only a cook and a scullery maid to tend to the kitchens. Ladies' maids were for the rich and highborn, of which Ru was neither.

"I'd like you to send for my brother Simon Delara."

Pearl lit up at the name. "Oh!" she exclaimed. "I am familiar with Mr. Delara. Didn't know he was your brother. I believe he's staying in the courtiers' wing. What a lovely talent he has!"

"Yes, very talented," Ru said, excited and impatient that she knew her brother was indeed here at the palace. "Would you send for him, immediately? Tell him it's his sister calling," she added, unsure whether Simon would brush off a random summons without his sister's name attached.

"Of course, Miss." Pearl gave a little curtsey and departed to fulfill her mission.

It wasn't long before a knock came at the room's main door. Ru sat up from the bed, where she had been curled up next to the artifact.

"Simon!" she cried, throwing open the door.

She barely had time to take in her brother's tall frame, coiffed coppery hair, and ridiculous puff-sleeved getup before she was throwing herself into his arms. The tears came without preamble, neither hot nor painful, but rushing out of her like a dam bursting. For a moment every tense muscle in her body relaxed, and she let her brother's arms hold her up as she sobbed, ruining his lovely silk jacket.

"See, I told you," said Simon, "that Tower will turn you into a certified wet blanket. I'm never wrong. And look where we are now. Shameful." His words were full of love and laughter, and Ru was instantly cheered — but the tears still came.

"Close the door," she managed between sobs. "I have so much to tell you."

Simon stood back, taking her in, her pale features and bloodshot eyes. His usually laughing mouth pulled into a thin line, his heavy-lidded hazel eyes shining with worry. He allowed Ru to direct him to a chair across from a velvet couch where she now perched, drying her eyes.

"Shall we call for tea?" said Simon, eyebrows knit together in concern, as if tea would solve everything. He raised an elegant hand to call for it, his collection of gold rings glinting as he did.

Ru shook her head. "Later. I'd rather avoid interruptions for now. I think I've ruined your lovely jacket."

He glanced down, seeing the wet stain she left on his silk flower embroidered attire. Even his frothy white neckcloth was mussed.

"I have three more jackets just like it," he said, treating her to a pained smile that said he didn't. "But what's this about, Ru? I haven't heard from you in months. And suddenly you turn up at the palace, sobbing wildly."

Ru's bottom lip quivered.

Simon let out a long, dramatic sigh, his bright gaze never leaving Ru's. "You're the academic who blew up the dig site."

Relief and shame coursed through her at the revelation. "You've heard?" She shouldn't be shocked; it made sense that Simon would already know every detail, from start to finish. He was a minstrel, after all.

Simon leaned forward, a self-confident smirk playing at the edges of his mouth. "Isn't it impressive? I've been hosting a salon for the better part of the day, performing music, discussing philosophy, science, and yet while doing all of that, I managed to learn not only that there's been an explosion at the dig site, but also that it was caused by some mad academic from the Cornelian Tower."

Shame won over relief, and Ru felt the telltale sickness rise in tandem with the memory of what had happened in the Shattered City. "Everyone must think I'm a monster," she said, twisting her hands in her lap.

"On the contrary," said Simon. "I'm delighted to learn it was you. Finally, another Delara makes something of herself."

"Don't joke about it," said Ru.

Simon was quiet for a moment, his somber expression a glaring contrast to his brightly delicate clothes and the fashionably styled curls of his hair. "Well," he said then, brightening, looking about the room with sudden interest. "I suppose you wouldn't let me have a look at that artifact?"

"Simon!"

"What? The way you've built it up, I feel entitled to at least a peek." He gave her his best, disarming smile, to which Ru had long since become immune.

She glared at her brother. "I know you're allergic to sincerity, but could you at least *try* to take this seriously? I didn't call you here for comedic asides."

Simon hung his head slightly in acquiescence. He took after their mother, with fairer skin and lighter hair than Ru, but he had the same nose, and the same slightly large ears. Ru noticed how he had aged in the time since she'd last seen him, a few lines forming at the edges of his eyes. She knew his joking exterior was armor, a front to keep everyone guessing, to paint himself as a harmless clown. But he, like every other minstrel in the kingdom — and there were very few — was probably more informed about political goings-on in the city than even the regent herself.

"You know it's only my nature to be terrified of feelings," said Simon. "But I'm sorry anyway. And before you ask, I think I know exactly what kind of information you're looking for."

Ru sat back. "Who says I'm looking for information? I needed a shoulder to cry on. You're my brother."

"Yes, a brother who, as you've just made clear, has no idea what to do when faced with a genuine emotion. I'm the last person you'd want as a comforting shoulder. But I know you, and I know you're absolutely *dying* to find out about the Children."

"The wh—"

Simon held up a ring-laden finger, silencing her. "Information for information, beloved sister. First, you have to tell me where to find this Fen Verrill character so that I might subject him to a thorough interrogation."

Ru snorted. Simon *would* use this as an opportunity to distinguish himself as some kind of overprotective elder brother, when she knew full well that he not only couldn't care less about who Ru associated with, but he had also never been the sort to feel entitled to protect her from amorous advances. She knew how to do that on her own.

"I don't think so," she said. "He's not coming to the Tower with me, anyway." She tried to sound casual, as if the words didn't feel bitter on her tongue. The regent was now involved — she didn't need Fen to escort her throughout the kingdom. He had his own life.

Simon tilted his head to one side. "Is he not?"

"No."

"Why not?"

"Because I don't know why he would," said Ru. "Anyway, who are these children I'm supposed to be dying to know about?"

"Not just any children," said Simon, smiling conspiratorially. He was in his element now, sharing gossip, passing on the little details he made it his business to know. "*The* Children. You will have seen them in the throne room, the creeps in white. They're new. Some kind of spiritual group. They claim to be from Mekya, but I imagine they came crawling out of the forest one day like little wriggling stoats."

Ru raised her eyebrows. "They're that bad?"

"Worse." Simon fiddled with one of his rings, spinning it around his finger as he spoke. The tips of the fingers on his left hand were red and calloused, the mark of a lutist. "They're not cruel or violent or anything, not like those ancient, bloodthirsty gods you read about. But these Children certainly have their fingers in a lot of pies, considering they're a group of strangers who came out of seemingly nowhere only months ago. They have their own temple, supposedly, *somewhere*, although it's unclear exactly who or what they worship."

He paused to fix a copper curl that had fallen out of place. "Anyway, the creeps have taken up residence in the palace, as you can see. Somehow their leader, a character called Hugon — *blech*, even the name's revolting — ingratiated himself with Regent Sigrun almost immediately, and within weeks she appointed him as her unofficial *advisor*. Can you imagine? He's the only one of them who has anything interesting to say, but even he's wretched most of the time. Too charming. Smiles like a snake. Has plans... though I'm not sure what they are yet. I'm working on it."

"Do you have any actual information about these people other than your general dislike for them?" Ru asked, impatient.

Simon sniffed. "They're harder to crack than your average foppish aristo. And *you* still haven't told me where to find Mr. Verrill."

"He's got nothing to do with this," said Ru, leaning back on the sofa, desperate to get out of this uncomfortable gown. The boning had done its job in keeping her standing straight; now it threatened to crush her slowly. "I doubt I'll even see him again after dinner tonight."

"Fine, have it your way," said Simon, shaking his head as if his sister had driven him to his wits' end, when it was in fact, he who was being tiresome. "But I do have one more tidbit for you. That dig site at the Shattered City. I don't believe the regent could have cared less about that sort of thing. She would never have considered digging around in the crater like a lunatic. But the second those white-robed Children arrived, she decided to fund a dig. Not one of them will open up to me; I've tried all my tricks. I can't understand it. And what I understand even less, little sister, is twofold. Perhaps you'll enlighten me?"

Ru sighed. Her brother had a way of using fifty words when two would do. "Yes, Simon, what is it?"

"Why do you suppose they uncovered this black rock, this misshapen object, and immediately thought: *magic*."

"How can I possibly know that?" said Ru. "Lady Maryn said their technology was... acting up. Their watches weren't working properly."

He gave her a long look. "And scrambled clockwork says magic to you?"

Ru shrugged, hoping her nonchalance was believable — if he suspected she was hiding something, he wouldn't let her leave until he got it out of her. He couldn't know about the artifact's connection to her. No one could. It was too dangerous, too *wrong*.

"I suppose not," she replied. "There are plenty of things that could cause a reaction like that. All I know is that the regent and her advisor read my paper and actually found it intriguing. If anything, this raises my opinion of Hugon."

Simon pursed his lips. "Well, I *also* read that paper, and all I can say is that I was left with more questions than answers."

They glared at each other for a moment.

"And what was the second thing?" Ru asked, finally, losing patience.

"What *was* the second thing," replied Simon, staring up at the ceiling, brows furrowed. "Ah, yes. How did Hugon get hold of your paper in the first place? How did he convince the regent to take it seriously? What have they got against you?"

Ru rolled her eyes. She wasn't safe from even her own brother's mockery. "You can't be serious."

Simon actually laughed at that. "I swear I'm not trying to insult you. I'm genuinely intrigued, and you should be too. That paper was... well, to put it mildly, the jokes among the palace scholars went on for weeks. What's the reasoning behind Hugon dredging it up after how many months? Where do you fit in? It all smells a bit foul. And from what I've heard, it sounds as if Hugon himself convinced the regent to allow you to bring the artifact with you to the Tower. Why?"

"That's what I'd like to know," said Ru. So the blonde man in white, lurking behind the regent's chair, that had been Hugon.

"Well," said Simon, standing abruptly, his hair bouncing with the movement. "It's getting late, and I can see your maid is eager to have you dressed for dinner."

Ru turned, seeing Pearl hovering near the servants' entrance, clearly waiting for a break in the conversation to intervene. Turning back to Simon, she fixed him with a wide-eyed pleading look.

He hesitated for a moment, as if he might pull her

into a hug, but instead he extended a hand and patted the top of her head. "Don't worry, sister. I'll be performing at dinner tonight, flitting from guest to guest like an invisible little butterfly. Your brother has your back. We'll speak again soon."

He left with an obnoxious wink and a flourishing bow, and Ru slumped on the couch, wishing her brother was a bit more open and a bit less flashy when it came to... well, everything. But she knew he had heard her, had taken everything she told him seriously. If he was to be performing at dinner, he would pick up on things that others missed.

She only hoped she would have another opportunity to speak with him, one on one, before she departed for the Tower.

"Pearl," she said, forcing herself to stand despite an intense desire to take a very long nap. "Would you help me dress for dinner?"

CHAPTER 12

Much to Ru's surprise, she was seated to the right of Regent Sigrun at dinner, a place of honor. She wasn't sure what she had done to earn such a thing, nor was she certain she wanted it, but there was no getting out of it. The regent would sit her guests where she pleased.

Worse, though, was that Fen sat across the table from Ru. Normally such placement would be ideal — they could converse throughout the meal easily. But the dining table was so large that Ru would have to shout to be heard by Fen over the loud conversation of the room. Not to mention her brother's addition to the noise, strumming his lute and singing a raucous ditty as he drifted about.

The seat to Ru's right was thankfully empty; for now, at least. She took this as a gift, and since the regent's attention was constantly being vied for by her various dinner guests, Ru found herself sitting and eating in peace.

The room at least was beautiful to look at, with dark wood paneling along the walls that belied an older part of the palace. The regent's banner hung at one end of the room under an arched ceiling, flanked by brightly burning oil lamps in iron sconces.

The table itself was long and took up most of the room. Bedecked with summer foliage and flickering candelabra, it was a feast for the senses, the smell of roasting meat and fresh bread wafting in from an antechamber where the servants prepared to bring out each course.

While she took in her surroundings, Ru wondered why the regent had invited them to dinner at all, beyond perhaps a sense of duty to her guests. She made a toast at the start of the meal, thanking everyone for their work and loyalty, but never once acknowledged Ru by name, or the artifact, or anything to do with Ru's traumatic experience at the dig site.

She felt almost snubbed at first, but Ru decided that she would rather not be the center of attention at a palace dinner. And it was all the easier to enjoy the sight of Fen. She wanted nothing more than to let her gaze rove over him greedily, from head to nimble fingers.

She first saw him as she sat down, catching his eye across the table, causing her to stumble as she settled in her seat. His effect on her was almost embarrassing, the way he made her regress to an awkward pubescent girl. Heat flushed her cheeks, her hands clammy and awkward as she tried not to stare.

If he'd been a prince before, now he had the aura of a king and he was dressed to match.

He wore deep green velvet, so dark it was almost black, with patterned threads of dark gold sewn through, catching the light when he moved. His jacket hung open, and a waistcoat of the same color clung to his chest. A white neckcloth frothed out from a starched collar. He was frowning, pulling at the waistcoat's high collar until he loosened it enough to reveal more of his neck.

Ru watched him, mouth dry. His eyes were so fiercely wild, and his hair so impervious to styling that he appeared windswept and dramatic, even in this staid setting.

When Fen saw her looking, he smiled, and she dropped her eyes with embarrassment. Her brother's interest in Fen had made her both shy and agitated. She was confused that Fen was still here, and upset that he wouldn't be around for long. Was he truly so fascinated by the stone? Was he simply here to... protect Ru? Support her? She didn't understand his motivation, and that frustrated her. She wanted to speak to him privately, but since they'd arrived in Mirith, there hadn't been a chance.

Throughout dinner she kept trying to make eye contact, to indicate that she wanted to talk, but each attempt was fleeting, brief. During the soup course, Ru looked up briefly to see Fen watching her, but his eyes darted away as soon as their gazes met.

Her heart sank when his attention turned to a lovely young courtier sitting beside him, a woman whose golden hair was piled atop her head, adorned in white roses.

Ru kept trying to catch his eye, but to no avail. There were too many distractions, too much laughter and loud conversation. And by the time the venison arrived, steaming on gold plates and garnished with dark tart berries and sweet root vegetables, Ru finally decided that she should stop glancing furtively, and simply call Fen over to sit next to her.

Setting her shoulders, she leaned forward in her seat. "Fen," she hissed.

He didn't hear her, his attention once again taken by the courtier beside him. A horrible prickly feeling coiled in Ru's chest, and it wasn't the artifact.

In fact, the artifact had been quiet all afternoon, distant yet still present. Ru was almost used to it now.

"Good evening, is this seat taken?" said a smooth, accented voice.

Ru turned abruptly to see who had spoken. She was greeted by a man bowing, golden hair falling around his face. When he straightened, he held out a hand that was heavy with silver and jewels, putting even Simon to shame. He was very finely dressed in pale silks, countered by a strong jaw and seemingly even stronger hands. He grasped her hand gently as he brushed the faintest kiss across her gloved knuckles.

He was one of the most arrestingly beautiful people she had seen in her life.

She blinked up at him. "Please sit," she said, indicating the chair.

He did, delicately masculine, coattails sweeping out behind him. He turned back to her, a knowing smile creasing his face. A small dimple appeared on his left cheek, and it was almost as if he *knew* he was pulling Ru's attention straight to it.

"Allow me to introduce myself," he said, and Ru was finally able to place his accent — Mekyan. "I apologize for not doing so immediately; the lack of food has gone to my head. I am Lord D'Luc."

"Ah, you have arrived, my lord," said the regent, noting Lord D'Luc's appearance. "I thought you had left poor Miss Delara to sit alone all night."

He laughed, a deep, lovely sound. "I would never deprive her willingly. Miss Delara, what a pleasure to meet you." He met her gaze, and she was embarrassed by the effect he had on the state of her stomach. But there was something intense about him, magnetic.

Ru turned away from Lord D'Luc, glancing across the table at Fen. His eyes were dark, and he utterly ignored the golden-haired courtier, despite her attempts to regain his attention. Catching Ru's eye, he raised one eyebrow ever so slightly, disapproving. Ru's stomach twisted again — was he jealous?

"Why haven't I seen you before at court?" asked Lord D'Luc, pulling her attention away from Fen. She turned back to see him swirling his wine, his gaze sweeping over her appreciatively. "I would have remembered you."

Ru's insides tumbled again, her cheeks heating, despite knowing exactly what Lord D'Luc was doing. As much as she wished it were otherwise, she was anything but immune to the charms of handsome men. "I live at the Cornelian Tower," she explained. "I don't make a habit of being the Lady Regent's guest of honor."

"And yet I hear you've made quite a name for yourself in the world of academia," he drawled, his cupid's bow lips curving in a smile. "I read your infamous paper, 'From Sorcery to Science...'"

Ru reached for her wine, fingers tightening around the stem of the glass. "Ah. I thought only scholars would have read that."

"And who says I'm not a scholar?" he asked. "Even lords amuse themselves with academic texts, especially these days. I like to keep myself informed. And..." he lowered his voice as if sharing a great secret with her, "I have always been intrigued by the inexplicable, the occult."

Ru bristled slightly. "My paper doesn't at all address the..." she trailed off, suddenly distracted by the sight of her brother. He had meandered closer and was now staring so intently at her that it seemed as if he was trying to bore a hole straight into her brain. He continued to sing and strum his lute as he did so. She cut a glare at him as if to say, *not now*.

Lord D'Luc frowned. Even his frowns were lovely.

"Sorry, my lord," said Ru, hurriedly. "The minstrel distracted me."

"But you were saying, about your paper?"

"Well," said Ru, surprised to find someone who wanted to discuss her paper without mocking it, eager despite everything, "you must understand that not all magic is occult, and not all occult matters are truly magic. There is some overlap, but often what we call the 'occult' is folklore or religion. I find that to get to the truth, it is easiest to delve into where these two *do* overlap. There, we can locate the merging of story with reality, science with the impossible, as it were. Of course, I don't believe that magic is impossible – what many might call magic is actually science, perhaps performing or existing on a level we can't calculate or comprehend. Our technology is far too limited to measure it. But I wouldn't reduce the term magic to *advanced science*, as there is still a spiritual factor, an unknowing that we must accept as intrinsic to the practice."

Lord D'Luc was nodding as he listened, brow furrowed. Ru wondered if he'd actually understood anything in her ramblings. "So in a way," he said thoughtfully, "the occult is, ultimately, irrelevant, unless accepted as an intrinsic part of magic itself."

"Yes, exactly," said Ru, nodding eagerly. "I had planned to write another paper delving deeper into the areas where science and magic become indistinguishable, possibly introducing an element of spirituality to the mix, but I never came up with a thesis. And, well... the reception of my first paper wasn't exactly encouraging."

"You mustn't let the capriciousness of academia dissuade you," said the lord, his expression soft. He had such wonderfully long lashes, his jaw like carved marble.

A footman came sweeping over with desserts balanced on delicate trays, and in the brief chaos, Ru's attention was drawn once again to Fen. His eyes were fixed on her, his expression still dark as a storm.

The regent stood then, daintily pinging a tiny spoon against a glass, and everyone turned to her, expectant.

"Thank you all for attending my dinner," she said, smiling around as if everyone at the court wouldn't have fought tooth and nail for the privilege. "And special thanks to Ruellian Delara, who has so fearlessly agreed to escort our mysterious artifact north to the Cornelian Tower, and to study it there in an effort to ascertain its true potential."

There was polite applause about the table. Ru smiled uncomfortably. *Fearlessly* agreed? She also found it disconcerting that knowledge of this artifact had spread so quickly throughout the court, and that nobody seemed alarmed by it. Although, she supposed her audience with Regent Sigrun had been public, and there likely wasn't a soul left in the palace who hadn't heard of Ruellian Delara or the artifact.

Venison, pheasant, and far too much wine all roiled in her stomach.

Across the table, Simon appeared at Fen's shoulder and began whispering something into the man's ear. They both looked terribly serious. So serious, in fact, that Ru felt almost annoyed. Why should they be so grim? *They* weren't the ones who had to worry about the artifact, its incessant hum in her mind, even now. They didn't have to contend with the memory of Lady Maryn's face, the rising darkness, the horror of it.

Her fingers twisted in her lap.

The regent sat again, her announcements at an end. She directed a magnanimous smile toward Ru, who smiled wanly back. But Ru was no longer enjoying the dinner, if she truly ever had been. She regretted eating so much. Her stomach ached, and she suddenly felt too hot, suffocated by the close walls and elegantly dressed bodies and laughter and candlelight, all too close, too much.

She thought of the artifact, back in her room, which she had instructed Pearl to watch over but never touch. The black stone sat heavy in her mind. She needed to leave, to get out of this stifling room.

"Fen," she said, but he couldn't possibly hear, not over the clink of silver on porcelain, laughter, and voices.

"What's that, Miss Delara?" Lord D'Luc placed a hand on the back of her chair, careful not to touch her at the dinner table without her consent — the actions of a gentleman. "You look pale. Are you ill?"

There was a lull in the conversation then, and much to Ru's embarrassment, she realized the regent had overheard the lord's words. "Are you well?" Sigrun said, echoing the words from earlier in the day. "You've been through much, today."

"I'm fine," Ru managed.

"Escort her to her rooms, Hugon," said the regent. "She's obviously exhausted by the day's events."

Ru froze. *Hugon?* She remembered the man behind the regent, whispering into her ear. Golden hair, a glass-cut jaw... How could she have failed to recognize him?

"Of course, Lady Regent." Lord D'Luc rose from his chair, holding out an elbow for Ru. "Let's get you somewhere comfortable, Miss Delara."

She turned to where Fen sat, hoping for some kind of escape, and was met with the sight of an empty chair.

Where had he gone? And where was Simon? Exhausted and sick to her stomach, Ru had no choice.

She took Lord D'Luc's arm, allowing him to lead her around the table to the exit.

"You'll feel much better with some fresh air," he said. Ru couldn't quite believe it. This man in lovely finery, with a scientist's mind and the appearance and behavior of a highborn lord, was Hugon D'Luc, the leader of the Children and the regent's own advisor.

CHAPTER 13

The realization of Lord D'Luc's identity came as a shock, but Ru found herself more curious than intimidated. Now that she knew he was a man of science, he made an entirely different impression. Perhaps his interest in the Shattered City wasn't strange at all, but a true passion for discovery. How could he have known that the artifact would be not only discovered there, but also cause a horrific incident?

No, that was Ru's doing.

"You're white as a sheet," said the lord, steadying Ru with his broad arm. "You've pushed yourself too far today. Are your rooms near? Shall I call for water?"

Ru shook her head, directing the lord to her rooms. He kept up polite small talk as he practically carried her there, stopping once or twice so as to avoid her completely passing out. She apologized repeatedly and profusely, but he would hear nothing of it.

When they finally made it to Ru's room, Pearl met them at the door with a mug of steaming hot liquid and a cold cloth, which she immediately pressed to Ru's head. Waving Lord D'Luc away with one hand, Pearl shut the door with the other, leading Ru gently over to a cushioned divan.

"One of the footmen said you weren't feeling well at dinner, Miss," she explained, when Ru made a questioning noise at the steaming mug. "I could only guess you've overextended yourself."

"That's what Lord D'Luc suggested," said Ru, sipping at the liquid. It was strong and spicy, just hot enough to hurt a little as it went down.

Pearl instructed her to sit and relax while the bed was turned down.

Eyes closed, Ru slumped on the settee. She was now convinced that Simon must be personally biased against Lord D'Luc. He had behaved like a gentleman. Not once had he handled her inappropriately. Yes, he was a bit overly charming, but Ru found it almost refreshing after days of sleeping on cold ground, contending with fear and danger at every turn. And his conversation about science had been stimulating; the idea of that same man being the leader of a religious group? Nonsense. The Children must be scientifically enlightened, just as Hugon was.

When the bed was ready at last, she shed her gown and crawled between the sheets without bothering to change into pajamas. "Thank you, Pearl," she managed to mumble before sleep took her.

A VIOLENT KNOCKING on the door wrenched Ru from her slumber, tumbling her out of bed like a rabbit from a hole, heart pounding. She rubbed her head, blinking.

"Who is it?" she called out, her words thin and croaking.

"Sybeth," came the clear, determined voice. "We depart in thirty minutes."

Ru groaned, feeling as if she'd only just fallen asleep. The curtains on the windows were so thick it was impossible to tell the time of day based on sunlight alone. Squinting and rubbing her eyes, she yanked on the tassel for maid service.

Pearl arrived only moments later, pushing a cartful of morning accoutrements: a pot of hot coffee, toast, and jam, and on the lower level of the cart were stacks of folded clothes and a pair of boots.

"We must hurry," said Pearl, laying out the coffee and toast. "I lost track of time, Miss, I'm terribly sorry."

"It's perfectly fine," said Ru, dragging herself to the coffee. "Are these clothes for me?"

"Yes, Miss. A gift from the regent. Traveling clothes for your journey to the Tower."

After drinking her coffee as quickly as she could without burning herself, and chewing a piece of toast as quickly as she could without choking, Ru got dressed.

The clothes weren't exactly what she was used to at the Tower. They were more luxurious, adorned with details and ornamentations that Ru had absolutely no use for. Her jacket was velvet with a brocade collar, her skirts and bodice woven with fine wool, and ornately embellished at the bust with buttons and embroidery.

Even though they looked a bit too luxurious for a traveling outfit, Ru found that the clothes were very comfortable, and fit her perfectly.

"You look radiant," breathed Pearl.

"I look *something*," said Ru, peering cynically into a full-length mirror. The full look was somewhat more palatable than she had predicted as she was putting the clothes on, but even so, she felt overdressed for days of riding. "These sleeves are too puffy," she complained, pulling at the fabric and frowning. "And these boots, they're lovely, but they'll be ruined immediately. Not to mention the *skirts*…"

Pearl tutted and steered Ru away from the mirror before she could launch into a full-scale rant.

"It's time to go," said the maid, practical and useful as always. "Take your artifact. The horses and carriage are packed with everything you'll need, and I made sure the footman included some of those little sugar cookies you like."

Ru almost wanted to cry at Pearl's thoughtfulness. "How did you know about the cookies?"

Pearl blushed. "Your brother sent a note."

"Simon *would* send a note about my favorite cookies

rather than coming to see me off himself," Ru grumbled. She gathered the artifact in her arms, trying to ignore the way it almost seemed to purr at the edge of her consciousness.

Lyr was waiting in the hall, arms crossed over his broad chest, his eyes almost completely obscured by his heavy, dark brows. "Finally," he said when Ru emerged from her room. "Come on. We're late."

"By a few minutes," protested Ru, but she was rushed through corridors and down flights of stairs until they emerged into a gray morning.

The palace was almost ethereally quiet, its facade lit softly by angled sunlight through mist. The hour was so early that hardly anyone was about — servants and cooks would be preparing for the day in their wings of the palace, hurrying through servants-only corridors. The lower streets of Mirith would be teeming with market crowds, but the aristocracy had no reason to be up and about yet.

A miniature convoy waited for Ru at the foot of the palace's main stairs. She had foolishly, briefly imagined that she and Fen would be riding a horse together all the way to the Tower, a fantasy swiftly quashed by the reality that lay before her: half a dozen horses, three kitted out with King's Riders regalia, and four with simpler but much more robust harnesses and armor at the chests — these were horses of the King's Guard. In the center of everything sat a carriage, simple on the outside, but Ru caught a glimpse of a heap of pillows and blankets within.

"I don't need seven guards," she said, looking around for Fen. She saw Sybeth and Rosylla, preparing their horses for a long journey. She was comforted by the fact that her riders would be with her, at least. But four King's Guards? Did someone foresee a battle taking place on the northern road? "And who on earth is going to ride in there?" she asked, pointing at the carriage.

"Obviously you," said Lyr.

Ru balked. "I'd rather ride."

Sybeth approached then, one hand resting casually on her sword pommel. "Problem, Delara?"

"I was telling Lyr that I would much rather ride a horse than sit around like an old woman, alone in a carriage."

"No you wouldn't," said Lyr, matter-of-fact. "I've seen you ride. You hate it. You're terrible at it. Nearly fell off the saddle countless times."

"Where's Fen?" Ru asked, changing tactics. "I'll ride with him."

Lyr shrugged, and Sybeth frowned. "He'll not be joining us."

Ru's heart sank. It wasn't a shock, not really — why should he come with her when he had no reason to? She was being escorted by the regent's finest guards. She wouldn't need Fen anymore. But the fact that he hadn't come to see her off, had made no attempt to say goodbye… She hated how much it hurt.

Just then, the regent came sweeping out of the palace. She was in her usual military regalia, her face fresh and energetic even in that early hour. Just behind her left shoulder, looking elegant and handsome as ever, followed Lord D'Luc.

"Good morning," said Sigrun, approaching Ru. "I would like a word with you, Miss Delara, before you depart."

Shivering slightly, even under her layers of clothes, Ru followed the regent to stand a small distance away from the gathering. She hugged the artifact to her as if it could warm her, despite the mist that clung to them like ghostly wisps.

"Lady Regent," said Ru, dropping a curtsey.

"None of that," said Sigrun, waving a hand. "You must be on your way, but I hoped I might steal a moment of your time."

"Of course," said Ru, wondering what the regent could possibly impart at this point. She wouldn't call off the journey to the Tower, not now, would she? Ru shivered a little more violently.

"I must impress upon you," said the regent, "that it is

of the utmost importance that you and the artifact reach the Cornelian Tower safely. Do not do anything rash on the way. Do not begin your research prematurely. Do not handle the artifact without cause."

Ru felt defiant, insulted that she was being warned like this, treated as if she were a child. Hadn't she been the only person in Navenie with the relevant knowledge to inspect the artifact? Hadn't the regent sent for her, by name, and trusted her enough to visit the Shattered City itself? And now the regent was behaving like an over-bearing mother when Ru's own brother hadn't even bothered to see her off. That thought cut through her defiance, replacing it with a defeated loneliness.

She nodded. "I understand, Lady Regent."

"And we absolutely refuse to hear of you falling from your horse and injuring yourself gravely," added Lord D'Luc, flashing a handsome smile.

"Of course," sighed Ru. "Anything else?"

"You will write a weekly report of your research, hypotheses, findings, and anything else you believe relevant, and send it via pigeon to Lord D'Luc," said the regent. "Should you need any additional devices, books, or accoutrements of the scientific sort, we will provide either the funds or the things themselves. We only ask that you specify as to *why* you would need said items."

"We're all terribly excited to hear what you discover," said Lord D'Luc.

"I'm sure we are," said Ru, desperate for either more coffee or a bed to sleep on, and maybe a little cry — she felt so alone. On second thought, the carriage wasn't such a bad idea.

The regent departed then, flowing sedately up into the palace with Lord D'Luc trailing after. Almost puppy-like, Ru thought, and she liked him a little less for it.

Defeated and tired, she returned to the group of riders and the carriage. Only three of the King's Guards had arrived so far and were already mounted, looking around sternly with furrowed brows. Ru thought it must be difficult to be so serious and focused all the time. King's Riders mostly delivered important messages or escorted people around the kingdom, while guards were employed to deliver violence in some form or other.

Their presence made her uneasy.

"Ah, Ru!" Rosylla said, coming around the carriage. "We're only waiting for one more guard. Why don't you get settled in the carriage? Your maid had coffee and some cookies sent for you."

Unendingly grateful for Pearl, Ru finally admitted defeat and scrambled into the carriage, settling herself on the forward-facing bench. It was soft as anything, with warm blankets piled on both seats, and tasseled velvet pillows to cushion the jostle of travel. And there, nestled between two of the pillows, was a large leather flask and a colorfully painted tin.

Ru busied herself with the coffee and cookies until the general conversation outside the carriage grew a little more purposeful. She poked her head out the window and looked around. There were four guards now, all mounted, all wearing their plumed helmets and frowning — and all men.

Sybeth was speaking angrily with one of them, and Ru was sure it was the one who had come late. He kept shaking his head and gesturing as if explaining himself, while Sybeth's expression of disapproval grew deeper by the second. After a moment, they seemed to conclude their confrontation, and by that time everyone was mounted up and ready to go.

Ru leaned back in the pillows, holding her coffee. She stared out the window as the carriage began to roll forward, pulled by a pair of dutiful palace horses. The opulent palace gave way to trees and hedges of the palace drive, which eventually gave way to the lovely homes that circled the palace to the north, in the highest part of Mirith. Soon enough, the buildings became more colorful and less clean, the streets more narrow, the gardens wilder and brighter.

Ru took it all in with eyes glazed, her excitement to study the artifact greatly tempered by the absence of her brother and Fen. Why had they abandoned her?

She recalled, suddenly, dinner the night before. She

had seen them talking, Simon leaning over Fen's shoulder, the two looking almost conspiratorial. And then they had disappeared, at least Fen had — gone from his seat when Ru left with Lord D'Luc. At the time, so distracted by Lord D'Luc and her own illness, she thought he must have been tired or bored by the whole thing. But now... what had they been up to?

All of a sudden, there was a violent surge of the carriage as something slammed against it. The carriage driver cried out, and someone — it sounded like Lyr — swore loudly.

"Sorry!" came a familiar voice from just outside the carriage. "Only be a minute."

And then Simon was swinging through the open carriage window, somehow as elegant as an acrobat. He flopped into the seat across from Ru with a "*hup*," all while the carriage continued to speed through the city.

"One minute!" called Sybeth.

"Absolute madman," said the carriage driver, loud enough for everyone to hear.

Ru stared at her brother.

"Good morning," he said, swiping the leather flask from her grasp and taking a long swig. "Oh, that's hot."

"That's the point of coffee," said Ru, handing him the cookie tin. "Since when do you swing into moving carriages like that? Why didn't you just see me off at the palace?"

"I have a death wish."

"Right. And where did you go last night? I was looking for you."

He laughed, a forceful puff through the nose. "Didn't look like you were, little sis. I saw you arm in arm with that ghoul Hugon, going toward your rooms."

She knew what would come next. "He behaved like a perfect gentleman, Simon. I was tired and needed to sleep."

"Lucky he was there, eh?" said Simon, managing to cover himself in cookie crumbs as he nibbled. "I trust you, dear sister, far more than I trust any lord at court, let alone *that* one. And mind you, I've no real reason to distrust the fellow other than general dislike and a sort of slimy feeling in my stomach, but I will feel ever so validated when I do figure out what he's up to. Anyway, I do entreat you to take care when it comes to wandering hallways with strange men and so on."

"There are no strange men for me to wander halls with at the Tower. There's nowhere I'll be safer."

Simon's eyes narrowed. "So you say."

She pursed her lips. "I'll be *fine*. Is this the reason you leaped into my carriage like a mad acrobat? To remind me to keep myself intact? It's a bit late for that."

He made a disgusted face. "Ru, I hate it when you reference things of a... *carnal* nature. I only want to make sure you're safe. At least promise not to explode again. I don't know what Father would do."

"I promise," she said, leaning forward and wrapping her brother in a tight hug. He returned the hug briefly and then patted her back, indicating he was finished with this display of intimacy.

When she pulled away, though, he was smiling.

"Safe travels, sister," he said, positioning himself halfway out of the carriage window. At her look of horror, he said, "Don't worry! I've done this many times with ladies' carriages, and almost always stick the landing."

With that, he leaped onto the street as nimble as anything, and just managed to dodge Rosylla's horse as she rode past. Lyr swore again, Simon laughed, and then he was gone, no longer visible through the small carriage window.

Ru leaned forward to peer after him, but he had already disappeared into the city's morning crowds.

CHAPTER 14

An hour or two past midday, Ru woke with a start. She didn't remember falling asleep. She was crammed into an uncomfortable position in the carriage, one pillow under her head, and the rest had fallen onto the floor.

The carriage itself was no longer moving. The sudden stoppage must have woken her. Bleary-eyed, she sat up. Raised voices drifted in from outside, and she reached instinctively for the artifact. It was still there. Relief warmed her as she pulled it close, settling it in her lap.

She listened. The carriage windows were open, but she had pulled closed the curtains after they left the city, the rising sun blinding her. Sybeth's voice was loudest, angry and forceful. There were other voices, men's voices that she didn't recognize. They must be the guards.

She was about to whip open the curtains to see what was going on when her instincts stopped her short. Something in the tenor of the voices was edged like steel; there was danger coming, or it had already arrived. Blood rushing in her ears, her heart shot through with sudden fear, she lifted the edge of the curtain just enough to peek out.

They had stopped in the middle of the road, the carriage angled slightly as if it had been about to pull off to one side before stopping abruptly. They were in a wooded copse, where the road cut through the forest. Everything was dappled in moving shadows, the sun glancing through trees.

An incomprehensible scene unfolded outside the carriage, at the edges of the wood.

Sybeth, Lyr, and three of the four King's Guards had dismounted, their horses standing by and shaking their heads in agitation. The riders and guards were facing off against each other, swords inexplicably drawn, exchanging heated words. Sybeth's dark eyes flashed, and Lyr, usually taciturn, had become a honed weapon, ready to strike.

Ru couldn't understand, couldn't hear the conversation clearly from inside the carriage. She only saw grim faces, the visible spit of angry words flying out from between gritted teeth. The scene was so nonsensical she almost thought she was seeing it wrong. Why would the riders and guards draw upon one another?

Only one of the King's Guards remained mounted, his sword still sheathed. And near him was Rosylla, looking both wary and stricken, also mounted. Her fingers, though, were curled firmly around the grip of her sword, arm tensed to draw. She said something to the others, but again, Ru could decipher no clear meaning.

The artifact pulled against Ru's mind, vibrating with what felt like fear. Was it warning her? Or was Ru's mind affecting its voice?

At last, the wind turned, carrying Sybeth's words toward the carriage.

"Fools," the rider growled. "I said, drop your weapons."

"Excuse me," said the carriage driver, cutting in from above, his voice much clearer to Ru despite a quaver in it. "If we could all perhaps—"

"You, *quiet*," barked the guard whose sword was drawn on Lyr.

"Shout at him one more time," growled Lyr, his voice so low Ru could barely make it out. "I'd love a reason to disembowel you."

Each guard and each rider was a coiled snake ready to strike, a bloodbath held at bay only by controlled, taut muscles. The trees waved above them, casting shadows on bright armor. Seven bright helmet plumes fluttered in the breeze.

Ru found herself unable to move or react, she was so glued to the scene. Still trying to make sense of it. Her heart beat a staccato of dread against her ribs.

One of the guards turned toward his colleagues, whose bright blades were angled toward Sybeth and Lyr. With tight-jawed aggression, he hissed, "Get the *doors*. Get the *bloody* doors, one of you! I told you louts not to wait. She'll have already crawled out the other side—"

A sweat broke out on Ru's forehead, her throat tightening with the beginnings of panic. In the haze of waking up, the nonsensical tableau outside had been more confusing than anything, not clear enough to give her reason to flee.

But the guard's words shook her into sharp awareness, grounding her with a flash of fear to her nerves. They wanted *her*. Swords were drawn, threats exchanged because of her. Rational thought demanded to give way to panic, but Ru couldn't let it.

Her gut in a knot, breaths jagged and shallow, she tried to think of a plan, a logical way to put an end to this confusion. But the need to arm herself, the desperation to get away, engulfed all other thoughts.

If they wanted the artifact... She had to get away. And there stood the forest, old and dark, practically untouched for millennia. She could hide there, lose herself in the ferns and shadows. She would crawl out the far door of the carriage, disappear into the trees, and wait. Wait to see who would reveal themselves as friend and who was foe.

Because Ru wasn't no longer sure she could trust the riders. What if *they* were trying to hurt her, and the guards were attempting to keep her safe?

Another incalculable problem without an obvious solution. Almost every variable an unknown, jumbled by emotion. The only surety came in the form of Ru herself, and the artifact. She would defend herself at all costs, as the laws of human nature and a panicked mind demanded. And the artifact, as the regent had ordered, as Ru's instincts demanded, also needed protection.

Shaking, staving off waves of panic with sheer force of will, Ru clutched the artifact to her chest. As quietly as she could, she undid the latch on the far door of the carriage.

How many steps to the edge of the road? How many steps to reach the forest's full darkness? How many guards would it take to find her? Pointless calculations rattled against her skull, doing nothing to soothe her.

Then came another shout, sending a burst of terrified energy through Ru. In one movement, she opened the door and half-jumped, half-rolled out of the carriage. Her hands smarted in pain as her palms slammed against sharp gravel.

Not waiting to see if anyone had heard or seen her, she dashed pell-mell toward the forest, spraying bits of gravel as she did.

She only made it three steps before a figure slammed against her from behind, flattening her under the weight of a body. She gasped at the metallic press of steel against her back — not a blade, but armor.

Her attacker was one of the guards.

"Got her!" he cried, his voice unfamiliar, hoarse from exertion.

Ru's chest screamed beneath his weight. His hot breaths fell on her hair and exposed neck, and she struggled wildly. Wedged between his breastplate and the artifact, the air had been punched from her lungs.

Panic, at last, overtook her.

And then, as quickly as he had come, the guard leaped to his feet, leather and armor creaking as he did, gravel moving under booted feet. His weight disappeared from her back, and gasping, Ru drew breath. Tears stung the corners of her eyes.

There was the sing of steel, an obscene squelch, and the guard fell to the ground with a heavy thud. From where Ru lay only inches from the man's body, she watched, frozen, as blood leaked from the corner of a bearded mouth. Unseeing eyes stared out from his white face. A breeze moved against him, the plume on his helmet dancing.

Ru sat up and scrambled sideways, away from the body. The artifact pulsed against her, that ever-present tether taut and vibrating.

She couldn't pull her gaze from the guard's empty stare. He had come for her, come for the artifact, come for both — in that moment, it didn't matter.

Sybeth appeared in front of Ru, crouching, her eyes wide and wild. Blood spattered her front, red and wet and bright. Ru couldn't tell if it was hers or the guard's.

"Get back in the carriage," Sybeth ordered. "Now."

Ru stared. "This," she stammered, pointing at the dead guard, unable to form coherent thoughts. "Was it trying to kill me?"

"Get in the carriage," growled Sybeth. Then she stood, brandishing her red-slick sword. She turned to the sun, her dark skin flecked with blood, and strode around the carriage, leaving Ru alone.

Ru could hear the ring of steel, the shouts and grunts of combat. Then a horrible, guttural scream rose from the other side of the carriage. Ru covered her ears, terrified, a lost child in a nightmare.

Everything here was new, a horror unlike any she had witnessed before.

She understood violence. Understood death. She had destroyed a dig site, vaporized dozens of souls in a moment. But she had been unconscious. Separate. She had never been so near the realities of death, watched the light seep from a man's eyes.

Books, words, thoughts. They were nothing to the reality of what she heard now, the chaos of it, the suddenness of violent death.

Get in the carriage.

But her limbs were like jelly. Terror clamped on her muscles, holding her hostage.

New sounds snapped her to attention. Cursing, shouts, and someone bursting into the carriage from the other side. Ru tried to stand again, to dart toward the woods, but she was too slow. The guard scrambled through the carriage, seeing Ru as he leaped out, and tackled her to the ground from behind.

"Got 'er!" he snarled.

Thoughts fled from Ru as instinct took over. She screamed and kicked, struggling against the much larger man.

She had lost her grip on the artifact. In the force of the attack, it had rolled from her grasp, coming to a stop at the edge of the road. Its blanket had unfurled, and the sun glanced off its black surface.

Ru scrabbled uselessly for the stone. It was miles away. The guard was a grown man in full armor, his weight on her back holding her easily in place. She was completely helpless as he lifted her to her knees, pinning her arms behind her.

She tried to bite him, tried to use her skull to bludgeon his nose, but it was pointless. He only laughed at her attempts.

"Help me with the bitch!" he called out. "She's wriggling like a cat in heat."

An icy fist gripped Ru's heart. She had only seen one of the guards die; where were the other two? Surely the riders could hold their own. She had seen Lyr's flashing eyes and Sybeth's confidence with a blade.

But where were they?

She began to shout, to call for help, but the guard quickly clamped a gloved hand over her mouth. She spluttered, the taste of dirt and old leather suffocating her.

Caught in a nightmare, unable to speak or move, Ru watched as a third guard, still mounted, rode around the carriage toward them. Blood dripped from the tip of his sword, spattering on the dusty road.

In what felt like slow motion, he dismounted and walked toward them. Dust rose from each of his heavy footfalls.

"Hurry up," grunted the guard who held her, one

hand holding her arms roughly behind her, the other still clamped on her mouth.

The approaching guard made no move to hurry. And as he came, Ru couldn't bring herself to look away. With wide-eyed horror, tears running down her cheek and over the guard's glove, she choked a sob.

She didn't want to die like that guard, her eyes staring, unseeing, up at the sky.

"Stop *wiggling*," her captor barked in her ear, yanking her close, her back to his chest.

His hand disappeared from her mouth, and a sudden pain exploded across her face as he struck her with the back of his hand. The blow was awkward, but the glove was reinforced with steel, the edge of it catching her skin. Stars spotted Ru's vision and she stilled, breathing hard. Hot blood dripped down her face.

The other guard never stopped stalking toward them. Ru watched him coming through blurred vision. From what felt like far away, she heard herself let out another strangled sob.

The artifact thrummed in her, a hot wave of emotion she couldn't place.

And then the guard was there, standing over them. His helmet's visor was drawn, his features hidden behind cold steel. A blood-soaked angel of death.

"Give her to me," he said, holding out a gloved hand.

"All yours," spat the guard holding Ru, shoving her forward.

She stumbled. The other guard caught her arm before she fell and pulled her roughly to her feet, drawing her toward him. She balked at the touch, his arm around her, pulling her close until the steel of his chest plate pressed against her back.

Then, smooth and sudden as a viper, the guard holding her struck out with his weapon. In one deft motion, it cut through the other man's neck. Cleanly as a wire through clay.

Ru watched in silence as blood pumped wetly from the guard's severed neck. His head, still in its helmet, rolled on the road. His body slumped, then fell with a sickening thump.

Ru's vision wavered, her knees hitting the road with force. She tried to vomit, to extricate what she'd just seen and endured. But her stomach refused to empty, and only a spatter of blood hit the gravel as she doubled over, spitting and sobbing.

The remaining guard's grip on her loosened. He would kill her now as well, she thought. No matter that he'd just turned on one of his own. He must be a madman. A monster.

A metallic crunch sounded as a helmet landed on the ground beside her. Dust billowed where it fell, as it rolled to a stop in the sun. Ru stared, watching with detached confusion. Why had the guard dropped his helmet? Did he want to free his face before killing her, to look her in the eyes?

She squeezed her eyes shut as he moved around to face her. She couldn't bear to watch more blood stain the road.

"Ru." The voice was familiar, deeply accented.

Gasping, stars of panic still bursting at the edges of her vision, she tilted her face up to see. There stood Fen, his face streaked with dirt and sweat, his chest heaving. His black hair, finally freed from his helmet, was plastered messily to his forehead. His fingers loosened on the grip of his sword, and it fell with a clang at his feet.

He knelt before Ru, taking her face gently in his hands as she wept.

"You're safe," he said in an unsteady whisper. "You're safe. Breathe, Ru. I have you."

She fell into him then, the relief overwhelming her until she could hardly breathe from crying. She didn't care how he was there, or why. All she knew was that everything was back in place now, where it belonged.

And there, warming her from within, the artifact's touch flickered against her mind. Comforting.

"I've got you," he kept saying, trying to get her to return to her senses. "You're safe."

She couldn't wrap her mind around it. Fen, here, the

whole time. Ru had been sure she was about to die. She had been *certain*. And now that she was safe, her body couldn't cope; there was too much fear stored up. She couldn't stop crying, shaking and—

"The riders," she said between breathless sobs, a new terror nearly blinding her. There had been cries of battle on the other side of the carriage.

"They're fine," said Fen.

Ru sat back to look at him, his dirt-smudged face, those familiar gray eyes under dark brows. His full lips curved in the beginnings of a reassuring smile. Tears still streamed down her face, blurring her vision. "Don't lie."

"I'm not. Can you stand?"

He helped her to her feet slowly. She stumbled at first, still dizzy from the blow dealt by the other guard. Still shaking from panic and fear.

When she was fully upright and able to stand on her own, Fen went to retrieve the artifact. He wrapped it carefully in its blanket, handing it to her wordlessly. She took it in her arms with a relief she didn't want to show. And then, wrapping his arm around her waist for support, Fen guided her around to the other side of the carriage.

What Ru saw made her knees so weak with relief she thought she might collapse again.

Sybeth, Lyr, and Rosylla were there, all visibly the worse for wear, but alive. Lyr and Rosylla sat in the grass, wrapping up wounds and passing a flask back and forth. Sybeth paced behind them, an angry gash across one of her eyebrows. Even the driver had survived, standing near the carriage and taking deep swigs from a hip flask.

Scanning the scene, Ru caught sight of a flash of armor in the grass near the trees — the body of the third guard. She looked away quickly, swallowing bile.

When the riders saw Ru and Fen, they exclaimed with collective relief. Sybeth shot Fen a look of appreciation, nodding firmly once.

"Thank fuck," said Lyr, spitting blood and saliva into the grass.

Rosylla stood, brushing off her trousers. It did nothing to dislodge the blood stains. "Ru," she said, voice shaking, "we thought…"

"Fen," Sybeth said, her dark eyes hard. "Is there a reason you lied to me?"

"He saved our lives," said Rosylla.

Sybeth remained unmoved. "Well, Verrill?"

"I wasn't certain the guards would betray you," Fen said, loosening his arm from around Ru's waist. "I needed them to think they had a chance."

Sybeth's expression was carved in granite, unmoving. "Why suspect a betrayal from the king's own guards?"

"I'm naturally distrustful," said Fen. "They proved me right."

"I see. And where did you get the armor you're wearing?" Sybeth asked. "I trust you didn't steal it."

"'Course he stole it," muttered Lyr.

Sybeth shot the other rider a look, and he shrugged, turning away.

"I'll let you pick whatever explanation you like best," said Fen. A muscle in his jaw flexed, tense.

Ru watched them with confusion, head reeling. Her mouth was sour with vomit and her entire body ached. Betrayal… stolen armor… "I need more context," she said, swaying.

Fen caught her before her legs buckled.

"You're going to need a doctor," he said, his tone softer now. He tossed Sybeth a sharp look. "We have to get her to the Tower. As quickly as possible."

The rider sighed, still frowning deeply. "This matter is now far beyond my purview," she said, her tone tinged with annoyance. "Rosylla, you will ride back to Mirith and alert the regent that there are traitors in her midst. I'll follow behind and escort the carriage. Lyr, ride with Fen and Ru. The artifact must be kept safe. It can't fall into the wrong hands. Ride through the night if you have to."

Lyr frowned, thick brows falling heavy over his eyes. A smear of blood angled across his large nose, and the skin around one eye was swollen, darkening. "Long ride to the Tower."

"Yes, and you'll ride your horse to its death if you have to." Sybeth's gaze was glacier cold.

"Please don't," said Ru, wanting to cry again and feeling more useless than she ever had in her life. She hugged the bundled artifact to her, its blanket warm in her arms. "All on account of this? Of the artifact?"

Fen shot her a pained look. "I suppose it never occurred to you that your life also matters."

"To *me*," she shot back, though her voice still shook.

"You underestimate the people who care about you," said Fen.

Ru glared at him, the remnants of her terror morphing into a sick self-loathing. "Sybeth said it herself. This is bigger than me. Than all of us. Why would the guards betray the regent's orders? Were they trying to get to me, or the artifact? Or both? Or—"

She coughed, her throat hoarse, doubling over as a sudden pain sliced through her chest. Blood drained from her face as pain overtook her.

"Broken rib," said Lyr, observing.

"We're leaving," growled Fen. "Now. Ru will ride with me. Lyr, are you well enough to ride?"

The rider tapped his bandaged shoulder, winced, then nodded. "Surface wounds."

"Are you ready?" Fen's low voice was for Ru alone, gauging her, asking for honesty.

She hated this. Images of death played, unending, through her head. Lady Maryn's face, a head rolling, blood, the artifact seeming to pulse beneath her bare fingers and then darkness.

She trusted Fen, but what he had done to the guard unsettled her. The ease with which he cut short a man's life. She was an academic, not a fighter, nor a soldier. She wished she hadn't seen it happen, wished she'd never been called to the dig site, had never written that paper. Maybe she could give the artifact to Fen; let him take it away.

She didn't want it.

But the wretched thing seemed to feel her angry thoughts and responded, grasping at her desperately, refusing to let her go.

It was too much. She couldn't fight anymore. She needed rest, needed to be home. She belonged at the Tower, and that was where they would take her.

At last she spoke, her voice low but firm. "I'm ready."

CHAPTER 15

Ru remembered almost none of the nightmarish ride to the Tower. She drifted always in and out of pain, in and out of wakefulness, but blood was always on her mind. Fen kept one arm wrapped tightly around her as they rode, a reminder that she was alive and protected. His body heat, his breath on her neck… he was the only thing that felt real to her.

She knew that night fell after a time, and even then they continued riding. They stopped long enough for Lyr to share his dinner, and for the horses to drink, all of them eating swiftly. Wordlessly.

And then they were off again.

Every once in a while, in fits and spurts, Ru returned to consciousness, her half-awake gaze taking in beautiful vistas that seemed like dreams. For a time, they passed through the depths of a dark forest, the smell of moss and damp wood filling her senses. And once, she woke and saw that they weren't far from the Tower — grand rock formations blanketed in lichen rose up around them as they rode, the early morning sun painted the rocks in that angled light.

No… the sun was setting, Ru realized. How long had they been riding? Had she missed the sunrise?

Fen spoke to her sometimes, but the words ran together in her head, and half the time she was certain it was a dream.

The next time Ru was jolted out of the fog of pain, they were coming to a stop in a flagged courtyard. Fruit trees whispered kindly in a bright afternoon breeze. There were voices, the sound of hurried footsteps.

Ru's entire being, from nerves to flesh to soul, relaxed as if she had sunk into a hot bath. They had finally arrived at the Cornelian Tower. Finally home.

"What have you done to her?" said a shrill voice, cutting through the morning air.

Ru knew Professor Obralle's voice immediately. As Fen helped her gently to the ground, she tried to turn, to see the Tower and the professors. But her stiff legs and broken rib wouldn't allow it. She stumbled, hand reaching for something, anything to steady her before she fell. Fen's arm was there, firm and familiar.

With his help, she turned to face the Tower at last. The great building rose up before them, shining gold in the light, and Ru breathed easy for the first time in what felt like ages.

Professors Obralle and Cadwick, plus a small contingent of academics, stopped short at the sight of the three travelers. Lyr and Fen were still catching their breath from the hard ride, and their horses were faring much worse.

"I asked you a question," snapped Obralle, her pink hair styled to resemble a cluster of mushrooms on the top of her head. "Delara, what have these criminals done to you?"

"Ready the dungeons," Cadwick ordered one of the academics. "One of our own has been treated ill."

"I'm perfectly fine," Ru said in a croak. She knew she must look gruesome, covered in dust and blood, and probably bruised where the guard had struck her across the face. "Lyr and Fen didn't do this to me. They're..." she doubled over, wincing in agony.

"Gods alive," said Obralle in a hushed voice. She darted forward and took Ru in her arms, steering her toward the Tower. "Delara, dear child. Come inside. Cadwick, tend to her boys!"

Ru, delirious with pain and lack of sleep, began to laugh at "her boys," until a stab of pain stopped her.

"I think I need a doctor," she choked out.

"You need a great many things," said Obralle. "I will be the judge of what, and in which order."

"Thank you," said Ru. "There's so much I need to tell you, Professor. All of you."

Obralle nodded and made encouraging sounds as they walked. "Not to worry. There's been a pigeon from the palace, an explanation from the regent. But what I *don't* understand is why you look like an unearthed cadaver, and why you've arrived a day ahead of schedule. No one said anything about grave injuries to one of our academics."

They passed through the courtyard slowly, the sound of Cadwick's no-nonsense chatter, Fen's deep voice, and Lyr's random interjections fading as they went. After what felt like an age of Ru stumbling and clinging to Professor Obralle to stay upright, they finally came to the Tower itself. Ru took the entrance stairs as slowly as possible, with Obralle helping her, steadying her.

Contrary to its name, the Cornelian Tower was not a single tower jutting up from the landscape. It was closer in style and size to a castle or an oversized abbey. It was an ancient structure, built nearly a thousand years ago. It had centuries ago fallen to ruin, rebuilt by an order of monks who sought a remote place to seek scholarship and enlightenment. Now it was run by the professors, part university and part research center, and it was vast and drafty and often too cold.

For Ru, it was home.

The moment they passed into the cool shade of the front hall, despite her pain, her entire being, from skin to bone to soul, relaxed.

"There we are," said Professor Obralle, noting Ru's relief. "Welcome home."

Ru's room was in the dormitory wing, where the academics slept. Most first- and second-years had to share rooms between two people, but Ru was in her fourth year at the Tower and had earned her own private space.

When they arrived at Ru's familiar dark wood door, its curving brass handle inviting Ru in, Obralle took out a rattling set of keys and unlocked it. Steering Ru inside with gentle firmness, the professor helped her to sit, settling her into a settee near the fireplace. The small but cozy room, including Ru's furniture, had collected a fine layer of dust in her extended absence in the field, but in her current state, she couldn't have cared less.

She closed her eyes and let the sounds of the Tower lull her to a light doze: Obralle bustling around the room; muffled birdsong drifting in the single window from the courtyard below; laughter in the hall; a heavy door slamming in the distance.

"There," said Obralle, and Ru opened her eyes. The professor had made a pot of tea and even produced a tin of biscuits, which she explained she always carried in her pocket "for emergencies."

"Now, stay here, drink your tea, and I'll summon the doctor."

Ru wasn't sure where Obralle expected her to go just then, as stiff and tired and injured as she was, but she nodded obediently.

When the professor had gone, when she was at last alone, Ru sat up slowly. Every muscle in her body ached. She gingerly touched her face and bit back a cry; it stung where the guard had struck her. He'd done more than bruise — he must have broken skin. She pressed three fingers to her ribcage, testing, and gasped in pain as she found the wounded bone.

As if in response, the artifact reached out gently, its touch hesitant but soothing.

It was still wrapped in its blanket and tucked inside her jacket, where it had been since the attack on the carriage. She sighed, staring into the small fire that crackled in the hearth. At last, she was here at the Tower, and a world of discovery lay spread before her. Soon the artifact would be an answer, rather than a question.

At least, she hoped it would.

Her thoughts drifted to Fen and Lyr, whether they were being treated kindly. The professors often tended toward suspicion of the palace and its messengers, so different was the culture in Mirith. But in their hearts, they were generous and compassionate, and the Tower was welcoming to all. If all else failed, Ru reminded herself, the mark of the regent's sigil on their chests would at least keep Fen and Lyr out of the long-disused Tower dungeon.

Sipping her tea, Ru found that it warmed her in a far more immediate and tangible way than the artifact's enigmatic touch. She was grateful for the walls of the Tower surrounding her at last, the embrace of her home these four years. But even in that knowledge came a faint sense of unease. She wasn't here to fall back into her academic studies. She wasn't here to reconstruct ancient vases.

She had returned to the Tower with a new purpose, and it filled her with a looming dread. Even more so now that she knew there were people who wanted the artifact, or who wanted her, or both. People who would use violence to achieve their ends.

Setting down her tea with a groan, her rib a slice of sudden pain, she lowered herself slowly to lie lengthwise on the settee. Her head throbbed like a drum against her skull. Her chest was on fire. Distant laughter drifted in from outside, the sound of a lute being strummed. She wanted to see Gwyneth and Archie. Even Simon's sarcasm would have comforted her at that moment.

Heaviness settled in her bones, replacing the brief sense of respite her return home had given her. She was a burden now, a liability to the Cornelian Tower. The King's Riders, those she considered friends, could have been killed if it weren't for Fen's forethought.

How *had* he managed to wrangle his way in as a guard? And why? He had to have known, to have had some kind of an inkling.

A tentative knock at the door shook Ru from her thought.

Sitting up slowly and painfully, she began to stand to get the door but immediately thought better of it.

"Come in," she said, her voice at least slightly more human than it had sounded earlier.

Professor Obralle entered, followed closely by Hartford, the Tower doctor. They made quick work of turning the settee into an examination center, with tools and instruments laid out on the table where the tea had been. A painfully bright lamp was brought in to aid the doctor in his examinations. He was matter-of-fact in his practice, giving Ru little taps and prods all over her body, asking whether it hurt and how much.

Most of her body was in pain to some degree, some areas far worse than others. Hartford frowned when he gently palpated her ribs, as she sucked in a hissed breath with suppressed agony.

At the end of it all, Ru was diagnosed with a cracked rib, some extreme bruising, and countless cuts and scrapes. Hartford supplied her with a bottle of soothing ointment for her abrasions and bruises, and bandaged her torso to keep her from damaging the rib further.

The entire exam was over in less than half an hour, and Hartford swept from the room afterward without a thank you or a goodbye.

"He's efficient," said Ru.

Obralle nodded, lips pursed. "He was also very aware of that... *artifact*," she said, nodding toward the blanketed bundle. "None of us particularly like the idea of it, you must understand. The regent has ordered that it be studied here, yes, but..." she shrugged, looking as if she wanted to say more but restrained herself, eyeing Ru.

Ru knew that she had brought danger home with her. She knew the risks, she had seen the worst of it at the Shattered City. But in her eagerness to uncover the artifact's secrets, she hadn't spared much thought for what the professors or her peers might want, whether they would see it her way.

But would she have acted differently if she had more carefully considered the consequences? Or would she have done it anyway, determined to find answers? The artifact was, more than likely, magic.

Unwilling to admit what she knew was the truth,

that she had put herself and her curiosity above the safety of those at the Tower, Ru lapsed into silence.

"I'll leave you here to rest, then," said Obralle, her tone subdued. "There's to be a deliberation tomorrow morning. Get some sleep until then."

"A deliberation?" Ru asked. Deliberations weren't overly common, and Ru had only ever attended a handful in the time she'd been at the Tower.

"Yes, naturally," said Obralle. "We must decide how to go about studying the artifact. Everything must be debated, and then agreed upon via vote."

Ru knew this as an academic, but the reminder was oddly steadying. It wasn't as if they would let Ru appear at the Tower with a dangerous artifact, and allow her to do whatever she wanted with it. There were procedures. She wouldn't be completely alone in this. The Tower would stand behind her and ensure the correct steps were taken.

"Will they let me head the research?" Ru asked. She was happy to follow rules, happy to delegate, and conduct her research within agreed-upon standards. But allowing someone else to take charge of the artifact, to separate her from it... that, she couldn't bear to contemplate.

Obralle sniffed. "Perhaps, perhaps not. Thus, the deliberation. I'd prepare a speech, Delara, if I were you."

"In less than a day?" Ru groaned, lying back on the settee, wondering if she'd ever stop being in pain. "Can't you delay it?"

Obralle gave her a sympathetic look. "Now that the artifact is here, we can't simply allow it to lie around without guidelines. There must be rules."

Too exhausted to reply, Ru closed her eyes for a moment. She would have to speak tomorrow then, lay out her plans clearly, even if it meant dredging up old humiliations.

An afternoon breeze from the window washed over her, cooling her hot forehead. She lay quietly for a while, and when she opened her eyes again, Professor Obralle had gone.

Not wanting to fall asleep on the settee, conscious of her already stiff muscles, Ru tottered over to the bed, carrying the artifact and her bottle of ointment. Then she stripped to her undergarments, crawled into bed, and dreamed of blood and darkness.

CHAPTER 16

Ru woke before sunrise. She had slept, un-waking, from afternoon to morning. She went blearily to the window, bare feet padding on hardwood, to look out over the courtyard below. Birds sang a cacophony in the trees, and dew clung to the windowsill where she pressed her fingers. She had left the window open all night, the northern winds cooling her as she slept.

Even though the sun was still just behind the horizon, there was no point in going back to sleep. She felt rested, though her bruises and scrapes were still a pattern of aches across her body. Hartford had done his job well, even her rib no longer sending jagged spikes of pain through her torso.

Going back to the bed, Ru pulled the covers over her legs, sitting up against a pile of pillows. She reached for the artifact, swaddled in its blanket at the far side of the bed. It hummed against her thoughts, a steady vibrating presence. She felt a great, inexplicable surge of fondness for the thing. It was volatile, it had to be. A weapon. A magic object. A focus of unspeakable destruction.

And yet…

Slowly, delicately, she unfolded the blanket. In the work of a moment, the artifact was free. For the first time since the dig site at the Shattered City, she was able to look at it, to drink it in, with no distractions. She ached to touch it, to draw her finger gently along the black-on-black whorls that curved across its surface. She marveled at its smoothness — there were no edges, no breaks where molten stones would have snapped apart, no signs of erosion.

It wasn't a naturally formed mineral, then. No stone dug from the earth looked like this, felt like this. There was one explanation for such a thing. A thing that spoke treasured curses at the base of her skull, caressing at the edges of her mind.

Magic.

But there was no proof, no way to tell. And while she yearned to pick it up with her bare hand, to cradle it in her palm, a voice in the back of her head told her no. It wouldn't be safe.

And yet...

Ru extended her fingers toward it slowly, thoughtlessly, half awake in the gloom of early morning, almost intoxicated by it. The artifact wasn't insistent, not like it had been at the dig site. It was quiet, soft, as if it was breathing. As if her lungs were shared between the two of them, Ru and the dark stone.

Closing her eyes, fingers hovering above its surface, she imagined it in her mind's eye. A humming pulse around the end of a thread, from stone to woman. *Yes*, it seemed to say. *I'm here.* As if it knew her, had been waiting for her. For *her*, Ruellian Delara. No one else.

How she wanted to hold it.

Thoughts of Fen rose unbidden then, his clear gray eyes and rugged features. Hair lifted by a gust of unseen wind.

Her eyes flew open, and she caught herself, her fingers millimeters from the stone. Breathing hard, she wrapped it snugly in its blanket.

She would have to be more careful, wary of the effect it had on her. Yet, while fear lanced through her in response to the artifact's stupefying influence, her limbs and mind almost alcohol-heavy, she also felt a thrill of connection.

The artifact had chosen her, and she had chosen it.

A gentle knock sounded at the door, and Professor

Obralle poked her head around it. "Awake already?" she said.

Startled, Ru turned to look out the window. The sun had already risen, the birdsong so loud she could no longer hear the wind in the trees. How long had she been staring at the artifact?

"I just woke up," said Ru, not even sure what time it was. "Is the deliberation soon?"

"Very," said the professor, coming into the room. There were few true formalities in the Tower, and little need for professors and academics to maintain distance when it came to Tower life. They were friends and colleagues — the rigid boundaries of Navenian society were meaningless at the Tower, where science and progress of thought reigned supreme.

"Get dressed," said Obralle, bustling about, starting a fire in the small hearth even though it was the height of summer. She wore trousers and a waistcoat of navy blue wool, her neckcloth held in place with a large gold brooch — her version of the utmost formality. "I'll collect the artifact."

Ru froze. "The artifact?"

Obralle gave her a look as if she were being willfully ignorant. "Of course, Delara. The artifact. It must be taken somewhere safe, somewhere isolated, until the deliberation has concluded."

She understood the need for it, but the thought of handing over the artifact to someone else, someone who didn't *know* it like she did... a pale flicker of something like panic moved through Ru. Just as quickly, she tamped it down, knowing that the professor was right. Grudgingly, she gathered the bundled stone and handed it to Obralle, who took it with slight hesitance.

"Thank you," said the professor. "Now. The deliberation is in an hour. See that you're not late, and come prepared."

With that, the professor was gone again, the artifact in her arms. Ru bit her lip, worrying that something would happen — to the artifact, to Obralle. Fear swirled through her, sudden terror that the artifact might somehow be cut off from her if it were removed from her presence. But as she waited, the artifact's soft touch never faded, never faltered. That alone quelled Ru's anxiety.

Eager for a distraction, Ru set about getting dressed. She chose an unassuming dress of brown wool with a square neckline, lace-up bodice, and buttons at the cuffs. Quickly braiding her hair in one long plait down her back, she glanced in the mirror before heading to the Great Hall.

She wondered if she would ever look alive again. Dark circles still hung under her eyes, and a bruise bloomed purple across one cheekbone. Her skin had become too pale, almost sickly, and her long brown hair was dull, even in the firelight.

It frightened her a little, the physical toll the last several days had taken on her. So much had happened, with hardly any rest in between. It occurred to her for a fleeting moment that her connection with the artifact might be nothing but a delusion, a hallucination brought on by sudden trauma.

But she *knew* it was real. Felt it in her marrow.

Ru sighed and turned away from the mirror, accepting that she would look like a risen corpse at the deliberation. Her mind was going to be the thing on display after all, not her appearance.

When she eventually moved to leave, she paused on the threshold, her thoughts turning to her friends, Gwyneth and Archie. They'd know she was at the Tower by now — why hadn't they come to find her?

And Fen. Her thoughts strayed inevitably back to him, an anchor. A source of comfort from the moment she'd first heard his boots against dark earth, the deep timbre of his voice.

A sudden desire to find him, to seek him out in the Tower — if he was still there — filled Ru, and she started hurriedly down the corridor. His reassuring presence, his steady hands… And then the bells rang out, a musical chiming from one of the Tower's highest spires, signaling the start of the deliberation.

There was no time. Cursing, Ru spun toward the Great Hall. Fen could be there, waiting for her. And Lyr. It was possible the two men had gone, knowing she was safe now, knowing she no longer needed them... but she desperately hoped not.

Ru was gnawing her lip, a sore forming between her teeth, when she finally arrived at the Great Hall. It served as the location for any kind of debate, celebration, presentation, or any other event that would draw the majority of the Tower's residents together. For the purpose of the deliberation, the room was set up as a round table discussion. Simple wooden chairs were set up in an oval shape around a central podium, upon which stood a dark wood lectern fitted with a brass speaking horn.

Even as the bells' echoes still rang through the Tower, Ru saw that most of the seats around the room had already been filled. She hovered just inside for a moment, taking it all in. Even amidst the unknown, the trepidation that this deliberation set curling up inside her, she felt grounded in the Tower. She had missed it. After her fieldwork at Dig Site 33, and everything since then, it was almost six weeks since she had been home.

Taking in her surroundings like a tonic, she tilted her head to gaze up at the great chandelier lamps, which hung in a cluster at the center of the ceiling. They were designed to look almost organic, as if a light-up brass and gold flower had bloomed and begun to shine right there, out of the stone of the castle.

Everything in the Tower was a bit odd — compared to what was considered normal in Mirith, at least. While the palace in the capital was all finely carved stone, the interiors clean and elegantly grand, the Tower was old and worn. Time-worn rugs were strewn across wood floors, books piled in random corners, and paintings and strange taxidermy hung along the corridors. Unlike the palace, which was grand yet distinctly distant, the Tower invited one to touch. To find comfort there.

The walls of the Great Hall were painted to represent a forest, with golden curling trees that hid unearthly creatures even Ru couldn't name. Above the trees rose a depiction of the dark beyond, with celestial objects and stars forming pictures of animals and humans and gods.

Across the painted walls hung many tapestries, gold-framed paintings, and various medals, awards, and diplomas. Nothing here was sacred, but everything was treated with equal respect. The professors felt deeply that the Tower should be a place of learning, acceptance, and equality. In contrast to the culture of the palace, which valued station, privilege, and wealth.

Even though most of the seats were full, academics continued to trickle into the hall, laughing and jostling. Ru felt strangely disconnected from them, that carefree life gone forever now in the wake of what she'd endured. A surge of regret welled up in her, curdling into self-pity as she scanned those already seated. Looking for a familiar face.

Ru started as someone appeared at her side. Someone petite, with long blonde hair. With a rush of relief, she realized it was Gwyneth. And there was Archie, just behind her, both of them beaming.

CHAPTER 17

"Ru!" cried Gwyneth, throwing herself into Ru's arms, squeezing until Ru swore, her rib flaring in pain. "Oh no, your rib! I heard, I'm so sorry," gasped Gwyneth. She held Ru at arm's length then, her brown eyes filling with tears.

"Don't start crying, you know I'm allergic to it," said Archie. But Ru could tell he was just as glad to see her as she was to see him, his green eyes bright with relief. "Give her room to breathe."

"I don't need room," Ru said, her voice cracking before she threw herself into Gwyneth's arms again. All of her pain, the heaviness that clung to her body and mind, seemed lighter now. It was still there, like a shadow, but the presence of her friends eased its weight. "Come sit with me?"

"Obviously," said Archie. The freckles on his nose had darkened from weeks in the field; the shadows under his eyes said he hadn't been sleeping well. "The moment we heard… the dig site. And everything else. I've been sick with worry, and you know worrying doesn't complement my eyes."

"*We've* been sick with worry," Gwyneth corrected, pursing her lips and turning to scan the assembly. "We heard you met Regent Sigrun."

"It wasn't as fun as it sounds," Ru muttered as they began to make their way through the assembled chairs, looking for three empty seats together. She was self-conscious of anyone overhearing. This deliberation was going to be embarrassing enough without people thinking she was a braggart.

She knew she would have to speak to the crowd, to defend herself as the most qualified candidate to lead the research of the artifact. But the thought of it made her want to melt into the floor and disappear. She had never been good at public speaking, her paper would be brought up and...

Gwyneth touched Ru's arm lightly, interrupting her thoughts. She pointed to three seats right at the front. The three friends hurried to sit as the room grew quiet, laughter and chatter fading as Professor Thorne made his way to the lectern.

He tapped the speaking horn. "Welcome," he said into one end, and his voice was projected across the room clearly

Ru peered around at the seated academics, searching the crowd for Fen and Lyr. For a shock of messy black hair, or a pair of heavy dark brows. But they were nowhere to be seen, and in a small rush of dread, she worried again that they had left the Tower. Left her. They had no reason to stay. Fen had fulfilled his promise to take her to the Tower, and Lyr's duty was to the re-gent. He would be needed back at the palace if there were traitors in their midst.

Traitors... Ru bit her already sore lip, the memory of the attack rising unbidden, unwelcome. She had tried not to think of it, but it was impossible not to. Had the guards been working alone? If not, who sent them? And why? Ru wished fervently that news of the artifact hadn't been allowed to spread so widely. Anyone with the right access could have waylaid the real guards and taken their places by Ru's side.

The other possibility — that someone within the palace had ordered the attack — wasn't worth contem-plating. Not now.

Again she scratched at the itch of persistent ques-tions: where did Fen fit in, and how had he known there would be a betrayal? She had no idea where his loyalties lay, but she hoped... she hoped selfishly they might be with her.

"Thank you all for attending this deliberation on short notice," Professor Thorne was saying. He ran his fingers through his hair, pursing his lips. "As you may or may not be aware, depending on the level of gossiping you engage in—" he leveled an accusatory look at the seated academics. "One of our own, Ruellian Delara, was involved in a deeply regrettable event some days ago. This event involved an item, a relic that was recovered from the earth below the very site where the Destruction took place."

A low murmur broke out among the academics. Ru was certain most of them had already heard about the artifact; news traveled like wildfire through the Tower. It was impossible to curtail the spread of information between young people living in such close quarters, especially when that information was shocking or involved death in some way.

To the academics, this news was exciting, a distraction, something to think about other than their usual studies. For Ru, it was a reminder that she had been there, she had done.

Thoughtlessly, Ru reached into her pocket for the stone, remembering belatedly that it wasn't there. Its presence in her mind was still so clear she had forgotten it wasn't with her.

"You may wonder specifically what all this has to do with the Cornelian Tower," Professor Thorne was saying, and Ru realized she'd tuned him out completely; she had no idea where he was in his speech. "...And you are right to do so. The artifact is, in fact, at the Tower today."

Another rumble of chatter arose, and a few gasps came from scattered academics.

Thorne peered around at the seated crowd until his gaze met Ru's. A faint smile softened his face. "And so is Ruellian Delara. She was returned to us by the regent, specifically to fulfill the role of the artifact's keeper. This fact cannot be contested, nor do we have a say in whether we *want* this highly unpredictable and very likely dangerous item in the care of the Tower. However — quiet, please." He glared out at the assembly until the commotion died down.

Ru had been dreading this part. She could tell that he was drawing his introduction to a close; then would come the speeches and the vote. She hadn't prepared enough, should have written something down. She found herself wishing that the deliberation could have been between professors only, to spare her the judgment of her peers. But the rule of the Tower was that everyone had a say of some kind, that one person's decision could affect them all equally, and vice versa.

"Is all this *true?*" Archie said under his breath, leaning toward her. "The explosion, the regent…"

Gwyneth heard this and shot Ru a questioning look. Ru nodded. Her friends glanced at one another, and then Gwyneth reached across Archie and squeezed Ru's knee. The simple gesture was unspeakably comforting to Ru. She belonged here. No matter what the professors and academics thought of her, good or ill, this was her home, too.

"Now we shall begin the deliberation," Thorne said and stepped down from the podium as Professor Cadwick took his place.

"Greetings," said Professor Cadwick, his white hair standing up in the lamplight. He, like Thorne and Obralle, was dressed for the occasion in a yellow silk jacket and breeches, his waistcoat sky blue.

"How many are going to speak?" Gwyneth hissed, impatiently flicking a golden ringlet. "This is already getting dull."

Ru smiled despite herself. She was anything but bored, but she was glad that her friends didn't seem worried on her behalf.

But Cadwick wasn't there to drone on about the background and context surrounding the artifact. Instead, his words were brief and to the point. "Thank you, Professor Thorne. May I remind you that we hold deliberations in order to make a decision. This particular deliberation will address one item of concern, of which there are three sub-categories. One: To determine *how* the artifact will be studied. Two: To determine *where* the artifact will be studied. And three: To determine a *hypothesis* of study. In order to answer these three questions, we must appoint a head of research for the project."

Already there were loud objections from the gathered academics.

"Shouldn't the hypothesis come later, after initial analysis?"

"Study it in the *sea!*"

"Why haven't we got a say in it staying here?"

"Can I touch it?"

"I nominate myself as head researcher!"

Cadwick produced a miniature wooden hammer from within his waistcoat and rapped it on the lectern. This produced such an ear-splitting sound that the room went almost immediately quiet.

"Thank you," he said, without an ounce of gratitude in his tone. "Please respect the rules of the deliberation. To address the first topic of concern, I will turn it over to Professor Obralle."

Ru didn't like where this was going. She had been to deliberations before. They always took hours, with various votes and lengthy arguments from whoever decided to pipe up with an opinion. As humiliated as she felt, she also knew, with a prick of indignant anger, that *she* should be the one deciding it all. The artifact was tied to her, and she to it, and only she should be tasked with determining its nature.

Professor Obralle was speaking into the brass horn now, explaining in more detail that the regent would be fully funding the study of the artifact, that every amenity would be granted to the research team, and that all safety precautions would be taken.

A line of Ru's peers began to form at the lectern now, each academic granted a minute to speak on each topic.

"Aren't you going up there?" Gwyneth asked, giving

Ru a piercing look. "Your voice should be weighted most heavily in the debate."

"Yes," said Ru, unable to look away from the lectern, from Professor Obralle as she stepped aside, giving the floor to the first academic in line. "I just need a minute to…" she trailed off, distracted.

Academic after academic went up to speak, so confident in their ideas, their plans. Ru barely listened after the first one, unable to focus in the face of her anxiety.

"Well?" said Archie, nudging her shoulder with his. "You've got to, you know, actually go up there."

Against the core of her nature, which begged her to stay in her seat and hide from the inevitable derision, Ru stood. The lectern seemed miles away as she shuffled awkwardly through milling academics until she came to the end of the line. She stood there hunched, arms crossed, hoping nobody would notice her.

Meanwhile, the academic currently on the podium was going on about numbers and weighing safety against potential danger. "If you look at the statistics regarding explosive items, whether they be contained chemical concoctions or crude bombs meant for warfare, we must acknowledge that—"

"Yes, thank you," said Professor Obralle, edging sideways to place her hand over the speaking horn. "Your minute is up, Westley. Back to your seat, please. And—ah, I see Delara has finally joined the queue! All of you, out of the way. Delara, come up."

There was an outcry of protest at this, and Ru's face burned as she shook her head frantically.

"Don't be silly, you ought to have been first in line," said Obralle. "You have firsthand experience with the artifact. How do you think we should study it?" She handed the lectern over to Ru, who made her way there in a haze.

"Go on," said Obralle so that only Ru could hear, patting her gently on the shoulder.

This gesture was received with a few derisive snorts from the academics who stood in line, loudly offended that Ru had been given precedence.

Already sweating in her too-hot dress, Ru cleared her throat. The sound echoed throughout the room, and she was certain, at that moment, that literally anything in the world would be better than standing up there.

As she opened her mouth to speak, a new sensation took hold of her. It started in her chest and spread outward, subtly but definitely there — a calming warmth, like honeyed tea drifting through her veins. It was the artifact, no longer humming quietly in the background of her mind as it usually did, but making itself known. As if it knew she needed soothing.

"Um," she said into the speaking horn, distracted by the artifact but no longer shaking with anxiety. She caught Gwyneth's eye in the crowd, her friend nodding encouragement. It was the push she needed.

"Ruellian Delara," she said, her voice quiet, even through the horn. "Fourth year, Archaeology. As you know, I was… present at… at the site. Where the artifact was uncovered. I believe, and have accepted, that I should have died at the time."

The hall filled with sudden anticipatory silence. Each academic, despite the muttering and shouting out earlier, was now at the edge of their seat. Ru didn't know what to do with this sudden attention. She had expected jeering, or catcalls, but not this.

"I should have," she continued, "but I didn't. Instead, I woke up blind with a stone in my hands. And everyone around me, the dig site…" she took a breath. "Well, you all know what happened. I wasn't lucky or blessed. I still don't know what happened, exactly. But… I've come to accept that I am intrinsic to the study of the artifact, and vice versa. The regent sent me here with the artifact under orders to discover the nature of it, and to answer two questions."

Every time she spoke about the dig site, she thought of Lady Maryn. Panic threatened to choke her. But as her throat constricted with it, she focused on the artifact's touch. Its steady, humming voice against her nerves.

With a steady voice, she said, "I ask the same questions as all of you no doubt, the same questions as the regent: Did the artifact cause the dig site's destruction? And if so, why did it spare me? We can't begin to study the nature of the thing without answering these questions."

Some of her peers nodded, while others furrowed their brows thoughtfully. Some still frowned and whispered behind their hands.

"I believe I'm the best person to do that," she finished. There was a faint smattering of applause, mostly from Archie and Gwyneth.

Obralle appeared again on the podium, leaning over to reach the speaking horn while Ru moved out of her way.

"A moving and convincing argument," she said. "May I speak on behalf of everyone here when I ask, Miss Delara, what might be the nature of your hypothesis?"

Ru froze. "Hypothesis?"

"Yes. Everyone who speaks must post a thesis statement, a conjecture as to what you believe the artifact to be and how you will come to the same conclusion via the scientific method."

I know what a hypothesis is, thought Ru, her brain scrambling to come up with something. But she had no choice — there was only one hypothesis she believed, one possibility that explained the stone and its detonation, the inexplicable way in which it had spared Ru.

"Ah yes, I forgot," she said into the speaking horn, sweat beading on her upper lip. "My hypothesis."

She caught Archie's eye for a moment, then Gwyneth's, both of them smiling encouragingly.

"My hypothesis," she said again, slightly more confidently this time, "is as follows. The artifact was present during what I believe to be a particle-level explosion, and remains intact. I, too, remain intact. Therefore, if the artifact is an explosive device, then it must be selective in nature. Discerning. Calculating."

"Are you saying it's *alive*?" said one of the academics in line for the lectern. It was Grey Adler, smirking.

Ru gave him a pitying look. "If that's what you think I said, then I apologize for not simplifying my words."

Almost everyone laughed. Grey was notoriously arrogant. Extremely smart and cunning, but entirely lacking in personality and generally disliked.

Ru, buoyed by this reception, continued. "I am not saying the artifact is alive, nor am I arguing conscious thought. What I *will* attempt to prove is that the artifact — its physical makeup notwithstanding — was constructed for a purpose, and whatever that purpose was must be inherently mechanized into the thing itself, enabling the artifact to act without orders or guidance. However, such advanced engineering would be beyond our ability to identify it. Beyond, even, our understanding. The artifact must be, for lack of a better word... a magical object."

The room was deathly silent for a moment. Then someone snickered, muffled, and another small laugh broke free. Ru set her jaw. They could mock her as much as they liked. It was the only explanation for the artifact. And more than that, it was a chance for her to finally reclaim her dignity in academia.

The artifact had come to her, whether by fate or by chance, and she wouldn't take that for granted. She could use the artifact for progress and the advancement of scientific thought. It could change the world. And most desperately, most urgently, she needed to know what had happened at the Shattered City and why.

Obralle, who was still hovering near the edge of the podium, stepped forward and asked, close enough to the speaking horn so that her voice carried through the room, "Is this your hypothesis, then? To prove that the artifact is... magic?"

"Yes, it is." Ru felt utterly confident in her hypothesis. It would sound like madness to everyone there, but she knew it was true. She only had to prove it.

"I see," said Professor Obralle. "And once you determine whether it is magic, do you aim to seek out its purpose?"

"Of course," said Ru. "Although, over the course of

study, I may discover outliers or contradictions which steer my research in a new direction. But if my hypothesis is proven, then the natural next step would be to seek the source of the stone's magic. And, from there, to determine its purpose."

The low murmur of the room, the half-laughs and whispers, grew to a low roar. Ru tried to drown it out, tried not to let shame and humiliation drown her. She was right. She knew it. She only had to prove it.

Obralle smiled hesitantly, her eyes slightly pained. "A clear plan of action, then. Thank you, Delara. You may sit."

The deliberation continued for another three hours. The mockery and jeering that followed Ru's presentation was brief, the topic of the artifact too grim to maintain jokes for more than a few moments.

Sitting with Archie and Gwyneth, waiting for everyone to argue their point as the morning wore on, Ru realized that she had far underestimated the ability of academics to talk about themselves and their ideas. She thought maybe a dozen would stand up as volunteers, no more than twenty, but *this*? It seemed as if the entire Tower was vying for the post of head researcher.

It made her oddly jealous, possessive of the artifact in a way that felt foreign to her. But the artifact *was* hers. It didn't want anyone else.

She was so wrapped up in thinking about the artifact that she didn't notice Gwyneth had left her seat until her friend appeared at the lectern.

Only a handful of academics were now awaiting their turn, and everyone in the room was restless with impatience.

"I don't have a hypothesis," said Gwyneth matter-of-factly, as soon as Obralle turned the speaking horn over to her. She ignored the ensuing grumbles, flicking her hair over one shoulder. "I only have a question. Have any of you truly considered the fact that Delara is the *only* person who survived the explosion at the dig site?"

There was an irritable rumble of assent.

Ru leaned toward Archie, whose eyebrows were

raised so high they threatened to merge with his light hair. "What's she doing?" she hissed. But he only patted her arm, distracted, listening to what Gwyneth said next.

"So I suppose you've also considered," Gwyneth continued in her warm, engaging voice, her large eyes wide with animation, "that Delara might be the only person alive who is immune to the artifact's destructive capabilities." She paused, staring around at the seated academics, a fearless challenge. Despite her small frame and doll-like features, she radiated confidence. "And I *suppose* you've all weighed the danger of being stuck in a room with an explosive object all day against your eagerness to prove yourself smarter than everyone here, correct?"

She smiled sweetly, tossed her hair, and descended from the podium, her skirts bouncing as she went.

Archie punched her arm as she slid back into her chair, grinning. "Well said, Gwyn."

"Thanks," said Ru. "But these idiots will do anything for academic prestige."

"If you say so," said Gwyneth, shrugging. "But I think I've put an end to it."

Ru opened her mouth to protest, but even as she did, the remaining academics in line at the lectern hesitated, then scattered, returning to their seats. Gwyneth beamed.

Professor Cadwick, seeing that no one was left to argue their point, approached the lectern. "It is time now for the vote," he said. "I will read out, in order, the names of all those who have put themselves forward for the role of head researcher of the artifact."

Ru looked around, expecting to see eager faces and jovial banter, the usual competitive academic behavior. Instead, everyone around her shared nervous glances. Some faces had even gone pale.

"Does anyone wish to withdraw their name at this time?" said Professor Cadwick. The gathered academics continued to exchange looks of unease, but nobody spoke up.

Then someone from across the room raised a hand.

Ru recognized her as a third-year named Pip Williams. She was first in her class and had been one of the first to line up at the lectern.

"Professor," she said, "I'd like to officially request that, as a matter of respect for the harrowing experiences she has endured thus far, we vote on Delara first."

Professor Cadwick frowned slightly, clearly irked by the unexpected request. "Fine." He leaned forward so that his lips were nearly touching the speaking horn. "All those in favor of Ruellian Delara as head researcher, in charge of studying the artifact, raise your hands."

Every hand in the Great Hall shot up.

"Ah," said Cadwick. "I see we have a shocking consensus. Very well. By unanimous vote, it is decided that Ruellian Delara will take on the role of head researcher of the artifact, here at the Cornelian Tower, in keeping with the orders of the Regent Sigrun. Henceforth, all decisions regarding the artifact's research will fall to Delara."

Elation and relief washed over Ru. She'd done it. No... Gwyneth had done it, really. But with that relief came new questions. Did she really know what she was doing? Was this the correct course of action?

Professor Cadwick whacked his little hammer against the lectern. "The deliberation has concluded."

CHAPTER 18

More than anything, Ru needed lunch and a nap. And, though she would never say it aloud, she longed for the artifact. But there was no hope for any of these at the moment. As soon as the deliberation came to an end, Ru was swept out of the Great Hall by the professors, serving as a sort of human shield, protecting her from the congratulations and questions tossed at her by the thronging academics.

She was herded into a small parlor that was most often used for receiving visitors, adjacent to the Great Hall. Ru seated herself in an armchair by the fire, which was already lit and crackling away. Professor Acorn sat across from her, his golden-brown hair catching the firelight. He was the youngest of the professors at the Tower, and the most emotionally minded, his gaze laced with compassion. The rest of the professors stood in a semicircle, their expressions deeply serious. Only Thorne seemed to be lost in his own world, pacing about the room, muttering to himself.

"Now listen," said Professor Cadwick without preamble. "I'm sure you know that you've put yourself and the Tower in a difficult spot with all this…" he waved his hands, "magic artifact business. We *know* why the regent initially sent for you. We know she agrees that this item could indeed be *magic*." The last word spat like a curse.

This gathering felt immediately to Ru like an off-the-cuff interrogation, and it set her teeth on edge. She understood where Cadwick was coming from; of course she did. But his seeming lack of empathy rankled. It wasn't as if Ru had asked to be called to the Shattered City. She would have been much happier if none of this had happened.

Even the artifact? A tiny thought pushed its way to the surface. *Even Fen?*

"I'm aware of all that," said Ru, crossing her arms defensively. "I've considered the dangers. We'll need to take precautions, but I feel confident that I can prove my hypothesis."

"Don't forget the matter of the attack on your journey here," said Professor Obralle. The others nodded, and Thorne paused in his pacing to frown deeply in assent. Obralle continued, "We've already spoken at length with Lyr and Fen Verrill. They know very little, as it stands. But whoever those guards were, whoever they worked for, there's no reason to believe they won't come back. Looking for the artifact, or you, or whatever it is they're after."

"Both, perhaps," muttered Thorne, running his hands through a mess of hair.

Dread seeped into Ru's veins like a sickness.

"I didn't want to bring danger here," she said, as if she were a young girl being admonished. "But the Tower is a fortress. It's the safest place for the artifact, even safer than the palace. Particularly now that we know there are traitors in Mirith." She avoided bringing up the fact that there could also be traitors here, in the Cornelian Tower.

"Very well," said Professor Cadwick, sighing. "I suppose we must abide by the regent's wishes in the end."

The talk turned to more practical matters: where the research of the artifact would take place, who — if anyone — would be assisting Ru in her studies, and what sort of tools and mechanisms she might need for the work. It was agreed that the research center should be in the depths of the Tower, far underground in what had once been a dungeon. The dungeon would be fixed up to

Ru's specifications, fitted with lighting, workstations, along with basic comforts.

It was up to Ru's discretion who would join her team of researchers. She knew that she wouldn't demand that anyone join her. She would only accept volunteers, those who understood and agreed to the risks they would be taking.

More than anything, she found that she wanted Fen there with her. She couldn't imagine studying the artifact without him. And the thought of being close to that smooth, dark stone with Fen's body so near she could feel his warmth, hear him breathe… the artifact's silky press against her mind, soothing anxious nerves, softening taut muscles…

"She needs rest."

"She needs *food*."

"Delara, wake up."

She started, coming back to the moment. She had been so lost in thought, spurred on by the artifact, overcome with exhaustion and delirium, that she had drifted into a doze.

She straightened, blinking and shaking her head to clear it. There was now only one thing on her mind.

"Where is Fen?"

ACCORDING TO PROFESSOR OBRALLE, Fen was still at the Tower along with Lyr. Once they had been thoroughly questioned, the two men had been encouraged to rest and allow their horses to recover from the grueling journey. They were staying in the guest wing.

Ru hadn't seen Fen since yesterday. She had barely seen him in days, she realized. He had been evasive, there but not, disappearing from the regent's dinner and reappearing as a King's Guard in disguise. And now this, avoiding the deliberation.

He owed her nothing. She hardly even knew him. Ru wasn't sure they were even friends, or if they were simply two people thrown together by chance, ultimately fated to be wrenched apart by the same. Ru couldn't say what he felt, how he saw her. But somehow, in such a short time, Fen had become dear to her. And not just familiar, as he had felt on their first meeting when she first saw those gray eyes, the immediate sense that she was safe with him. It was something more than that.

Something she wasn't ready to face. Not yet.

These thoughts chased each other through her head as she made her way to the guest wing. When she arrived in that long stretch of hall, narrower and lower-ceilinged than the dormitory wing, she realized she had no idea which room was Fen's.

She stood awkwardly near the first door, wondering what to do. She couldn't go down the hall and knock on every door until she found him. Still sweaty and shaken from the deliberation, and desperately in need of food, she found herself deflating. She couldn't see Fen in this state.

Exhausted and somewhat dejected, Ru turned and walked back to the dormitory wing. She needed a bath and a hearty meal, and then... then she would look for Fen.

"If it isn't the notorious Ruellian Delara."

That deeply accented voice could only belong to one person.

Ru stopped in her tracks and looked up, beaming, to see Fen. He was coming from the direction of her room, black coattails swinging behind him as he strode briskly toward her.

"What are you doing here?" she said, her heart lighter just at the sight of him. "I thought you were staying in the guest wing."

He stopped before her, so close she could see the delicate hairs curling out from his slightly open shirt, a faint freckle on his nose. Motes of dust drifted through a beam of sunlight, bathing them in faint colors.

"I was looking for you," he said.

Her heart leaped. "And I was looking for *you*. Why weren't you at the deliberation?" She hadn't meant to ask immediately, wanted to seem nonchalant as if she wasn't so desperate to know where he'd been. But the question came to her lips despite herself.

"The professors wouldn't let me attend," he said, smiling apologetically. He tilted his head slightly, a lock of black hair falling over one eye. "Lyr and I tried, you know, to support you. But outsiders aren't allowed to witness the mysterious inner workings of the Tower, apparently."

Then his face fell, his expression hardening. He moved closer still, and she wondered if he felt her heart pounding. Lifting a hand, he traced a thumb gently over her cheek.

She hissed in pain as his thumb brushed against the bruise.

"I wish I could kill him again," he breathed, voice low and angry. "He deserved worse than a beheading."

Ru's breath caught at the darkness in his tone. "It's fine," she said. "It only needs ice."

Fen gave her a look as if he couldn't imagine anything worse than a bruise on Ru's cheek, which made her feel too hot, too close. And yet there was nowhere else she would rather have been.

"Where have you been since the deliberation?" she asked, trying to change the subject to something less intense.

"Looking for you," he said again. He made no move to increase the distance between them, his thumb still soft against her jaw.

She felt almost weak in the knees, but she was sure it must be her hunger. "You found me," she said.

"I'd prefer you less battered and bruised," he said, his smile returning, "but it's a relief to see you up and about."

There were so many things she wanted to ask him about — how he had known the King's Guards would turn on them, how he managed to sneak into their traveling party in disguise, why he was still there, who he was… really. Instead, her brain stumbling at the simple touch of his thumb and his gentle smile, she said, "I'm leading the research team. To study the artifact."

He hummed approvingly. "I expected nothing less of you."

She swallowed, suddenly nervous. But she had to ask. "Will you... stay and help?"

He gave her a long look. "Do you remember when I said I'd die before letting any harm come to you or your little rock? I don't know where else you think I'd go."

Ru could have floated away on a beam of sunlight.

They spent the rest of the afternoon together. First, with tea in Ru's rooms, and then walking the grounds of the Tower while Ru gave a rudimentary history of the building and its uses over the ages. Fen was fully engrossed, which only encouraged her further. She told him about her studies and how the concept of magic had initially captivated her.

"It was my brother," she admitted under the shade of a swaying fruit tree in the eastern courtyard. "He used to play these songs for me when I was young. We had a family lute that was passed down from our grandmother; she's where he got the talent. He taught himself how to play and he'd practice his own compositions for me in the back garden. I remember, on days like this when it was bright and warm, I would doze in the sun while beautiful melodies swept over me. The only way I could describe how I felt was... well, magic. I was so sure in those moments that the music itself was, somehow, altering my state of being."

Fen listened closely and quietly, his eyes fixed on her. Ru looked away.

"It's silly," she muttered.

"It's not," he said. "Nothing you say is silly."

The way he looked at her was unlike any man she'd met. Even Archie, devoted friend and once lover, had never regarded her with such intensity. As if Fen was seeing through to the core of her, as if he understood more about Ruellian Delara than anyone else ever could. She couldn't hold his gaze, it was too open, too honest.

"You don't have to stay here, you know," she said, at

last, staring out across the courtyard, at the billowing clouds. "The promise you made, about protecting me. I'm home now. I'm perfectly safe."

"Are you?"

The question rang in her ears. If there were traitors at the palace...

"Fen," she said, turning to him with a slight frown, "why did you travel with us in disguise? How did you know the guards would turn on us?"

"I didn't," he said. "But I suspected. Simon pulled me aside at dinner with a warning. He had noticed guards acting out of character, even members of the court. Ever since the arrival of the Children, he claimed that things were... off-kilter. He asked — no, he ordered me to keep you safe on the journey to the Tower." Fen's mouth curved upward in a rueful smile. "He loves you, your brother. And he sees what others can't."

"He has the gift of intuition," said Ru, reeling slightly from this revelation. "But why wouldn't Simon have told me this directly?"

"He didn't want you to give away his plan. If the guards had known I wasn't one of them, had suspected something was afoot, they might not have acted. Had that been the case, it would have been impossible to predict their next move."

Ru chewed her lip. "But who... why would they betray the regent? Who turned their loyalty? Surely the regent herself wouldn't send us away only to have us attacked on the road."

"You now know as much as I do," said Fen, leaning back, hands braced in the grass behind him. "Whoever the guards worked for knows about the artifact, knows you were on your way north with it."

"But that could be anyone," Ru said, her voice rising in agitation. "The entire city of Mirith will know about the artifact by now. And my whereabouts. Any power-hungry, murderous madman will be after me." She reached for Fen thoughtlessly, needing to feel anchored to reality as her thoughts were increasingly unmoored.

Fen took her hand and squeezed it, gently. "I won't

break my promise. I will protect you. If anyone so much as looks at you wrong..." he made a slitting gesture across his throat with one finger.

Despite herself, Ru laughed. "You'll be after the entirety of the Cornelian Tower, in that case. I suspect everyone has it in for me now. Bringing a dangerous item to the Tower, declaring it magic. I'm practically a pariah."

It was meant to be a joke, an exaggeration, but Ru knew in her heart that it was partly true. The professors allowed the artifact's study because the regent ordered it. She was unspeakably grateful that nobody knew the truth of it — that she had just short of begged the regent to let her take the stone back to the Tower.

Regret bubbled in her, threatening to rise like a wave in a storm.

"If I have to fight them all, one by one," said Fen, half-smiling in the golden light, the planes of his face softened, "then I will."

"My protector," Ru said, smiling. She kept her tone light, but the depths of her gratitude were incalculable.

CHAPTER 19

When they returned to the Tower, the sun had set and evening fell in swathes of muted blue over its stone walls. Fen accompanied Ru to her rooms. She was silently grateful, the growing shadows and chill in the air raising goosebumps on her arms. Logically, she knew there weren't assassins hiding in every corner, waiting to spring. But there was just enough uncertainty to make her wary, and glad of Fen's presence.

Outside her room, Ru hovered in the open doorway, unsure what to say. She wanted to thank Fen for staying, for distracting her all afternoon and allowing her a much-needed mental rest. But it wasn't just that. She enjoyed talking to him. He was attentive and interested — she never felt ignored. His presence was innately comforting to her, and somehow since she'd met him, he had become more than a friend. He was a safety net of sorts.

He felt almost like home.

And she realized then, looking up at the dark-haired man who had found his way so seamlessly into her life, that she had hardly noticed the artifact all afternoon. She was struck by the sense of relief that came with this discovery, that she was still Ru, that the artifact didn't define her. Even so, she probed in her mind and found it there, the thread between them intact.

With Fen, she hadn't needed the artifact; and somehow, it hadn't needed her.

"Remember," said Fen, smiling, "there could be traitors in our midst. Don't open the door for just anyone."

"Not even you?" Ru teased.

"Always open it for me," he said, catching her with an intense gaze, and Ru tried to ignore the sudden heat that sprang up in her. Then he turned away and ran a hand through his messy dark hair. When he looked at her again, his expression was soft but determined. "That is, if you want to."

He was so tall and so close that Ru had to crane her neck slightly to meet his gaze.

"Why do I feel like I've known you my whole life?" she said. The words fell off her tongue before she could stop them. She tensed immediately, assuming he'd step away, laugh, and brush the comment aside for the nonsense it was.

Instead, for just a brief moment, a desperate sadness passed over his face. And then it was gone so completely that Ru wondered if she had imagined it.

"Ru!"

Gwyneth's voice. She came dashing around the corner, her golden hair streaming, a stack of books hugged against her chest.

Startled by Gwyneth's sudden appearance, Fen backed into the hall, and Ru shook her head to clear it, to douse the rising heat, the lingering intensity of his gaze. He was a friend. He had implied nothing more.

"There you are," Gwyneth said, breathless, skidding to a halt. "I've been looking all over for you. Have you eaten? Come to dinner." She paused, turning to Fen. "You must be Fen. Pleased to meet you. I'm Gwyneth."

The corners of his mouth twitched. "A pleasure, Gwyneth. Ru thinks very highly of you."

Gwyneth beamed, adjusting her grip on the pile of books. "Join us for dinner? Archie is meeting me there. *Us* there. We can discuss our plans for the artifact's study." She was practically vibrating with excitement.

Ru blinked, not quite believing what she heard. "You want to be on my research team?"

Gwyneth laughed. "Don't be thick, Ru. As if Archie

and I wouldn't join you. Anyway, who else do you think is going to volunteer?"

"After your little speech at the deliberation, you mean." Ru raised an eyebrow, half-laughing.

Gwyneth sniffed dismissively. "I took the liberty of collecting your paper's entire bibliography. What I could carry, anyway."

Looking closer, Ru saw that it was true — Gwyneth's arms were full of books that Ru had read and cited in her paper. "Gwyn," she said, "you're incredible."

"I know," Gwyneth replied. "But this means you're now honor-bound to help me gather sources when I start on my next hideous paper."

"The lamb one?" Ru asked. Gwyneth was often planning full-scale treatises and then pivoting to a new topic at the last minute, her enthusiasm so easily piqued by the latest bit of intriguing research or historic anecdote.

"No," said Gwyneth, holding the pile of books out to Fen, her gaze still locked on Ru. He took the books without protest. She wiped her hands on her skirts, attempting to smooth them, but only succeeding in smearing dust on the fabric. "Goats as transportation. Did you know they once pulled little carts? Thousands of years ago? I have to know if the carts were for an adult's use, or were they transporting goods... or perhaps children..." she trailed off, a length of shining hair twirled around one finger, her delicate brows knit together in thought.

"As soon as you decide on a subject, I'll help you research," Ru said laughingly. "I promise."

Gwyneth nodded once, a jerk of her pert chin. "Agreed. Fen, are you joining us for dinner?"

He stood looking down at them, his arms now full of books, bemused. "I—"

"He is," said Ru, steering her friend away from Fen and toward the direction of the mess hall. "But Gwyn, I'm not sure you've considered all the possible dangers. Remember your inspiring speech at the deliberation? Don't be so eager to..." she trailed off, not wanting to say aloud what she meant.

"Die?" Gwyneth finished cheerfully.

Fen, following behind, his chin resting on the tower dusty of books, grumbled to himself at the mention of death.

"Never mind," said Ru. "Let's eat, at least, before we discuss our deaths at length."

"Wonderful," said Gwyneth, her tone completely at odds with Ru's feelings of rising dread and the fear of exposing her friends to danger.

When they came at last to the mess hall, Ru's reception was just as she had expected. Some academics gave her awkward nods, some ignored her altogether, while most shot her suspicious or even frightened looks. At least, she thought, they weren't laughing at her. Better to be feared or hated in the academic world than mocked.

Her rumination was cut short by the sight of Archie, who had found a table and was waving them over, his bright hair like a beacon in the throng. Ru and Gwyneth made a beeline for him, settling themselves on the long wooden benches, where each place was already set with dishes and utensils.

Fen, trailing behind, set the pile of books on the table with a thump, sending a plume of dust into the air. Gwyneth coughed, waving a hand in front of her face.

Large portions of food were laid out at the center of each table. There were tureens of hearty stew, fresh loaves of rustic bread, selections of cheese, roasted game hens, various dishes of vegetables, and sticks of butter laid out for convenience.

Ru had missed the Tower's simple but hearty food. While the Tower employed no servants like at the palace, there was a contingent of cooks who lived in their own section of the Tower, near to the kitchens. Ru rarely wandered into the kitchens as she worried she might come out smelling like stew, but Gwyneth and Archie often visited the cooks and were always coming back to their rooms with little treats.

"So what's the research plan?" Archie asked eagerly, while the others loaded up their plates. Then his gaze lit on Fen, and his smile stiffened. "Have we met?"

"Don't be rude," said Gwyneth. "This is Fen. Ru's friend. *Remember*? I *told* you…"

"Ah yes, of course. How could I forget the way you lovingly described his artfully disheveled hair?" Archie gave Fen an appraising once-over. "You're a… historian, I'm given to understand? "

"I am," said Fen, raising an eyebrow in response to Archie's tone. "My reputation precedes me." The two men were roughly the same age, but Fen's deeply accented voice and dark, intense presence made Archie seem younger by contrast. Almost delicate.

"Archie Hill," said Archie. He pressed his well-formed lips together in obvious disapproval.

Neither of them made to shake hands.

Gwyneth and Ru shared a look. They knew what Archie was doing. Because he and Ru had shared a bed in the past, because she knew he cared for her more deeply than he would ever let on, he was feeling protective. Even jealous. In any other man, such behavior might have put her off. But Archie had been her friend from the start, and while he was guilty of more than his fair share of buffoonery, she cared about him. And just like any true friend, she was even fond of his flaws.

"Archie loves knives," Ru offered, pausing in buttering a slice of warm bread. "Kitchen knives — ancient ones. He's not going to stab you."

Archie shot Ru a look of exaggerated betrayal. "How dare you say such a thing when you know full well I'd happily stab Fen. Anyway, my knives are special. I prefer not to discuss them with the uninitiated."

Ru stopped herself from rolling her eyes. "Would you rather me talk about your obsession with that musician from Mirith?"

Gwyneth snorted.

Archie shifted, his smile strained to the point of near breaking. "On second thought, the knives are fine."

Gwyneth smothered her laughter and leaned forward, commanding attention. "Don't worry, Arch, we would never reveal that little tidbit. Your secret stays safe with us."

Archie was clearly desperate to turn the conversation away from his favorite musician, the famous harpist he had written letters to as a teenager, repeatedly asking for her hand in marriage. Ru and Gwyneth hadn't known him at the time, but he had told them the story once while drunk and would never live to hear the end of it.

Ru bit back a laugh. Color was high in Archie's cheeks, his jaw clenched so tightly she worried he'd break a tooth, yet still feigning a cheerful smile. Fen, across the table from him, looked on with mild dark-eyed bemusement. She had missed her friends. She hadn't realized until now how hungry she had been for their joy, the peace their laughter brought her.

"Good," said Archie, "in fact, let's forget all about that little tidbit, shall we? Simply erase it from our minds. Knives are *so* much more fascinating than... than other things. With their serrations and their various uses." He stabbed a small potato with his fork, nostrils flaring defensively.

Fen cut in then, saving Archie from further embarrassment at the hands of his friends. "As a historian," he said, holding up his bread knife as if it were a prop, "I've always been interested in the domesticity of past lives. The blades they may have wielded in safety, rather than on the battlefield. If you'd be willing, I'd love to read any papers you may have written on the subject."

Ru beamed at Fen.

Archie, on the other hand, seemed unmoved. He raised his eyebrows and nodded, pointedly avoiding Fen's gaze. "Wonderful. Yes. No doubt that will be stimulating for us both."

"If we're going to work on this project *together*," said Gwyneth, cutting in with thinly veiled ferocity, steering the conversation away from stabbings, "first on the docket should be a research plan. Ru, do you have an idea of how you'd like to approach things?"

"Slowly," said Fen.

"Yes," said Ru, considering, "but the pace will come naturally as we build out a schedule. I have a list of everything I believe we'll need to start, equipment-wise, and a list of questions we should answer. But above all, I think we need to remember that this is incredibly dangerous. We're going to be in close proximity to a potentially volatile object that could be... well, magic."

Archie and Gwyneth shared a glance, then, a look that said they were preparing to finally voice something they had been talking about behind Ru's back.

"We've been meaning to ask you, Ru," Gwyneth said, hesitant. "After what happened at the dig site... will you be alright? Studying the artifact, I mean. It won't... dredge up memories?"

"We'll quite understand if you need to—"

Archie's words faded to a meaningless hum in Ru's ears. She set down her fork, her appetite fleeing. She had expected trepidation about her belief that the artifact was magic, doubt from her friends, but this...

Dredge up memories.

"I'll be fine," she said. Her hands shook, twisting in her skirts.

Memories of black dirt at her feet, a remnant of unspeakable destruction. A smooth stone beneath her touch. Lady Maryn's cry of fear.

Nausea clouded Ru's senses, a sudden terror that she would vomit there in the mess hall. She tried to breathe more slowly. Archie had said something else; they were waiting for her to respond.

The artifact, as if waking from a slumber, caressed her mind, filling her with that spreading warmth. But it wasn't enough. Not enough. Her breaths came too fast, too shallow.

She glanced up at Fen, just for a half-second, and he caught her gaze with firm reassurance.

"I'll be fine," Ru said again. "I need..."

"It's just," Gwyneth went on, pushing. Her expression was free of malice, yet her words turned like a knife between Ru's ribs, "you knew those people. Spoke to them. And now they're gone."

An image flashed in Ru's mind, a memory of a nightmare — Lady Maryn's body, molecule by molecule, coming apart... blackening... turning to dust and fading... until it was nothing.

She wouldn't lose control; she wouldn't vomit. Not here. Bile rose in her throat nonetheless, choking.

"I'm fine," she heard herself say, the same words coming again and again. Meaningless.

"She's a bit pale," came Archie's hissed voice.

Another voice, Gwyneth's, saying something soft, her delicate hands against Ru's shoulder.

"She needs rest," said Fen, his words cutting through the fog. Then he was at Ru's side, urging her to her feet.

He said something to Gwyneth and Archie as he steered Ru away from the table and out of the mess hall, but everything was muffled in Ru's head. All she knew was the rush of blood in her ears, increasingly blurred vision, the artifact calming her — calming her, and yet it wasn't enough.

Finally outside the mess hall, Ru stumbled toward the nearest wall, leaning against it, sliding down until she was half-crouched. She turned to press her bruised cheek to the cool stone. She closed her eyes and tried to breathe.

"You're taking in too much air," said Fen. "You're hyperventilating."

"I know that," Ru hissed through gritted teeth. "You think I don't know that? Who's the scientist here?" She still couldn't unclench her hands. "I don't need you to tell me anything."

Hot tears streamed from the corners of her tightly shut eyes.

A strong, warm hand found hers. Frightened and embarrassed, hoping none of the academics had seen or understood what was happening, Ru allowed Fen to help her upright again, to lead her slowly back to the dormitory wing. It wasn't far, and by the time they got to her room, her breathing had steadied a bit.

"Listen to me," said Fen, taking her shoulders in his hands, ever so gently. His gaze was so intense that he almost looked frightened. "You're right. You don't need me, not for anything. You're Ruellian Delara."

She sniffed, dissuading the tears that desperately wanted to fall.

"But I promised I would keep you safe," he continued. "And when you panic... when you lose control like that..." he shook his head. "If the artifact truly is magic, it could react... *poorly* to strong emotion. Not just yours. Anyone's."

"Why do you say that?" She was shaking, clinging to him shamelessly.

"Because I've studied magic."

Ru stared up at him through tear-soaked lashes, taking in his disheveled black hair and his fraught expression. Had she heard him correctly? Was she delirious? "You've what?"

He sighed and closed his eyes for a moment. When he opened them again they were far clearer, the fear gone, replaced by a steady resolve. "I've studied magic. I told you I was interested in the occult. I've read extensively on the subject. Magical objects, in theory at least, can react to all sorts of stimuli. Emotions, words, temperature, the touch of water. Anything."

A hot tear ran down Ru's cheek. "My skin."

"Ru," said Fen, his voice low. "It wasn't your fault. Magic can be wildly unpredictable. Whatever the artifact is, whatever it responds to..."

"I understand," said Ru, exhausted, drained, weak. Even the artifact felt quiet in her mind, as if it, too, was overwhelmed. "I can't lose control of my emotions around the artifact."

"That's not—" he began, but Ru interrupted him.

"That is what you meant. It's all right. I agree." She sniffed, wiping her eyes with the back of one hand. "I didn't realize you truly believed in magic. I thought you were just..."

He smiled faintly. "What, appeasing you? I wouldn't lie about something like that." Then his eyes glazed as if remembering something long past, a memory he would rather forget. "*Believe* isn't the right word. I accept it. Despite the harm it can cause."

"You mean the Destruction," she said.

His eyes snapped to hers.

"Yes," he said darkly. "How else can we explain it? Take what we know, what was found there, what we've seen."

"It would be foolish to assume anything different," Ru said. "But the others won't. And intuition won't prove anything, not to Archie and Gwyn or the regent. Even if you and I believe… We have to prove this strictly by scientific method."

"I hadn't doubted that," said Fen, his expression softening. "Ru, you are…"

He straightened then, stepped back, away from her. The few inches of distance seemed to yawn like a gulf between them. Disappointment flooded Ru's chest; she wanted to close the gap.

"I'm what?" she asked, resisting Fen's pull.

He swept a hand over his face. "You're probably exhausted. Get some rest. We'll all need it if we're going to confront that rock tomorrow."

He left Ru standing in the doorway of her room, his coat and hair waving darkly behind him as he stalked away. She knew she would see him in the morning, so why did her chest ache at his departure?

Lonely and seeking solace, she reached out to the artifact. As always, it answered, squeezing her heart as gently as a butterfly might alight on a flower petal. But now, alone outside her room with the remnants of panic pumping through her, even such a light, delicate touch felt like ice in her veins.

CHAPTER 20

"I guess I don't understand the relationship dynamic," said Gwyneth. She pulled another book from the shelf and handed it to Ru, who was already hefting a heavy pile of books.

They were in one of the many Tower libraries, hunting for more tomes that might assist in their research. It had been two days since the deliberation, time during which Ru devoted every free moment to preparing for their research. She had made a meticulous list of every tool, device, or item they might need from the palace that wasn't already available at the Tower, and sent it by pigeon to the regent.

Ru had tasked everyone in the research group with studying her paper on magic, noting anything that could apply to the artifact. Even Ru had forgotten some of the paper's nuances and was eager to reread it, to apply her own methodology to this new project.

But the paper was only a basis — they would need more books, more avenues of study than what Ru had presented. So, she and Gwyneth paid visits to the libraries, one by one.

This particular library was in one of the Tower's smaller turrets, a circular library with books all the way up to the ceiling. There were several levels and a spiral staircase right in the center, like a black metal corkscrew. Ru and Gwyneth had started at the top and gradually made their way down, picking up books in any subject or genre as long as it sounded even somewhat promising.

Ru looked skeptically at the book Gwyneth had just handed to her: *Matters of the Mind and Heart* by Lady Isabella Bosomme. "I'm pretty sure this is smut," she said.

"It's romance, actually. You didn't answer my question." Gwyneth continued pulling books from the shelves, returning them when they didn't pass whatever test she was using to select them.

"You didn't ask one," said Ru. "Why have you added a romance book to the pile?"

"Because I want to read it," said Gwyneth, her tone airy. "I *asked* about your relationship with Fen."

"What about it?"

Gwyneth sighed and stepped down from the short ladder she'd been standing on as she perused the shelves. "Ru, sometimes I want to shake you until your stubbornness falls out. What is going *on* with you two? Are you... *you* know." She fixed Ru with a wide-eyed, meaningful stare.

Ru feigned ignorance. "You'll have to speak a dialect I understand, Gwyn."

Gwyn made a sound of frustration, which elicited a shushing from other academics using the library. "It's just bizarre," she said in a lower voice. "You come back from the Shattered City with a strange man in tow? I mean, he *is* handsome. His hair is..." she cleared her throat. "But the way he behaves around you, tracking your movements, it's almost as if he's your bodyguard or your very attractive manservant or something. And the way he looks at you. His attraction to you is so obvious it's almost unseemly. I just want to make sure you're not rushing into something."

Ru carefully schooled her expression to hide the fact that Gwyneth's mention of Fen being attracted to her made her skin tingle, her heart speed. Avoiding her friend's gaze, Ru removed the romance book from the pile and handed it back to her. "You've been reading too many of these."

"I'm not blind," said Gwyneth, returning the novel to the stack of books in Ru's arms. "And I'm not trying to be overbearing, I just want to *know*. We're best friends, Ru. Spill your heart to me. You've been so... different since you came back."

A painful sadness rose in Ru, and she wished she wasn't holding so many books; she would have pulled Gwyneth into a hug.

She knew she *looked* different. She was bruised and battered, her face still marred from the guard's attack. And when she'd looked in the mirror that morning, she had been struck by the depth of pain that stared back from her brown eyes. Her skin was no longer pallid, but she was still paler than she was used to. And with her long dark hair and the faint purplish shadows under her eyes, she felt like a creature of the underworld.

But that wasn't what Gwyneth meant. She'd seen the inner change in Ru, seen her lose herself to panic at dinner, seen what came after the loss of the dig site. A small destruction of Ru's own.

"I know," Ru said quietly. "I'm sorry. I owe you more, I owe you—"

"You don't owe me anything," said Gwyneth, her tone softening as she spoke. "You're like a sister to me. I only wanted you to know that you can talk to me. About anything."

Ru sniffed, valiantly holding back tears of gratitude.

She knew Gwyneth would never judge her, never think any less of her no matter who she associated with. No matter what she did. But when she imagined telling her best friend about the artifact and the way it spoke to her... the way it had influenced her mind at the Shattered City. She couldn't. The terror of Gwyneth pulling away, of frightening her friend or losing her trust, was too painful for Ru to contemplate.

"I know," said Ru.

She stared down at the cover of the romance book, the illustration of a woman leaning over a shirtless man, expressions of lust on their beautiful faces. When Gwyneth had first come to the Tower, she and Ru had often spent hours looking for the lewdest books they could find in the libraries. They had read passages aloud on benches in the courtyard, or sat crowded together on one of their beds, giggling and blushing in the lamplight.

"If I'm being honest," Ru said finally, seeing Gwyneth straighten in anticipation, "I *do* think Fen is handsome."

Gwyneth deflated. "That's it?"

Ru shrugged.

"That's you spilling your emotional insides to me?"

Ru was torn between her desire to gossip with her friend and her heart of hearts, which told her that Fen wasn't some silly crush, some handsome traveling historian. He was more than that — she felt it in the air between them, the way he'd felt familiar to her from the moment they met. She was afraid to voice it aloud, and even more afraid that if she did, he might not reciprocate.

Ru tucked her hair behind an ear. "I just don't think I should be talking about our research colleague like that."

Gwyneth looked deeply unimpressed. "So you wouldn't mind if I make a move, then?"

Ru froze, her stomach lurching. "A move?"

"On Fen." Gwyneth's smile was brightly innocent. "You won't mind?"

"Not at all," Ru managed, jaw clenched.

"See!" exclaimed Gwyneth, eliciting another mass shushing. "You *do* like him."

"Of course I do," Ru replied airily, pushing delicately past Gwyneth toward the library's exit, stack of books precarious in her arms. "He's my friend. And now he's our colleague. So if you don't mind, you'll keep these romance book questions to yourself from now on."

Gwyneth snorted. "Whatever you say."

They left the library and made their way down the hall, toward the staircase that would eventually lead them to their makeshift laboratory in the dungeon. Fen and Archie were down there now, setting up lighting and making the place as serviceable as possible.

Ru rolled her eyes. "Hurry up," she said, pulling

ahead of Gwyneth with a hurried gait. "These books are heavy."

~

WHEN THE SUN had set and the very last remnants of indigo clung to the western edges of the sky, Ru slipped out of her room and into the hall. She had spent most of the afternoon holed up alone in her room, rereading her paper, taking notes as she read.

But as she worked, her thoughts drifted constantly away from her, and by the time evening fell, it was impossible to stay focused. The rigidity of scientific fact had always come so easily to her; she had never before found it so difficult to read and think for hours about a single scientific problem. But now, with the artifact so close, her thoughts were ever drawn toward a darker, more unknown place.

She had needed something solid, something staid in the face of everything. So she'd set aside her reading, pulled her messy hair into a bun, hastily shoved her feet into boots, and tied the laces carelessly.

What she needed now, she thought, she would find in the laboratories.

The dormitory wing was lively at this hour, academics hanging out of open doorways and shouting to one another, some even sitting on the carpeted floor to chat, backs leaning against stone walls.

Ru avoided their gazes as she passed, but she could feel them watching. Not with malice, or even judgment, but with sharp-eyed curiosity. She was almost to the broad staircase that would eventually lead her to the laboratory wing when a voice called out.

"Delara."

She spun to see Archie, hanging out of his door, teeth flashing in a grin. He'd obviously seen her pass and darted to the door; his cheeks were ever so slightly pink with exertion.

"Come on," he said, jerking his chin as an invitation.

"I've just made tea." She sighed, shaking her head with a smile. The laboratory wing could wait.

Archie's room, like Ru's, was cozy and small but private. One of the walls was still painted with a centuries-old mural of a deer hidden in a copse of trees, the paint chipping and faded, but still beautiful. A small fire burned in the hearth, crackling comfortingly. Archie handed Ru a cup of tea. Steam curled lazily up from the hot liquid, chamomile and citrus with a hint of honey.

They settled onto the soft, somewhat musty couch that faced the hearth, a worn velvet thing that had been there since, Ru could only assume, the beginning of time. Books were strewn about the room, a staple of most academics' living spaces. But Archie's were stacked neatly, each stack differentiated by subject.

"I know everyone must be asking," Archie said, sipping his tea, eyes on Ru. "But... are you... you know, all right? Not taken by madness or ready to leap out a five-story window or anything like that?"

Ru smiled despite herself. She and Archie hadn't had a moment alone together since Dig Site 33. He'd been around her, cracked jokes with her, and made casual conversation. But it was always with the others, or in a crowded hallway. A pang caught at her heart; she had missed him.

"I'm sorry I left Dig Site 33 so suddenly," she said, glancing away. That moment had played over so many times in her head, waving goodbye to Archie as she rode off with the king's riders. She had ached for his presence while she'd been away, his irreverent remarks, his trusted and brilliant mind. And most of all, she'd wondered if she shouldn't have stayed. With Archie, the professors, all of them. None of this would have happened.

"Oh, my mistake," he said. "I thought I'd asked you if you were all *right*. Silly of me to mishear myself."

Ru couldn't stop the laugh that escaped her, tea sloshing in its cup. "Don't make me spill, Arch. I just... I've been wanting to say that for days."

He made a dismissive noise with his mouth, the air

from his lips puffing up and ruffling his light brown hair. "Don't be silly. I never once held it against you."

"I know," said Ru, trying to find the words and failing. "But so much has... I feel different, Arch. As if the woman I was at Dig Site 33 is gone, and I'm a new Ruellian Delara. The world feels bigger now." She looked up to see that Archie's smile had faded, mirth replaced with concern.

"So you're not all right."

Ru wasn't sure, and that was the worst part. She knew what she wanted, who she was. But everything else, Lady Maryn, Fen, the attack on the road — none of those things were *all right*. And the artifact, even now its presence thrummed in her.

"I don't know," she said at last. A log in the fire cracked and fell, sending up a bloom of orange embers.

"You will be," Archie said, his tone far too confident for someone who had no idea what Ru had gone through. But that was Archie, either making light of something heavy or kicking up a fuss over something truly minor.

She smiled, grateful for his confidence. She could use every bit of support now, especially from her friends.

Archie set down his tea, then reached for Ru's, setting it gently on the table. He moved closer to her on the sofa until their knees were touching. Close enough to take her hand, to run his thumb over her knuckles. Ru sat unmoving as he made these slow, deliberate movements. *Not this again,* she thought.

"I've missed you," he said.

Ru knew what that meant — he missed touching her like this, he missed her in his bed. But they would never have worked as a couple, and he knew it. There had been enough arguments in their short time together, neither one able to give themselves fully to the other, both too stubborn to relent. And Ru knew that Archie would have wanted her heart, her feelings. He wanted her to spill forth for him. That was something she couldn't do.

She studied his face, his delicate freckles, his cut-glass jaw. He was painfully handsome. There had been a reason she'd been so eager, once, to bite those plush lips. But that feeling was long gone now, and even in the face of his obvious lust, she felt no answering attraction.

"Arch…"

"Ru." He said her name with a smile, his gaze fixed on her mouth.

"We're not doing this again." She tried to make the words sound softer than they were, but there was no room for subtlety.

He sat back, blinking. Let go of her hand and cleared his throat.

"I care about you," said Ru, "obviously. You know that. But…"

His mouth curled petulantly. "It's Verrill, isn't it."

She spluttered, sitting back, away from Archie. "Don't be ridiculous. It has nothing to do with Fen. I thought we agreed it was best not to continue… whatever we had. We're not right for each other."

"That was then. Could it be different now?" His eyes were searching, hopeful. Unusually earnest.

Ru hated this. At that moment, she would have given anything to return Archie's feelings. It would have been so easy to fall back into his arms, into the safety of a familiar lover. To seek comfort in what was known, what was simple. "I don't feel that way about you anymore," she said, the words tasting sour on her tongue. It was the truth, but it hurt to say it.

He swallowed once, nodded, and pushed away from her until he was at the far end of the sofa. "I see," he said, almost as if to himself.

"I'm sorry," she murmured. She was. "We're friends, Arch. You're my best friend."

He lifted a sardonic brow. "And what's Verrill?"

"Also a friend."

"At least be honest with yourself," he said, "if not with me."

"I told you, Fen isn't relevant." She bit out the words, her jaw clenched in frustration. She had meant what she said. Fen had nothing to do with her feelings toward Archie.

"For someone so intelligent, you certainly miss the obvious."

Ru rolled her eyes and reached for a cookie, biting the lemony shortbread and chewing it in annoyance. The last thing she wanted was to continue this argument, but there was no escape now, not unless she fled from the room like a coward.

"I don't know what you mean," she said, her voice muffled by the cookie.

"I mean it's painfully obvious that Fen's infatuated with you."

She stared. He wasn't. "He's just protective by nature."

"Of *you*."

Archie didn't understand. He couldn't possibly, not unless she explained the way she and Fen seemed connected, drawn together by the strings of fate. They weren't lovers, they were... friends. Colleagues. Something else even Ru had yet to fully comprehend. Something she couldn't explain without sounding mad.

"Can we talk about something else?" she asked, brushing crumbs from her lap.

"It's getting late," Archie said, even though it was only just past eight. He stood then, making a show of gathering the tea.

Ru heard the unspoken words quite clearly: he wanted to be alone. "Thanks for the tea, Arch," she said. He gave a little nod, a forced smile, and went back to tidying up.

Heart in her throat, full of too many emotions to sort out and name, Ru left Archie's room and continued on her way to the laboratory wing.

~

THE LABORATORY WING was quiet in the evening, most academics preferring to move their studies to libraries or the dormitory wing as darkness fell, seeking comfort and the warmth of a hearth. Even at the height of summer, the Tower was so far north, nestled at the foot of the mountains, that nights were chilly.

Ru could hear the sounds of voices drifting into the hall from open doors as she passed, but they were few and far between. When she pulled open the heavy wooden door of the archaeology lab, its brass handle cool beneath her fingers, she was relieved to find it empty.

The lab had two full walls of gothic-style windows that, during the day, let in copious amounts of natural light. The room was large and airy, its ceilings vaulted. A dozen large wooden tables stood equidistant from each other, each outfitted with a full array of tools.

At the far end of the room was a smaller door, with a wooden sign hanging from a brass hook: *Artifact Storage*. If Ru's black stone hadn't been dangerous, it would have lived there. Crossing the room, her skirts sighing about her legs as she went, she pulled open the door.

It swung open with ease, its hinges regularly greased, the wooden sign bumping softly against it as Ru wedged it open with a nearby doorstop. The smell of ancient earth, of stone and time, filled Ru's lungs as she inhaled deeply. This room was her favorite in the Tower, and she mentally chided herself for waiting so long to return after her weeks away. Shelves upon shelves of artifacts greeted her, steeped in the memories of those who had come long before.

Sighing, releasing the pent-up tension from tea with Archie, Ru walked slowly through the rows of shelves until she came to her section. There were small plaques affixed to the shelves, indicating whose discoveries were housed where. Some artifacts were exposed to the air, while others were so delicate they had to be kept in small boxes, or under glass domes.

Ru's vases were all there, from shards of pottery to near-complete vessels. Her throat tightened as her eyes fell on a large, squat vase with a wide mouth — the vase from Dig Site 33, the last one she had found before everything changed.

Eyes burning with unshed tears, she ran a finger along its curved edge, rough to touch but solid, a thing so easily quantified and understood. So unlike the artifact, the vase had no connection to Ru, pressed no subtle touch to the edge of her consciousness. It simply existed.

Ru had come here for solace, a respite from the chatter of an unsettled mind. But no matter where she went, the artifact followed. And there was no comforting warmth emanating from the thread between them now, no radiating calm. Simply a low steady thrum, ever-present.

How many vases were in this storage room? How many relics of lives long past? If she calculated the number of shelves...

But Ru's mind skittered at the thought, unfocused. She squeezed her eyes shut for a moment, clenching her fists.

How many shelves in the room... if each shelf housed roughly a dozen items and the volume of...

Again, she found herself unable to think clearly, to follow the solid framework of numbers and space and calculation to a logical end. Her anchor, that constant mental escape — she couldn't reach it. She was lost and spinning, and even the artifact seemed distant when she needed something here and now, something to steady her.

Spitting a curse, Ru turned away from her vases. She hurried back into the lab, the room still empty, her footsteps echoing on the stone floor. When she was out in the corridor, she closed the door and leaned back against it, exhaling slowly.

She had never felt so lost, so unlike herself. What she'd said to Archie now hung all the heavier over her — she felt like a different Ru, reborn, as if the events at the Shattered City had been a metamorphosis. Her world had tilted ever so slightly on its axis, shifting her center of gravity. Who could she go to, now? Who understood?

Straightening then, she set her shoulders, smoothed her skirts, and set off along the corridor toward the guest wing.

CHAPTER 21

F en's room was at the end of the hall, near a tall window that looked out onto one of the Tower's surrounding courtyards. Ru had never been to his room, had only been told where it was should she need to reach him.

Standing before the closed door now, palms growing sweaty with anticipation and nerves, she hesitated. What would he think of her coming to his room at night for no clear reason? Instinct had brought her here, the need to be near someone who understood, even in the smallest of ways, what she'd been through with the artifact. And maybe, something in Archie's words had rung true. Maybe he'd seen the way Fen was able to steady Ru when nothing else could and had misinterpreted it as infatuation.

She knocked, a soft rap of the knuckle.

There was a thump, footsteps, and a moment later the door swung inward. Fen stood in the doorway, one arm braced on the door frame, his hair fluttering slightly in the wake of the door flying open. He wore tight black trousers and a loose black shirt, hanging open at the collar. His sleeves were rolled up to the elbow, revealing forearms corded with lean muscle. The angles of his jaw were shadowed with the beginnings of a true beard, as though he'd been too distracted to shave.

Ru stared up at him, momentarily lost for words. He was so tall and broad-shouldered, yet slender and elegant in the way he held himself. Ru herself wasn't exactly petite, she would have described herself as *average* in every category, but Fen towered over her. When she stood near him she felt engulfed by him. It wasn't a bad feeling.

"Hello," he said, a momentary expression of surprise replaced quickly by a smile, soft and welcoming.

The artifact, waking from some slumber, lit up inside her, an affectionate flame at the edge of her thoughts.

"Hello," she said, echoing his words due to loss of her own.

He stepped aside, giving her space to enter. An invitation. Wordlessly, she slipped past him and into the room, acutely aware of his proximity, the heat of his body, his gaze on her.

Fen's room was even smaller than hers, not much larger than the bed itself, with just enough room for a small hearth, a washbasin, and an armchair. And almost every surface in the place was covered in books. Stacks of tomes sat on the floor, piled on the armchair, and lined the bed. Some open, some closed, all different subjects. Archie's room was neat and well-kept in comparison. Scanning the room with surprise and approval, Ru saw several rolled-up parchments — academic papers, most likely.

A gentleman of Mirith, an aristocrat raised to abide by social mores, would have hurried to clear the armchair for Ru. Perhaps offered her a drink, asked how her evening had been so far. But Fen, a force unto himself, leaned against the door to watch Ru, fixing her with a half-smile, a raised eyebrow.

"To what do I owe the pleasure?"

She hesitated. She ran a finger along the cover of one of the books strewn on his bed, a burgundy tome with a worn leather cover. The entire room smelled of old leather, of words on dusty pages. She chewed her lip, her gaze meeting his once again. "I was..." she paused.

He pushed away from the door, moving toward her, nonchalant. But she saw interest shining in his eyes, and concern. "You know you can trust me," he said.

"You've been reading quite a lot," she said, picking up the burgundy book and reading the title aloud. "*Kings and Gods: Tales of the Immortal?*" She shot him an incredulous look.

His lips parted in a true smile, shaking his head as if Ru had said something funny. "You're deflecting," he said. "Again."

She set the book down, frowning. "I'm not." She knew she was — she didn't want to explain it, her unsettled feeling, the sense that everything she understood was somehow changed forever. And least of all, her need to be near him, his familiar steadiness, the way he had already become a pillar of safety in her life.

He stepped closer, crossing his arms, looking down his nose at her. Disapproving. "I saw you when I opened the door. Your eyes were even more troubled than usual. What's wrong?"

There was no use avoiding it. She had come here for comfort, and now he wouldn't let her leave without it. She flopped onto the bed, in the one empty space where, she guessed, Fen had been sitting until she knocked on his door. He watched her patiently, not moving from where he stood. Firelight danced in his eyes, on his black hair, against the partially-hidden planes of his chest.

"I need someone to talk to," Ru admitted, staring down at her hands. "Things have been different since I came back. The Tower... it feels like home, it *is* home, but something's missing. Or maybe there's nothing missing, and I've just... changed."

"You've endured unspeakable pain in the last few days," Fen said gently, his accent seeming to roll the words over his tongue. "More than anyone should experience in one life. It will take a long time for those wounds to heal. And even then, your world may never fall back into place."

She caught his gaze, those deep gray eyes that

seemed to hold so much more experience than they should. "How can you be so wise?" The question sounded silly even as she asked it.

He snorted. "I'm far from wise. But I've experienced my share of hurt, and I know how it feels to wake up one day and wonder if it's the world that's changed, or you."

"The way you talk..." Ru said, turning to watch the fire dancing in the stone hearth. "I'm not surprised you believe in magic. You seem like that sort."

He smirked. "What, a strange old man? An eccentric hermit?"

"Hardly," she said, laughingly. The artifact seemed to respond to her laughter — comfort from within, through an unseen thread. And there in Fen's room, with a warm fire crackling in the hearth, the connection to the black stone felt immediate, more familiar than ever. "You see things from a new perspective," she clarified. "So different from mine, my facts and figures, numbers and calculations."

"I like your facts and figures."

Ru's heart sped beneath her ribs. Fen's closeness was affecting her, his long lashes, that triangle of bare skin below his throat. She swallowed thickly. "You've been reading my paper?"

"Three times," he said, "and I plan to read it several times more. With each read, I find something new. A shining tidbit of fascinating information. The way you write, it's clear and factual, nothing but rational thought, and yet... you weave a story. I'm entranced by it."

Heat surged in Ru's cheeks, her stomach forming pleasing little knots. She found she couldn't meet his gaze, smiling instead down at her hands. No one had ever said something like that about her work, not even close.

Apparently taking her silence as an invitation, Fen moved to the bed, stacking the books that lay scattered on the bedspread and setting them aside. Then he settled himself to face Ru, one foot braced on the floor, the other folded under him. When she glanced up at him, he was smiling.

"I'm serious," he said. "I can't begin to understand why the academic community has decided to dismiss you out of hand. A collection of simple-minded fools, if you ask me."

"I never proved the hypothesis," Ru said, fighting the pleased grin that threatened to overtake her expression. "I came close, but..."

"You proved it to me," said Fen, matter-of-fact.

"You already believed in magic."

He grinned, one eye half-obscured by his hair. "Aren't we a pair? Probably the only two people in Navenie who believe in magic, thrown together by fate."

Ru's brows drew together in thought. This wasn't the first time Fen had mentioned fate, nor the first she had felt distinctly as if she were at fate's mercy. "The rational explanation for fate is purely science-based," she said as if reciting by rote. "A coincidence occurs every moment of every day, no matter who or where you are. But only a small fraction of such coincidences are so surprising, so notable as to be considered fateful — beyond the physical. Only explained by something *more*."

Fen arched a dark brow in amusement. "And you believe that?"

Ru pressed her lips together in thought. "Until recently."

He hummed, but whether it was an agreement or simply an acknowledgment, she couldn't tell. Then he leaned forward and lifted a hand to brush a stray hair off her cheek, tucking it gently behind her ear. His touch was warm, solid, familiar.

I mean it's obvious that Fen's infatuated with you.

No, Archie was wrong. A jealous past lover, seeing what he wanted to see. But Ru's heart hammered in her chest, and she couldn't pull her gaze from Fen's.

"Your paper is ingenious," Fen said, voice low. "The things you understand, the complexity... no one else sees the world like you do, Ru."

"I think that's a bit of an exaggeration," she murmured.

Thrown together by fate...

Fen shifted then, looked away, and cleared his throat. He glanced back at Ru, throat bobbing visibly as he swallowed. "You'd better get some sleep," he said at last, almost apologetically.

He was right — they officially began research on the artifact first thing the following morning. The dungeon was set up, everything in place... everything except Ru's head, apparently.

She nodded, determinedly looking at anything in the room but Fen; she realized she had been staring, entranced like a flower reaching for the sun. Flustered and inexplicably disappointed, impatient with herself for losing control of her feelings so easily, she slid off the bed, smoothing her skirts with self-conscious precision.

Fen stood too. "If you ever need to talk again, I'm here."

"Thank you," she said, hurrying past him to the door. The room was so small she had to brush against him, his body heat clinging to her. "Good night," she said, closing the door firmly behind her.

Out in the corridor, she paused for a moment, catching her breath, willing her pulse to slow. When her breathing was even again, she set off down the hall.

Back in her room, stripping to her undergarments, Ru climbed into bed. Groaning with confusion and frustration, she pulled the covers up to her chin. She couldn't lose control around the artifact. Her emotions had to remain in check. So how was she supposed to study it, to be confined to a room with it every day, with Fen so near? His effect on her, on the artifact's connection to Ru, was undeniable. But that didn't make it any less confusing.

Thrown together by fate. The words echoed in her head.

She closed her eyes, hoping sleep would take her quickly, but it didn't come. Her only thoughts were of Fen, his eyes, the way he could somehow see through to the truth of her. She felt she might never sleep. But almost as if it heard her, the artifact pressed a soft caress to her mind, soothing.

So at last, slow and heavy like a fog descending from the mountains, sleep overcame her.

~

RU LAY IN BED, enveloped in blankets. All was still and quiet. The night sky hung clear and bright outside her window, a dark expanse scattered with stars like salt on black velvet. What time was it?

She mentally reached for the artifact and felt nothing, no thread. No connection. But somehow it didn't alarm her; she didn't miss it.

And then, "It's all right," said a deep voice from the shadows of her room. "I'm here."

Fen moved as if he were a shadow himself, one moment across the room from her, and the next, his weight was on the bed, his knees pressing divots into the mattress on either side of her, leaning over her like a predator. He was dressed in the same black trousers and shirt he'd worn in his room. His eyes were dark, seething with want.

Ru's body, still heavy with sleep, responded to his proximity — a flare of need in her belly.

"What do you want?" Fen asked, his hands planted on either side of her, his arms flexed as he leaned down.

She lifted her hips to him, unbearably slowly. And then the blankets were gone, exposing her skin to the night. Nothing lay between them, then, but thin garments and a distance that Ru ached to close.

Stars wheeled in the night. A cold wind danced in Fen's hair and cooled Ru's heated skin.

"What do you want?" Fen asked again, bending down to kiss her neck, his hot mouth seeking, caressing.

She groaned, arching into him, and at last, achingly slowly, he lowered his body against hers.

The sensation was almost unbearable, his hips pressed against Ru's, the heat between her legs expanding, overcoming. He bit her ear, his hands roving, every inch of her on fire. She rocked her hips against his and he groaned, reaching between them with one hand, a finger catching her undergarment and pulling it aside.

"Is *this* what you want?" he said, his fingers moving into her, his voice a low growl.

Ru woke with a start.

Birdsong drifted in the open window — morning had broken, the sun just beginning its journey across the sky. She blinked, sat up, and rubbed her eyes. Her blankets were tangled around her body as if she'd been thrashing in her sleep. Arousal still pulsed through her, and she was wet between her legs.

Shocked and embarrassed, despite being alone in the room, Ru slid out of bed in a rush, dressing quickly, eager to cover herself. To think that she had dreamt of Fen like that. Fen in her room, in her bed... The heat in her belly began to fade as she buttoned her dress, the light of day cooling her like a douse of cold water.

This was somehow Archie's fault.

But she couldn't shake the image of Fen leaning over her, skin against skin, his mouth... his fingers…

"Ruellian Delara," she said aloud, stern and disapproving. "Pull yourself together."

The dream had come from his proximity to her the night before, the way he'd comforted her, just after Archie had made such silly claims about *infatuation*. And it had been so long since she'd bedded anyone, her body and mind were simply reaching for the nearest man, bringing him to her in sleep. That was all.

Ru brushed her hair with agitation, then braided it into a loose plait that hung over one shoulder. There were far more important things to think about, to focus on.

Shoving her feet into the nearest pair of boots and lacing them hastily, Ru stood to regard herself in the mirror. A young woman stared back at her, a new confidence in the depths of her brown eyes. Her color was returning, her skin regaining its usual healthy glow. Her hair shone darkly in the morning sun, and for the first time in a long while, she recognized who she saw there.

Turning on her heel, head high, she left her room and shut the door behind her with a click. Even if her world had turned on its axis, her gravity upended, she knew one thing: She was Ruellian Delara, expert archaeologist, and head researcher in the study of the artifact.

CHAPTER 22

An assemblage of carriages and riders arrived from the palace that morning. There was a well-packed wagon filled to the brim with scientific instruments — including an astrolabe, an equinoctial compass sundial, a graphometer, a device with which to create a small atmospheric vacuum, and even some microscopes — all of which were expensive, delicate, and in short supply at the Tower.

In addition to the wagon of devices was a small contingent of King's Guards, a King's Rider, and three solemn figures in white robes belted with gold. Ru, who had been summoned from her breakfast at the arrival of the small convoy, paused when she caught sight of the Children. Why were they here?

But she was quickly distracted by the King's Rider, who dismounted at her arrival. "Miss Delara?" the rider said, her voice carrying across the courtyard. "Letter for you."

Ru skirted around the somewhat large gathering of professors and first-year academics who had been called to assist in carrying the wagon's contents down to Ru's laboratory.

When she was close enough to see the rider clearly, Ru was slightly disappointed to see that it wasn't Rosylla or Sybeth. She took the letter from the rider's gloved hand, looking for an obvious sender, but the seal belonged to the palace, not an individual.

"Do you know who sent it?" Ru asked.

The rider shook her head.

Curious but distracted, Ru shoved the letter into one of her skirt pockets for later, when she could focus. She had other more pressing things to attend to at the moment.

"Delara, there you are!" said Professor Obralle, emerging suddenly from the small crowd, her hair quivering in the breeze. Today it was shaped like a cumulus cloud, but the pink hue and fluffy texture were such that it almost looked like spun sugar. "Your things have arrived. And look, they've sent us a trio of... what were you called, again?" She turned to one of the white-robed figures, all of whom were hovering at the edge of things, looking utterly detached.

"The Children," Ru answered for them. Unease began to writhe in her stomach. She couldn't begin to understand why they were here, these pale, white-robed oddities.

"They're here to keep tabs on the progress of your research," said Obralle, as if reading Ru's thoughts. Ru now understood that the professor's overly cheerful tone was for the benefit of the robed visitors.

"We are simply observers," said one of them, overhearing. His voice was strangely devoid of emotion, a deadpan drone. "We have no wish to interfere."

"No, no, of course not," said Obralle, grinning far too brightly. "I never thought otherwise, dear boy."

Professor Acorn, his floppy golden hair shining in the sun, approached the trio in white and began welcoming them to the Tower. Seeing that she was free of their attention for the moment, Professor Obralle turned to Ru so that her back was to the three Children, took Ru's arm and steered her back into the Tower. Her forced smile had evaporated.

"Do you know anything about these people?" she hissed.

Ru glanced at the three Children over her shoulder

as she and the professor ascended the wide stone steps. They were all about the same height, blandly attractive, and so unadorned in their flowing garments that it was impossible to determine gender from this distance. But unlike the Children she'd seen at the palace, gesturing animatedly and bright-eyed, these three were so devoid of visible emotion that Ru thought them almost corpselike.

"I had no idea they were coming here," said Ru, slightly defensive, her voice low to match Obralle's. She was trying to slow the beating of her heart, the rising worry in her throat. The sight of those blank faces, the white robes... she shuddered despite herself. "I thought the regent trusted me to send accurate reports of our progress. Apparently not."

"Hmm," was all Obralle said, clearly deep in thought. She turned down a corridor, and Ru saw they were going to the professorial wing.

It occurred to Ru that perhaps, since the attack on the road, the Children were some kind of safety measure. The regent's attempt to exert as much control over the situation as possible. Maybe the regent had second-guessed her decision to let Ru bring the artifact here, and wanted more direct oversight.

But Ru also wondered — with a pang of guilt, because she was loyal to the regent — whether Sigrun had her own secret motives with regard to the artifact. Ru still couldn't understand why the regent had funded the Shattered City dig in the first place, or whether Lord D'Luc had been directly involved. A piece in the story was missing, some important fact.

"Did the regent send a letter?" Ru asked, Obralle ushering them into her office and closing the door. The office was a blessed relief from the hot morning sun and the bustling halls of the Tower. By contrast, it was cool and dark, lined with books and hanging lamps of brass, almost everything coated in a fine layer of dust.

Grumbling to herself, the professor pulled a folded piece of parchment from her robes. "Here," she said and settled herself in a high-backed leather armchair while Ru read the scrawled note.

Professors of the Cornelian Tower,

Along with the requested items to aid in the artifact's research, I have sent three representatives of the Children. They, like me, have a great interest in what you uncover. I have selected these three personally to observe your progress with the artifact.

While I still expect regular written updates directly from Ruellian Delara, I also ask that you allow the Children complete and unrestricted access to any laboratories, libraries, or other areas wherein pertinent research may take place.

You will also oblige the regency by housing and feeding my personal guards, who have been tasked with the protection of the artifact. Additionally, should Lyrren Briar still be at the Cornelian Tower, you may request that he remain as an additional member of security.

To address your inquiry regarding the matter of the traitors who waylaid your traveling party on the road — all remaining traitors have been dealt with, and the matter is closed.

I look forward to Miss Delara's first update.

Regards,
   Sigrun

By the time Ru had finished reading, Professor Obralle had pulled a long-stemmed pipe from a drawer in her desk and begun puffing on it meditatively.

"Well?" she said, seeing Ru fold the paper and set it on the desk.

Ru lowered herself into the chair opposite the desk where Obralle now rested her feet, crossed at the ankles. She stared at the letter, the bit about the traitors playing on her mind. Admittedly, she had no idea how such things were handled — the kingdom had been in a state of relative peace for centuries, and the concept of political betrayal was only theoretical to Ru. But the regent had been almost dismissive in the way she addressed it, as though treason was a regular occurrence and not a grave matter of Navenian security.

Obralle puffed smoke rings into the air, which caught the light from the shuttered window and circled around the professor like a hazy halo. "I'm curious about these Children," she said, drawing Ru's thoughts to more present, immediate worries. "I've never heard of such a group. Are they... religious?"

"I believe so," said Ru, trying not to cough as pipe smoke billowed toward her. "But they're led by Hugon D'Luc, a man of science. So, perhaps not at odds with our aims."

Professor Obralle's expression didn't change. She took an extra long drag on her pipe before offering it to Ru. "Puff?"

Ru shook her head.

"Very well," said Obralle, putting away the pipe and sighing heavily. "We are under the watchful eye of the regent, whether we like it or not, by way of these white-robed... *Children*. What do you think of them? Be honest." The professor's gaze was sharp, discerning as always.

And it was a question to which Ru didn't quite know the answer. She had liked Lord D'Luc; she couldn't understand what Simon had against him. Lord D'Luc clearly had an intelligent mind, his interest in Ru's paper proved to her that he was invested in learning new concepts that could be ahead of their time. His Children must hold similar beliefs.

Even so, for reasons she couldn't explain, they made Ru's skin crawl.

"I don't know them well enough to say," she answered finally.

"Hmm," said Professor Obralle. "Best not to allow too many cooks in the kitchen. But while I have you here, what about that Fen fellow? The regent's note didn't mention him."

"What about him?" asked Ru, her thoughts skittering off-track at the mention of Fen.

Professor Obralle leaned forward, steepling her fingers and studying Ru's face. Ru felt blood rising in her cheeks at the memory of her dream. *Not now*, she thought desperately, and had to look down at her hands again.

"We had believed him to be a King's Guard at first," said the professor. "He was wearing the armor when you arrived here. But now he's joined your research team. Who is he? An envoy of the palace?"

Ru considered several possible explanations for Fen, and finally decided that she should be truthful with the professors. "He's a friend," she said. "He came to my rescue after... at the Shattered City. He's a traveling historian. He saved my life. Three times, in fact."

Professor Obralle's face remained passive, but Ru could tell she was rolling this information over and over in her mind. "I see," she said at last. "He's a wandering man who appeared seemingly out of nowhere, just after you experienced an unspeakable trauma, became immediately inseparable from you, and then proceeded to save your life multiple times."

"Yes," said Ru, knowing how it sounded.

Obralle sighed and leaned back again, eyes to the ceiling. "Well, I can understand why you'd be so taken with him. And you trust this man completely?"

"I do," Ru rushed to reply. She had only known Fen for a matter of days, but they shared a connection now that no one could question or undermine, a resulting trust that defied reason. Their bond was for her and Fen to understand, and nobody else.

"Very well," said the professor, somewhat resigned. "I take it you believe he'll be a useful mind at work in your studies, and not just..." she waved her hands, "a distraction?"

Heat rose in Ru's face again. Why was everyone so eager to interrogate her about her feelings for Fen? Yes he was handsome, yes they shared a bond, but their interactions had only ever been platonic.

While waking, anyway.

She chewed her lip, willing the blood to drain from

her face; she knew she was blushing furiously. "He won't distract me."

Obralle raised a skeptical eyebrow.

"I promise."

The professor shrugged and stood, pushing her chair back from the desk. "Very well, very well. You're an adult, and a fourth year at that, I can't stop you from being silly." This was all said in a mutter, almost to herself, which Ru pretended not to hear.

Obralle continued on as they exited the office, "Keep an eye on those Children for me though, will you? Don't let them observe anything too closely."

"I won't." Ru had no reason to fear the Children, but she also had no reason to trust them. When it came down to it, she only trusted three other people with the study of the artifact, and they were already on her research team.

CHAPTER 23

Ru hurried to the dungeon. Arriving at the stairs that would lead down into its cool depths, she found that two King's Guards already stood sentry there. She nodded a silent greeting to the stoic figures, heading down the narrow steps.

Cold air embraced her almost immediately, the sound of her boots on centuries-worn stone echoing before her, announcing her presence. As she came out into the long open room that had once been a dungeon, she braced herself for the presence of the Children. But they were nowhere to be seen.

Ru would have to use her time wisely now.

Fen and Archie seemed to have formed a kind of tense truce, and while they weren't friends by any means, they had been efficiently productive in setting up large tabletop oil lamps throughout the lab, which provided a bright glow in the circle of workspace. At the center of the room, with four worktables situated around it at even intervals, sat the artifact, still wrapped up like a present on a circular wooden table. If Ru hadn't known better, she might think it a loaf of bread, wrapped up to keep its warmth intact.

Almost as if in greeting, as if it sensed her nearness, the artifact swept a delicate touch along the edges of her senses, like a tickle along the curve of her skull.

Gwyneth, Archie, and Fen were already there,

moving about the warmly lit room. They were busy setting up the various devices sent by the regent, all talking in slightly hushed tones. At the sound of her footsteps, they quieted, looking up.

"*There* you are," said Gwyneth. Then her eyes widened questioningly, and she gestured behind Ru, indicating the guards at the top of the stairs.

"Just ignore them," said Ru, picking up a spherical brass instrument and twirling one of its little extrusions with her finger. "They don't care what we're doing down here. If anyone does, it's the Children."

"The Children?" demanded Archie, fuming in a way that suggested he'd been fuming for a while now. Ru suspected he'd been that way since she turned away his advances the previous night. "You mean the creeps in white?"

"How can we possibly ignore anything about this?" Gwyneth demanded, her voice a crescendo.

"They're not *really* creeps," Ru said futilely. Archie and Gwyneth had clearly whipped themselves into a small frenzy while she was with Professor Obralle, unlikely to listen to reason. "They're—"

"I don't trust them," interrupted Fen, setting down the intricate metal device he'd been setting up — an astrolabe. "I didn't trust them in Mirith, and I don't trust them here."

"Everyone calm down," Ru said, frustrated by what felt like a subtle mutiny of thought from her own team. "We should keep our emotions under control around the artifact. If it's magic, we don't know what it might react to." She lowered her voice. "And of course we can't trust the Children. They're here to keep tabs on us for the regency, that much is obvious. But we don't know why, do we, so there's no reason for antagonism. Besides, I met their leader, Lord D'Luc. He was very progressive."

Fen bristled and Ru felt it, even across that large stone room. "Lord D'Luc is very charismatic," he said, "to the point of it seeming purposeful."

"How can a man be charismatic without trying?" reasoned Gwyneth, loyally taking Ru's side even though she had never met the lord before in her life.

Ru smiled at Gwyneth, grateful for her support.

"I say he sounds like a stand-up fellow," said Archie, joining in.

Fen gave him a long, withering look.

"Archie, you're only agreeing with me because you don't like Fen," Ru said. "A fact which had better not affect your research, by the way. And Fen... don't hold back on my account. I know my brother told you everything he said to me at the palace."

Gwyneth and Archie shared a look, and Fen grinned. "I should know better than to hide anything from you," he said, watching Ru intently as if everything else in the room was suddenly nonexistent. "You're right, Simon did have a lot to say on the subject of Hugon D'Luc. He warned me that he wasn't to be trusted."

Ru made a sound of impatience. She didn't like the idea of Fen and her brother deciding things together, as if they couldn't trust her judgment. "Simon has a superfluity of opinions on everything," she said, "from fashion to music theory to political intrigue to the facial hair trends of the day. I've never known him to form an opinion in his life that wasn't based solely on his own senseless tastes."

"You think so little of your brother?" Fen asked, but he was still smiling. Ru got the distinct sense that he was enjoying her frustration.

"Simon's wonderful," said Gwyneth, "but he's... Simon. If you knew him better, you'd understand."

"Trust me," said Ru, directing this at Fen alone.

Fen's smile faded, but he nodded slightly, and the heavy energy in the air seemed to dissipate. "I trust you."

"Good," said Ru, "because I have more to share before the Children get here."

She told them in a hurry everything she knew that could pertain to the artifact, everything that she didn't want to say in front of their new guests. She explained the situation at the palace, and how the regent claimed the traitors had been put down. She even told them about her uncertainty regarding the regent's motivation to fund the Shattered City dig site, and her decision to send the Children here to oversee them.

Fen, though, was unconvinced. "Why blame the regent when it's Hugon's lackeys who have come to keep tabs on our progress?" he said, leaning forward so that his elbows were braced on the table where he stood, hands folded under his darkly stubbled chin.

"I spoke to him directly," Ru replied, "and I trust him. Enough, at least, to know he has this project's best interests at heart. I saw his eyes light up when I spoke of the artifact, the possibility of a convergence of science and magic. The Children are a formality to keep the project above board. That's all. I don't believe Lord D'Luc would truly stifle us, not like this."

"I see," said Fen, raising one eyebrow slightly.

There was a spark in his gaze, something dark and unexpected, and with it, the memory of her dream came rushing back, the vivid recollection of his mouth on her neck. His breath on her skin, his fingers... She glanced away quickly, her cheeks burning. *It was just a dream*, she chided herself.

"Lord D'Luc sounds like a man of contradictions," Archie said airily, his hair fiery in the lamplight, his jaw even sharper than usual in the contrast of shadows. "But if Ru says he's on the up and up, then that's all there is to it."

Fen shot Archie a look but shrugged acquiescence.

The group was far more subdued now than they had been when Ru arrived. Yet there remained a hum of anticipation in the air, an excitement that came from the fact that they were about to begin research of a completely new, wholly mysterious item. To prove the existence of magic.

Even the arrival of the Children gave the project a sense of something like adventure, as though the four of them were embarking on a secret mission under their jailers' noses.

That energy carried them through to the end of the day, organizing tools into categories, ensuring reading materials were on hand, laying out notebooks and pencils, and confirming that there was enough oil for the lamps. They assembled and cleaned the remainder of the regent's gifted devices, and laid them out. Each researcher claimed a table, a workspace where they might take notes and conduct individual measurements, or observe the artifact from afar.

It was late by the time they finished, and Ru couldn't stop yawning.

"Meet here after breakfast tomorrow?" said Archie, rubbing his eyes.

They stumbled upstairs and mumbled goodnights to the guards, who were still stationed at the top of the stairs. And for a moment, laughing and walking through the Tower halls with her friends, Ru felt the heaviness of everything begin to lift, as though looking up through a thick cloud and finally seeing a touch of blue sky.

At that moment, Fen turned to look at her, smiling, as if he felt it too.

The artifact thrummed warmly.

~

IT WASN'T until Ru was back in her room, settled comfortably in her bed, that she remembered the letter from the palace. How could she have forgotten? Springing up at the recollection, she went to the wardrobe and fished the letter out of her skirt pocket.

There was no return name or address, only her own name scrawled across the front of the envelope. She read the missive in a rush:

Ru,

By now you'll have met the repulsive trio of Children they sent to keep an eye on your research. No idea what they expect you to find. Who knows with these religious types. Are they hoping the artifact will prove to be god himself descended from the heavens?

Whatever their aim, I do happen to know that they expect

you to deliver results. And quickly. If they don't see that you're making progress (toward summoning god??), I have it on good authority that they'll send even more of the white weasels to the Tower, and who knows what *they intend to do to ensure you keep up your end of whatever ridiculous bargain you've bumbled your way into.*

Your devoted and loving brother,
   Simon

Ru's heart sank. When she had realized the letter was from Simon, she had hoped he might have shed light on the regent's comment about the traitor and how she'd dealt with the situation. Surely it couldn't have been that easy. Even a clear answer as to what exactly the regent expected Ru's team to discover about the artifact would have been nice. Instead, she was still mostly in the dark when it came to Sigrun's motivations. And now there was added pressure.

If she didn't "deliver," there would be further oversight, and it would be impossible to work under those conditions.

CHAPTER 24

The next morning, Ru went straight from her room to the dungeon, eager to get started. She was thrumming with nerves and anticipation. They would finally be able to begin proper research. And who could say, maybe the artifact would open up to them like it hadn't opened up to Ru yet, like a blooming flower, and they would discover something incredible.

It could also be a weapon, a sudden thought intruded. *Why would something wonderful come from an object that wiped out an entire dig site? What if it had been there since the Destruction itself?*

"You sick, Delara?"

Ru stopped in her tracks at the top of the dungeon stairs. Two different guards were posted there now. With a burst of recognition, she saw that it was Lyr who had spoken. He no longer wore the plumed hat and uniform of a King's Rider, now fully outfitted in the armor of a King's Guard.

"Lyr!" she said. "I didn't see you under all that armor. Are you a king's guard now?"

"Am indeed," he said, lifting his chin ever so slightly as he spoke. "Regent Sigrun thought you might need an extra sword." He frowned slightly, peering down his oversized nose at Ru. "You all right? Look a bit green in the face."

She chewed her lip. "I'm fine. Just... thinking. Anyway, I'm surprised you'd want to stay here when your friends are at the palace."

He frowned. "Don't make me admit to liking you."

Ru couldn't help but smile at that. "Does this mean we're friends, Lyrren Briar?"

The rider-turned-guard glowered, heavy black brows crowding over dark eyes. "It's Lyr," he said.

Ru laughed, stealing a faint smile from the guard's lips. "Thank you for staying, Lyr. You and the others saved my life."

He nodded once. "Doing our job. Just so happens you attract trouble."

"Let's hope that phase of my life is over," Ru muttered, passing between the guards and down the cool steps that led into the dungeon. Lyr's presence was a surprising relief to Ru, a balm she didn't know she needed. He was reticent verging on surly, not as warm and trusting as Rosylla, but even so, she was buoyed by his familiar presence.

When she stepped out into the cavernous room, Ru saw that Fen was already there, lighting a lamp on the artifact's table. The contrast of light on his face sharpened his cheekbones, his nose in profile almost regal. His hair hung over his eyes as he bent to adjust something, and when he brushed it off his forehead with a hand, he saw Ru standing there watching.

"You snuck up on me," he said, a smile slowly spreading across his face. "Did you bring coffee?"

"No," said Ru, smiling back. "But I'm sure Lyr would love to fetch you some."

"Somehow, I think that's inaccurate."

Ru joined him at the table, picking up a pair of thick woolen gloves. The Tower kitchens had generously donated a pile to the cause. Ru had declared it unsafe to handle the artifact without some form of protection. It would be difficult verging on impossible to handle it in any delicate or meaningful way with their hands stuffed into oven mitts, but Ru wouldn't take any chances.

She found her gaze drawn to the artifact, even wrapped up in its thick blanket.

"Does it scare you?" Fen asked, somehow knowing where her thoughts lay.

"Yes," she said. She would have been a fool not to be frightened of it.

"Me too," he said. Somehow, that small admission felt like a revelation. Ru still understood so little of Fen, but she was hungry for more. She craved to know him.

She wondered, not for the first time, whether she ought to tell Fen and her friends about the way the stone spoke to her. What harm could the knowledge do? With their minds at work alongside hers, maybe they could come to understand the connection more quickly. But if word got out, if the Children found out... There were too many what-ifs, and too much at stake.

The chatter of voices and footsteps on the stone steps announced the arrival of Archie and Gwyneth, with a tray of coffee and pastries carried between them.

"We missed you two at breakfast," said Gwyn, her golden hair shining like honey against a blue woolen dress. "We thought you might need sustenance."

"You're the heroes we needed this morning," said Ru, their happy moods contagious. Knowing she'd need the energy, she reached for a sticky cinnamon roll.

Archie set down the tray and poured two steaming mugs of coffee, handing one to Ru with long-fingered hands. She saw in his easy smile, in his interactions with Fen, that any lingering wounds between them had been healed. "What do you say, Ru. Is today the day? Are we finally going to get a look at the thing we're supposed to be studying?"

"All will be revealed soon," she said laughingly, "but first, I want to go over my plan of action. I've divided our research into three steps, each of which must be completed before we can move to the next. The goals, as we all know, are to identify the nature of the object, to identify the purpose of the object, and to prove that it is a magical object. I'd like to start by focusing on its physical traits. What chemicals is it composed of? Is it a known mineral, for example? If so, where does the mineral come from? And so on. That's step one."

The group was listening intently, chewing their breakfast and sipping steaming coffee, nodding along as Ru spoke. She felt her confidence grow as she explained the process, all due to the attention of her friends — the way they hung on her words, even taking notes as she spoke. This was the first large-scale research project she had been in charge of, ever. She had conducted experiments with one or two other academics for various subjects of study, but never once had she had full reign over something like this.

The sense of pride made her skin tingle, and her heart beat quicker. Her voice was almost breathless as she spoke. Fen's gaze didn't leave her once, and for a brief moment, Ru almost felt as if they were breathing in sync.

"Remember," she said when she came to the end of her speech, before any of them could cut in with questions. "The artifact will, by necessity, be moved and lifted, especially during the first phase of our studies. We can't possibly determine its physical properties otherwise. In all cases, we should take the precaution of using these oven mitts to handle it. If an exception must be made, clear it with me first. Questions?"

Fen, Archie, and Gwyneth all looked at each other, but nobody spoke or raised a hand.

"Nothing?" Ru said, a bit surprised.

"You were very thorough," said Gwyneth. The others nodded in agreement.

"Well then," said Ru, "let's get started."

Everyone watched with bated breath as Ru turned to unwrap the artifact. No one but she and Fen had seen it, and even though Ru had already described it to them in as much detail as she could, there was no comparison with the object itself. Ru wondered suddenly, if anyone else might react to the artifact as she had, if Archie or Gwyneth would begin to hear it, to feel it, once it was revealed to them.

A pang of jealousy shot through her at the thought. The intimacy of her connection to the stone, the sense that she had been chosen in some way, gave everything — the horrors she'd seen — a sort of meaning.

Ru stopped this line of thinking in its tracks. Of course her friends wouldn't feel it like she did. Her imagination was running wild, spurred by excitement and nerves.

As she pulled the blanket away from the artifact, she was struck once again by its beauty. It had been so long since she had seen its curves, the depth of its black sheen. It was smaller than she remembered, small enough to fit perfectly in the palm of a hand. Every curve of it, every slight oddity in shape, the way its dark surface caught the light and pulled it in like a deep well... it was perfect.

"Ru?"

She started, the voice jerking her out of her thoughts, and straightened. The artifact was fully uncovered now, lying on the blanket in the middle of its table. "Yes, what?"

She turned to see Archie and Gwyneth exchanging a look. "You were standing there staring at it," said Gwyneth. "For a long time."

"How long?" asked Ru, heart racing. Had she done it again? Had she gone comatose for what felt like seconds to her but was really minutes?

"Not long," said Fen, his tone reassuring despite the tense set of his jaw. "A few seconds."

"Well, you were acting strangely," persisted Gwyneth. She tucked a curl behind her ear, her eyes large with worry. "Are you sure you're going to be all right? Studying this, I mean. The things you've been through..."

"I'll be fine," Ru said, as much to convince her friends as herself. She would just have to be more careful around the artifact from now on, consciously shut it out — or try to. She hadn't realized how obvious it was, the effect it had on her.

The morning flew by, and Ru's reaction to the artifact was almost immediately forgotten. Ru assigned specific tasks to each member of her team, which they were to perform at their dedicated workstations. She would bring the artifact around to everyone, allowing them to take a measurement or weigh it or look at it through a magnification lens.

At one point, Archie asked if she could shave part of it off for him to study under the microscope, a request that filled Ru and the artifact with a twinge of horror, but he was sternly dissuaded. The artifact was to remain completely intact, no matter what. They had no way of predicting what would happen if they tried to alter its structure in any way.

Despite several hours of work and discussion, the progress they made that morning was tantamount to nothing. They measured the artifact's weight and ability to refract light, and began a series of trials that would — in theory — reveal its density. But everything had to be done with the aid of Ru's hands clumsily swathed in oven mitts, which added further time and frustration to tests that should have been completed in a matter of moments.

The arrival of the Children at midday ground everything to a momentary halt.

The three white-robed figures entered the room so quietly that no one noticed they were there until one of them cleared their throat.

At the sound, the research team froze in what they were doing. The artifact safely on its table for the moment, Ru slid off her mitts and set them on her workstation, moving to greet the three Children. She didn't want them there; she disliked the idea of such oversight. But rudeness wouldn't help anything.

"Good afternoon," she said, shaking their hands one by one. "I don't believe we've been formally introduced. I'm Ruellian Delara, Fourth Year, Archaeologist, and head of this research project."

"You may call me Inda," said the one in the middle, who Ru now saw was a woman, with hair and eyes so light they almost matched her white robes.

Inda gestured to the others, identifying them as Ranto and Nell. All three were equally pale, verging on sickly, with close-cropped hair. Ranto's hair was reddish in hue, and Nell's was a dirty blonde. And just like the Children in the palace, they wore white hats that would do nothing to stave off the chill of the dungeon. Especially not in those floaty robes.

Ru felt oddly sorry for them; surely they hadn't *asked* to be sent to a far-off dungeon in a Tower full of uncooperative academics. But here they were, and Ru felt obliged to put them at ease.

"We're all so pleased to meet you," she went on. "If you have any questions, don't hesitate to ask." She smiled brightly, assuming the three would keep to the edge of things, observing from a distance.

On the contrary, and much to Ru's annoyance, the Children immediately began drifting from workstation to workstation, asking idiosyncratic questions in hushed, deadpan voices.

"And what are you measuring here, Miss Delara?" Inda droned, singling out Ru from the start and hovering around her as she worked.

Ru set down her pencil, straightening up from the paper she had been notating. "I'm making a diagram of today's results," she explained, waving a hand at a detailed illustration of the artifact. "We've begun our research by measuring the artifact's basic attributes — weight, dimensions, and so on. As you can see, this is a depiction of the artifact itself. My colleagues are keeping their own records as well, but my job is to collate their findings and look at them as a collective, watching out for any possible conclusions, based on the overall progress of our findings."

Inda said nothing. In a few minutes, she drifted away and began asking Fen about the instrument he was using to measure the artifact's light refraction, asking whether it was made of brass or copper, and how cold he thought it was in the dungeon, down to the specific degree.

Archie became visibly agitated as this went on, to the point where Ru was forced to take him aside under the guise of adjusting one of the lamps near the far end of the room. Her own warning echoed in her mind — they must control their emotions around the artifact. And even though Archie appeared calm enough to those who might not know him, Ru could tell he was cultivating a rage.

"Arch," she said in a low voice, when they were mostly out of earshot of the Children, "pull yourself together."

"How can I?" he hissed. "These reprobates won't let us work without peppering us with inane questions."

"Figure it out," Ru said with forced serenity. "They'll be able to see if we're upset, and I'd rather not give them a reason to suspect anything… untoward."

"We're not *doing* anything untoward," countered Archie.

"And we don't want them to think we are."

Ranto appeared suddenly at Ru's elbow like a ghost; she hadn't heard him approach. "What are we discussing?" he asked, in a tone that suggested he didn't care one way or another.

But Ru knew better. "The lighting," she replied. "Archie and I disagree on… the placing of the lamp."

"Place the lamp as Miss Delara instructs," said Ranto, before drifting back to the workstations.

Archie glared at her for a moment, then returned to his own table.

Ru sighed. This research project was going to be even more difficult than she had initially thought. And proving the existence of magic, in a world dictated by science… they were already attempting the impossible.

CHAPTER 25

Night hung low and unseasonably gray over the Cornelian Tower. Only through slivers of thick fog could the stars be seen, winking in and out as the clouded sky drifted slowly past. Three lamps and a lively fire burned in Ru's room, doing their best to drive out the chilling damp. Rainwater dripped restlessly from the eaves outside, emphasizing the cozy warmth within.

Archie lounged across Ru's bed, one arm bent to prop up his head, light hair tousled from a day of running his fingers through it. The other hand thoughtlessly picked at a loose thread on his waistcoat — his favorite, bottle-green wool with yellow embroidery flowers at its collar. Lamplight drenched him in soft gold, which made him look softer, younger than his twenty-four years.

"And what are you writing now?" he said, a careless tone that Ru knew was a cover for some other emotion. He hadn't spoken of the night he tried to rekindle their flirtation, and she was all too eager to pretend it had never happened. Though every once in a while, she caught a curl of his lip or a tilt of his jaw that said he was still thinking about it.

But she wasn't about to let that get in the way of their friendship, and she knew Archie would agree. She sat perched at the head of her bed, cross-legged on the patchwork quilt, a worn wooden lap desk balanced across her knees. They had been trying to write a letter for the past hour, but the parchment unfurled across Ru's lap was woefully empty, save for a few words.

"Nothing," she said, resisting the urge to crumple the paper and lob it at Archie's head. This was the third time he'd asked in a quarter of an hour. "All I've written is the salutation, I *told* you. Are you going to help me think of something useful to write, or just lie there like a lump on a log? I should have asked Gwyn to help me instead."

"She wouldn't have come," Archie said airily. "She's busy reading up on magic. The lengths we go to for you, Delara."

"And I'm endlessly grateful, really, but I *do* need to put something in this letter."

It had been a week since the three Children arrived in the dungeon to oversee the team's research. Since the first day, Inda, Ranto, and Nell had taken to arriving in the dungeon not long after dawn each day, their pale countenances hovering in the shadows when the rest of the team arrived. And now, even after seven painstaking days of subjecting the artifact to countless pokes and prods and measurements, no meaningful progress had been made.

Lord D'Luc expected an update, a letter detailing the team's discoveries. And even though there was nothing to report, Ru had no choice — she had to write *something*. Anything. Even if it was pure fiction.

"Writing the letter is your job," said Archie, sniffing. "Mine is to simply be pretty. My presence alone infuses you with inspiration."

Ru fixed him with a withering gaze, fighting the smile that tugged at her lips. "It does, does it."

"I've been thinking," he said, rolling onto his back to stare up at the ceiling, his delicate features drawn together in thought. "Trying to sort out what the Children expect from us. Why they're hovering about, asking questions, and so on."

"What the regent wants, you mean," Ru muttered. "I'd give my right arm to know."

Archie snorted. "At least donate the left one, your right arm has that adorable cluster of moles."

"You're actively hindering my progress at this point, Hill."

He turned his head to grin at Ru, his eyes alight with the full knowledge of how much he was irritating her. "Surely, by now your brother will have come to some conclusion, spied on the correct people. I thought he knew *everything*."

"So did I," said Ru, "but he never warned me against *you*, so…"

Archie laughed, closing his eyes for a moment, brown lashes brushing against his cheeks. "Don't make me fall in love with you again, Delara."

She tried hard not to roll her eyes at that. He had never loved her, just as she'd never loved him. What he felt for her had always been pure infatuation. "Don't make me kick you out of my room forever," she tossed back. "What's brewing in that unknowable mind of yours?"

"Oh, nothing," he sighed. "I haven't come to any true conclusions. Only… mulling, I suppose. Testing ideas. But I'm convinced of one thing, and it's that these Children aren't scientists."

"That much is obvious," said Ru. "Every question they ask about our progress…"

"We offer a lie and they buy it, I know," Archie said impatiently. "What I mean is, they're not looking for a purely scientific breakthrough. If they were, they'd see right through our nonsense. And then I thought, well I suppose they must be quite eager to witness the first ever proof of magic in Navenie."

Ru tilted her head, thoughtful. "But they haven't once alluded to magic," she said slowly, voicing her thoughts aloud. "They ask rudimentary, irrelevant questions. Physics, mineralogy. We're not the only ones hiding something."

"I never told you this," said Archie, still gazing up at the ceiling, his expression far away, "but when I was very young, my mother took me to one of those ancient temples. I don't remember which, or where — somewhere near the sea. It was terribly wet, I do remember that. My socks were absolutely sodden at the end of it. But something about it was deeply intriguing to my young self. A strange, decrepit building where people came to speak to beings who lived in the sky, thousands of years ago."

"Where are you going with this?" Ru asked, tapping her quill on the parchment. "Should I be writing this down?"

He laughed. "What I mean to say is, these religious types are different from the rest. They see things, believe in things that we don't. Maybe what the Children are looking for is something we can't even put into words."

"Archie," Ru said, her words drenched in exasperation. "I'm touched by this revelation, thank you, but... the *letter*."

He rolled over onto his side to face her again. "Just list a series of random facts and statistics. Whatever we've said to the Children, repeat it to D'Luc. He won't know the difference."

Letting out a long-suffering sigh and tucking her hair behind her ears, Ru set about penning the letter while Archie watched, peering at the parchment. It was utter nonsense, outlining the stone's physical properties in great fictional detail.

Because no matter the strength of Ru's connection to the artifact, no matter how many measurements she took, the artifact would not reveal itself to her.

The black stone was a restless creature waiting in the darkness of her mind. And even while it might send her a comforting touch, resonate with her on some deep emotional level, always at the core of her was fear. And a pang of something else. Something painful, bitter. A memory of Lady Maryn's horror-stricken face.

～

TWO TEDIOUS WEEKS of research passed, neither much different than the first. Ru and her team continued their work, and the Children continued their questioning. The lies and misdirection set Ru's nerves on edge to the point of near breaking. And even some experiments' results, with a bit of planning and foresight, were faked — less for the benefit of the watchful, emotionless eyes of Inda, Ranto, and Nell, and more for the benefit of Lord D'Luc's letters.

Late in the third week of studying the artifact, without so much as a hint that it might be anything but a black rock, the Children approached Ru, their glazed eyes fixed on her in the cool of the dungeon.

"Miss Delara," said Inda, "we would like to make a request."

Ru stopped scratching pointless notes with a pencil, standing and turning to face the trio of moon-faced Children. She could feel Fen's crackling gaze on her and heard Archie and Gwyneth set down their pencils, pausing to listen.

"Yes?" said Ru, the hairs on the back of her neck beginning to prickle. "What sort of request?"

Inda gave a slight, slow nod as if to indicate that she had heard Ru and appreciated the response. "We would like you to conduct a new experiment."

"Sorry," said Archie, from across the room. "Ru makes the decisions here."

"Shut up, Arch," muttered Gwyneth, sipping her coffee.

Ru glanced at Fen, her attention inevitably drawn to him in moments of uncertainty. He sat slightly hunched, elbows braced on the tabletop, chin planted firmly on his clasped hands. His lips, always so expressive, had tightened in a tense line. His eyes shone darkly in the lamplight as he regarded the Children.

He turned then, noticing Ru's gaze on him. His expression softened subtly, but the frown remained. He raised one eyebrow, ever so slightly.

"What's the experiment?" Ru asked. She braced herself for something irritatingly dull, something that would fit what she knew of the Children.

Ranto stepped forward, robe swishing on the stone

floor, nodding as Inda had done. "We would like you to speak to it."

The room was silent for a moment.

"Sorry, what?" said Gwyneth.

"I'm not sure if you've noticed, but it's a *rock*," Archie deadpanned.

Fen's other eyebrow rose to meet the first. He blinked at Ru, his intense stare sending a message she didn't understand.

"…Why?" asked Ru, tongue leaden. She was frozen to the spot, her blood seeming to curdle in her veins. Did they know? Had they guessed, extrapolated somehow the existence of an invisible thread, a connection that stretched between Ru and the artifact? Or was it a sick coincidence, a demand for the one thing Ru knew she could carry out successfully if she tried?

"We'd like to know," said Nell, stepping forward to join Ranto and Inda, "whether it is reactive to human speech."

"It's clearly not," said Fen, his voice a warning. "We've been talking around it all week. It remains dormant."

Inda, Ranto, and Nell all turned as one to regard Fen with emotionless stares.

"No one has spoken directly to it," said Inda. "With purpose. That is what we would like to see."

Archie snorted loudly. "Surely you can't suppose that will accomplish anything."

Gwyneth shot him a look. "It might if it's a magic object."

"Exactly our thoughts," said Inda. "Miss Delara, you may now proceed with the experiment."

Ru stared, disbelieving. She hung in stasis, refusing to accept her surroundings, the Children, or the request.

They wanted her to do this, right now, at this moment? Reach out to the artifact, speak to it, in the hopes that it would respond? As if it was so easy, so simple. None of them knew. None of them *could* know. And logically, Fen was right — the artifact had been in the presence of voices, laughter, and arguments, since the moment it was unearthed at the Shattered City. If it was going to respond to human voices, it would have done so.

But Ru had never spoken aloud to it. She had not once reached out across that connection with intention, never tried to speak to it, whether silently or aloud. In her rational mind, she knew it would make no difference. Why should it? Yet in her heart of hearts, in the deepest part of her, she was afraid.

Some part of her believed that this might, against all logic and evidence proving otherwise, induce a reaction from the artifact.

"I'll do it," she announced.

The words rolled off her tongue like venom spit from a snake. Sudden, dire. She couldn't do this. Couldn't subject her friends to even the smallest possibility of danger, couldn't risk the Tower... but even as these thoughts crawled through her head, pulling at her will with blazing fingers, she pushed back. Because the artifact was there, waiting, their connection taut like a coiled spring, a feedback loop of understanding, of anticipation.

And as she wrestled with herself, her friends watching, the artifact's effect on her grew. Its presence, at first simply waiting, became insistent. Forceful, confusing, a cloud of hazy emotion, as it had felt in the Shattered City.

Ru couldn't understand, not really, why she *shouldn't* speak to it.

Her friends understood the danger. Surely they would be safe. She wouldn't touch it, not like at the dig site. It was her skin on the stone that had caused the small destruction. Not her voice. She licked her dry lips, unsteady on her feet. The pulse of the artifact was strong, eager, that finger once again hooked against her consciousness, urging her.

And what if this small action, a simple question posed to the artifact, was all that she'd been waiting for? Proof of magic?

The artifact seemed to purr in response, an excited thrum against the base of her skull.

"I'll do it," she said again in the shocked silence, the wordless nods of the Children.

"Spectacular waste of time if you ask me," said Archie, speaking, at last, to cut through the tension in the air.

"Ru," Fen warned, "you don't have to do this."

Inda blinked rapidly. "On the contrary," she said, "you are required to."

"On whose orders?" Gwyneth said, paling visibly in the lamplight.

"The regent's," said Ru. "Who else? That's why they're here. To push for results. But it's all right. I said I would do it and I will."

There was a jumbled protest, Fen half-standing at his table, the chair toppling back onto the stone floor. Archie began talking too fast, gesturing aggressively at the Children. And Gwyneth, still pale but holding herself together, quietly admonished Archie and Fen for their behavior.

Ru pushed it all aside, a background hum, irrelevant, and focused on the task at hand. The Children wanted her to speak to the artifact, and she would. If she changed her mind now, the regent would no doubt remove Ru from the research project, order the artifact sent back to the palace, and place it under her own direct watch.

Ru wouldn't let that happen. And she was tired of failing, tired of lying, tired of all of it.

Not waiting for the clamor to die down, ignoring everyone else, Ru went to the center table. The artifact sat unwrapped, shining like onyx. With deliberate movements she approached, leaning forward until her hands were braced on the dark wood of the table. She gazed at the black stone, opening herself up to it, letting it in.

The artifact responded eagerly, flowing into her being like syrup, coating her from the inside out.

Around her the sound died out, fading to nothing.

"Move away," she said, never once looking away from the stone. "Just in case."

Everyone but Ru retreated to the far edges of the room, clinging to the shadows.

It was too easy, speaking to the artifact. Ru only had to angle her thoughts toward it, a soft touch of the mind, and immediately the artifact was filling her thoughts, her feelings, a vibration of energy at the core of her being as if her body were brimming with light.

Her breaths came faster, shallower. The sensation of it nearly overwhelmed her.

"What are you?" she whispered aloud.

At the same time, she asked this question through the connection that tethered her to the stone. No words, only emotion: *What are you?*

In the middle of an inhale, like a brick to the head, she was slammed with a wall of sensation — color, light, shapes, images. She saw a sky, blackened with soot or thick storm clouds; she saw a dark figure, a cloak spreading across her vision; she saw a flash of light, or darkness, or both. Then the images came faster, warping until all she saw was a blur flashing through her mind, useless information, nothing she could parse, impossible to calculate.

There was a feeling of disconnect, then. As if she couldn't hold what the artifact gave, as if she overflowed with it, her pores leaking its magic.

Her vision faded and went dark.

CHAPTER 26

Ru woke on the floor of the dungeon, her cheek pressed against the stone. She opened her eyes — only blackness. She was blind. Terror seized her heart, rendering her mute, the horror of one thought crashing against her like a wave: She had killed them. They were dead.

And then, as if from far away, voices came. They were talking over each other, jumbled, meaningless. The fist of terror loosened on her heart, and she breathed again. But everything hurt, and she was alone in the darkness. She curled into a ball then, arms over her head, her skull engulfed in waves of pain.

"She hasn't eaten breakfast," said Archie, the fragments of his distant voice converging into something Ru could understand.

"...for the doctor?" said another voice. Gwyneth, drifting in from a distance.

"I'll take her," said another voice, much closer, deep and accented. Strong arms wrapped around her, pulling her to her feet before sweeping her off them entirely. "Archie's right. She hasn't eaten yet. She's not used to this grueling schedule."

"This must be documented and reported," said a toneless voice that came to Ru's ears, almost warped, as if she were underwater.

Then her head bumped against something hard, and she hissed in pain.

"Shit, sorry," said Fen.

And a moment later she was on her feet again, her vision returning, but blurry and spotted. She rubbed her eyes, swaying. Again, she found herself at Fen's mercy, when she was at her most alone and confused. A familiar terror began to course through her.

What had she done?

But no, she had heard their voices. Her friends were alive. She pressed a hand to her forehead, finding it feverishly hot and sweat-drenched.

"Can you walk?" Fen asked gently, so close that she could feel his breath on her ear. "We're on the stairs leading up from the dungeon. I don't want to carry you past the guards if I can help it. They'll ask questions."

Ru nodded, the movement causing her to wince in pain.

"Shit," Fen swore again. "If they ask, you fainted because you haven't eaten anything today."

Ru groaned slightly.

"Up we go."

The walk up the stairs was slow and painful. Ru's weight was mostly supported by Fen, who seemed unhindered by her disorientation, her stumbling. When they came at last to the top of the stairs, Lyr turned to greet them.

"She's unwell?" the rider asked, flicking up the visor of his helmet.

"Fainted," said Fen. "She didn't eat breakfast. She's been working so hard."

"Too hard," said the other guard. "Morning to midnight, all of you. Unnatural, down there in a dungeon. Days on end."

"Be quiet," said Lyr. "Need help, Verrill?"

"She just needs rest. Her room's not far."

Then they were walking again, and with every step, Ru found her strength returning. By the time they came to her room, her vision had returned, but her head was pounding, and her stomach roiled with nausea like a stormy sea.

Fen helped her inside, closing the door gently behind them.

"I should sleep," said Ru, making an unsteady beeline to the bed. "My head's killing me."

Fen caught her waist before she could get there, spinning her around to face him. "No," he said in a low voice, "you should tell me what happened down there."

She pressed a hand to her eyes; that was where it ached, just behind them, where she had seen... her breath came quicker. What *had* she done? She hardly knew. She had uttered three words, and...

"Ru, look at me."

Fen's voice... He was upset. Frightened.

Ru made a sound of irritation, pulling away. She wanted to be alone. To sleep, to forget. Her head ached, and her stomach was in watery knots.

But Fen's grip on her tightened. "*Look at me.*"

He had never spoken to her like that. Angry, desperate to the point of breaking.

Ru opened her eyes, finally meeting his gaze. She saw anguish in his face. Torment. And the longer he looked at her, the more pained he seemed, until he let go of her and turned away so violently it nearly made Ru lose her balance. He had looked at her as if he'd seen something, recognized something in her eyes.

"*Fuck,*" he spat, hand running through his hair. He began to pace the room.

Ru stood watching. His behavior confused her. No one had died — that had been clear from the moment she woke up, heard voices. They had sounded more worried about Ru than about themselves; she had only fainted.

"Fen," she said after a moment, her voice small in the high-ceilinged room. He didn't hear her. Or he ignored her, stopping every few moments in his pacing to rub a hand over his face or to mutter an expletive.

"You're scaring me," she said, louder this time, loud enough that there was no way he couldn't hear.

He stopped dead, and when he faced her his expression was absolutely wrecked. "What did you do down there?"

Despite her throbbing head, despite everything, Ru became defiant. What did *she* do? She had followed orders. She'd done what she thought was best. Fen had no business demanding things from her, had no business pacing about, his hair and eyes wild.

"What do you mean, what did I do?" she spat. "You were *there*. You tell me, Fen. I fainted. I missed everything. All I did was speak to the stone. As ordered. Everyone heard me. And then..." she waved a hand, lost for words.

Fen's face went from agony to ice in a moment. He closed the distance between them and lifted a hand to her face, touching a thumb gently to her lip. There was something strange in his gaze, something... different. Detached. The glaze of a man too deep in his drink, or of someone waking the night, awake but disoriented.

Ru swallowed and tasted bile.

"You're not being entirely truthful, Ru." Fen's voice was like dark honey, no longer demanding or shaken. This was new. This was... different.

And the artifact was there at all once in her mind, filling her as it had just before she spoke to it, caressing her thoughts, goading her. And though she didn't mean to, didn't fully understand it, she felt herself begin to melt, become malleable.

"I didn't do anything," she said. "I asked the artifact a question."

"Did it answer?"

The words hung heavy between them. Ru was desperate, then, to tell Fen the truth. She wanted to tell him everything. He deserved to know — he had been with her since the start, had saved her life, promised to protect her. But this was too much. The truth could rend them apart, he'd think she was mad, or cursed, and she would not risk opening a fissure between them.

"No," she breathed.

Fen's nearness in concert with the artifact's warm

tendrils along her spine, was affecting her, making her light-headed. She was already disoriented, weak from her spell in the dungeon.

"You're lying," he said, eyelids hanging heavy over dark eyes.

He dragged his thumb from her lip to the edge of her jaw, a lazy caress. His eyes shone like glass. She felt a strange pull toward him, inevitable as the thread that pulled her to the artifact. As if the artifact itself were pushing her, urging her closer to him.

"I'm not lying," Ru said, increasingly breathless. She leaned into Fen's touch, relishing the light brush of his thumb against her ear, his hand in her hair. Her head spun.

"Tell me," he growled, his body so close to hers she could feel his chest rising and falling as he breathed, "exactly what you did."

His other hand moved to her waist, feather-soft, fingertips pressing ever so lightly against her jacket. The artifact's touch blazed like a sudden beacon, nearly engulfing her.

Now, she felt truly drunk, her limbs heavy, Fen's body so fiercely close. Heat flared in her, deep in her belly. And the artifact stoked the flame.

"I know you," Fen said, leaning down until his lips just brushed her jaw, right where his thumb had been. His voice was low and gravelly. "I can tell you're holding back. I'll get the truth out of you, one way or another."

She inhaled sharply as his hand made its way to the nape of her neck, his fingers tangling in her hair. Were they really doing this? Was she still unconscious, her cheek pressed to the cold stone in the dungeon?

The artifact's touch coursed through her like molten gold, from her spine to her fingers to every point that Fen touched, flaring where his skin met hers. The floor could have fallen away; the sky could have crashed down around them and she wouldn't have noticed. There was only Fen. Fen, and the ceaseless, devastating pull of the artifact.

Then, ever so slowly, he pulled her hair. "You spoke to the artifact, didn't you?"

For a fraction of a moment, Ru froze as fear cut through the haze. She should pull away, keep up the lie. But it was nearly impossible to think, to drag her mind out of whatever fog of Fen and artifact and *need* it had sunken into.

"Of course, I spoke to it." Her voice was practically ragged and sounded as if it came from miles away. "You heard me."

Fen pulled her toward him until their bodies were pressed together, caught in an inexorable dance, unable to move away from one another. She was certain that somehow he was as caught up as she was, drunk as she was, though it made no sense. The artifact was doing this to her... yet Fen...

The thought skittered away, fading until it was lost.

"No," Fen said, lips moving against Ru's neck, the sensation burning in tandem with the artifact's fire under her skin. "You *spoke* to it. It felt you."

Struggling against what felt like the weight of the earth itself, Ru pulled back, pushing Fen away with both hands. His words had once again cut through the fog, clear and bright. *It felt you.*

"So what if I did," Ru said, blinking hard, trying to put her thoughts in order. "What if I did speak to it? What if it did feel me, in some unfathomable, impossible way?"

Fen's eyes were still glassy, pupils blown wide. His black hair was disheveled, his shirt rumpled and hanging open at the throat.

"You're going to be the death of me," he gasped, chest heaving. "Did it *answer*?"

She gave him the coldest look she could muster, despite her bright-hot face, her own heart beating in time with his. Could he see that she wanted him? Could he feel the magnetic pull between them, of the artifact, just as she did at that moment? But how would such a thing be possible?

She pressed a palm to her eye and breathed deeply.

Her skin began to cool, and the haze that shrouded her thoughts and movements seemed to be fading.

"It's none of your business," she said at last.

They stared at each other, wide-eyed as if neither understood what had happened. Ru remained unsteady, her mind foggy with the artifact's insistence, that fog reflected in Fen's gaze.

"Be honest with me," he said at last. "I'm trying to protect you."

"What from? The Children? The artifact? Yourself?"

"Pick one."

Ru didn't know how to respond to that. With every moment, the artifact's effect diminished. And as Fen rubbed his face, stepping back slightly, blinking, she knew his senses were clearing as well.

As she stood there, trying to think of a way to respond, a half-truth that would appease him, she faltered. But as her faculties returned, a chill fell over her. The pain in her head was growing, and with it came the memory of what she had done in the dungeon. She remembered only snippets of it, her guts in turmoil, as though she was remembering a night of heavy drinking. Everything was jumbled, hazy.

But even through the fog of memory, one detail burst suddenly into harsh, breathtaking clarity: darkness, rising from the surface of the artifact. A millimeter, maybe less. But she had seen it, *felt* it, like a wave before the crest, and the next thing she remembered was her vision going dark before the fall.

Ru felt as if a fist closed around her lungs at the realization of it, stopping her breath at the source. She had almost done it again. First the dig site, now this. And all she had done was ask a question.

The last of her energy fled at once. Stumbling, Ru lowered herself onto the bed, staring into the middle distance, biting back a sob.

"I could have killed you. All of you."

The heavy truth of it fell on her like a hammer, and she chewed her lip until she tasted blood. She hadn't even touched the artifact. She had only spoken three words.

Fen went to her side then, settling wordlessly on the bed, a safe distance from Ru. As he did, she realized with a jolt that the room was cold, uncomfortably so. No fire was lit in the hearth, and one of the windows was open. She shivered slightly, both from the cold and the fact that she hadn't felt it until now. She had been too over-come with madness, that wild draw toward Fen, and she couldn't help but think he'd been overtaken by the same.

But it made no sense. Ru's breath came fast and shal-low, her hands grasping at the bedcovers, tightening into fists. She had lost control again, in the worst way.

Beads of sweat dotted her forehead. "If I hadn't lost consciousness…"

"But you did," Fen said, softly. Soothing. "Nothing happened."

Nothing happened. She felt sick, the bile of self-loathing and the remnants of fear rising in her throat.

For a while, they sat in silence, until Ru's heart slowed its pace, her breathing settled, and her fingers loosened on the bedclothes. They were safe. No one had been harmed. *Nothing happened.*

But the two words rankled, stuck to Ru like a burr. She had seen the artifact's reaction, seen that almost im-perceptible sheen of darkness. That wasn't nothing. Her thoughts drifted to the dig site, the researchers, Lady Maryn…

"I'm sorry," Fen said, breaking the silence. "I should have stopped it. The Children pushed you, and I could have stopped it. I'm to blame."

His words brought Ru back to the present. "No," she said, voice soft as if hoping that Fen might not hear her. As if his not hearing would make it easier. "It was my fault. I spoke to the artifact. Not just with my words. I… reached out to it, with my feelings. And it answered me."

He turned to her, studying her, his lips parted slightly in wonder — or fear. "I saw something in your eyes after you fainted in the dungeon. Something that scared me. I thought you might have been poisoned by the artifact somehow. I'd suspected, thought maybe there was more to it. Something you weren't telling me."

"What do you mean?" said Ru. She pressed her fingers to either side of the bridge of her nose, stifling the headache that wouldn't give her peace.

A series of facts flitted through Ru's mind — Fen had encouraged her to control her emotions near the artifact. He believed sincerely that it was magic. He was first to react when she fainted in the dungeon, hiding her blindness, the reality of what had overcome her.

She stared at him in disbelief as the realization washed over her. "You knew all along."

CHAPTER 27

Outside Ru's room, a summer sun crept slowly upward, arching across a cloud-flecked sky. Bees hummed and darted between colorful flowers in the Tower courtyards. Academics strolled between fruit trees, lounged on stone benches, and walked the hallways of the Tower, windows drenching the corridors in sunlight.

And in that moment, perched on the edge of her bed with a thousand thoughts and questions clawing inside her for purchase, Ru could have been in another world entirely. All that existed to her was Fen. He had known about the artifact, her connection to it, all along.

"I guessed," he said, his chin angled down in slight contrition. He looked up at her through dark lashes. "Extrapolated. It's not as if there's a way to prove that someone is communicating telepathically with an inanimate object."

Despite the maelstrom of emotions that threatened to consume Ru, relief crept through her, melting tense muscles one by one. She no longer had to lie to Fen. And with the lifting of this weight, in the wake of the artifact's intoxicating effect, came a strange sense of emptiness. No, of being untethered. As if the world Ru knew had changed, by even one molecule, altering its course forever.

"Why didn't you say something?" she asked.

"I didn't want to frighten you unnecessarily," Fen said. "I hoped I was wrong."

He wouldn't meet her gaze now; he had turned to stare at his hands, the wall, the ceiling, anywhere but Ru.

"Fen," she said, afraid to utter the words: "do you still trust me?"

"Yes." His answer came so easily. "Of course."

"Why?" she asked, hesitant. "I mean, trust you. I trust you to help me study the artifact, and I trust you to keep this... this knowledge to yourself, whatever it is, whatever it means. I trust you with everything, Fen. But why should you return that trust? I hardly trust *myself*, not with that stone—" She cut herself off, afraid that one more word would set loose a flood of tears.

He reached for her, his fingers gently bracketing her chin, turning her head to face him. His gaze was steady, clear. "I would have done everything the same, in your shoes. And I repay trust, given freely, in kind."

She closed her eyes, leaning into his touch.

"Promise me something, Ru."

"Hmm?" Fen's touch relaxed her, comforted her in a way that no one else had ever done. She was fading fast, the need for rest, for a dreamless sleep, overtaking her. But she couldn't bear to be alone, not when Fen's presence was such a balm.

His fingers tightened on her jaw, ever so slightly. "Don't take a risk like that again."

He shouldn't have to ask, shouldn't have to force a promise from her. "You know I won't."

"Promise me."

She let out a slow, exhausted exhale. "I shouldn't have to say it, but I promise."

He relaxed, letting his hand fall.

"Fen," she said, still reeling from everything that had happened, the words they'd spoken, the touches they shared. "What happened between us..."

"I was worried," he said, almost too quickly. He ran his fingers through dark hair. "Overcome with emotion."

"Is that all it was?" Ru studied his profile, that handsomely arched nose, the purse of his lips, his clenched jaw. She could ask him outright, voice the nagging question that had been on her mind since the artifact's haze subsided: Did he feel it too? The artifact, its wild frenzy of emotion? Had it somehow extended beyond her at that moment, warping Fen's actions as much as her own? But… she was ashamed. Afraid to admit her own vulnerability, the undeniable power the artifact held over her.

"I didn't sleep well last night," he said, turning to glance at her. His eyes were like dark glass. "I was on edge, and I behaved in an ungentlemanly manner. I apologize for the way I…" He cleared his throat. "I was frightened for you. And angry at myself, wishing I'd been able to help you, to protect you from the artifact."

It was a reasonable but inadequate explanation. Ru saw a shadow in his eyes and she knew he was hiding something, holding back.

"I wasn't myself either," she said. They would each pretend everything was fine, then, and move on. As if it had all been nothing. As if his mouth on her skin, his hands on her waist, had been nothing.

She longed, suddenly, for him to touch her. To tuck her unruly hair behind her ear as he'd done in his room, to take her in his arms, and… she stopped the thought there. That strange moment when they'd come here tonight, the fire in her belly, it had all been the artifact. Hadn't it? But what she had felt that night on Fen's bed, what she felt now, those feelings were pure, all hers.

"Ru…" He moved toward her, catching her gaze with his.

Something tightened in her stomach, a knot of excited nerves, and it had nothing to do with the artifact. Her eyes flicked down to his lips, slightly parted. Fen. He had been her colleague, her friend, her protector, her companion. He had tumbled into her life as unexpectedly as the artifact, yet, she couldn't imagine a life without him in it. His solid presence, his laugh, the way he smelled like winter snow.

And here he was on her bed, so familiar, yet her heart was pounding, her breaths uneven.

"Fen," she said, smiling slightly.

And then, as if he'd read her mind, he gently brushed her hair away from her face, his hand lingering.

A thunderous knocking at the door startled them apart, and Fen leaped from the bed like a startled animal. Before they could react further, the door swung open and Archie and Gwyneth burst in.

"Ru, thank god," Gwyneth gasped, seeing that Ru was perfectly healthy. "We've been absolutely *mad* with worry, but the Children wouldn't stop asking questions, made us write out the whole thing—"

"In painful detail, might I add," Archie cut in, eyeing Ru and Fen, no doubt noting their proximity, the fact that Ru was on the bed. "Including a description of your eyes rolling back in your head before you hit the floor."

"Archie, don't. I'm going to lose my breakfast," Gwyneth said, clutching her chest. "Fen, is she all right?"

"I'm perfectly fine," Ru said. But even as the words left her mouth, she knew she wasn't. Her head was throbbing now, and she wanted everyone to leave her alone, to let her sleep.

"She should see a doctor," Fen said.

"We called for Hartford," Gwyneth said. "He'll be here any moment. But we had to see you, Ru, had to know you were safe."

"I'm safe," Ru said, blinking hard. "But I'm…"

"Archie, Fen, get out." Gwyneth's words were sharp as steel. She waved her hands, long golden hair flying about her face as she spun, herding them from the room. "Can't you see she's unwell? The last thing she needs is a pair of useless louts hovering about. Go!"

With no small amount of grumbling, the two men retreated from the room, leaving Ru and Gwyneth alone. Despite her repeated assurance that she was fine, Ru was quietly glad Gwyneth was here. She was desperately tired.

"You need sleep, Ru," Gwyneth said, already turning back the covers. "Go to bed. Take off your dress and get under the blankets. I'll let the doctor in."

"I'm fine," Ru said again, pointlessly. The events of

the morning were catching up with her at last, physically and mentally. Finally giving in, she undressed until only a thin chemise remained, then crawled dutifully into bed.

Gwyneth settled herself at the edge of the bed, pressing the back of her hand to Ru's forehead. "You're burning up."

Those were the last words Ru remembered before she tumbled into a restless sleep.

~

DUSK WAS FALLING by the time Ru woke. She recalled snippets of wakefulness, opening her eyes to find hot tea by the bedside, Gwyneth's voice, a cool cloth on her head. But what she had done in the dungeon, the intoxication that had overcome her afterward, her conversation with Fen... it had drained her so completely that she fell almost instantly back to sleep every time she was roused.

Now that she was finally rested, able to keep her eyes open, the day was gone. Reaching across to her night-stand and downing the last of her cold tea, Ru stood and set about getting dressed. She could hardly remember getting into bed, the weight of exhaustion had fallen over her so suddenly.

The artifact would always, it seemed, take its toll.

She shuddered at the memory of her last view of the stone, blackness seeping from it like water squeezed from wet cloth. Even its touch now, unassuming and tranquil, sent a shiver down her spine.

Never again.

Then a wisp of an image flitted across her memory, the faces surrounding the artifact as she spoke to it, and all at once she saw the dungeon again as clearly as if she were there — Archie and Gwyneth looking on with eager trepidation; Fen's face stern as he watched. The Children, hovering at the edges of the shadows, their expressions empty.

But as soon as the artifact began to react to Ru, just

before she lost consciousness, she remembered the Children's eyes. Dark and shining, predatory.

Ru blinked hard as the flashback faded, as she came back to herself.

The Children had seen something in that moment, something they'd been waiting for. She was sure of it. That nearly imperceptible shell of darkness expanding from the artifact. They had seen the change, had seen what Ru could do with the stone. They were hungry for it. But what did it mean to them? What could the Children, and what could the regent, possibly want with the artifact's cursed darkness? Who *were* the Children? Ru was struck with a vibrating need to do something, to find answers. Any answer would do.

Ru pulled on her shoes, quivering with barely contained agitation, and set out for the nearest library.

Hurrying past the Great Hall, Ru pushed her way through a brass-handled door into one of the largest of the Tower's libraries, containing the widest selection of historical and nonfiction texts. In the evenings, it was always bustling with activity, lit with myriad oil lamps and full of the whispers of academics, the rustle of pages, and the smell of old leather and dust.

Ru made her way to the section on Religion and Spirituality, which was near the back corner of the library. These shelves were so seldom visited, so dimly lit, that Ru had to retrieve one of the oil lamps from the wall to carry with her as she perused the shelves, holding it up to illuminate leather spines.

She pulled out books on rare religions, new and up-and-coming spiritual groups, even cults. When her arms were full of volumes, she shuffled over to an empty table and began to flip through them. Hours later, she found nothing that even hinted at a group that resembled the Children.

Determined, not ready to give up yet, Ru returned the books to their places on the shelves. She would read every vaguely relevant book in the Cornelian Tower if she had to.

The next library she went to was the tall, circular one

where she and Gwyneth had gathered books for the research project. This library was far less organized than
the last and much busier. The books here were mostly
fiction, memoir, or biography, and the academics who
needed a break from their day-long studies lined the
aisles and picked their way along the shelves, looking for
entertainment.

Ru tried every genre she could think of. She picked
up memoirs written by religious leaders and scholars,
novels about handsome yet mysterious priests, biogra-
phies of spiritual and occult practitioners, and even a
romance novel that involved a cult.

She carried the books with her to the top level of the
library, where there were soft chairs and couches dedicated to reading quietly. Most of the academics there
were chatting and laughing, but Ru continued unperturbed. She spent nearly three hours skimming each of
the books she had pulled from the shelves, but found
nothing whatsoever that pointed in the direction of the
Children.

It was nearly midnight, and she was becoming frustrated. Who *were* these people in white robes? What did
they stand for? Their request in the dungeon had
seemed so innocuous, so outwardly simple — speak to
the artifact. But it had been the one thing that elicited a
reaction, that had brought the still black stone to life.

With a shiver running down her spine, Ru wondered
if they had known somehow. Or had even guessed at the
connection she shared with the artifact. She shuddered,
remembering the hard glint in their eyes, just before she
fainted.

She was determined to find out exactly who they
were, what they wanted from her research, and what
part the regent played in it. But they couldn't know
she suspected them of anything untoward, of not
trusting them. They might remove her from the research project, or worse — take the artifact from her.
She couldn't bear the thought of losing the artifact, as
dangerous as it was. She hadn't yet come to understand it, to prove what it was. And now, more than

ever, she was aching to know the nature of her connection to it.

If they took it from her, if they stalled her research, then all of her pain, the loss of innocent lives, would have been for nothing.

Increasingly restless as the night wore on, coming up empty time after time, Ru made one last stop at the only remaining library. It was located in the laboratory wing and was not much larger than Ru's own bedroom. It contained almost entirely books of diagrams and illustrations, a surprising number of them fantastical or fictional. She thought perhaps she might find a collection of celestial or at least esoteric diagrams, something in the spiritual vein. Anything that might point to the Children. It was a long shot, but she wasn't about to give up.

Yawning, Ru flicked through oversized leather-bound books about constellations and cloud formations, seeing nothing that caught her eye. Finally, her fingers brushed a book that might be useful: *Ancient Gods and Demons Depicted: A Pictographic History Of Natural Occurrences Through the Lens of Miracles and Curses.*

She knew it was a long shot, but it was the only vaguely religious or spiritual book she'd come across in the library. And now, it was well into the small hours of the morning, the sounds of the Tower having faded to quiet stillness.

Stifling another yawn, Ru decided to bring the book with her.

Returning to her room in a sleepy haze, she set the book on her bed and flipped briefly through it, but its illustrations were almost meaningless at that late hour. There was a drawing of a dragon under the earth, blowing smoke up through the crust that appeared to be geysers from above. She flipped to another page to see an ancient god forging weapons in the clouds, his hammer strikes forming shards of lightning, and booming thunder. There was a painting of a night sky scattered with crescent moon and stars and thin wisps of cloud, and something that looked like trees at the very bottom edge of the paper.

The book's text was so small and Ru was too tired to read it. They were all lovely depictions, but useless.

Still driven by a need to do *something*, despite the heaviness of her eyelids, Ru was struck with a sudden thought. Setting the illustrated book aside, she went to her desk and pulled out a parchment and quill. If there was no information to be gleaned about the Children here at the Tower, *surely* there would be something at the palace. And if there was something at the palace, her brother would know of it.

Hastily scribbling a letter, Ru made certain to omit any specific mention of the Children. When she was satisfied that Simon would understand exactly what she meant, and that any other readers would see nothing but innocent questions from a sister to a brother, she rolled up the parchment and slid it into a small leather tube.

She made her way, heavy-limbed, across the Tower and up several flights of narrowing stairs to the dovecote, an octagonal stone structure set with circular windows and humming with the coos of sleepy pigeons.

A low whistle left her lips. In response, a pigeon came fluttering out and landed on her outstretched wrist. She tied her letter to its leg, gave it a kiss on the head, and said, "Please bring this to my brother Simon Delara, at the palace in Mirith."

Instantly the pigeon was off, southward bound toward the palace.

CHAPTER 28

When she rolled out of bed the next morning, a cacophony of birdsong in her tired ears, the last thing Ru wanted to do was face her research team. There would be concerned gazes, questions, and... Fen. So much had been shared between them in the past day. That small moment on Ru's bed, before Gwyneth and Archie had barged in...

But it wasn't worth dwelling on, not now.

The thought of the Children overshadowed everything else, their hovering inevitable presence, hanging over her like a storm cloud. What if they wanted her to perform the experiment again? What if they made even more sinister demands?

Increasingly dreadful scenarios played out in her mind until her gut was in such knots that she doubted she'd be able to eat anything.

Her stomach twisting as she made her way to the dungeon, coffee in hand, Ru began to mentally determine how many square meters of oxygen must fill the Tower at any given time, accounting for the exhalation of carbon dioxide by a given amount of academics, and the possibility of open windows and breezes interfering with said exhalations...

Think of something else. Make a rational calculation. Come to a solid conclusion. It will calm your mind, settle your nerves. But, as before, her thoughts scattered at the attempt, as if balking in the face of logic and reason.

She was so engrossed in her attempts to calm herself, frowning at the floor as she went, that Ru didn't notice Professor Cadwick until she was almost on top of him. He was hovering near the stairs down to the dungeon, talking to Lyr, so thin and dressed in such somber tones that he had almost seamlessly blended into the stone wall behind him.

"Ah, there you are," Cadwick said, smiling, his white hair standing up as if caught in an unseen gale. But there was something nervous behind the expression, a tightness. "Would you mind terribly if I joined you all in the, uh… dungeon for a few moments? I've an announcement to share."

The way Cadwick said 'announcement,' through slightly gritted teeth, smile fading as if it was too much work to keep it in place, made Ru's stomach churn even more.

"Yes, of course, Professor," she said. "You're always welcome."

He followed her down the narrow staircase as she tried, unsuccessfully, to keep her hands from shaking, droplets of coffee sloshing over the sides of her mug.

Even though their presence was expected, Ru's heart sank when she saw the Children in the room. They were drifting about the workstations, prowling, until they saw Ru and Cadwick arrive, at which point they drew away from the center of the room and waited in the shadows, expectant.

"Good morning, Professor Cadwick," said Gwyneth, greeting him with what Ru could see was forced cheer. Gwyneth's eyes darted to Ru after she spoke, which said more than any words could — she was worried.

Archie looked much the same, only he kept leveling unsubtle glares at Fen, who stood with arms crossed, expression unreadable. Ru fervently wished she could erase what had happened between them last night. Just the sight of him made her skin hot, her breaths shallow.

How was she supposed to work with him in a professional capacity now?

Her wayward thoughts were cut short by Cadwick, who cleared his throat loudly, pulling everyone's attention.

"Good morning all," he said, nodding at the academics and blatantly ignoring the Children. "I thought your team should be first to know. This morning we received a pigeon from the palace. Though I am not following your work on the artifact closely enough to have been privy to this knowledge," — he shot a glance of admonishment at Ru — "it seems that, as of yesterday, you've made some kind of major breakthrough. So major, in fact, that as of this morning, the regent's advisor is on his way to the Tower to witness said progress in person."

"Lord D'Luc?" said Ru, hoping she had heard wrong. "Coming here?"

"Yes," confirmed Cadwick, "and with only a few days' notice. I suppose you thought it best not to keep your professors apprised of your progress down here?"

Archie and Gwyneth glanced at each other.

Ru's brain whirred with heightened anxiety. They had made no progress. There was only the horrible mistake she had made in speaking to the artifact, in obeying the Children's orders. It hadn't been a breakthrough, it had been madness. But if the Children had sent for Lord D'Luc, then her suspicions were correct — whatever they had seen, their eyes glittering dark, was exactly what they'd been looking for.

An uneasy weight settled in Ru's gut. Would he want her to replicate the experiment himself if he knew the truth of it? If he knew the destructive possibilities, the death that lay in the wake of that thin sheen of darkness? It didn't matter – there was no world in which she would replicate it for Lord D'Luc. She wouldn't dream of even attempting such a thing.

Ru turned to Inda, Ranto, and Nell. They were still half-shadowed, watching Professor Cadwick with expectant expressions. She had to put a stop to this, to whatever the Children might share with Lord D'Luc. She took a breath and put on her best cheerful but confused face, looking around at Cadwick and the Children.

"I think there's been a misunderstanding," she said. "We haven't made any major breakthroughs. Unless Lord D'Luc sees determining the physical density of the artifact as *major*, then I fear he's been misinformed."

Inda stepped fully out of the shadows then, her expression serene. "On the contrary, Miss Delara. We witnessed something extraordinary yesterday morning. A reaction. The artifact seemed to have been... activated, in some way. This is a major step toward discovering what it is. What it does."

"I'd agree with you if that had actually happened," Archie cut in, to Ru's relief.

"Yes, the Children seem to be mistaken," Gwyneth said, in a sweet but determined tone. She twirled her hair around one finger. "We attempted a new experiment yesterday, which was rather... unorthodox, shall we say. The Children themselves requested it. Ru tried speaking to the artifact, you see, to determine if it would respond to human voice. But it didn't. The experiment failed."

"And Ru was sick anyway," added Archie. "She couldn't have put pencil to paper, let alone produce a major breakthrough."

Professor Cadwick adopted a thoughtful expression, directing his gaze first on the research team and then the Children. "Delara, you were sick?" he finally said.

"I fainted," she clarified. "I didn't eat breakfast."

Fen nodded along as the others spoke, submitting his agreement, making no attempt to communicate with Ru. The artifact, at least, thrummed reassuringly against her consciousness.

"I see." Cadwick shrugged, apparently convinced. "There you have it, then. Inda, Ranto, Nell, shall we send a pigeon to Lord D'Luc? It appears there's no need for him to travel all the way to the Tower for a misunderstanding."

"Do not worry yourselves," said Inda, and her impassive face — off-putting at the best of times — sent a chill down Ru's spine. "We are certain of what we saw. Lord D'Luc, as you call him, will be eager to see the replication of your experiment when he arrives."

Professor Cadwick frowned. "If he's hellbent on it, we can't deter him I suppose. Though I do hope you'll warn him that you may have misunderstood the—"

"We didn't," interrupted Inda.

"Very well, very well." Cadwick turned his back on the Children and said to Ru, "Don't fret. The conclusions you've already drawn will no doubt be fascinating data for the regent's advisor to pore over."

With a smile and a nod, he hurried out of the dungeon.

Uneasiness rolled through Ru like a sickly wave. It was still so strange to her that Lord D'Luc led these people, so inhuman in their mannerisms. What had happened to the animated Children she'd seen in the palace? Lord D'Luc, by contrast, was so vibrant, so charismatic, and thoughtful, that the disconnect was vast enough to be farcical. She wondered when Simon would respond, and hoped it would be soon. She hadn't heard from him since his first letter of warning.

And now, she realized with a weight in her stomach, despite Simon's attempt to protect her, everything would be revealed in three days. It would be immediately obvious to Lord D'Luc that every detail, every description she had sent in her weekly updates, was nothing but a lie. She didn't want to think about what would happen then. He would alert the regent, and the research, the artifact, would fall out of Ru's control entirely.

They conducted the last of their tests in research phase one, as if the day previous hadn't happened at all. As if Ru hadn't nearly vaporized the dungeon, her friends, possibly even the Cornelian Tower.

Ru moved by rote, her mind flitting from one thought to the next, each more troubling than the last. She was afraid to probe for the artifact, to move a thought against its presence in the darkness of her mind.

Even so, she knew it was there — she could feel it, always.

To worsen Ru's day further, Fen seemed to be avoiding her. When she went to his station to ask for a spare notebook, he handed one to her wordlessly, not meeting her gaze. While Ru would normally have joked with him, made excuses to touch him, casually brush against him as she passed, every time she came near him, he moved away. As if she disgusted him.

He said he still trusted her, but beyond that... had she lost him?

By the time evening fell, everyone packing up their stations for the night, Ru's disappointment and hurt had curdled into resentment. Fen had no reason to avoid her. She had been just as frightened as he had yesterday. She needed reassurance. Support. His distance was confusing, painful, and cold. If he had made a mistake in almost kissing her, as she'd thought... then he should have said. Been honest, outright with it.

It was pure bad luck that as Ru packed up her desk, her fingers slipped and she dropped a glass vial. It shattered on the floor, tiny shards of glass scattering across the dark stone.

The Children were filing quietly up the stairs, just behind Archie and Gwyneth. None of them seemed to hear. But Fen, still at the foot of the stairs, stopped and turned back.

"Go on," said Ru, waving a hand. *Not now.* "Just a vial."

He didn't move. "You're angry with me."

"I'm not."

There was a long, tense pause. Fen leaned against the wall near the stairs, arms crossed, studying her. His grey eyes were narrowed, lips pursed ever so slightly. "You *are* angry, though."

"Why would I be angry?" His accuracy annoyed her. Sometimes it felt like he understood her better than she understood herself. She grabbed a broom, busying herself with sweeping up the shards of glass.

"I can think of a few reasons." He pushed himself off

the wall, easing toward her, slowly, as if trying not to startle a wild animal. "Some of which pertain to me."

His low voice cut straight to her belly. Avoiding his gaze, she swept the glass into a wicker bin and set it aside, wiping her hands on her already dusty skirts. "That's very self-aggrandizing."

Fen finally caught her eyes, smiling, and Ru's resolve weakened.

"Don't you want to know the reasons?" he asked, now standing across the table from Ru. He leaned forward, resting his palms on the wood so that their eyes were level.

"Not really," she said, glancing away. She didn't need Fen to tell her that she was hurt by his avoidance when she was feeling especially vulnerable with him.

"Seriously, Ru," he said, his voice painfully open, genuine.

She almost cracked then, almost crashed into him like a wave, the way she'd been wanting to for days and days. But she didn't.

"This news about Lord D'Luc," Fen said, nudging the subject into slightly less frightening territory. "We need a contingency. A plan of some kind."

"I'm well aware," said Ru. "If you're worried about me losing control again, I won't." Her voice was like ice.

Talk to me, she thought desperately. *Why did you avoid me all day?* All she wanted from him was a hint that he might feel the same way about her, that he had felt it last night. But she couldn't voice it. What if it was nothing, a side effect of the artifact? Or worse, what if Fen felt nothing for her at all? His friendship meant too much to her. And feelings were... difficult.

"If this is about last night," said Fen, "I apologize again for the way I acted. I'll apologize tomorrow, the next day, and every day for the rest of my life."

That was the last thing Ru wanted: Apologies, regret. *I acted in an ungentlemanly manner.* She wanted to throw it all back in his face. Because the most hesitant part of her said that they had shared something true, something real. He had wanted her, just as she had wanted him. The artifact had only watered a seed that was already planted. Hadn't it?

Or, said a louder part of her, it had all been the artifact, intoxicating her, and by extension Fen. That was all. Why else would he keep his distance now?

"No need," she said, turning away to collect her things, a chill settling on her heart. "I've already accepted your apologies. Good night."

She swept past him and up the stairs, into the hall, and finally to her room, where she threw herself on the bed and screamed into a pillow.

CHAPTER 29

A great party was going to be held in honor of Lord
D'Luc's arrival in two days.

This had nothing to do with the professors, who
hated the idea and were against it at every step. They
were finally swayed by an endless onslaught from the
academics, who were so deprived of real parties and the
kind of pomp that took place in Mirith that they clung
to the arrival of the regent's advisor as if for dear life.

The party would take place in the Great Hall and
would consist mostly of music — performed by the few
enthusiastic musical academics who studied at the
Tower — and dancing and drink. There would be a
chance for Lord D'Luc to make a speech if he desired,
and despite the fact that he was visiting for the purpose
of checking up on Ru's experiment with the artifact, nobody bothered to ask her to take part in any of the fes-
tivities.

It was clear to Ru that the academics had generally
lost interest in the artifact, beyond the fact that it was
now bringing in an exciting dignitary from the palace.
She guessed this was because nothing entertaining or
outright grisly had occurred in the dungeons, and therefore the attention of the academics had drifted
elsewhere.

This should have painted Ru in a slightly more favorable light in the eyes of her peers, but instead, she had effectively returned to square one: a woman who continued to fail at proving the existence of magic.

The event had sprung up overnight like wildfire, and now the Tower was outright buzzing. Every mention of the party was like a little punch in Ru's stomach, a reminder of the inevitability of Lord D'Luc's arrival. Ru knew she would have to discuss the party with her team, who she had avoided the night before in favor of brooding in her room, and she dreaded the conversation.

It wasn't that Ru couldn't handle emotions, but they weren't something that she processed easily. She couldn't speak of them clearly, didn't know how to express herself. So she had laid in bed all evening, staring up at the canopy and formulating hypotheses, calculations as to why Fen might be so repelled by her.

Each calculation, each formula, came to the same conclusion: Unknown.

And all the while, the artifact attempted to soothe her mind, whispering to calm her nerves, all for nothing. Nothing would have lifted her out of that dire mood.

And now, surrounded by the boisterous energy brought on by the impending party, Ru became inconsolably stressed. Too much was happening — and at the same time *not* happening — all at once. She felt lonelier than she had in a long time. She couldn't talk to Gwyneth or Archie about the way the artifact spoke to her, nor could she talk to Fen — for entirely different reasons.

She needed support, advice, a calm and objective point of view to set her back on her feet.

So, both in an effort to seek solace and to further avoid the topic of Lord D'Luc's party, instead of heading to the dungeon to begin faking experiments for the benefit of the Children, Ru turned and strode down the hall in the opposite direction — toward the professorial wing.

This part of the Tower was quiet in the mornings,

dimly lit and comforting. The ceilings were high, arched with dark wooden beams, the walls wood-paneled and hung with paintings, diagrams, and the odd piece of taxidermy. Distant voices echoed through the corridor, and somewhere a door opened and shut, muffled. Ru passed a cluster of academics as they strolled in the opposite direction, only one of them shooting her a curious glance as they went.

Professor Thorne's office was locked when she arrived. He had always been her favorite after Obralle, a steady, thoughtful man with sharp insights and a sharper mind, and a sense of emotional intelligence that rivaled only Professor Acorn's. She thought Thorne would best provide the balance of logical and emotional advice that she sought.

She knocked. There was no answer.

"Professor Thorne?" she called through the door. She had never known him not to be in his office during his official office hours.

"Good morning, Delara."

Ru turned to see Professor Acorn walking toward her with a steaming mug, clearly on the way to his own office down the hall, his gold-brown hair falling to one side, framing a softly oblong face. "Looking for Thorne?"

She nodded. "Do you know where he is?"

"Sick with a little ailment." Acorn sipped his coffee, his tone jovial despite the subject matter. "I hope I haven't caught it myself. Far too many people, far too close to one another in this Tower."

"I see." Ru's heart sank. She had been sure Thorne could provide her with the sense of solidity that she desperately needed.

"Might I assist you in some way?" Acorn asked, steam drifting up from his coffee.

Ru briefly thought of declining. She knew Acorn would be far more inclined to see past her words and come to conclusions about her feelings and state of mind, which she wasn't particularly keen for anyone to see at the moment. But she needed immediate reassurance, a logical but empathetic mind, and Acorn was here now.

"Thank you, Professor," she said, and with a broad smile, he showed her to his office.

The room felt almost claustrophobic. Mismatched shelves lined the walls from floor to ceiling, brimming with various books, minerals, potted plants, and artifacts. An enormous, delicately carved cuckoo clock hung from one of the few clear sections of the wall, painted in bright colors, waiting for the hour to strike.

"How can I assist the brilliant Ruellian Delara?" Acorn asked, once they were settled — he at his desk and Ru seated across from him in a velvet-upholstered swiveling chair. Sunlight streamed in from a tall window behind the desk, illuminating motes that spun about the professor's head, a corona of dust.

Ru thought for a moment. She had been so determined to seek advice, and reassurance, that she hadn't considered how to voice those needs. She decided to veer as closely to the truth as possible without rousing any needling questions.

"We're having difficulties," she said, gripping the armrests of her chair, hiding the fact that her hands shook slightly. "With the study of the artifact, that is. It seems there's been a mistake in communication. The major breakthrough that Lord D'Luc was told about, well, it... doesn't exist. There was no breakthrough."

The professor regarded her with a thoughtful expression, and rubbed the bridge of his nose with two fingers. "I see. But you have made progress in your research, otherwise?"

"Yes," Ru said, hating that the lie came so easily. "I mean... mostly."

Acorn squeezed his eyes shut, pushing his hair back. "I seem to have a headache coming on... sorry, Delara. Right. So you're saying the regent's advisor has a rather exaggerated view of what sort of discoveries you've made so far in your research of the artifact."

"Yes, exactly."

He stood suddenly and closed the curtains, drenching the room in immediate gloom. "That's better," he muttered. "Bit of a migraine. You were saying?"

"It's just that I'm concerned the advisor will be... I don't know, *angry* upon discovering that he traveled all the way here for nothing. What do you suggest we do?"

"Hmm," said Acorn, staring at nothing. "Yes. A good question. Lord D'Luc is an understanding man, though, is he not? Mix-ups happen. No need to worry. Apologies, but you must excuse me, as I seem to have quite suddenly taken ill." He frowned, rubbing the spot between his eyebrows.

"Maybe you've caught Thorne's ailment after all," Ru said, hurrying to stand, moving away from the professor. He only nodded, pressing a hand to his forehead, as she slipped out of his dark office and into the corridor.

She strode back through the professorial wing wracked with grim thoughts, her anxiety even worse than before. Thorne's illness, and now Acorn... But that concern was quickly pushed aside to make room for the more pressing matter, the arrival of Lord D'Luc. Ru realized with growing despair that she and her team would have to make a play of it, construct an entire experiment based on nothing at all, and somehow fake the artifact's reaction when she spoke to it directly. Or she would lose the artifact altogether, she had no doubt.

But how? What could they do?

On her way back to the dungeon, Ru tried to focus on the number of flagstones in the hall, the number of doors in the entire Tower, the number of pages inside books in all the Tower's libraries, as a way of calming her thoughts. But her mind circled constantly back to an image of Lord D'Luc forcing Ru to speak to the artifact, threatening her, holding her hand to the thing, until blackness exploded from the surface and darkness fell.

Of course, that won't happen, she thought, *don't be ridiculous. The worst that will happen is he takes away the instruments, revokes funding, and cancels the experiment altogether. And the artifact is taken back to the palace.*

But the fear remained, gripping her when she

thought of losing the artifact. As hard as she tried not to, the dread of it spun endlessly in her mind.

By the time she descended the dark stone steps into the dungeon, it was late morning and her team was busy at their stations. Fen held the artifact with a pair of thick gloves while Archie moved a small brass instrument over its surface, something they had done several times already for various invented purposes.

The energy of the room was subdued, as if Archie, Gwyneth, and Fen had absorbed the Children's somber demeanors at the molecular level. They grunted greetings when Ru started setting up at her station, but were otherwise absorbed in their own projects. She wondered if the impending arrival of Lord D'Luc had crushed everyone's spirits — it had certainly crushed her own.

Ru went to her workstation, pulling out one of her notebooks, and flipping to the most recent page of notes, most of which were utter nonsense. Then she settled into her chair, resting her chin on her hands, elbows braced on the table, watching Fen and Archie with the artifact. They spoke in low tones, focused on their performance, aware of the Children's sharp gazes.

Their measurements finished, Fen went to return the artifact to its central table, setting it gently on the folded blanket. Ru watched intently as he slid the oven mitts from his hands, flexing long, sun-tanned fingers.

He turned, sensing her eyes on him, catching her gaze. His lips curved in the beginnings of a smile and she glanced away, pretending to focus on her notebook, the pointless numbers and letters she scribbled there. She felt him watching her for a moment, palpable anticipation stretched between them.

Ru didn't dare glance up again until she heard his boots moving away, his chair dragging across the stone, until she knew he was back at his workstation. Her heart in her throat, she waited three beats, then glanced up.

Fen had turned to fiddle with one of the instruments on his desk, his profile catching the lamplight, hair falling over his eyes. She felt something melt in her, a softening of a shell she hadn't known was there. What was this distance that had sprung up between them? Was it Ru's fault? Her inability to understand what even she herself wanted? Was it Fen's inability to return Ru's stunted feelings?

She sighed, tucking her hair behind her ears. Brooding and worrying would accomplish nothing. Greater things were at stake than Ru's silly attraction. They needed a plan of action in anticipation of Lord D'Luc's arrival, and time was running short. She needed to speak to her team in secret, without the Children hovering, without them knowing. There was no other way to formulate a strategy of misdirection.

Ru ripped a page from her notebook and scribbled a note, folding it while the Children were distracted by Gwyneth, who had gone to hold a mirror and a candle over the artifact.

"Arch," Ru said, "come here. Does this formula look right to you?"

As Archie sidled over to her workstation, Fen shot her an unreadable look. A shiver traveled down to the base of her spine. A simple *look* and he had her unbalanced. Biting her lip, she turned to Archie and slipped the note into his hand as he bent over the desk, studying one of her old notes.

"Looks good to me," he said, closing his fist around the note.

"Thanks, Arch," she said, her heart thundering in her chest. If he read it and followed the instructions without giving himself away, Archie would pass the note to Fen, and Fen to Gwyneth, without their white-robed overseers being any more the wiser.

Now, all Ru had to do was formulate a plan. But nothing came to her. She made random scratches on paper with pencil, willing her fingers to bring forth some knowledge that her mind would understand and follow. But her brain was like a dried-up prune, sapped dry, absolutely useless. Her team would be counting on her to inspire them, but she had nothing.

There was a sudden clatter on the stone stairs, and

Lyr appeared in the room. He had never come down into the dungeon before, and his plumed helmet, his shining armor, seemed almost comically out of place in the ancient room.

"Letter for you, Miss Delara." He held out a rolled-up parchment.

Ru sprang up so quickly, she almost knocked over a slew of delicate scientific instruments. Brass bits jangling in her wake, she hurried over to Lyr in the doorway. This had to be a letter from Simon, at last, the answers she'd been looking for.

"Thank you," she breathed. A bit more loudly, she said over her shoulder, "I'll be back in a moment."

The Children fixed her with narrow-eyed stares, but the others nodded and went back to their work as Ru hurried up the stairs.

It wasn't that Ru believed her brother to be anything but subtle when it came to sending delicate information via pigeon, but she wanted to be alone when she read his reply in case the Children took an interest in it, in case he'd written anything sensitive. Clutching her skirts in one fist, the other holding the letter, she hurried breathlessly to the dormitory wing and her room.

Flinging herself onto the settee by the unlit hearth, she unrolled the letter. A separate sheet of paper fell out and fluttered to the floor. She bent to pick it up, setting it aside as she read the letter itself.

Ru,

Forgive the brevity. Some intriguing goings-on at the palace these past few days. I've sent you a leaflet that might pique your interest. If you don't hear from me, I'm perfectly fine, but may be unable to write for a while.

Your devoted brother,
Simon

Apprehension settled like a stone in Ru's gut. She

didn't like Simon's tone, his forced brevity. What could be going on at the palace that would give Simon pause, deter him from writing? His attempt at reassurance had the opposite effect on her — if he felt compelled to spell out the fact that he was fine, Ru felt certain that he wasn't.

Hoping the leaflet would shed light on the letter, she unfolded it. In large curled lettering, the top of the leaflet read:

The Children

welcome you into their loving arms

It was an advertisement of sorts, although Ru thought it odd that a spiritual group would lower themselves to putting out leaflets as if they were a barber shop or a butcher. She read the leaflet in a few minutes, front to back. Most of it was pure rhetoric, convincing ordinary people that their lives were incomplete or deficient in some way, that the Children could help them begin the journey to a new life, some kind of spiritual "paradise." There was a list of services they offered, meditations in various parks and public areas throughout Mirith. Ru imagined Inda, Ranto, and Nell sitting in a park having conversations with the workers and commoners of Mirith, and the image was too absurd.

The only part of the leaflet that was even vaguely interesting to Ru was a small illustration on the back, a night sky lit by the moon, and a strange pattern at the bottom that looked like trees, or mountains. Underneath it was a string of words in a language Ru didn't recognize; she would have to ask one of the linguistics academics to translate it for her.

With growing frustration, Ru read the leaflet again, searching for clues — there was nothing. No hint of an answer to the questions that plagued her. The leaflet was as useless as the Children were somber. Sometimes Simon could be so hopeless. Why hadn't he just answered her clearly? Why be so vague and deflective? Surely whatever "goings-on" he'd mentioned weren't so dangerous that he feared for his life — the regent had declared the traitors dealt with. But what if the regent hadn't been entirely truthful? What if the threat continued? What if some new danger had sprung up in the past weeks?

She grit her teeth, folding the letter and leaflet with shaking fingers.

A knock at the door startled her, and the letter fell from her hands, fluttering to settle on the velvet settee. Before she could answer or hide the letter, the door opened a crack and Ranto's bland face appeared around it.

Ru's mouth went dry in an instant as she held her breath, waiting for him to speak.

"Miss Delara," he said in his monotonous tone, "we ask that you please return to your research presently. Lord D'Luc will be expecting results upon his arrival in two days' time."

She let out her breath slowly, shakily. Simon's letter had put her edge, set her nerves on fire. She forced a smile.

"Thank you, Ranto. I'll be down in a minute."

"I will wait here," he said, closing her door with a click.

Wait here, outside her door? Ru grimaced, feeling suddenly like a child being punished for disobeying some rule she hadn't been aware of. Filled with dread that she couldn't shake and a burning resentment toward the Children, Ru stood. Smoothed her skirts. Willed her hands to stop shaking. And, taking a deep breath, she went to join Ranto in the hallway.

He walked her back down to the dungeons as if herding a wayward sheep. By the time they were descending the stairs, Ru had at least managed to get her heart to slow its pace, her hands to steady. But a knot of dread still sat heavy in her stomach.

The dungeon was just as she'd left it — buzzing silently with nervous energy and a distinct air of discontent. But as she returned to her workspace, Gwyneth caught her eye and smiled, and her expression said everything: they had all read Ru's note without interference, and they would be ready to meet at the specified time.

CHAPTER 30

The rest of the day passed without incident.
Gwyneth made a detailed and arresting diagram of
the artifact reacting to one of her experiments — dripping water, blowing sand, and producing minor electric
shocks all around it to simulate the natural elements —
which the Children were very taken by.

"Lord D'Luc will be greatly stimulated by this depiction," Inda had said, leaning over the diagram.

"I hope not," Archie muttered.

When it was time to pack up for the day, Ru expected
the Children to begin filing out of the dungeon along
with the rest of them, as they had always done. Instead,
they made their way to the stairs and stood in a cluster,
waiting.

Gwyneth was ready to leave first, but when she made
to leave, Inda blocked her path at the foot of the stairs.

"Please wait until all are ready to depart," droned
Inda.

"Why?" asked Gwyneth, adjusting her satchel with a
glare.

"Lord D'Luc would like every precaution to be tak-
en," said Nell in her small, inflection-less voice.

"That explains nothing," Archie said, joining
Gwyneth at the stairs.

Ru glanced at Fen. He had paused in gathering his
things, listening.

"Precautions for what?" asked Ru, joining the others to face the Children.

"The safety of your team and of the artifact," said Inda. "It is unsafe for any one of you to be alone with the artifact. It is unsafe for any of you to traverse the Tower alone, without supervision."

Gwyneth, Archie, and Ru all stared at each other, grasping for meaning.

"That's a bit much," said Archie at last.

"No, it's perfectly sensible," Ru cut in, realizing that she ought to play along with this new rule as loudly as possible if she was planning to break it at every opportunity. "We're understanding the artifact more and more every day. With that comes a level of risk. Especially if we know that there have been traitors who might kidnap or murder in order to attain the artifact. Who knows what word might be spreading in Mirith?"

While she spoke, the Children nodded solemnly, oblivious to her misdirection.

Fen appeared at her shoulder, his presence at once steadying and distracting. "Well put," he said, his breath warm on Ru's hair.

Archie and Gwyneth remained silent, clearly disagreeing with Ru, but smart enough not to protest.

"Very well," said Inda, her hands clasped before her as if in constant prayer. "We will remain at your sides throughout the day. Should you go your separate ways, we will separate also, one of us with each of you. Miss Delara, the King's Guard Lyrren Briar has been assigned as your designated bodyguard."

Gwyneth snorted. "Ru doesn't need a *bodyguard*."

But Ru was relieved by it, glad to know that Lyr would be her protector and not one of the dead-eyed Children.

With no small amount of grumbled protests from Archie and Gwyneth, the group ascended the stairs together, first the research team and then the Children. Ru felt like a schoolgirl on a trip to the Mirith Market, being forced to hold hands with her classmates so that nobody got lost in the chaos of the city.

The plan had been to meet at Ru's room directly after they'd finished research for the day, but if they all traipsed collectively there now, the Children would be curious as to why. The team had never before gathered like that in anyone's room. And while there were countless innocuous explanations they could give as to why they were doing it now, Ru preferred that the Children had no idea the team was meeting at all, let alone where.

And anyway, Ru still had no plan. Lord D'Luc would arrive at the Tower in two days, and in that time they would need to formulate a ruse clever enough to fool him, his Children, and the professors. If they put their heads together, maybe they could think of something. But it couldn't be now.

"Shall we go and have dinner?" Ru suggested. The mess hall would be loud and busy; as long as the Children weren't sitting on their laps as they ate, they could talk more freely there. Ru hoped it would give her a chance to explain why she wanted to meet outside of the dungeon, to plan a place and time, while keeping in mind the fact they were now going to be shadowed everywhere they went.

As promised, Inda, Ranto, and Nell followed the four of them to the mess hall, their robes billowing behind them like ghostly wisps. Lyr also peeled away from the dungeon as they passed, hanging behind the Children, his large features painting his expression in a dour light. Ru could sense his disapproval, his reluctance to follow her about as if she needed parental supervision. But at least she hadn't been assigned one of the Children.

As they entered the warm, crowded mess hall, the smell of fresh bread and roasted meat made her stomach growl. Ru saw a mostly empty table and started toward it, her team following in her wake. She assumed the Children would fall away and wait by the door, like guards. Ru saw that Lyr was already stationed outside, the glint of his armor visible just past the entrance. Instead, the three white-robed figures clung to the research team like leeches. None of the three took food for themselves, but simply sat nearby, hands in their laps, as if they were in a church pew.

When Ru and her team were finished loading up their plates, they sat in awkward silence for a moment, the Children staring at them unabashedly.

"Isn't this lovely," said Fen, glancing at his food, then at the Children.

"It's for our safety," said Ru. She was determined to seem as compliant as possible lest the Children take even more extreme measures. Ru clenched her hands in her lap, even as a smile lit her face. She imagined Inda, Ranto, and Nell standing over her bed as she slept, lidless eyes staring…

She shuddered, blinking, returning to the moment.

The team made stilted small talk over dinner, from what they'd each wear to the advisor's party, to what sort of pencils everyone preferred to use for their research notes. The Children showed no indication of interest, nor of being bored. They simply sat, observing.

Throughout dinner, no matter how much she fought it, Ru found her attention inexorably drawn to Fen. They hadn't shared a meaningful exchange since their brief spat in the dungeon.

Anger wasn't the word for how Ru felt toward him. No; that had been a mistake before, an inaccurate assessment of her own emotion. It was a need that had been growing in her for days, weeks, since the moment she'd met him. But now, his seeming indifference, his vehement denunciation of the way he had touched her, pulled her close… as much as the artifact had been stoking her feelings, Fen's dismissal and subsequent avoidance had cut through her like a shard of ice.

It certainly wasn't anger that burned in her — it was something hot and instinctual, something that threatened to overtake her senses when Fen was near. But she tamped it down as much as she could, avoiding Fen's gaze.

When they had finished eating, Ru stood up first and made to leave the table. Inda moved with her.

"I'm going to my room," said Ru, exasperated. "Is that allowed?"

"I only wish to accompany you," said Inda.

"Isn't that what Lyr's for?" asked Archie.

"Are you going to cuddle her to sleep, then?" Gwyneth added cuttingly. "I don't understand why you've taken to following us about as if we're infants." Her voice rose to a fever pitch at the word *infants*, and she continued in a rage, "We're perfectly safe. Ru will have Lyr, and he's actually armed. What do you think you're accomplishing by invading our personal space at every turn? What are you planning to do if real danger arises, stare blankly at it? You're suffocating us. At this rate, you'll hinder the progress of our research. It's mentally exhausting seeing your empty faces staring at us every day from underneath those hideous hats. I beg you to go *away*." She stopped then, her cheeks pink with anger, breathing hard.

Her outburst was met with a brief, shocked silence.

Then Archie grinned, his face gleefully shocked. Fen's eyebrows went up slightly, impressed.

Ru was exhilarated, proud, but slightly struck with horror. Hadn't Gwyneth realized what Ru was trying to do, to keep the Children oblivious to their rebellion? How would the Children react to such antagonism? How would they relay this outburst to Lord D'Luc?

But the Children collectively turned to look at Ru, as if she were Gwyneth's keeper. "Is this accurate?" droned Inda.

Ru didn't think about it, didn't mean to, but her gaze snapped to Fen. He watched her steadily, and she could almost *feel* his calm, his warmth, as if his body was pressed to hers, wrapping his arms around her.

Everything became clearer in that moment. The Children, this research project, Lord D'Luc's impending arrival, whatever was going on at the palace, even her need to prove the existence of magic... all of it was background noise, secondary, distraction.

The artifact and the devastation it had caused, the lives lost, Ru's bare hands pressing lightly on that cold stone, Lady Maryn's eyes before the darkness fell. And Fen. Fen, by her side since that moment, keeping her from capsizing on the wave of her anguish — These things blazed brightly, painfully, a white-hot fire in her veins. These were the moments, the things that mattered.

Anger, determination, and a sudden sense of clarity galvanized Ru. "Yes," she said, leaning over, palms braced on the table so that her eyes were level with Inda's. "This is accurate. We *do* want you to go away. You three are a blight on the research project, on our lives, and you've done nothing of worth since you arrived here. Your one contribution has been to ask for an experiment that made me sick. You'll leave us alone to conduct our research in peace until Lord D'Luc arrives, or we will cease the work altogether. If the regent chooses to rescind funding as a result, then so be it."

She took a long, steadying breath, trying to stop herself from shaking. "I'm going to my room now. Fen, you're coming with me."

As she left the table, she caught a glimpse of vague shock on the faces of the three Children — the first hint of emotion she had seen in them since their arrival. Fen stood as she passed, following her obediently from the hall without a word of protest.

As they passed Lyr on the way out, Ru shot him a single look — *Don't* — and he stayed exactly where he was.

Fen said nothing until they came to a stop outside Ru's room. He had trailed behind her like a trained predator, capable of slicing a man's head off in a heartbeat, yet behaving as meekly as a puppy, just for Ru. Now he stood watching her as if waiting for a command.

She opened the door. "Inside."

He obeyed without hesitation.

Slamming the door, she finally allowed her feelings, so pent-up and painful, to burn through her like wildfire, like water bursting through an opened dam. A wave of intense emotion crashed through her, battering her edges in its velocity.

And the artifact, always there, always waiting, responded. It burned in sudden response, building in her belly and vaulting upward through her bones, intoxicating her from the inside out, egging her on. Daring her.

This wasn't what she'd wanted. She had wanted to speak to Fen, to be honest with him, she… she blinked, hard. The artifact's caress had become a violent force, fueled by her own emotions, and she was helpless to it now.

"Sit," she ordered, breathless.

Fen sat. He looked up at her through dark lashes, and for a moment yet another heat rose in Ru, deep in her belly, and her heart skipped.

"I've had enough of us avoiding each other," said Ru, every nerve in her body reaching for Fen. "Enough awkward silences between us. It stops now."

"You've been avoiding *me*," Fen said. His tone wasn't defiant, but there was a glint in his eye as he said it.

"The semantics are meaningless," said Ru. It was hard to think… she was overheating, the inside of her skin itching, she needed… "You are a living headache, Fen Verrill. For countless reasons."

He opened his mouth to respond.

"*Don't* speak over me."

He closed his mouth and swallowed, his dark gaze never leaving hers.

"Better," said Ru, trying… *trying* to make the artifact relax, to push its influence away, back into the shadows of her mind as she spoke. "We need to talk. About the artifact. The Children. Lord D'Luc arriving in two *days*. Fen, the artifact still…" she paused, her thoughts fuzzing as if wine were making a slow, syrupy journey through her veins. *Stop that*, she thought, but it wouldn't. "It *talks* to me, in a way. I can feel its moods. It used to scare me, but now it feels almost comforting. It calms me when I'm agitated. Do I sound mad? It calls to me, Fen."

She chewed her lip, continuing on, barreling forward

because she could, because Fen was listening, because she'd let go of her feelings and now they were over-whelming her. "But when Lord D'Luc comes," she said, "he'll want to... to know the stone, to understand it. The artifact *can't* be known or understood. Not by anyone but me, don't you see that? The research project, these experiments, it's all so insignificant, so irrelevant. Mean-ingless. What we're looking for can't be found with numbers, calculations, or tests. It's in me, Fen. Me. The artifact will tell me what it wants, what its purpose is, how it works. I only have to listen."

During this sudden flood of words, Ru had begun to pace in front of Fen. Her breaths came faster as she went, her complete conviction in what she said over-whelming all other feelings. And all the while, the arti-fact hummed inside her, spurring her on, her thoughts flickering in and out like a flame caught in a breeze.

Fen listened with an expression of neutrality. In the ambient light of her room, shadows cut across his face in angles, and Ru thought briefly that she had never seen anything so perfect.

"Ru," said Fen, when she had finished. His words were low, cautious. "May I speak?"

"Fine." She paused before him, chest heaving as if she had just run a mile.

"What do you want from me?" His expression was almost lazy as he spoke, his eyes half-lidded. As if he was reveling in this. As if, somehow, he felt as untethered as she did. The last time they had been in her room to-gether, it had felt like this. Too much, not enough, an unclear haze between feeling and reality, brought on by the artifact.

Ru took an unsteady breath, pulling herself toward the light of rationality. What *did* she want from him? Support. Guidance. An ally.

"I want your honest opinion," she said at last. "On everything I've just said."

He smiled in a way that veered dangerously close to lascivious, so much that it almost knocked Ru breath-less. "Am I allowed to disagree with you?"

"You're not taking me seriously," she said, frustration flaring in her.

"I'm perfectly serious. It's just that you're giving off a distinct... *energy* at the moment. I think I'm better off letting you ride it out before I start sharing opinions."

"Listen, Fen," she went on, completely ignoring his comment, her vision slightly blurred. A strange sense of unfocused power had sprung up in her, from an ember to a roaring wildfire, and now she grasped in vain at threads of reality.

What had she been saying? "As of today, the artifact belongs to me, not the Tower. Its fate is up to me. You'll help me protect it from anyone who interferes with that."

Fen remained on the settee, seated as obediently as a trained attack dog. His expression was unreadable to Ru. He tilted his head, hair falling away from his eyes, to fix Ru with a clear gaze. "You don't think that might go over a little... badly?"

"With who? Inda and her minions? I don't care." Ru couldn't take her eyes off Fen's mouth, his full lips slightly parted, the stubble along his jaw.

"You don't care," he repeated.

"All I care about is the artifact," said Ru. *And you.* She wanted to say it, yearned to say it, but the artifact, its boundless energy, the power of it, was threatening to overtake her. "You promised you would protect me and my little rock. I'm asking for that now, again."

Fen rose to his feet, ever so slowly, his gaze never leaving hers. By the time he stood to his full height, he was looking down at her with hooded eyes. "And if I refuse?"

The fire in Ru roared forth, filling her with desire, defiance, and rage. She was intoxicated, drunk on the artifact that burned alongside her, its voice in her mind. Telling her she could do anything, get away with anything. That Fen was hers.

As if through a break in the cloud of smoke and flame that raged inside her, Ru peered out at a night sky, a clear world, and she was frightened – it was so far away.

"I hardly even know you," she said, reaching up and tangling her fingers in the hair at the base of Fen's neck, as he had done to her last time he was in her room. "I have no qualms about threatening you."

For a moment his eyes fluttered shut. "Ru," he said, his voice a warning. But she heard a raging fire behind his words.

Practically on tiptoe to keep hold of his hair, she pulled him closer, pressing herself against the length of his body. He tensed, his breathing shallow. She had been so angry when he apologized to her before, after he ran his thumb along her jaw, after his fingers pressed against her, his arms around her. As if it had meant nothing to him, as if he regretted it.

And she had been hurt. It hadn't been passion, desire, or the burning need she felt. He had done it because of the artifact, a mistake. And now... now, she realized, staring into his eyes, clear and gray like a winter sky, he was unaffected. His gaze held no reflection of her own raging fire, of the artifact fanning the flame of her emotions. He was free of it.

"Fen," she murmured, burying her face in his chest.

"Don't," he said, breathless.

"Don't what?" Her free hand moved to grasp the back of his jacket, holding him to her, the fingers of her other hand still tangled in his hair. He could have pushed her away if he wanted — he was strong enough, and she wouldn't have stood a chance. But he stood motionless, submitting.

Her mouth was level with his perfectly formed neck, where dark hair curled against his skin. She felt almost as if she deserved, she was *owed* the kiss she pressed against his throat.

The groan this elicited from him made her burn even brighter. She wanted to throw him onto the settee, to see what else he would submit to.

"Ru, stop," he said, and each time he spoke his voice came from further away.

"Why," Ru said, pressing her nose against his jaw, inhaling him, the inferno inside her railing against rational thought, burning it away, consuming her until she could hardly think. "So you can leave me here alone again? So you can hurt me?"

"God, no. Listen to me." Strong hands grasped her arms, gently. "You said you hardly knew me. But you *do*. Because I know you. I understand you. Every twitch of your mouth, every light in your eyes, every joy you feel, your face when I make you laugh… it's part of me. I'm part of you. I know you've felt it. We're entwined, you and I. What you're doing now, whatever you're feeling, it's not the Ru I know. Come back to me, now."

Come back to me.

Why did his words feel like home? How could he, this man she found at the Shattered City, hold her heart in his calloused hands? But her emotions ebbed and flowed like a hot sea, and she fought him, her thoughts scattering.

We're entwined, you and I. Come back to me, now.

His fingers tensed around her arms, firm and unrelenting. He was an anchor, the eye of her storm. Gradually, through the overwhelm of the artifact's noise, came a slow clarity. A speck of light, cutting through a thick fog.

"Doesn't make sense," she mumbled, her face still nestled in the space between Fen's shoulder and chin. She was on fire, but the flames flickered and subsided, pulling in on themselves. "Agree with me. Do what I say."

"I will," he said, sounding infinitely sorry for it. "I will if *you* ask. Come back to me."

Hot tears streamed down her face. The fire inside was eating at her, it was too hot, too painful, too much. But with every moment it lessened, pulled away, returning to the darkness.

She was leaning against him now for support. One of his buttons pressed painfully into her cheek. His hand moved to curl in her hair, his fingers making slow, soft strokes against her neck.

Minutes passed. Eventually, her breathing slowed, her tears with it.

Gently, tenderly, Fen separated them, holding Ru with reverence as if she herself were a priceless artifact. He took her face in his cool hands and looked into her eyes.

"You're burning up," he whispered. "Are you back now?"

Ru stared back at him, shaking, her face plastered with the salt of dried tears. The fire inside her was gone at last, and in its wake rose a distant unease. "Fen?"

"Ru," he said, as though her name were a prayer, his voice heavy with relief.

His hands on her face were so comforting, such a salve after that fire... the heat. She felt feverish, light-headed. "I'm sorry," she managed, unable to meet his gaze now. "The stress... it got to me. I think the arti-fact... it was fueling me, pushing me. I just felt so *angry*, and..."

"And some other things," Fen said, smiling a little.

Ru closed her eyes. Her words and her actions came back to her in figments. "Please tell me I didn't do any-thing embarrassing. I remember coming in here, telling you to sit — I'm so sorry, Fen — and I ranted about the artifact and asked you to protect me, and..." she shook her head. "You must think I'm mad. Maybe I am mad."

Fen looked conflicted for a moment, his expression unreadable. Then he pulled her into a hug. "Everything's fine. You're safe. You were under the artifact's spell for a while, that's all. And I think... part of me was, too. For a moment. But if it puts your mind at ease, nothing you could say would ever..." he let his words trail off, and in a matter of heartbeats, he broke the hug, stepping back to run a hand through his dark hair.

"I should... you need rest. We can talk about it to-morrow if you'd like. If you need anything, I'll—"

"Wait," said Ru, cutting him off. "You're not leaving, are you?"

He blinked, uncertain. "Do you want me to stay?"

A chasm yawned between them, and Ru knew...

hoped she could close it with a word. And whatever had happened between them — twice now, twice caught up in a mad push and pull, a magnetic draw that defied logic and explanation — she couldn't let him leave again, not like before. Not now, when she knew exactly what she wanted.

"Yes," she said, and the relief of speaking it was like a drink of cool water on a summer day. "To sleep," she clarified, heat rising in her cheeks. She wouldn't touch him like that tonight, wouldn't think to. "I don't want to be alone."

His expression softened, and she almost thought she saw the same relief mirrored in his expression.

"You only had to ask," he said.

Ru's heart overflowed in her chest.

CHAPTER 31

Consciousness found Ru slowly, first with the glance of morning light across her closed eyelids, then the movement of her curtains in a light breeze. The window was open, letting in the noises from the court-yard. Then came the hum of insects, birdsong, and laughter drifting in from early risers on their morning walks.

And as she rolled over in bed to make herself more comfortable — she had time to sleep for another half hour, at least — her outstretched arm knocked against something warm and unexpected. Fen.

Everything from last night came flooding back. She remembered being so tired she could hardly keep her eyes open, crawling into bed with her clothes on, Fen's arm draped over her as she fell asleep.

Ru's eyes shot open, and she was met with Fen's lazy, sleepy smile.

"Morning," he said. He lay at the far edge of the bed, on top of the blankets, still fully clothed. But his lids were heavy with sleep, and his expression was so gentle it almost hurt. "You talk in your sleep."

"Do I?" She was having difficulty not inching closer to him. She couldn't remember the last time she had woken up feeling so safe and rested.

"And you kicked me in the shins at least twice," he

added, his smile widening. "I'd kill to know what you were dreaming about."

"Probably oversized men taking up the whole bed," she laughed.

"A terrible nightmare." His expression softened. "How are you feeling?"

"Like I drank too much wine last night. My head is very upset with me."

He hesitated, his hand almost imperceptibly moving as if he was about to reach out to her. Then, as if thinking better of it, he rolled out of bed, stretching his arms wide.

Ru sighed. He was going to pretend it had never happened, just like before. Was she truly that repulsive to him?

"You need to eat," said Fen, pulling on his boots and running a hand through his hair, which was even messier than usual. "Shall we get breakfast before heading down?"

"Heading down where?" asked Ru, sitting up in bed, pulling at her dress bodice, wishing for something more comfortable. "I meant what I said at dinner last night. I'm not doing anything with or for the Children."

Fen paused in his attempts to tame his hair, expression surprised and mildly impressed. "You know the regent will revoke funding if we don't show Lord D'Luc something world-changing. Or at least *something*, which is the opposite of what we have now."

"I know," said Ru, sliding gently out of bed. "He'll certainly want to take the artifact back to the palace with him."

Fen frowned. "What you said last night, about the artifact. Will you be... okay with that?"

Ru chewed her lip. Since finding the artifact, it had never truly occurred to her to be apart from it — what such a thing would feel like, whether the connection would stretch, or break altogether. At that moment, she acknowledged for the first time that she had simply, from the very moment she had touched it, *known* that the artifact was part of her in some arcane, soul-deep, unknowable way. And she suspected that while being separated from the artifact wouldn't kill her, it would take a toll on her.

"No," she answered finally. "I won't. Which is why I won't allow him to take it."

"I hope this isn't the artifact talking again," Fen said, and she knew he was only half-joking.

"I'm serious," she protested, smoothing her skirts and wriggling her feet into her boots. "It's safer here than at the palace. My brother sent me a letter that was more than a bit worrying, despite his insistence that he's safe. There's something going on in Mirith, or at court, that we haven't heard about. The regent said she'd taken care of the traitors who attacked us, but... maybe they weren't the only ones. Or maybe she was lying. Can we truly trust Sigrun? And what about Lord D'Luc? I want to trust him, but the Children..." she trailed off, shivering slightly at the thought of them, the memory of their glittering eyes.

Fen sighed. "I'm finding I don't trust anyone these days, with the exception of you."

A sudden knocking at the door made Ru jump, reaching for Fen's arm by instinct.

"Ru, wake up, please be awake," came the frantic sound of Gwyneth's voice.

Fen crossed the room and flung open the door.

Gwyneth froze at the sight of him, her wide-eyed stare traveling from his disheveled hair to the unmade bed to Ru, who was tying her boots and probably looked just as unintentionally debauched as Fen did.

"Gwyn," said Ru, staving off the inevitable flood of questions with a pointed look, "what's wrong?"

Gwyneth blinked, shaking her head a bit as if clearing a slew of sudden new thoughts from her head. "Right, I'm glad to see that you're both... here. Archie and I were having breakfast, and on our way to the dungeon, we heard raised voices from the vestibule. We went to investigate, and Ru, it's terrible. The worst possible thing."

All manner of possibilities rushed through Ru's

mind: someone had died, someone had come to kill or kidnap her, more Children had arrived; there was no end to the jumble of anxieties that flew through her. She reached thoughtlessly for Fen again.

"Spit it out," Fen said.

"It's Lord D'Luc," Gwyneth exclaimed, her face a mask of anguish. "He's already here."

Ru and Fen shared a brief yet intense look. Ru saw in his eyes that he would act with her no matter the cost. The artifact would stay at the Cornelian Tower.

"I guess we'd better prepare for the party," Ru said.

Gwyneth stared. "Are you joking?"

"I was perfectly clear last night at dinner," said Ru. "We'll continue our research *without* the Children, until Lord D'Luc arrives. It seems he's here. Research is concluded for now."

"But Ru," Gwyneth protested, her large dark eyes shining, "we don't have anything to show him! He'll get the regent to stop funding us, he'll take the artifact, it will all have been for nothing. You'll never know why you..." she caught herself, swallowing hard.

"I may never know," Ru said, putting on a face of determination even though she felt a myriad clambering emotions beneath the surface. She knew what Gwyneth had been about to say. *Why you killed them.* "You're right, Gwyn. But I have to accept that. In the meantime, what I really need right now is a party to cheer me up."

Gwyneth did not look at all convinced, but allowed the other two to herd her from the room obediently. She offered to accompany Ru and Fen to breakfast but they declined, and Gwyneth's intuition doubtless made clear that Ru wanted to be alone with Fen.

～

THEY SPENT the morning and afternoon together, a perfect ease between them. And even with the early arrival of Lord D'Luc; even with the artifact's constant inexplicable pull on her; even with the ever-present memories of the Shattered City dig site, memories that clung to her subconscious like flies, never to be eradicated, Ru felt settled. Almost happy.

For the moment, at least, she had let go.

"Do you remember when we first rode into Mirith?" Ru said, the wide northern sky threatening to swallow her.

They were in the western courtyard, sitting under one of its fruit trees. Sunlight fell in irregularities across their faces, dancing in concert with gusts of soft wind. Only a few wisps of cloud drifted across the otherwise clear blue sky.

Fen murmured assent. "You were happy to be home. I remember you craning your neck in the saddle, grinning at everything. Even the mundane things."

"And you told me you didn't have somewhere like that. A home to return to." Ru turned to Fen, who was gazing at the sky with a far-off expression. "You said you didn't deserve something like that."

He glanced at her from the corner of his eye, then let out a sigh. "If I told you I'd been joking, would you believe me?"

"No."

Fen sat in silence for a moment, thoughtful. "There's a reason I haven't opened up to you about... well." He motioned to himself as a whole. "It's been a long time since I met someone like you. Someone I *wanted* to know. I was alone often as a child. Left to whatever whims and devices I fancied. My mother died when I was very young, and my father was always away, or locked in his office. He rarely spoke to me or my brothers, so I spent a lot of time with my nose buried in books, as you know. When I was tall enough to handle a horse on my own, I would ride into the nearest city to visit its libraries. I shouldn't have to tell you, I also managed to get myself into plenty of ridiculous scrapes."

He laughed softly, and he was so lost in recounting his memories that Ru said nothing, worried that any word from her might snap him out of this reverie. She wondered what city he'd grown up near; his accent wasn't Mirithan.

"Once, I broke into an old woman's house," he continued, a gentle breeze ruffling the collar of his shirt as he spoke. "She was supposedly a witch, according to the legends of children. It was on a dare from some of the orphans who ran the streets of the city — they'd said she was out, that I'd be safe from curses. She was home, of course. Scared the living daylights out of me when she appeared, silhouetted in a doorway. I'll never forget the pure terror I felt then, still wet behind the ears. But she was surprisingly kind and made us tea and fed me cookies.

"Her name was Althea. I saw her many times after that. She became a sort of mother to me, in the absence of my own. She taught me... she taught me about the world and how it worked, how powerful families like mine often took every opportunity to crush anything and anyone weaker than ourselves. It was as if a whole universe opened up to me and I felt, for the first time, that I might amount to something in my life."

Fen paused then, rubbing a hand over his face. "Althea made me promise to *always* fight for others less fortunate than myself, for good. No matter what. But as I grew older, I visited her less and less. And I found myself in a situation that... Well, I strayed from that promise. In the worst way. I'll never do enough penance to cleanse myself of it."

Sensing that the story had come to an end, Ru reached out until her little finger brushed against Fen's in the grass. "You're a good person, Fen. I sensed it from the moment we met. Everything you've done for me, the danger you put yourself in, surely it's made up for whatever mistakes you made in the past."

With a sharp intake of breath, as if just remembering Ru was there, he pulled his hand away and sat up. "You can't know that."

"I know that you shouldn't punish yourself for the rest of your life," said Ru, an unbidden sadness rising in her. Only she deserved that.

Fen stood, brushing grass from his trousers. "I can,"

he said. "There are some things I will never deserve, and you are one of them."

He left her there in the courtyard, under the wide sky. She sat for a long time afterward, cross-legged in the grass. What could he have done? How long ago had it been? But no answers came, of course, and when the sun began its descent toward the horizon, she brushed herself off and went back to the one thing she kept returning to, again and again.

CHAPTER 32

The artifact was quieter than usual. Its incessant gravitational pull on Ru could be ignored at a distance, when she wasn't overcome with emotion. But close to the stone, she could almost feel a physical vibration against the core of her, needy, pulling at that invisible tether. Sitting across from it as she now did, alone in the gloom of the dungeon with only one lamp lit, she imagined what it would be like to hold it again.

She would never again be so thoughtless, and she guessed the artifact knew it too. Nor would she speak to it through their connection. She'd more than learned her lessons. But now, her chin resting on her arms as she looked at the amber reflection of lamplight on its irregular surface, she tried to remember what the stone had felt like, cool against her skin.

And as she gazed at that small black thing, no larger than a man's closed fist, she was convinced the artifact sensed her, understood her.

The thought was pure fantasy, but so was the artifact. It shouldn't exist, shouldn't do the things it did, shouldn't be a *part* of Ru the way that it was, and yet... there it sat.

The hum of the Tower's residents preparing for Lord D'Luc's party didn't penetrate this deep into the bowels of the building. The dungeon was quiet, almost comforting in the wake of the previous day's events.

It was all so silly, she thought, the welcoming party. There was no reason for it to take place tonight, or at all, and yet there would be music and drink and dancing. She loved parties, normally, but this one filled her with an unnamable unease. So instead of braiding her hair and putting on her best gown, she was here. Saying what amounted to goodbye.

She was determined to keep the artifact at the Tower. She would do anything in her power to keep it there. But there was always the possibility that her stubbornness and determination would amount to nothing, that the artifact would be wrenched from her nevertheless.

It was this possibility that had brought her down to the dungeon, for one last look at the thing that had caused her so much wonder, so much pain. One last look before everything changed, one way or another.

A step sounded on the stone stairs behind her.

She spun, slightly alarmed, not expecting anyone to come here so close to the start of the party.

Least of all Fen.

As he stepped into the dim light, Ru's breath caught in her throat. His tall, slender figure was emphasized in a dark green waistcoat, starched cream shirt collar, frothing neckpiece, and polished black boots. A brocade jacket hung at his elbow. His hair was wild as always, but Ru had become unspeakably fond of it.

"Fen," she said, her heart speeding. "Were you— are you going to the party?"

He gave her a look that said she'd asked the most obvious question in the world. "How else would I contrive an excuse to dance with you?"

Ru felt herself blushing, and hoped he wouldn't see in the low light. She was still in her day clothes, grass-stained and sweaty. She knew she should go back to her room and change, and do her hair, but she was rooted to the spot.

"Oh," was all she managed to say.

Fen's face fell slightly. "You were busy. I'll leave you."

"No!" Ru's outburst was so instinctual, so unplanned that it set her cheeks burning even hotter. "I mean, come

sit with me. I'm saying goodbye, should things go horribly wrong."

Fen sat, draping his jacket across his knees. The
bench at the table wasn't very long; they were forced to
sit thigh to thigh, their shoulders almost touching. He
smelled of wind and earth. "You're saying goodbye to
the artifact?"

"I'm not talking to it, don't worry. Just... thinking.
Looking."

"Your connection with this rock," said Fen, "the
things it seems to make you do, the way it makes you
act... nothing good and true could do that to a person.
Yet, you act almost as if you..." he shook his head, hair
falling around his face.

"As if I love it?" Ru finished for him. There were only
so many possible ways he could have finished that sentence. He knew how she felt about the artifact.

Fen turned sharply to meet her gaze. "In the worst
way," he said, his voice almost a whisper. "Like someone
might adore a cruel lover. This bond you've formed, it
was born from destruction. Death. I'm worried—"

"I know," Ru interrupted, turning away. "Imagine
how I feel."

A moment passed in silence. Ru thought Fen might
stand then, leave her alone once more. He was so good
at that. Instead, he let out a deep sound of resignation
and said, "How do I join you in saying goodbye? Should
I just... look at it?"

Ru laughed a little. "If you want to. It's quiet today,
though I'm not sure why."

"Very well," said Fen, leaning forward to stare at the
artifact.

Nothing happened, of course. Fen had no tie to the
object. Ru felt the stone's distant touch, the warmth of
Fen sitting next to her, but other than that faraway pull
from the artifact there was nothing unusual there.

Until there *was*.

The strangest sensation, like a mild electric shock,
flared briefly between them, where their legs touched.

Ru turned to Fen, wide-eyed.

"Did you feel that?" he said, returning her stare.

Ru nodded. Acting on instinct, she took his hand in hers and placed their entwined hands on the table, closing her eyes.

"Shut your eyes, Fen." And even though she couldn't see, she knew he obeyed. "Keep doing whatever you were doing," she murmured. She didn't know what would happen, and had no way to prove that their combined presence wouldn't activate the artifact, destroying the Tower in the process.

But something in her gut, something entirely separate from the artifact, told her this was right. This was pure, it was good.

Fen's hand was warm in hers, broader than hers, her fingers stretching to accommodate his. His forearm flexed slightly where their arms touched — she could feel it through his thin shirt. His breathing was slow, deliberate, regular, as though he was counting between each inhale and exhale.

Somehow, the more Ru allowed Fen's closeness to invade her senses, the more of him she was able to feel, to understand. His pulse, too fast and didn't match his breathing. His jaw, tense. His other hand, still clasped tightly around his jacket, crumpled on his lap.

"Ru," he said, his voice slow as if emerging from a deep sleep. "What…"

"It won't hurt you," she said.

As she spoke, she caressed the artifact with the smallest, gentlest stroke of her thoughts. She said no words, asked no questions, she simply acknowledged it. Welcomed it. She felt, squeezing Fen's hand, that it was the natural and obvious thing to do.

And as she reached out, so did the artifact.

They met in the middle, and its pull held no desperation, no anger, no fear. It simply existed. The more she allowed her connection with the artifact to grow, an exchange of energy expanded between them, and her heart opened up like a flower to the sun.

Fen's breaths rose and fell. Blood rushed through his veins.

Her own body, her thigh pressed to his, seemed to float into a dreamscape. She could have expanded into a thousand galaxies. Every plane, every slope of her skin sparked with life. She felt that, if she asked, the world would crumple inward for her at a word. If she asked, the stars would come to greet her in the darkness. The mountains would march for her, the sea would boil.

She burned with the sensation. Her mind was tinged with fire, just like the night before, only this time it wasn't a flame of rage or desire or frustration. It was pure, clean, and easy.

Fen's body, too, seemed to radiate heat, and she wondered what would happen if she asked him right now for everything. *Everything.* His body in hers, their souls melded, no longer two individual people, but something more.

Fen's grip on her hand tightened, and as it did he inhaled sharply.

"Ru," he murmured. "Open your eyes."

She did and was met by a spectacular sight.

The artifact was glowing.

Not a hovering darkness, like it had exuded in the dig site, but a thick golden glow, as if it had been dipped in honey and lit by a thousand lamps. The light flowed around it like oil, white-gold, and writhing, achingly beautiful. And bursting out from the artifact were two ropes of the same white-gold light, thick and bright, curving and rippling from the black stone, connecting to Ru and Fen.

Ru looked down at their clasped hands, at Fen's body and at hers, and saw that they, too, were glowing, arcs of light curving around them, until they were wreathed in that fluid, gold-burning light. He turned to her, and for a long moment, they gazed at one another with a wonder that overwhelmed all other feeling.

Fen had never looked more perfect to Ru, and she knew he saw the same in her.

Fen's jacket fell from his grip and slumped to the floor.

The sound of it startled Ru, and with the distraction, a seed of fear pried its way in.

The artifact wasn't supposed to do this. It had never done this. Whatever this was, it had to be wrong. Dangerous. It felt too good, too perfect, too safe. And the way it made her want to press herself bodily to Fen, the flame burning hotter and hotter in her belly...

She wrenched her hand from his, standing and pushing herself away until they were no longer touching.

Instantly, like a flame being doused, the flares of golden light disappeared. The blackness of the room enveloped them, the silence overwhelming.

But the heat in her burned on.

"Ru," said Fen. His voice was rough. Her vision began to adjust, and she saw him reaching for her in the darkness. "Sit down."

"I can't," she said, and found that her own voice was hoarse, as though she had been running for miles. Her heart was hammering in her chest; she felt like it might explode, might burn up, if she didn't take a step closer to him. She set her jaw stubbornly. "What if— what if it happens again?"

He stood then, breathless, his eyes wide. "Do you know what that was?"

Ru shook her head. By now her eyes had adjusted to the dim light, but spots of white and gold burst in her vision.

"You did something." Fen was clearly trying to keep his voice low, but as he spoke, he moved toward Ru. Slowly, as if unaware he was doing it.

She took a step back.

"Don't," Fen said, but he stopped trying to move toward her. "Ru, whatever you did... my *heart*, it's... I can't stand here and—"

He would have been able to say more, but in that instant Ru closed the distance between them in a rush, pulling him to her as if he belonged to her, and claimed his mouth with hers. She had been kissed before, in all manner of ways. But none were like this.

None were remotely like this.

The kiss was slow at first, a plunge into pure desire. Fen responded eagerly to Ru, taking her head in his hands, and holding her close as he kissed her. His mouth moved hungrily against hers, needy, like he had been crawling through a desert and was finally allowed to drink.

She couldn't get enough of him, couldn't kiss him deeply enough. Fen's mouth, his body, moved with hers with increasing hunger. She burned so brightly she felt consumed by him, wanting him more completely than she could comprehend.

She pulled at his shirt, his waistcoat, his hair, trying to bring him closer. She thought he might rebel, try to move away, try to get her to relent. Instead, he only encouraged her, groaning when she bit at his lip, tilting his head to allow her to kiss his ear more easily, his hands moving slowly down her body as she did.

"Ru," he said, so breathless it was almost a plea, and the agonizing heat in her flared, almost scorching her.

She fumbled at the buttons on his waistcoat, and in a breathless moment, it was on the floor. Pushing against Fen, pressing herself into him as he responded, his hands finding her own jacket buttons, his teeth grazing her neck, she lost herself in him.

And then he stumbled, his foot catching on a stool, and it snapped her back to a semblance of reality.

Fen looked so debauched in the lamplight, his chest heaving, shirt half-untucked, hair hanging over one eye, lips parted. His expression was so hungry, so lustful that she had to look away for fear of losing herself again.

Because this wasn't her, was it? It had to be the artifact. She'd never felt like this, never been so undone.

And surely, this wasn't Fen. Fen slept across the bed, fully clothed. Fen apologized for touching her, after making her want him so badly it was almost all she could think about other than the artifact.

He had made it clear he didn't want her.

The golden light had sent them both into some kind of frenzy.

"This isn't real," said Ru. "You don't want this. You don't want me." She gave him one last look and ran for the door to the stairs.

Taller and faster, he got there at the same time she did.

As she wrenched open the door, Fen caught it with his broad palm and slammed it shut, placing himself between Ru and escape; she was backed against the door, Fen's arms braced on either side of her, fencing her in.

She opened her mouth to protest, but he pressed his thumb to her lips before she could speak.

"Ruellian Delara," he said in a low, slow voice, "that will be the last time you ever accuse me of not wanting you."

Her defiance melted as he took her face in his hands, kissing her slow, luxurious. She felt herself weakening, succumbing to him, and obligingly he took control. His kisses grew deeper, hungrier; his hands more purposeful.

Her thoughts fled completely, leaving her alone in a dream with Fen. That telltale heat spiked in her belly, caught in her throat, and as it spread through her veins she realized... it wasn't the artifact.

She could *feel* the stone's touch, thrumming gold and lovely in the back of her mind, but the restless hunger that demanded Fen, that urged her to kiss him, touch him, pull him closer... It was all Fen's doing.

"Tell me if you want me to stop," he breathed as he pressed hot kisses down her neck.

Ru made a sound of frustration. "If you stop I'll—"

He chuckled against her throat, one hand reaching under her skirts, inching upward ever so slowly. His knuckles grazed her bare thigh. "You'll what?"

Her response was a small gasp as Fen's knee bent upward, pressing between her legs. His fingers traced tiny circles on the delicate skin of her thigh, his other hand pulling on her jacket until it hung open. Her thin chemise and his shirt were the only barriers between them, between the heat of their skin.

Pleasure blossomed deep within her, sharp and demanding.

The memory of a dream came to her suddenly, Fen leaning over her in bed, his fingers curling around her underclothes. *Is this what you want?*

She wanted this.

"Fen," she said, a plea and a prayer.

With one hand he cupped Ru's ass, pulling her roughly forward until she was pressed against the hard length of him, and with the other hand, he brushed his thumb feather-light across her nipple.

The sound she made would have made her want to melt into the floor with embarrassment at any other time, but not like this, not when it made Fen moan her name into her neck. She was shaking with need, desperate, pleading.

His mouth wasn't enough. His hands weren't enough.

"Fen," she begged.

"You are..." he breathed, hot against her ear. "I can't control myself with you."

"Yes," she said nonsensically, pulling him in for another kiss, arching her back against the door, her hips rocking into him as molten pleasure rose up from the base of her spine.

"No," he said, breaking the kiss. "I mean, if we keep—I won't be able to—"

"I'm perfectly..." she said, punctuating her words with nips along his neck, "able to decide..." she bit his earlobe, eliciting yet another deep moan from Fen, "what I want, for myself. And I want you."

"We can't lose control in here," he said, all in a rush, as if he had to get it out before he lost himself completely in Ru, and she in him. "*You* can't lose control."

He moved away very slightly, giving her room to catch her breath, holding her steady until she could stand on her own. Even so, her knees nearly buckled when he let go, her breath coming in pants.

Her mind was foggy with want; she could see that he wanted her too. She clung to his arms, despite the space between them, and tried to think.

"But it was good," she said. As she spoke she knew it was true, that her fears were just that — fear, confusion, a lack of understanding. When she'd felt that golden light, when she'd seen it curling around them, she had *known* it was right. "We *should* lose control."

Fen gently pulled her jacket over her chest, protecting her modesty.

"Believe me, there is nothing in the world I would rather do right now than lose control with you," he said softly. "But not here. Not like this."

Ru looked up at him with unbound affection, wondering if he could see through to her soul. It was as if a wall inside her had been demolished, baring a tenderness, a depth of feeling that was beyond even her own understanding.

He smiled down at her, raising her chin with a finger and studying her face as if it were the most beautiful thing he'd ever seen. She had never felt so vulnerable, yet so safe.

"We should get ready for the party," he said.

The magic of the moment was fading, that bright flame of Ru's desire guttering out, leaving sudden cold in its wake.

The party. Lord D'Luc. There were more important things at stake now than sucking on Fen's earlobe, a fact which Ru was very reluctant to accept. She sighed, pressing the heels of her palms to her eyes. Then she straightened, buttoning her jacket with shaking fingers.

Fen went to retrieve his waistcoat from the floor, and then his jacket. He waited expectantly by the door while Ru sorted out her mussed hair and her rumpled skirts.

"You go," she said, waving him on, her breath still shallow, her hands shaking with unspent lust. "I have to go back to my room to change, anyway."

"I'll meet you in the Great Hall, then," he said and caught Ru's mouth with his so tenderly that a lump formed in her throat.

As Fen went up the stairs, she had the fleeting urge to run after him, to wrap him in her arms, and never let go.

CHAPTER 33

R u had never seen the Great Hall so bedecked. The
Tower's parties could never match those of the
palace, but the academics had put their excitement and
powers of problem-solving to use, creating a truly
breathtaking array of festivity.

Colorful streamers crisscrossed the hall and fluttered
in the eddies of movement caused by the mass of bodies
below. Lamps and candelabra had been brought in from
all over the Tower, and were arranged on tables and
stools that had been draped with flowers and green
branches from the gardens and courtyards. There was
even a massive arch of flowers and greenery that led
into the Great Hall itself, all constructed and arranged
by hand.

On a raised dais near the far end of the hall, a string
ensemble played boisterously. Ru made her way to a
table along one side of the crowded room, where sweet
pastel-colored treats and fizzing drinks were laid out for
the taking.

Ru felt almost transported, as though she had
stepped out of the Tower and into a fairytale. Until she
backed into Archie and he yelped, bringing her back to
reality.

"Oh, Ru!" he exclaimed, wringing his hand, "you've
made me spill."

She retrieved a napkin from the table and handed it to him. "Have you seen Fen?"

Archie made a face. "Good evening Archie! So nice to see you, Archie. Are you enjoying the party, Archie?"

Ru shoved him with an elbow. "And where's Gwyn?"

With a long-suffering sigh, Archie jerked his head toward the center of the room. "Talking to Lord D'Luc. Trying, anyway."

"About what?" Ru scanned the milling bodies, looking for Gwyn. As she did, she reached mindlessly for a fizzy drink and downed it in one gulp.

"You feeling all right?" Archie asked, his own glass held halfway to his mouth as he watched Ru. "Don't worry, Gwyn's just buttering him up. Making him like her. Us. The team as a collective."

"He already likes me," muttered Ru, standing on tiptoe to see across the room.

"You *are* in a mood." Archie finished his drink and set the empty glass on the table. "What did Fen do to you now? Stare too hard with lovelorn eyes?"

Archie's tone reeked of irony, so Ru ignored it. And she wasn't in a mood; she was impatient, frustrated, still humming with the touch of Fen's mouth, his breath on her neck.

"I'm going to find Gwyn," she said, handing her empty glass to Archie, whose mouth hung open in shocked annoyance as she swept into the sea of merry academics.

The musicians played a fast-paced dance, working the partygoers into a tumult of dancing, laughing, drinking, and spilling of drinks. Ru dodged past the dancers, the now sticky soles of her shoes picking up bits of paper and flower petals as she went.

At last, through the milling academics, she caught sight of Lord D'Luc.

His golden hair and statuesque bearing made him impossible to miss. He was conversing animatedly with someone, and as Ru moved closer, she saw that it was just as Archie had said. Gwyneth, in full regalia of low-cut dress, blonde hair piled high, and dark pink on her lips, was putting on a spectacular show. She laughed coquettishly, brushing her décolletage with the tips of her fingers, hanging on his word with wide dark eyes and parted lips. Lord D'Luc would have seen through it instantly, Ru thought, but he seemed happy enough to play along.

Ru pressed through the last of the throng, until at last, she came to stand next to her friend.

"Ru!" exclaimed Gwyneth, smiling far too widely. "You've joined us at last. Lord D'Luc, you remember Ruellian Delara?"

He took Ru's hand, as he'd done in Mirith all those weeks ago, and brushed his lips to her knuckles. "How could I forget? A pleasure to be in your presence once again, Miss Delara." His dark eyes caught hers and held them.

"The pleasure's mine," she said, trying to adopt an air of exaggerated sweetness, though it paled in comparison to Gwyneth's performance. "I hope you're enjoying the party. We've been anticipating this visit with great enthusiasm, as I'm sure you've guessed."

Lord D'Luc's face lit with a smile, his cheek dimpling slightly. He was more handsome than she remembered, his features so perfectly formed, that in Ru's mind, he was objectively the most beautiful person in the room. With bright golden hair framing his face, his silken jacket and waistcoat the color of the moon, embroidered in gold, he appeared almost angelic.

"I'm practically euphoric in the face of such a welcome," he said, never taking his eyes from Ru. "Miss Delara, your letters have been the light of my existence these past weeks. Such comprehensive descriptions of the work you've done, your meticulous inferences, the thorough data... I beg you, come now and speak with me. I feel as if your mind is the only one in Navenie that can stimulate my own in matters of science. I have so many questions."

He held out a hand, and Ru took it.

How could she have forgotten what a pleasant, thoughtful man he was? Lord D'Luc had taken on the form of a specter in her mind since the first letter from her brother; since the Children had come to hover over her research like ever-present wraiths. Lord D'Luc, like the regent, had become a distant yet demanding overseer, one whose punishment could come swiftly and painfully the moment Ru's research stalled.

But she began to think that some of her fears may have been a figment of anxiety. He was a gentleman, a man of science and logic. Surely, if she put her best foot forward, she could still convince him to let her team continue research on the artifact here at the Tower.

Tossing Gwyneth a reassuring glance over her shoulder, Ru allowed Lord D'Luc to lead her to the edge of the Great Hall, furthest from the musicians and the dancing, where they could converse more easily.

"I am ever so eager to learn," said Lord D'Luc, without preamble, "why you have omitted your significant breakthrough with the artifact from your letters. I was forced to hear it from my colleagues, whose finesse with words are severely lacking in comparison to yours. Why deprive me so?"

Ru, expecting this line of questioning, had an answer at the ready. "I fell ill after the event," she explained, putting on an innocent tone. "And by the time I was well enough to write, I had already been made aware of the Children's report, and your imminent visit. I thought, wouldn't it be wonderful if, instead of being forced to read my ramblings in a letter, Lord D'Luc could witness the thing in person?"

He seemed satisfied with this, sipping his drink with a courtly elegance that was so out of place at the Tower. "I'm beside myself with anticipation," he said. "Would it be an affront to request a demonstration now?"

A tiny shock of cold ran through Ru. "Tonight?"

"But of course. Science and progress wait for no one."

She composed herself, willing her nerves to remain calm. "That would be impossible, my lord. We haven't arranged the lighting or set up the necessary precautions. We had planned to show you an official demonstration in a few days' time. While progress waits for no one, science requires meticulous preparation."

He smiled knowingly. "Quite right, Miss Delara. Please, call me Hugon. I've heard enough of Lord D'Luc this, Lord D'Luc that. This is a place of academia. We're all equals at the Cornelian Tower, are we not?"

Ru didn't know what to make of *that*; she had been under no illusion that most aristocrats would rather die than be called by their first name by a load of graceless academics. But she liked the sentiment, and if Lord D'Luc was determined to be as an equal, a peer, then she would be the last to deny him that. Even if it gave her pause.

"I think I agree," she said, "although some of Mirith's aristo families might not be of the same mind. I believe that science is for all and should be argued and discussed in the same manner by all, between every level of society without the fog of unnecessary social mores or prejudice. But... the fact of us believing that doesn't make it true."

Lord D'Luc chuckled, a low and charming sound. "You are sharp as a knife, Miss Delara. This is exactly why I am so eager to continue supporting the research of the artifact, here at the Tower. Contrary to the regent's way of thinking, I believe that while your research continues to yield strong results, its study is best conducted here. At the palace, more crude matters of state could interfere. I'm continually haunted by the tale of your attack on the road north, and—"

"How did the regent get to the root of it?" Ru interrupted, all sense of decorum falling away, making room for curiosity. "Do you know who sent the guards who turned on us, what they wanted?"

His smile was strained for a moment, as though she was a silly child asking too many questions. But the expression passed as quickly as it came. "The threat, as such, has been eradicated."

Ru could see that he was holding back, not sharing the whole truth. Maybe his openness with her was a smokescreen, a misdirection. After all, why should he let her in on courtly secrets? She was just an academic, not a member of the regent's trusted circle. Not even a courtier. Science may be for all, but matters of politics, of the kingdom's security, were not.

She wondered briefly if Lord D'Luc's tolerance, if his openness, would endure if she failed to show him what he wanted to see. But surely it wouldn't matter. He wouldn't knowingly put her in danger... would he? She refused to believe it. He clearly thought highly of her, highly enough, at least, that he wouldn't remove her from the post of head researcher.

While your research continues to yield strong results. She consciously stopped herself from chewing the inside of her lip at the words, the implication.

"I'm relieved to hear that you'd prefer to keep the artifact here," she said, attempting to sound calm, despite her relief. "The Tower has no equal when it comes to research and progress. We take this project very seriously, and I look forward to showing you how far we've come."

"That puts my mind at ease," said Lord D'Luc. "I should like to see the item in action very soon, as you know. If not tonight, then perhaps in the morning?"

"Tomorrow?" Ru knew this was coming, knew they would have to show him *something* or risk... would he enact any punishment at all? Or simply express disappointment when they were unable to show him what he believed he was here to see?

An idea came to her suddenly. What she and Fen had done. The golden light.

The thought of it alone made her blush, and to think of recreating such an intimate moment in front of everyone, her and Fen holding hands, the artifact glowing brightly... it didn't feel right, exactly. But it didn't feel *wrong*. And what else could they show him? Neither she nor Fen had been harmed. It would be safe and visually arresting.

And, she thought, with the help of Lord D'Luc, perhaps she could find answers at last. Discover what the artifact was, why it had chosen her, and what her connection with it meant.

She felt a growing surge of relief as the solution took shape.

"Indeed," he was saying, "tomorrow morning is rather ideal. What do you say?"

"We'll certainly do our best," replied Ru, distracted now. She scanned the academics all around her, still laughing and dancing, looking for Fen. He should have been there by now. "My lord, I mean Hugon, have you seen Fen Verrill? You may remember him from our dinner at the palace."

"How could I forget," said Lord D'Luc, and she almost thought the very corner of his lip curled. "Odd fellow. I saw him brooding near the edge of things before you arrived. Ah, there." He indicated the far end of the Great Hall.

Ru had to stand on tiptoe yet again and was only barely able to make out a shock of messy black hair across the room.

"Thank you," she said, eager to speak to Fen. "If you'll excuse me, I must inform my team that we'll be demonstrating the artifact in the morning."

Lord D'Luc inclined his head, and Ru made a hasty beeline for Fen.

He caught her eye immediately and started moving toward her until they met in the crowd, inexorably drawn together. There was no more flowing golden light, and the aching fire within her had cooled to smoldering embers, but something had changed between the two of them. She knew he felt it too. The party swirled around them, but Ru could have been anywhere in that moment.

All she saw was Fen.

She wanted to throw herself into his arms, let him lift her up, and carry her away somewhere, to forget about everything else.

"You're gorgeous," he said, as a greeting. "That color suits you."

Ru blushed. Her dress wasn't as elegant as she would have liked, but as an academic, she had no reason to own anything as nice as the gowns she'd worn at the palace. It was a simple thing of silk and lace, midnight blue, with a low-cut bodice and a row of buttons down her back. It had taken ages to put on. She would have loved to see how quickly Fen could get her out of it.

He took her hands in his, and leaned down so only she could hear, "I'm aching to kiss you."

"Later," she said, heart pounding. "I've just spoken to Lord D'Luc. About the artifact."

Fen looked as if he had to struggle to change focus from Ru to the more important matter at hand. "Not here."

They threaded their way through the great hall, away from the music and the dancing, out into the foyer and beyond, to the moonlit courtyard. There were plenty of other academics about, strolling and taking in the air and kissing on benches. They walked together hand in hand until they were mostly alone, the hum of the party now distant. Ru could hear crickets and watched as fireflies danced like miniature stars under the trees.

"Tell me everything," said Fen. "Before I become distracted." His dark, hot gaze raked over her, his expression so indecent that Ru felt a surge of the familiar heat between her legs.

Taking a deep breath of night air to settle herself, she recounted her conversation with Lord D'Luc. How he seemed dedicated to keeping the artifact at the Tower, no matter what; how he had nothing useful to share about the threat of traitors at the palace; and how he had asked for a demonstration of the artifact the next morning.

Ru thought it sounded sensible, the way she told it, but Fen's expression grew steadily darker as she spoke. By the time she was finished, storm clouds seemed to have collected in his eyes.

"Why are you so determined to put yourself in danger?" he said, his jaw clenching. "Do you value your life at all?"

"What on earth do you mean?" Ru asked. She felt she had missed something, as if she'd descended a flight of stairs only to stumble at the last step.

"You know exactly," he said, pulling restlessly at his neckcloth, loosening it about his throat. "How many times have I saved your life, or wrenched you from the grasp of that cursed stone? It's almost like you *want* me to be forced to watch you die."

"Fen," she said, confused by his sudden anger. "I don't know what you mean."

"Don't you?" he said, his voice becoming dangerously low. "You seem surprisingly eager to show Lord D'Luc his precious breakthrough moment with the artifact tomorrow. What a lovely morning that will be when something goes wrong, when you're overtaken by the artifact, when everyone in the dungeon is unsuspectingly..." he stopped himself from continuing, but his face was a mask of barely contained fury.

"When everyone in the dungeon is unsuspectingly *what?*" she demanded. "Killed? Ah. Yes, you're right. I did murder all those people in the Shattered City. I had completely forgotten. Thank you for reminding me."

Ru couldn't believe what she was hearing. Where was this animosity coming from? Was Fen... *jealous* of Lord D'Luc? And to use her connection to the artifact against her... knowing how tormented she was, and how much agony she felt.

It took everything in her not to slap him across the face.

His face paled. "I didn't mean..."

But she wasn't going to let this go so easily. He couldn't profess to be *entwined* with her one minute and then turn her deepest hurt against her like a dagger the next.

"Yes," she said, "you did. It seems you're perfectly happy to hurt me in order to get your way. I suppose you don't care that I have a plan. You couldn't possibly imagine that I would possess an *ounce* of intelligence in my tiny brain. There Ru goes again, voluntarily vaporizing all her friends! What a silly girl. It's too bad there were no brave men in her life to keep her under control."

Fen bristled slightly. "You know that's not what I meant."

"Do I?" Ru knew her chest was heaving ridiculously in her corset, knew her cheeks were pink with anger, and the reasonable side of her knew — of *course* she knew — that Fen would never intentionally hurt her. But she also knew that sheen in his eyes, the fear, the knowledge of what she could do if she stepped a hair out of line with the artifact.

But he *had* hurt her, and there was no stopping her now that she had been set off. "I hardly know you at all, Fen Verrill," she spat, "if that's even your real name."

He stepped back slightly, off-balance as if struck.

Ru exhaled sharply and bit her lip. She hadn't meant... not like that...

"I'm sorry," Fen said. "You're right to be angry. Forgive me. Tell me your plan."

Ru crossed her arms, shivering slightly in the night air. "I was going to ask you to... to help me demonstrate what we did earlier this evening. To summon that golden light, whatever it was. For Lord D'Luc."

Fen's expression closed off then. Unreadable. He took another step back, and even though Ru was full to bursting with indignant anger, the increased distance between them made her blood run cold.

No, she thought, *come back. Don't close yourself to me.*

"You thought to demonstrate... *that* moment. To Lord D'Luc." Fen's tone was flat, devoid of emotion.

"With *you*," Ru said, her words coming out all in a rush, "only with you, with your permission, with your agreement. And not because I want to. I *don't*. But we have to show him something."

A wind picked up and Fen's hair and neckcloth were caught in it, whipping against his neck, his forehead. His gaze remained steady. "We don't have to show him anything. You, Ru, don't owe him anything."

They glared at each other for a moment, Ru grasping for the remains of whatever affection had been between them, whether it was lust or love or something more. Was it gone now, lost forever to the night? The thought was so devastating, so unthinkable, that it nearly brought her to her knees.

"He'll take the artifact," she said at last, her voice small. It was her only explanation. The excuse she came back to again and again.

"Why does it matter so much to you?" Fen asked, and a vast sadness passed over his face. "A cursed black stone. What is it to you?"

"You know what it is to me. I'm... entwined with it. Just as I am to you, like you said. Or have you changed your mind about that?"

"Of course I haven't." His voice was so low she almost didn't hear.

"Then why fight me on this?"

He rubbed his face and ran a hand through his hair. "I saw you with him. In the Great Hall."

"Saw me with who?" Ru asked, impatient, cold, wishing desperately for Fen's arms around her, pulling her close.

"Hugon D'Luc, Ru, who else?"

A knot of thorns caught in her throat, choking her. "You *are* jealous." She hadn't meant her words to cut, but the realization slipped out of her in a rush, accusing.

"Can you blame me?" Fen said. "I see how he looks at you."

"We were discussing *science*," she hissed, arms still crossed, squeezing herself so tightly to keep from bursting or something worse — crying. "The artifact, Fen. The reason he's here. I had to be charming, had to be gracious."

"So gracious that you'd happily share what you and I created together, the two of us alone, an indescribably intimate moment. You'd like to perform that for Lord D'Luc's enjoyment. As a demonstration."

Ru moved toward him, aching for closeness, but he backed away. How had she lost the thread of this conversation so completely? How was *she* now the one desperate for forgiveness?

"Not *perform*," she said, "not... not all of it, just the

light. When we held hands. Not for enjoyment, for research. Fen, what choice do we have?"

Ignoring her question, he said, "I thought perhaps you would think more highly of this evening, of our moment in the dungeon, than to use it as a means of continuing your little project."

"*Our* little project," spat Ru, anger boiling up again. "You know how much it means to me. My plan isn't as terrible as you're making it out to be. I wasn't going to... to... *with* Lord D'Luc, I..." She paused to draw cool night air into her lungs, to try to collect herself. Her heart ached. "Whatever you're imagining, it's wrong. This is my life too, Fen. I need this. I need to know what the artifact is, what it does, why I... why it chose *me*. Why all of this happened. Part of me believes I'm no better than Taryel, and I need to know why. You're just a bystander. A stranger who fell into this mess by chance. You can't possibly understand."

There was a long moment of strained silence.

Fireflies continued their dance overhead. Moonlight fell on Fen's hair, painting it blue-black. As Ru looked up at his face, she almost felt as if her heart was breaking and reforming and breaking again.

"I would let you use me," said Fen at last, in such a quiet voice that Ru had to strain to hear him. "Without question, in any way you liked. I would be your instrument, your servant. Your machine. But this..." he shook his head, looking away. "You've asked too much."

He turned and strode toward the Tower before she could react or respond. She stood there in frozen confusion as if a blade of ice had stabbed her clean through the chest.

CHAPTER 34

Ru's pain and distraction were so great the next morning that she nearly ran full-speed into Gwyneth outside the mess hall.

"There you are," Gwyneth said breathlessly, reacting quickly enough to avoid a collision and catching Ru by the shoulder as she made to barrel aimlessly past. "You're late. Why do you look... like shit? God, forget food, we've got to get down to the dungeon. I don't know what idiocy you've contrived with Lord D'Luc, but he and his Children are there now, claiming you made some promise of a demonstration this morning? Confirm or deny?"

"Confirm," Ru said in a deadened voice. She did look like shit. She hadn't changed since the night before, hadn't fixed her hair, hadn't glanced in a mirror. She probably looked like death warmed over.

She should have warned the others, should have made an effort, should have been the first in the dungeons that morning with coffee and a sharp mind. Instead, she had gone straight to bed after her argument with Fen and drunk an entire bottle of her reserve wine, which she kept under the bed for emergencies.

Her head was pounding. She needed a very large and very greasy breakfast, and she had no intention of hurrying anywhere.

"Where's Fen." She sounded like a toad with a mouthful of gravel.

"How should I know?" Gwyneth said, her voice shrill. "I thought he'd be with you. Come *on*, everyone's waiting."

"Need food," said Ru, wrenching her arm from Gwyneth's grip and continuing into the mess hall. Her friend trailed closely behind, making sounds of anxiety and reminding her to please hurry as Ru picked up various items from the nearest table, plopping them unceremoniously onto her plate.

"Ru, Lord D'Luc is *waiting*," Gwyneth hissed as Ru reached for a cinnamon roll, hesitated, then went for a rasher of bacon instead.

"Doesn't matter," said Ru. "There's no demo... demonstr... there's no *thing*. Not happening."

"What do you mean, not happening? Ru, he's going to revoke his support. Everyone is there. All the professors — well, except for Acorn and Thorne, they're still sick in bed. But everyone *else*!"

Ru shrugged, grabbing the entire platter of bacon from the table and sliding its contents onto her own plate, ignoring the protests of everyone seated at the table.

"What happened?" Gwyneth said in a gentler voice, apparently just noticing that Ru wasn't exactly behaving like herself. "What's wrong?"

Her plate loaded up with bacon, eggs, and a last-second cinnamon roll balanced on top, Ru turned to face Gwyneth at last. "Gwyn... grab me a coffee, will you? My hands are full."

She had no desire to explain, no urge to clarify, no energy to do anything but eat and go back to bed.

Gwyneth hadn't seen Fen, which meant he wasn't in the dungeon. He wasn't going to come to the dungeon at all today, he wouldn't tomorrow, and he wouldn't the next. Ru knew this with an unshakeable certainty. He had angered her last night, frustrated her, made her want to slap a welt across his impertinent cheek.

But somehow, she had managed to cut him even

deeper, in a way she didn't understand. And in her hungover stupor, she now suspected that she never would. Whatever had begun to bloom between her and Fen, whatever delicate unfurling of the heart, she had crushed it with her stupid, clumsy hands.

"Ru," Gwyneth's voice was verging on desperate. "Lord D'Luc expects…"

But Ru was already heading for the door, breakfast plate held almost reverently, her one comfort. Gwyneth followed her for a while, protesting, bouncing from pleading to angry to worried. Their project would be scrapped, she warned. The artifact would be taken, she cried. Ru's reputation was on the line.

None of that mattered to Ru, now. Her academic career was nothing to her, the artifact a terrible footnote in her life. They could take it from her, cart it away to the palace, and give it to the regent to fondle and study. They could snap the tether between them and grind the black stone into dust for all she cared. She suspected such a thing would hurt, more deeply and viscerally than anything physical possibly could. But that pain would be nothing. A whisper, a scratch, a joke compared to what it would feel like if she…

Hot, angry tears blurred the edges of her vision.

The pain of losing the artifact would be nothing compared to the loss of Fen.

"Tell Lord D'Luc I'm unwell," said Ru, not bothering to glance back at her friend as she spoke. "We'll reschedule for tomorrow."

∾

So THIS IS *what love feels like*, thought Ru, staring glassy-eyed at the ceiling. She had eaten part of her breakfast before she felt compelled to lie down on the floor, lacking the strength or will to move to the bed. Now, hours later, she was still lying there.

The carpet was growing uncomfortable, but she couldn't move. Every once in a while, she tried to reach out to the artifact for comfort. The thread connecting them had thinned, though, frayed, and the pull was weak.

The artifact had abandoned her when she needed it most. Like Fen.

There was no point in going on with the research now, not when the connection between her and the stone was all but dissolved. Maybe this marked the end of her horrors, a fade to normalcy. She supposed she may as well give the artifact to Lord D'Luc and the Children. They could keep it. She didn't want it. They could do what they wanted with it, play with it, poke and prod it, she no longer cared.

Ru was convinced that Fen had left the Tower entirely. She imagined him saddling his horse and riding away, back into the wilderness, to his traveling life. She hated how her chest ached at the thought, his lone figure in the wilds, no city or village to call home. No one to keep him safe.

Weeping overtook her then, her eyes unexpectedly flooding with tears. She sobbed, choking and gasping, until she had to roll onto her side to avoid suffocating. She cried for the loss of Fen, the impending loss of the artifact, for the lives she'd cut short with a touch.

She wept until she had no tears left.

It was a long time before she stopped, before the tears dried on her cheeks. Ru sat up, rubbing a sleeve across her stinging eyes. Glancing at the window, she saw she had been lying on the floor all morning and well into the afternoon.

She needed to bathe, to change into fresh clothes. But the weight of Fen's absence hung heavy on her, unmoving; she was helpless beneath it.

A melody floated up from the courtyard through the open window, an old song. It was familiar to her. She went to the window, unsteady on her feet, aching, and looked out. A group of academics had gathered below in the grass, lounging, one of them strumming a lute. From so high up, he could have been Simon — his reddish hair caught the sun, gleaming.

Ru leaned out over the windowsill, closing her eyes.

The music and the sun and the breeze washed over her, clean and new against her senses. The song, so ingrained in her memory that she would recognize it anywhere, was a tune that Simon had played for her when they were young. It was one of the melodies that had felt like magic to her, wrapping her in the invisible, a palpable hum of pleasure, notes falling one after another in perfect harmony. A sad melody, but tinged with hope.

If magic existed, she thought, then music was proof enough.

She moved away from the window, renewed. That feeling of ease, the beauty in the melody... the *magic*. This was the oxygen that filled her lungs, the ceaseless rhythm of her heart, the reason she was here at the Tower. She had lost a part of herself with Fen, but...

No one, not even Fen, could take magic from her.

IT WASN'T until the sun's rays were lengthy, the western sky fiery red, that Ru finally ventured out of her room. She had bathed and changed into fresh clothes, eaten the rest of her cold breakfast, and washed it down with hot tea. She proceeded through the halls almost aimlessly. But where earlier that morning she had felt empty of all meaning, now she was awake again, felt like herself again.

The artifact's pull on her was so weak it might have been gone altogether, except she could still feel the faintest pulse, the lightest touch.

She found her way inevitably to the guest wing. Despite the lower ceilings and smaller windows, the sun still managed to burst through and paint everything in rich amber tones, despite the darkening shadows.

Fen's door was shut. If by some chance he was still here, she wanted to believe that she would be able to feel him there. But whatever bond had been vibrating between them at the party, whatever wonderful connection they'd shared, had faded to nothing. The loss of it wasn't debilitating, but it was as if Ru's world had lost the smallest fraction of its luster.

Ru leaned against the door and pressed her cheek against the cold hardwood. She was certain, now, that he was gone from the Tower.

Your little project.

His words echoed in her head, over and over.

Fine, then. She would do it herself. She would do everything herself.

CHAPTER 35

Ru had never seen the dungeon so packed with bodies. She was sure their instruments and devices would be knocked over and broken, or the lamps shattered, or her own feet trod on. Everything but the central table had been moved to one side of the room, away from the unprecedented gathering of people who now stood in a crescent, facing the artifact.

Archie and Gwyneth were there, dressed in their nicest clothes. Ru suspected Gwyneth had even styled Archie's hair, which she had never seen so coiffed. Professors Obralle and Cadwick had also come, the latter of whom was endlessly mopping his brow with a cloth. Obralle's pink hair was uncharacteristically plain, a simple bun at the top of her head.

Lord D'Luc stood still as a statue, dressed all in white, his fingers flashing with silver rings. His eyes glittered like cut sapphires, and a dozen white-robed Children had arranged themselves behind him like vacant specters. Ru saw Inda, Ranto, and Nell near the front of the group.

The only person missing was Fen.

Ru stood at the artifact's table, facing her audience. She had dressed in her most professional attire, a dreary brown high-collared dress that Gwyneth had once told her looked like it belonged at a funeral in a swamp.

It was morning, just after breakfast. In a fit of stubborn determination after leaving Fen's room the night before, Ru had sent out the summons — she would complete the demonstration or fail in the attempt, but it would be *her* choice.

"Thank you all for assembling again on such short notice," she said, directing this particularly at Lord D'Luc. He had been visibly disappointed in her when she'd tracked him down the night before. She had found him in his makeshift office in the professorial wing, and had plied him with contrite curtsies and remorseful apologies until he'd agreed to see the demonstration in the morning.

But she had known he would. For what other reason was he here?

"We're eager to see what the artifact can do," said Lord D'Luc. "Will you be giving us a summary of its chemical properties, perhaps even its purpose? I was most interested in your hypothesis, and am rather happily shocked that you've all but proven it. Magic indeed."

Magic indeed. The word alone sent shivers across Ru's skin. Would her questions about the artifact, her connection to it, finally be answered? If her demonstration worked, if the golden light appeared, her life could change in an instant.

But there was no way to explain the artifact's chemical properties as Lord D'Luc had asked, nor its ultimate purpose. The small black stone remained an enigma, even to Ru. All she knew was that the truth of it lay only in her mind, nearly impossible to convey. But she would try.

"I will begin by allowing the object to speak for itself," she said.

Gwyneth looked as if she might be ill, and Archie's expression was like carved stone; even his freckles had paled.

Her friends would be safe — she would make sure of it. The artifact was hers, hers to do with as she liked. Since she'd wept in her room, it was as if her worries, her sadness, had fled with the tears. Now, all that was left was determination and full belief in herself. The artifact would not harm her friends.

Ru took a deep breath. She laid her palms on the table and opened whatever small connection she still had with the artifact. It lay darkly on its blanket, silent and still, a helpless thing with unknowable power.

Ru closed her eyes.

She imagined that Fen was there next to her, his fingers entwined with hers, their bodies sharing space, breathing the same air until they were one soul. She imagined molten white-gold light pulsing out from the artifact, spilling like sunshine until it wreathed the black stone in an infinite brightness. She imagined the ropes of light connecting her to the artifact, the hot flame of want, the weightless energy.

She opened her eyes.

The artifact lay there, dormant. An ordinary stone.

More than anything, Ru wanted to speak to it, admonish the thing, demand that it shine for her, glow for her. But she would never speak to it again, not with words. Not after what had happened last time. And it was easy to stop herself, to resist. Because now, the artifact didn't seem to care; it didn't seem to *want* her to speak to it.

Beads of sweat broke out on her upper lip as she concentrated every corner of her mind on the artifact. She pulled on the thread between her and it, so thin it felt like gossamer, a spider's silk, and still nothing.

Nothing.

She could have stopped there, made up an explanation of some kind, wiped away her sweat, and constructed a complex lie. Countless possibilities sped through her mind, thoughts of how she might improve the situation, turn it on its head, transform it into something beneficial.

Lord D'Luc's eyes were hard in the low light. Professor Cadwick coughed wetly, his white hair lank in the dimness. She longed for Fen's reassuring presence, yearned for his wordless guidance, but he was gone.

A surge of uncontrollable frustration rose suddenly

in Ru, and with a sound that was something between a sob and a scream of anger, she slammed her fist on the table, pushed her way past Lord D'Luc and the non-plussed group of onlookers, and rushed up the stairs and out of the dungeon.

◈

GWYNETH FOUND her in the smallest of the Tower's courtyards. It was more of a garden, surrounded by tall leafy hedges, overgrown in a deliberate way that made it look like a painting of wilderness. Trees, blooms, and cascades of colorful flowers burst unpredictably throughout the garden; the stone paths were almost impossible to make out or follow amidst the greenery and moss underfoot.

Ru was perched on a stone bench underneath a weeping willow that took up almost a quarter of the courtyard. She stared absently into the distance as the sun climbed up the sky, hot and glaring, even through the willow's cascade. A golden-haired figure appeared then, picking its way through the foliage toward her.

"Hi Gwyn," Ru said, patting the bench methodically, her gaze far away. She had been there all morning. If she tried hard enough, if she made sense of the series of events leading up to this moment, she could make herself understand her sudden distance from the artifact.

"Ru..." Gwyneth began.

Ru held up a hand to stop her.

The solution couldn't be reached with the work of her brain alone; she urgently needed a second mind. "Gwyn, what would you say if I told you that I can, for lack of a more accurate term, communicate with the artifact?"

Gwyn opened her mouth, frowning as if to protest.

"No, let me speak," Ru cut in, her thoughts now flowing from her head to her tongue; if she stopped, she was afraid she might never speak this truth again. "More than that, I can feel it. I've been able to sense, as well as be affected directly by... its *thoughts*, per se, as much as we can assign conscious thought to an inanimate object. And the thing is, Gwyn, I've come to the undeniable conclusion, based on nothing but intuition and personal experience, that it is in fact magic. A magical object, beyond the categorization or analytical capabilities of our current technologies, which you must admit are severely limited.

"And what if I went further and said that only our *imaginations* could begin to decipher what this thing is doing to me? What it's done every day since I found it, what the ramifications of its effect on me have been. Even before I touched it, even before I saw it, I felt it, the pain in my head. It called to me, Gwyn. There were feelings I've never... I had to, there was no stopping it. Lady Maryn, I..."

Something hot and thick began to seep from Ru's nose. She lifted a hand to her face and it came away red and wet.

Loose strands of golden hair lifted around Gwyneth's face in a soft afternoon breeze. Her face was ashen, her eyes wide. "Your nose is bleeding," she whispered, pulling out a handkerchief and handing it to Ru, who took it thoughtlessly.

"Sorry, I got... there was a..." Ru held the cloth to her nose, trying to form a coherent sentence.

She knew what she *wanted* to say, but her mouth wouldn't do the job correctly. If she could sit here a while longer, she would be able to figure it out. She would understand everything about the artifact. She just had to open her mind more, let it *in*. It was being stubborn. She would force it to listen.

A searing pain burst across her face and Ru gasped, dropping the handkerchief. She turned to Gwyneth, whose eyes were wide as saucers, her hand frozen in the air, palm pink from the slap she'd just delivered to Ru's cheek.

"Gwyn, are you mad?" she demanded, pressing her cool hand to the burning flesh of her face. It had been a strong, vicious smack. "Is this how you greet people now?"

"Oh, thank god," Gwyneth breathed, sagging. "Ru, you were acting... Well, *you* were the one behaving like a madwoman. Rambling about how the artifact talks to you? What in the world *happened*?"

Ru slumped. Snippets of thought came to her from far away, coalescing into coherence. She remembered Gwyneth sitting next to her... telling her everything, all in a rush, like a clockwork toy that's been wound up too tight and suddenly set loose. It occurred to her that the artifact, withdrawn as it was, had been influencing her. But why?

Had it wanted her to open up to Gwyneth, to seek support from a trusted friend? Ru chewed her lip, ashamed that she had waited so long to do it.

"I didn't mean to frighten you," she said in a hushed voice.

It was far less than what she meant to say. But how could she explain everything she had experienced with the artifact in a meaningful way, even to her best friend? The way the stone played with her head, whether too much or too little, made her feel as if she *was* mad. She hardly understood it herself. How could Gwyneth?

"You don't have to say anything," said Gwyneth, a kind of slow realization dawning in her expression. "I believe you. I only thought... I was scared. Just tell me how to help."

Feeling suddenly exhausted, Ru leaned into her friend, resting her head on the other woman's shoulder.

"Fen and I got the artifact to do something," she said quietly. "The night of the party. Something different. Something good, I think." She sighed, closing her eyes. "I tried to show it to Lord D'Luc, but it won't work. Nothing works. The artifact is so far away. It won't listen. It's here, but... ignoring me. And when I try to reach out to it, it saps my energy." She glanced at the blood-stained cloth in her lap.

"You may not like this," said Gwyneth, hesitant, "but what if you just... I mean, what if we stopped our research? You said you believe the artifact is magic." She stumbled over the word but continued. "If that's true, you've proven your hypothesis. To yourself, anyway. Tell Lord D'Luc and Inda that we're finished. Whatever you're doing with the artifact that we can't see, it's hurting you."

"I'm hurting myself," mumbled Ru.

"Exactly," said Gwyneth. "For the sake of a *research* project. What's the point of it, really? To discover the artifact's purpose? To get to the bottom of why... of what happened at that dig site? We don't need the Children or the regent or any of them for that. You and me, Archie, we'll create new hypotheses. We'll study all the magic books together."

These words comforted Ru, despite the fact that they were meaningless. Gwyneth was only trying to console her. What she needed were answers, solutions, that only the artifact could provide. But more than that, more than anything, she needed... Well, he was gone.

"Thank you Gwyn, but..."

She trailed off as a figure became visible, approaching with an eerily steady gait, her robe trailing behind her and picking up bits of leaf and petal as she went. It was Nell, her expression solemnly empty as always.

"Miss Delara," Nell said, "Lord D'Luc requests your presence in his office."

"Give her a minute," said Gwyneth, wrapping a protective arm around her friend. "Her nose was just bleeding. She's unwell."

"Immediately," intoned Nell.

"It's fine, I'll go," Ru said, rising slowly and tucking the bloody cloth into a pocket. Her limbs were stiff and cold from the stone bench, her movements stilted.

She followed Nell silently through the garden and into the Tower, avoiding eye contact with everyone they passed. She wasn't ready to be human again. Not yet.

CHAPTER 36

Lord D'Luc's office was too warm. Afternoon sunlight streamed in through a tall window, and a fire burned in the grate despite the fact that it was the middle of summer. Resisting the urge to pull at her collar to ease her breathing, Ru stood just inside the door, glowering. Waiting for him to acknowledge her.

He leaned over a pile of paperwork, his hair falling around his face like spun gold, his pale, silver-ringed hands flipping pages with a graceful lack of urgency. He seemed deeply engrossed, despite the fact that he'd summoned Ru urgently from the gardens. What paperwork he could possibly be working on now, at the Tower, Ru could only guess.

Nell had already gone, leaving Ru alone in the office without an announcement or explanation. Finally, she cleared her throat.

"Ah, Miss Delara," Lord D'Luc said, looking up genially from his paperwork, white teeth flashing. "Do come in, take a seat."

She slid into the leather chair facing his desk, folding her hands in her lap, trying to look composed. Whatever intensity of thought had come over her in the courtyard had left a sick taste in her mouth, a pain in her head. She touched her nose briefly and was relieved to find that her fingers came away clean.

"I suppose you know why I've summoned you."

"To discuss my failure this morning." It wasn't as if his summons had been unexpected. She had gone to the courtyard to hide as much as to think.

He fixed her with an appraising gaze. Backlit from the window, his hair glowed almost white where the sunlight hit it. Haloed, like some figure from an ancient religion. Looking at him now, in the state she was in, Ru wondered why she had thought him so handsome. He was almost *too* perfect in appearance, ethereal, untouchable. Nothing like Fen, whose nose was a bit too large, whose hair was always a mess, whose beard was never fully shaved…

"Focus," said Lord D'Luc. "I see your mind wandering. I require every one of your faculties, please. I will need you to explain to me exactly what you attempted with the artifact this morning, why said attempt failed, and what you plan to do as preparation for your next demonstration."

"When?"

"When what, Miss Delara?"

"When do you want a summary, and when do you request that I perform a second demonstration?" Her words came out dully, without inflection or an ounce of enthusiasm. She had lost all interest in Lord D'Luc, his nonsense, whatever he wanted from her and the artifact.

She didn't need him. She didn't need the regent's funding, her fancy devices, or the Children's prying questions. All she needed was the artifact.

"You know my paper on magic was absolute shit, right?" she added before he could answer her first question. Maybe she could push him away, make him leave her alone, make him give up on the artifact if he believed it to be a farce. An impossible project.

"Everyone laughed when it was published," she went on, meeting Lord D'Luc's cold stare with a fiery one. "Not a soul took it seriously. Because it's a joke. I'm a joke. You'll make a joke of yourself, pursuing some progressive, wonderful outcome with this artifact. It's a rock. A fossil. A remnant of a city long destroyed by minds we can know nothing about, for purposes we'll only ever guess. We will never understand what happened at the Shattered City, whether it was an echo of what came before, or something entirely new. Whatever it was, the artifact is nothing, a pebble, unrelated. May I go now?"

As she spoke, Lord D'Luc listened without reacting in the slightest; no movement or expression betrayed him.

And when she finally finished speaking, he sat up a little straighter in his chair. Tapped a finger against the desk. "I require a written summary by the end of the day, and a second demonstration tomorrow morning. You may go."

∽

IN THE NEXT TWO DAYS, Ru attempted two demonstrations. Both ended as well as the first — in utter failure.

The artifact no longer spoke to Ru as it once had, its connection to her still so weak that she was terrified it would sever at any moment. And with that fear came the knowledge that she had come to rely on the stone's comfort. All that remained in its absence was a stark memory of Lady Maryn's face, a burst of darkness in that desolate crater... and then nothing at all.

Lord D'Luc's eyes chilled increasingly, icier each day that Ru failed to show him anything useful until they were icebergs in his ethereal face. It might have frightened her, once. But Lord D'Luc was no longer the source of anxiety, no longer holding power over Ru.

On the morning of the second demonstration, she had woken to find rusty brown stains on her pillow, her nose crusted with dried blood.

"You need to stop pushing yourself," Gwyneth said, ministering to Ru with the patience of a sister.

"I'm not pushing myself," Ru said, staring out her window at an unseasonably gray day as raindrops scattered the glass. But that was a lie. She was pushing herself — too hard, too far. The blood on her pillow said as much. What else could she do? Lord D'Luc wouldn't let her stop. He demanded demonstrations. He demanded results.

And more than that, Ru wanted to prove to herself that she hadn't lost the artifact altogether, that her convictions about its properties, its magic, hadn't been madness. That she was Ruellian Delara, and Fen's absence wasn't gnawing a pit in her heart with every moment he was gone.

∾

WHEN FEN HAD BEEN absent for almost a week, Ru began convincing herself that everything between them was imagined. That it had been a fever dream, every moment they had shared and every feeling that passed between their hearts was false, a phantasm born of the artifact. A lie.

"You've got to move on," Gwyneth urged her. "You deserve better."

Archie said, "He was a degenerate anyway. That wonderful hair of his was a smokescreen, a distraction. He was always going to break your heart, one way or another."

∾

ON THE TENTH morning since Lord D'Luc had arrived at the Tower, Ru woke, stretching stiff muscles. The sun shone through her curtains, casting soft light across her room. She dressed and went to the mess hall where she drank her coffee, and mindlessly ate a piece of toast.

Then she went to the dungeon.

Lord D'Luc and his dozen Children were there waiting. Pristine in white, they looked like a hoard of dark-eyed, staring angels. Archie and Gwyneth clattered down the stairs after Ru. Professors Obralle and Cadwick were sick and bedridden, along with the rest of their colleagues.

After Lord D'Luc's arrival, the spreading illness had

been the talk of the Tower, according to Archie and Gwyneth. But Ru couldn't be distracted by such things. Not now, not when she needed to focus.

A thick silence hung over the dungeon.

Ru pushed her hair behind her ears and sighed, placing her hands on the table. She stared at the artifact, her frustration with it so heavy and so implacable that she felt like a great wall of ice had grown up inside her, repelling everything in its path — passion, joy, laughter.

Why won't it listen to me, she thought viciously.

Just as she had done every day since Fen's departure, over and over, she tried to bring the golden light forth, to make the artifact react in the way it had done with Fen. It was the only course of action she could think to take, the only thing that wouldn't end in the certain destruction of herself, her friends, and the Tower.

Because no matter how many times she failed in this demonstration, every time she refused to do another, D'Luc forced her hand. He demanded, coerced, and argued. Every time she came to his office, shaking with exhaustion and rage, he demanded that she continue. And each time she tried to reason with him, his words became needles, his every word laced with threat.

And while he never threatened her outright, she read between the lines of his smooth words.

"If you don't do this, I hate to think..."

"If you can't comply, the regent shall be notified, and your place at the Tower... the risk..."

Ru woke often in the night in cold sweats, in the wake of a recurring nightmare that her friends had been emptied of their emotions, soulless and dead-eyed, just like the Children.

Lord D'Luc would not let her rest until either she broke, or the artifact did. So Ru continued to do the only thing she could think of, to desperately reach for that feeling of connection, the warmth, the flowing golden light from before... and instead always found herself in a freezing, empty darkness.

The pain was worse each time, as if the artifact retreated day by day, further from her grasp. She could feel it, still *knew* it was there, called for it, cried out in silence, but it gave her nothing in return.

Her eyes were squeezed shut, hands flat on the table, head beginning to pound with an oncoming migraine. She waited for the telltale warmth of blood on her upper lip.

Fen had abandoned her.

The artifact had abandoned her.

She pushed and pushed, reached and reached, until she came to a final impasse. All was dark and empty.

She was alone now in the black with the headless body of a nameless King's Guard. She was alone with his sightless eyes; alone with a dripping sword. She was alone with Lady Maryn's terror. She was screaming, crying for someone to come and take her, to bring her somewhere safe, to take these things out of her head.

I hate you. The words came from so deep within that she wasn't aware she'd thought them at first.

Fen, Lord D'Luc, the artifact... none were exempt from her ire.

I hate you. The words burned, blasting across the invisible thread between her and the artifact.

I hate you. Then there were screams, someone calling her name from far away, and she fell into a moonlit night licked with flames, white against the black sky.

CHAPTER 37

R u woke in the dark, drenched with sweat.

For a moment she thought she was still in a dream, falling forever into a sky of ink and flame, of paper-white trees on a vast horizon. And then she heard Gwyneth's soft breathing. Her friend was curled up on the settee, which she'd moved next to the bed. Soft blue moonlight caressed her peaceful face as she slept.

An overwhelming tenderness came over Ru. Gwyneth hadn't abandoned her. She had always been there, even when Ru was so unwilling to see beyond the artifact, beyond herself.

She lay back in her pillows, the image of a dream clinging to her waking eyes. She couldn't flush it away; it clung to her, persistent. Her nightclothes sticking to her sweaty skin, she slid out of bed as quietly as she could manage, padding to the chest of drawers where a water jug and a cup sat waiting.

As she lifted the jug, the swirling blackness rose in her mind again, broken only by a moon and stars and flames... and a thought appeared in her mind so suddenly it was like a crackle of white-hot lightning across a dark sky.

The dream, the dark night, and those flames... she had thought they were trees, white against a night sky, so small she couldn't have made them out properly. The illustration from the book she'd taken from the library and promptly forgotten about.

Ru found the book exactly where she'd left it, in a pile on the floor next to her desk. She flipped through it in the moonlight until she found the depiction she remembered. There it was as if ripped from her mind — a black night dotted with stars and an overly large moon. And far below, what she had thought were white trees, were really flames, licking upward toward the vast sky.

Underneath the illustration was a caption:

The ancient god Festra, symbolized here as "Infinite Night" (c. 840, Mekyan archives) visits fiery destruction upon humanity. No longer worshiped by any structured religions, some Mekyan folklore traditions believe that the Destruction of Ordellun-by-the-Sea was brought about by Festra himself, in the form of the traitor Taryel.

She read the caption several times, her sleep-addled brain taking far too long to grasp it. Meaning fell into place with a rush as she realized with a start that she had seen this image before, somewhere else. Fingers shaking, Ru pulled open her desk drawer.

Careful not to make too much noise, she fished around in the drawer until she found what she was looking for: the pamphlet Simon had sent from Mirith. Heart in her throat, she turned it over to the back. And there, just as she had remembered, was the same illustration from the book.

"What are you looking at?"

Gwyneth's voice nearly startled Ru out of her skin.

"Gwyn!" she gasped. "You nearly gave me a heart attack." Ru had been so engrossed in her discovery that she hadn't heard her friend come up behind her in the darkness.

But Gwyneth was distracted, peering over Ru's shoulder at the leaflet in her hands. "Praise the Destroyer, for He anoints with His cleansing fire," she said slowly, sounding out the words. "That's a bit grim."

Ru was already scrambling to her feet, pulling

Gwyneth with her. "That's what the caption says? You can read it?"

"Well, sort of. Everyone unfortunate enough to be born in a noble family learns all the ancient languages," said Gwyneth. "But I've mostly forgotten them, just like everyone else. Why, what is it? Are you all right? Ru, yesterday, the artifact, it knocked you out again."

Ru paused, the leaflet still clutched in her clammy hands. "And?"

Gwyneth's face fell, her expression fracturing. "It's just that... Ru, you've been sleeping for a day and a half. You can't just leap up and start wandering around at night, you have to take things slowly. You don't know what it's been like for Arch and me, we're..." she paused, her voice faltering. "I've been so worried."

Gwyneth shuddered with a quiet sob, tears streaming down her face, and Ru realized with a growing horror that this was her fault. She had allowed her repeated failure, her loss of Fen and the artifact, to overtake her mind and body until she'd become some-thing like an empty shell. She had become so self-ob-sessed, so overcome with the indulgence of her own misery, that she'd spoken directly to the artifact again. It hadn't even *asked* her to. She had simply done it out of spite.

Ru gathered Gwyneth in her arms, pulling her close. "I'm so sorry," she breathed into her friend's hair. "I've been a rotten friend. Rotten."

"You haven't," Gwyneth sniffled, pulling away at last. "I understand. We both do, me and Arch. We've just been so *worried*."

"I know," said Ru, a pang of regret twisting in her gut. "I knew it the whole time and didn't care. I put all of you in danger, *twice*."

"We understand," said Gwyneth. "Truly. I'm just glad you're alive and awake, and... Hartford said this last time you fainted... that it might have taken a toll on your sanity. I couldn't leave your side."

"You're a better friend than I could have asked for if given the choice," Ru said and meant it with every piece of herself. "But Gwyn, I have to show you something. Come sit with me in the moonlight."

Ru showed Gwyneth the two illustrations, explaining how she came across them. How she'd found the book, flipped through it almost at random... how Simon had sent the leaflet as some kind of clue. He had overestimated her ability to draw connections, and more than anything, her ability to read ancient languages. But Ru now finally understood.

When Ru was finished explaining, Gwyneth's expression was incredulous. She twisted a lock of hair around her finger, silvery in the moonlight. "Praise the Destroyer, for He anoints with His cleansing fire," she said, reciting the caption again. "How could we have missed something like this? The Children ... they worship Festra?"

"They worship *Taryel*. This illustration is from the Mekyan archive, and look — some Mekyan folklore traditions equate Festra to Taryel. You said this word means Destroyer? That has to be a reference to Taryel. Who else do we call by that name?"

Gwyneth frowned. "But why would they worship someone who destroyed an entire city? It doesn't make sense. Maybe the illustration is a warning."

Ru shot her a meaningful look. "Read the description again. Festra visits fiery destruction upon humanity. Why would they print this specific image on their leaflets? He anoints with His *cleansing fire*? That doesn't exactly sound promising, Gwyn. Fire doesn't cleanse, it burns. It destroys. Like what Taryel did to Ordellun-by-the-Sea."

"That seems like a bit of a leap to make," Gwyneth murmured, peering at the leaflet and frowning. "And I told you, my languages are rusty. It's probably one of those ancient religious things, frightening people into submission with grim rhetoric. Nobody's actually going to be cleansed with fire."

"Is that much better, in our particular circumstance?" Ru asked, jabbing the leaflet with a finger to emphasize her point. "Would you be more comfortable with Lord

D'Luc poking and prodding at the artifact — at *me* — now knowing the questionable basis of his spiritual doctrine?"

Gwyneth said nothing.

Ru folded the leaflet and held it in shaking hands, speaking her thoughts aloud. "You're probably right, Gwyn. The Children are probably just harmless oddities with outdated notions and antiquated practices. But I don't like it. I don't trust the Children, I don't trust the regent or Lord D'Luc. What he pushed me to do this past week, he was relentless, he…" She paused, shaking her head, willing away the bitterness that gathered in her like a storm cloud. "All I know is that I don't trust him. Whatever he wants from the artifact, from me, it's more important to him than I had thought. More than I can understand. The way he looks at it…"

"It's all right," Gwyneth said, "we won't let him push you anymore. The demonstrations are over."

Ru nodded, blinking back tears of anger and shame. She had trusted Lord D'Luc so fully. And now, looking back on the way he'd spoken to her, the way his eyes glittered in the lamplight of the dungeon… he cared only for himself, for the artifact and what it might give him.

And with a sickening realization, bile rising suddenly in her throat, Ru grabbed Gwyneth's arm. "Gwyn," she breathed. "The artifact."

"The artifact," said Gwyneth, echoing Ru, her expression going from incredulity to wide-eyed shock. "The Shattered City dig site… Do you think the artifact *caused* the Destruction? That they're planning to use it again somehow?"

Ru shook her head. "No. I mean, I don't know, but… Why would the regent, Lord D'Luc, the Children, all invest so much time and money in studying the artifact if they already knew what it was? They can't possibly know what it's for. Nobody does, least of all me." Ru's words spilled out in a desperate stream.

"But Ru, remember how they *found* it. They know *something*."

Cold dread gripped Ru from the inside out as if a frozen fist was squeezing her heart. The dig at the Shattered City, the discovery of the artifact, the specific request for Ru's knowledge of magic, the funding, and now these repeated demonstrations... Lord D'Luc, or the Regent, or both — someone had already suspected that the artifact was not only magic but also capable of producing a destructive force. If Ru's conclusions about the Children were right, if they truly did seek a cleansing fire of some kind... why else would they expend the resources on a dig site at the Shattered City? They'd known the artifact would be there.

And the moment the artifact had shown its true potential in the dungeon, the moment that swirling darkness seeped from it like death, Lord D'Luc had come running. After the very experiment the Children had urged — no, *ordered* — Ru to conduct.

"Gwyneth," Ru said quietly, "Lord D'Luc believes the artifact is a weapon and means to use it. We need to tell the professors."

Her friend's expression, the soft shake of her head, told Ru everything before Gwyneth spoke. "They're all sick," she explained. "Bedridden, delirious. Not one of them can stay awake for longer than a few moments, just enough to eat."

Realization curdled in Ru's stomach. "The Children. As soon as they arrived, the professors started falling ill. This has to be their doing. They want us helpless. We need to get out of the Tower, and the artifact is coming with us."

Gwyneth grimaced, glancing away, out at the moonlit night. "Do you truly think... Maybe we should sleep on it, Ru. Talk it over with Arch?"

"Are you mad?" Ru said, already moving to her wardrobe to pull out a pack, to change into traveling clothes. "I'm not waiting around a second longer to see what Lord D'Luc does with the artifact now that the Tower is essentially at his disposal. You saw what happened with the last demonstration. Do you think he'll stop there? He'll push me until I break, or until I lose control completely, killing us all in the process."

Not waiting for Gwyneth's response, Ru knelt to wrench her pack from the bottom of her wardrobe, hastily shoving shirts and underclothes inside. A few moments later, she felt Gwyneth's presence at her side, calm and quiet.

"How can I help?" her friend asked, and relief swept through Ru.

"There's a tin of cookies in the bottom drawer of my desk. For emergencies."

Gwyneth nodded, then scrambled to her feet to fetch the cookies.

By the time she returned with the tin, Ru had finished shoving clothes haphazardly into her pack. She shoved the tin inside, fastened the pack tightly, and set it aside. "Thanks," she breathed, catching Gwyneth's eye. They shared a solemn look, and Ru knew there was no need to say anything else.

"Do you need to change? Pack a bag?" Ru eyed Gwyneth's simple woolen dress and boots.

"I'm fine," Gwyneth said. Her expression was rock-hard, her lips set in a determined line. "I'll be... fine. But where will we go?"

Ru shrugged out of her sweat-soaked clothes, not caring about modesty. Hastily she pulled a pair of thick trousers from her wardrobe, a plain white shirt, and a gray wool waistcoat. Over that she threw on an overcoat, shoving her feet into dirt-caked boots.

"My family's house in Mirith," Ru said, pulling her hair into a bun, and securing it at the nape of her neck. Then she bent, picking up her pack and slinging it over one shoulder. "From there, we'll send for Simon."

Gwyneth shook her head. "No, not your house. If Lord D'Luc comes looking for you, if the regent sends anyone after you, that's the first place they'll look. We can stay at my second cousin's estate just outside the city. They couldn't possibly guess we'd go there, and she won't ask questions."

"Gwyn," Ru said, breathless, "you're an angel."

She smiled, despite everything. "I'm just a good friend."

"It's the same thing," said Ru. "Let's go."

The corridor was dark and quiet. The hour was so late that even the Tower's night owls had gone to bed, and in an hour or two, the first glimmers of sunlight would begin to edge over the horizon.

"We have to get Archie," Gwyneth hissed, stopping dead as soon as they slipped from Ru's room.

Ru had already begun to stride away in the opposite direction, toward the stairs. She spun on her heel, shaking her head. "He's terrible at riding," she hissed back. "He'll only be a hindrance. We don't have *time*."

"You're worse at riding than he is," Gwyneth protested in low but aggressive tones.

"We don't have time to explain everything."

Gwyneth stood her ground, hands on hips. "You *know* Arch, he'll understand immediately. We won't even have to explain. He'll just come. Don't you trust him?"

Ru sighed, accepting defeat. "Fine. Go get him, and make sure he packs food. I'm going to the dungeon. I'll meet you at the stables."

They exchanged a wordless nod, Ru knowing with certainty that she was plunging herself and her friends into more trouble than they'd ever encountered, more danger than they could probably contemplate. But if the alternative was cleansing fire... what choice did she have?

Chewing her lip, heart hammering so loudly she thought it would wake the entire Tower, Ru hurried toward the dungeon.

~

THE DUNGEON WAS horrible at night. Cold, echoing, drenched in depthless shadows; every pocket of darkness set Ru's nerves on edge. She imagined the Children bursting out from the blackness, their eyes dark and shining, and shuddered.

Fumbling to find the nearest lamp, Ru stumbled in

the blackness until she managed to light it, the wick catching at last. A steady orange glow lit her way, and she edged toward the center of the dungeon, between the workstations, until the lamplight illuminated the central wooden table.

And there, as always, sat the artifact, wrapped in its blanket.

But tonight, for the first time, the bundle of cloth looked like a threat. With as much care as she could muster with shaking fingers, Ru gathered up the artifact and shoved it into her pack. She hurriedly smothered it with clothes in case she was stopped, in case her pack was searched.

She wished she could leave a fake artifact in its place, shroud something else in a blanket and place it on the table, but she didn't have another blanket handy and there simply wasn't time. She should have thought, wished she had time to plan. A seedling of doubt began to grow – was she overreacting? Moving too fast?

No — there was no time to question herself. She was certain of what she knew, certain that Lord D'Luc and the Children were not to be trusted. Worse than that, they were dangerous. Death dressed in angels' clothes.

Dousing the lamp, her heart still racing, Ru hurried up the stairs and out of the dungeon.

∿

THE WALK to the stables from the dungeon wasn't long, a matter of minutes. But in Ru's agitated state, in the silence of deep night, it felt interminable.

She stopped at every corner, hugging the walls and clinging to the shadows, convinced she would run into one of the Children at any moment. Despite her terror, she made it all the way to the Tower's main entrance without coming across another soul. The front vestibule, high-ceilinged and lanced with moonlight, might have struck her as peaceful at any other time. Instead, it made her shiver, the silence of it, the shadows.

Ru crept forward and unlocked one of the great

double doors, pushing it open just enough to squeeze through. Then, turning, she eased it closed behind her. With luck, nobody would notice that the door had been unlocked in the night.

Then she spun, readying herself to dash through the courtyard to the stables. And found herself face to face with Inda.

Ru's heart stopped.

The woman in white caught Ru's gaze with her empty one, her robes billowing up in a night breeze.

"Miss Delara," Inda said, unruffled as ever. "What brings you to the courtyard at this time of night?"

Ru grasped for words. She considered bolting, pushing past the woman to the stables, and fleeing on horseback. But she couldn't abandon her friends, couldn't separate them. And all Inda had to do was raise the alarm — Ru wouldn't get far. She would have to lie, then. But what would Inda believe? What did Inda know of Ru that would convince her this was an innocent walk, taking the air, nothing more?

The artifact seemed to weigh a thousand pounds in her pack. Inda would know it was there. Surely she would suspect.

She would guess.

"Last I heard," Inda went on when Ru didn't answer immediately, "you were sick in bed."

"I was," stammered Ru, "but I felt a little better. I came out for some fresh air."

"With a bulging pack over your shoulder, I see." She blinked. "Why?"

Ru's breath came in shallow gulps, she was unable to think, it would be impossible to lie convincingly. "I..." she swallowed. "I was..."

"She was meeting me."

Both Ru and Inda turned to see who had spoken.

Ru knew the moment she'd heard the first word, but couldn't allow herself to believe it. Not until she saw him, not until she was sure.

It was Fen.

CHAPTER 38

Fen stood in the moonlight, hands in his pockets like a young schoolboy caught in the act of breaking a rule. He was taller than Ru had remembered, somehow, his hair caught in the breeze, strands of it caressing his forehead, his ears. He seemed almost nonchalant, as if his sudden appearance in the courtyard hadn't ripped the very breath from Ru's lungs.

"Meeting you," Inda repeated, staring at Fen. "Why?"

He smiled, rubbing the back of his neck with one hand. "For a nighttime picnic. I left her a note to meet me in the courtyard when she was feeling better. I've been waiting."

"A nighttime picnic," said Inda. "For what purpose?"

Without warning Fen strode forward, wrapping Ru in his arms, enfolding her in warmth. She froze. She had waited for this moment, yearned every second for his touch, the warmth of him. As if he hadn't held her heart in his hands, open and yielding, only to crush it. Then he curled a finger, resting it under her chin, tilting her face upward.

Ru held her breath and squeezed her eyes shut. His chest rose and fell against her, steady as he had always been, an anchor in the storm. She felt a soft exhale of breath, and then his mouth on hers.

Fen, her every nerve cried out. She was trembling, helpless in his arms. And though she wanted to resist him, to make it known how much he had hurt her, there was no stopping her lips from parting, allowing him to deepen the kiss. Tears stung the corners of her eyes, still held tightly shut.

And then he broke the kiss, stepping back away from her. She opened her eyes as his warmth fled her body like a ghost of a memory. She stumbled, her knees almost giving way in the face of it.

How dare he? How dare he reappear like this, kiss her so easily, like it was all nothing?

And all the while Inda, expression dull and lifeless, looked on.

"Do you really want to know?" Fen asked, winking lasciviously at Inda.

"No," said Inda.

"You don't want all the details?" Fen pressed, laughing. "I had planned to kiss her, as I did just then, and..." but Inda had already turned, white robes fluttering, and was hurrying back into the Tower, the tall wooden door slamming shut in her wake.

Ru stared up at Fen, her emotions warring in her gut, churning until she was sick with it. He was the last person she had expected to see tonight. She'd expected never to see him again. Angrily she brushed the hint of a tear from one eye, breathing hard, unable to look away.

He was fearsome now in the moonlight, his overcoat whipping against his legs. He watched her with clear grey eyes, unreadable. She wanted to bury her face in his chest, to cry until she lost her breath, to drown in the relief of his presence. She wanted to slap him, to make him hurt as much as she had, to shove a blade of agony through his heart. But she couldn't let herself feel it, she had to pull herself together.

There were bigger things to worry about, and unless Fen had come to help her, he was a distraction.

"What are you doing?" she breathed, still shaking, nearly choking on all the words she longed to say.

"Rescuing you from Inda."

There was space between them. Not too much, not so much that Ru felt compelled to move closer, but at that moment it felt infinite, a gap between stars. It had been over a week since she'd seen him. Since he had disappeared. She had given up on him. Yet here he was.

She bit the inside of her mouth to keep the tears at bay. "Why?"

"I could ask you the same," he replied, tossing a meaningful glance at her pack, her field clothes.

"You left," said Ru, spitting the words like venom, hoping they would find their mark.

Fen let out a long breath, glancing away. "I know. There was something I had to do."

Her bottom lip trembled and she hated herself for it, hated the way her words were soft and broken: "You left without saying goodbye."

"I'm sorry." Regret shone in his eyes along with something that might have been grief.

It was too late. "Isn't that nice," spat Ru, and with that she let her anger overtake her heartbreak, her relief. She grasped at the selfishness of him, the impertinence. How dare he disappear from her life for so long, without a word, and reappear just in the nick of time. To *rescue* her.

He had no idea what she'd been through.

She bit back tears, standing firm as he tried to reach out to her. She backed away, teeth almost clattering with pent-up emotion. "No." Her voice shook. "You *left* me."

"I never meant to stay away that long," he said. There wasn't a warning of a lie in his eyes, and Ru hoped she knew him well enough to know. "I was angry. Confused."

"So was I," she bit back.

"Yes, but... Ru, I'm sorry. I should have told you I was going, but... I had time to think while I was gone, too much time. Some things became clear to me, things about you, about us. I need to speak with you."

Ru snorted, her fingers clutching the straps of her pack, white-knuckled. "Funny how you had to disappear, to abandon me, in order to find some personal clarity."

"Ru..."

"What?" she hissed. "Tell me. We're speaking now. What lovely revelations did you have on your trip? I'll tell you what revelations *I* had. At first, I was fine. I found my way, found direction. But Hugon pushed me... I pushed *myself*, too hard. I reached my limit, and you weren't there. I needed you. And everything went wrong. I did the one thing I promised never to do again. I spoke to the artifact. And you know what, Fen? If you had stayed, if you hadn't abandoned me..." her voice cracked on the word *abandoned*, and she had to take a moment to compose herself. She wanted him to regret it, wanted him to feel responsible for what he'd done, leaving her alone with Lord D'Luc's fervent demands. She had been pushed too hard and too far, desperate for something the artifact couldn't give her.

She pressed a palm to her eye, willing the tears not to fall. She didn't want Fen to see her vulnerable, not now. She wanted him to hate himself. "If you hadn't abandoned me, it wouldn't have happened," she said through gritted teeth. "If you had stayed, I wouldn't have done it."

They stood in strained silence, Ru's breaths jagged, her eyes stinging. Where were Gwyneth and Archie? She needed to leave, to get away from Fen, even though her heart was screaming at her to close the distance between them. Her hurt was too great to open herself to him again.

"Ru, look at me."

She shook her head. She could bear to look at the moon shadows on the flagstones, at the fireflies in the distance, but not at Fen.

"I understand if you can never forgive me." His voice was so quiet she could hardly hear him. "I... if I'd known... Everything I've done since I met you, Ru, has been for you. It may seem otherwise, and I know I've been a fool, I know I hurt you. But I'm still yours. *Yours*, you understand? Nothing can change that."

She took a shaky breath and finally looked up to face him. He wore his old black leathers, and except for a slightly fuller beard and the warmth that came with looking at someone familiar, he looked the same he had as the morning Ru had first met him.

Yet, there was something more to him now, a depth and a sadness that only became apparent as Ru got to know him. He watched her intently, a worry line forming between his dark brows.

Ru thought she would have come to love him if he had only stayed.

"Thank you for everything you've done," she said. "I will always be grateful that you saved my life."

There was a sound from the Tower, and she and Fen turned to see Archie and Gwyneth inching their way outside.

"Ru!" Gwyneth hissed, hurrying toward her. Then she stopped short, seeing the second figure in the moonlight. "Fen, *good lord*. Where did you come from?"

"That's what I'd like to know," said Archie, following after Gwyneth, his expression tight with mistrust.

Ru turned back to Fen, clenching her jaw. "He was just saying goodbye."

"Where have you been?" Gwyneth asked, her lip curling as she gave Fen a once-over. "You left Ru exactly when she needed you most. She almost *died*."

A look of agony crossed Fen's face, so quickly Ru thought she almost imagined it. "I know," he said. "I'm sorry."

"It doesn't matter anymore," Ru managed to say, pulling her pack securely onto her shoulder, busying her hands with pointless things so they wouldn't see her shaking. "Let's go, Arch. Gwyn. Now."

Without waiting for Fen to reply, she took off through the courtyard, toward the stables. She heard hurried footsteps behind her, Gwyneth and Archie rushing to catch up.

Gwyneth pulled at her sleeve. "Ru, what... why is Fen..." she gasped, but Ru sped onward, ignoring her friend's questions, until they arrived at the stable.

They would have to saddle their horses and set off without delay. Ru knew Inda wouldn't go back to bed after seeing her in the courtyard. She would tell the others, and they would come looking for her. If any of the Children went to check on the artifact now, they would know exactly what Ru was doing and where to find her.

"Get your horses," Ru hissed, "we should be gone already. Inda saw me in the courtyard. With Fen. She left us, but she won't keep this to herself. I would rather not be here to find out what the Children will do if they catch us."

Ru made her way into the dark stable and began saddling a taciturn gelding. She had ridden him before, knew he was good-mannered and able to travel for long distances.

Looking around to make sure none of the Children had crept into the stables behind them, she fished the bundled artifact out of her pack and slid it inside her waistcoat. It would be safer there, more secure. She was in the process of shoving it into one of the saddlebags when Fen strode up beside her.

"Where are you going?" he asked.

She jumped. Why wouldn't he just leave? She didn't need him now. He had forfeited his right to her.

"Nowhere," she said, her tone icy.

"It's the middle of the night. You've packed for a journey. You're clearly sneaking out, trying not to be seen." He reached for her, and before she could move away or protest, he cupped her face in his hands. His voice was low when he spoke, his fingers cool on her hot, angry face. "What did I say about putting yourself in harm's way?"

His skin against hers, the deeply accented voice that played in her mind at the darkest hours of the night, his return after days of believing she might never see him again… her heart continued its slow, slow crumble.

She closed her eyes, trying to wish him away. "You said don't."

"Let me come with you," he said, desperation in the shadows of his words. "I'll protect you. I'm your instrument. Use me. Just tell me where you're going."

"Ru!" came the hushed call from Archie, outside the stable. "We're ready, let's go."

"I will do *anything*," Fen murmured, lowering his head until their foreheads were touching. "I'll spend my life repenting for leaving. Let me come with you."

Weakness. That was all Ru felt now, hating herself for it, but welcoming it. Her knees were unsteady from the closeness of him. Her stubbornness was relenting for Fen, and he knew it, but she didn't care. Just as she had always given way to the artifact, she did the same for Fen. And it felt right, it was comfort. It was home. She needed Fen. Her body demanded him, and she wouldn't be the one to refuse.

Something in Ru unfurled, a bloom at the touch of spring, the artifact's voice against her. The closer Fen came, the brighter it burned. She couldn't resist it completely, though her mind was still clear. She raised herself up on tiptoe, relenting just enough to curve her arms around his neck, inhaling him, the smell of snow and storm.

"We're going to Mirith," she breathed, her lips brushing his windswept hair, the shell of his ear. "With the artifact. It's not safe at the Tower. It doesn't matter why. Fen..." she buried her face in his neck, pressed her mouth to his throat.

Then she lifted her face to take his mouth with hers, slow and soft, savoring the joy of it, the feel of his lips, his hands in her hair, at her hips, under her waistcoat... she bit back a moan. She had wanted this every moment since the night he left, yearned for it, and her body was too eager to respond to him.

"Fen," she gasped, using every ounce of her mental strength to return to the present moment, the need for haste. "I have to go."

"Take me with you."

She pulled away, eyes stinging. Though everything inside of her was drawn to Fen, though she yearned to crumble before him and lay her soul bare, she held back. It took all her strength to do it. And in her heart she erected a wall, cutting him out, putting an end to it. Letting him go.

"I'm sorry," she said. "If you had stayed..." She swung

herself into the saddle, gripped the reins in her still-unsteady hands.

Fen watched her silently, his face an unreadable mask.

"Goodbye, Fen."

As she rode out of the stable, she took a long breath of night air. She hadn't believed she could do it, hadn't been sure she would. But there were bigger things at stake. Her heart would heal. Biting back hot tears, ignoring the gaping hole in her chest, she gave the nod to Archie and Gwyneth. They turned, urging their horses forward, toward the road.

Instinctively, thoughtlessly, Ru reached for the artifact. It was a habit now, born of constantly looking for it, aching for it, her need to be close to it in its absence. The same absence as Fen's. She frowned as the tether between her and the artifact seemed to pull, to lengthen as she rode.

"Wait," she said, voice faltering, calling out to her friends as a sickness gripped her stomach. Sour terror rose in her throat as she realized something was missing; something was wrong.

They halted and turned to stare at her, eyes wide; they must have heard the alarm in her tone.

Wordlessly, she pressed the spot where she had nestled the artifact, safely against her ribs, and felt nothing. Nothing. Refusing to believe, she wrenched open her waistcoat and held it wide.

The artifact was no longer there.

As if in slow motion, Ru twisted in the saddle, turning back to the stables where Fen had been. There he stood, bathed in moonlight, as if waiting for this moment. His expression was unreadable to Ru, but even from a distance, his eyes seemed to glitter, hard and dark.

For a split second, Ru's world stood still.

Then Fen broke the stillness, tracing a strange motion in the air with his fingers. There was a loud crackle, a wavering, tight feeling in the air. Like the static shock before a lightning strike.

One second Fen was there, dark eyes shining.

In the next, he was gone.

All that remained was a blooming sphere of what appeared to be black lightning, just where he had stood. It was so nonsensical, so inexplicable that Ru almost *laughed*.

The lightning flickered for a moment and then it, too, sputtered and disappeared.

Ru turned back to the others, numb with shock. "He has it," she said. "Fen has the artifact."

CHAPTER 39

As if in a trance, Ru rode up to where Archie and Gwyneth waited, a few yards away. Archie's brows were furrowed, his lips pursed with indignation. The moonlit road stretched out beyond them — they should have been on it by now, riding at breakneck speed to put distance between them and the Children.

"How?" Archie demanded when Ru was close enough to hear his lowered, stricken tone. "When?"

Gwyneth was staring at Ru with wide-eyed disbelief. "Where... What did he do? Where did he go?" She glanced at Ru, then back at the stable where Fen had vanished into a sphere of crackling black lightning.

"He pickpocketed me," Ru spat, remembering with perfect clarity the sensation of Fen's deft hands inside her jacket, distracting her so thoroughly that she had been completely taken for a fool. It had never once occurred to her that he might lie to her. That he might *use* her, like some piece of machinery to toss aside once it had served its purpose. All those words about how much she meant to him, how he was hers, her *instrument*... They were lies. A trick to worm his way into her heart, to gain her trust.

She had been so naive. So unbelievably foolish.

Tears threatened, a twisted knot in her throat making it hard to breathe. But she wasn't going to cry, she couldn't let her emotions get the better of her now. They only had one choice.

"But what happened?" Archie was saying. "Where's he gone?"

"Magic," said Ru, half distracted as she wracked her brain with what felt like a thousand calculations of a thousand possibilities. "He used magic. He *vanished*. I hadn't been sure that my exact theories were correct, the displacement of particles... but he must have hidden it from us the whole time..." her mind was reeling, the truth of it coming slowly, bit by bit.

Fen wasn't a traveling historian. He was a mage, a sorcerer, a thing of myth. And he had known it, hid it from her. He could have *shown* her, he could have turned her world on its head. Instead, he had kept secrets. Lied to her. And now, betrayed her.

"Ru?" Gwyneth ventured, twisting her reins in one fist, anxious. "Did you say magic?"

Ru shushed her, frowning.

She considered every knowable solution. Fen was a wielder of magic. And he had found her at the Shattered City, at the center of the crater, naked and alone with the artifact. Fen hadn't come there by chance — he was looking for something. The dig site, he had said, out of curiosity. But that was a lie.

He had come for the artifact. How he could have known it was there, how he might have guessed, she had no idea. But instead of whatever he might have expected to find, he'd found Ru. And for some twisted purpose, he had decided to follow her all over Navenie instead of immediately taking the stone from her. He had waited until the last possible second, waited until they were in the stable, ready to leave.

But why?

He'd asked to come with them, almost begged for it. And Ru had told him where they were bound: Mirith. He wouldn't be going to Mirith, then. If he wanted the artifact, and didn't care about Ru's involvement, he wouldn't have waited so long to take it. Ru's admission that they were taking it to Mirith... that was when they embraced, when he reached into her waistcoat.

She bit her lip, thinking.

Fen didn't have a home to go to. Then... factor in the revelation that he could use magic and, based on her theories on displaced matter, if that was his method, then he could be... well, anywhere. But where would Fen want to go? Where would he bring the artifact? He had seemingly been as dedicated as she had to the research, had been truly curious, interested...

"I think he's gone to the Shattered City," Ru said, finally.

Gwyneth paled. "He's what?"

"He brought it back to its place of origin. He needs it for something, something he can't get at the Tower or at Mirith. He stayed with me, he helped us study it. I don't think he knows what it is, or if he does he only has a theory. This is his last chance, his final option to get whatever he needs from that stone. And if I were him, I would take it back to the Shattered City, where I found it. That's where he's gone."

She expected her friends to be skeptical, perhaps to argue, to question the magic, to delve into detail that Ru deemed irrelevant. Instead, they accepted her word. Ru led the way, Gwyneth and Archie following behind, as they set off on the road southeast toward Ordellun-by-the-Sea, the Shattered City.

～

THE JOURNEY from the Cornelian Tower to the Shattered City was a little longer than three days, four at a leisurely riding pace. Ru was determined to get there in two.

They would ride past Dig Site 33, continuing south on that road until they came to the miles-wide crater on the southern coast. The journey she had taken with the King's Riders, when Rosylla had tossed her sweets as they rode... it felt to Ru like several lifetimes ago, a distant past that had been so easy and kind.

There had been so much death, confusion, and pain in the past weeks that Ru felt as if an entirely new Ruellian Delara made the journey this time.

Gwyneth and Archie conversed intermittently as the three of them rode. Their voices were always low, and when they spoke to Ru, they seemed, at times, afraid of her.

Ru understood why. A combination of rock-hard determination and rage had bloomed up from within and curled around her from the inside out, a sort of armor, a shield from anything that might deter or distract her from the only thing that mattered: finding Fen and the artifact.

There was plenty of time, *too much* time, to mull over everything that had happened as they rode. Every interaction with Fen, every moment they'd shared that had felt meaningful and real and which, now, Ru understood to have been false.

Even the swirling golden light, the night of the party... for all Ru knew Fen had used his own magic to trick her into succumbing to him, trusting him. She fought down a constant swell of nausea every time she recalled her inexplicable attraction to him, her need for him, the way her heart had opened up for him without restraint.

Every urge she had felt in his presence could have been manufactured.

Ru tried not to drown in such thoughts, in a miasma of her own making, and blocked them off as best she could. Pushed them aggressively aside, locked away at the darkest corner of her mind, behind the wall she'd built around her heart.

After nearly a day of hard riding, darkness fell once again over Navenie. Ru barely remembered yesterday's sunrise, had hardly noted as the sun made its crawl across the sky. The night was loud with bats and insects, and the panting of their horses. A few hours after sundown, they rode past Dig Site 33. Ru gazed out over the uneven dirt, shadowed now, a desolate landscape. She thought of the vases she'd uncovered there, each different and perfect in its own way, simple and unassuming. An easier life, perhaps, but... she wouldn't let herself finish the thought. Questions of *what if* would only torture her.

"We'll stop to water the horses," Ru said, calling a halt. "There's a stream just over that hill."

The three friends dismounted, wordlessly wiping down their sweating horses before leading them around the dig site to where a small creek flowed through a bed of ferns. The water was cold and clear, probably runoff from a mountain glacier. Ru cupped some in her hands, splashing it over her face.

When they had all drunk their fill, they returned to the road. Ru found it hard to move away from the dig site, the place that represented an old life, an old Ru. There were still holes in the ground where tents had been pitched, where Ru had stored her vases for safekeeping. Night breezes carried dirt in eddies and swirls over the site, and the moon blanketed everything in a soft haze of white-blue.

"Let's go," Ru said, nearly choking on the knot that rose in her throat.

They rode in silence until the sun began to rise, cresting over woodland. A flock of birds took to the sky in the west.

"I think we should start considering the implications if Taryel really did use the artifact to destroy Ordellun-by-the-Sea," said Gwyneth, her words startling in the soft light of sunrise. Her horse made a soft sound of disapproval, shaking its head with a jangle of metal and leather.

Ru knew this had been coming, that it was a concern they had doubtlessly all been mulling in her heads, never uttering it aloud. Ru had almost hated to let the likelihood of it sink in. Festra, Taryel, the artifact... When it came down to it, were they one and the same?

"I bloody well hope you're wrong," said Archie, turning in the saddle. Sunrise shone pink-orange against his face and gleamed in his hair. "To think of that stone sitting in the Tower, in the same room as us, this whole time…"

"But what could Fen possibly want with it?" mused Gwyneth. "Is he in league with Lord D'Luc?"

"No," said Ru, a cool wind buffeting her face. In the distance, she thought she saw a fox darting between the trees, where the woods thickened. "He wouldn't have taken it from the Tower if that were the case. He has his own purpose."

"And what could that purpose *be*?" persisted Gwyneth, twisted in the saddle to frown at Ru, who rode between and slightly behind her friends. "What could he want with his own magical stone? How many other young women do you suppose he's terrorized on his way to finding it?"

Ru almost smiled at that. "None, I hope. I suspect he doesn't know what it is. Or he didn't, when he found it. Found me. And I believe our goals were aligned for a while. But something changed when I told him where we were taking it. He didn't want to be parted from it. He begged to come with us, and only when I refused did he steal it."

"Well if he's looking to destroy another city," Archie said, "follow in Taryel's footsteps or something equally pointless, then I don't see what he'll accomplish at the Shattered City."

"He's looking for answers," Ru said.

"To what?" Gwyneth asked, indignant. She had been bristling with visible anger since they'd left the Tower, and Ru knew it was aimed at Fen. "I'll never forgive him for what he's done. The hurt he's caused."

"Not to mention the magic," Archie added. "Aren't you astounded, Ru? What will this do for your paper? Your academic career?"

The magic. Archie had been asking as they rode, and Ru always deflected. She had asked herself the same question: *Aren't you astounded*? And she had to own that she wasn't. Perhaps it was the fact that she'd always believed, despite the lack of evidence. Perhaps it was the artifact's pull on her, that invisible thread that said *magic*, every time she reached out to it. But more than that, a cloud hung heavy over her feelings, over the wonder of it. How could she feel wonder, excitement, or curiosity, when all that Fen had left to her was a broken heart?

Ignoring Archie's question, Ru squinted as the sun crested the horizon, bright and eager. "Time to go," Ru said, nudging her gelding gradually into a canter, then a full-on gallop. She heard the others responding in kind, their horses kicking up dust in the morning light, nearer and nearer to the Shattered City.

THEY ARRIVED at the crater just after nightfall. Their horses were exhausted, and Ru's legs shook from the exertion of pushing her horse so near to his limit. But there would be no more pell-mell gallop to the Shattered City. They were here.

The sea was so mutinous that night, so loud in its endless crash against the rocky shore, that its roar could be heard far inland, where Ru and her friends rode slowly down into the crater. Stars pricked a velvet black sky. As they rode, a dark shape formed, rising up from the center of the crater. Ru thought at first it was a cluster of the stone fingers that dotted the landscape, but as they approached she saw with confusion that it appeared to be... a city.

Like giant crystals or stalagmites, still distant and difficult to see in the darkness, rose the towers and spires and steeples of a great city. Ordellun-by-the-Sea, the city of legend, somehow in the here and now.

"What *is* that?" Archie said, standing up in his stirrups to peer into the gloom. "Buildings?"

But there was something wrong. The light of the moon cut through the city like glass, and for a second the entire city wavered, like a reflection in a still pool when something disturbs the water.

"It's Ordellun-by-the-Sea," breathed Gwyneth, voicing Ru's thoughts.

"It's a projection of some kind," murmured Ru. "A facsimile of the real thing. A ghost."

"It's cursed, is what it is," added Archie.

"Come on," said Ru, dismounting and starting forward toward the ghostly city on foot. They were near enough that she could see it all clearly, the spectral windows, wavering stone walls. "Leave the horses, they'll get spooked."

She heard them asking questions as they dismounted and followed, offering theories, but their voices were muffled and distant — her own thoughts were far too loud. Calculation after calculation tumbled through her brain, one after another, none of them answering the simple question: *How?* A projection of a destroyed city, in the middle of the night...

Fen was here. And so was the artifact. But where had this vision come from?

As they continued toward the city, Ru felt the artifact's touch, its tether growing brighter, stronger by the minute. The connection was still weaker than it had been in the past, a background noise, a sound she had to focus on to hear. Yet the certainty of its presence inside that unearthly city was foremost in Ru's mind, driving her forward.

And wherever the artifact was, Fen would be.

They made their way slowly through the city, as if in a dream. They passed through a great arched gateway, along roads, through markets, and past shopfronts, all perfectly realized, all as ephemeral as a cloud or a warm exhale in cold air. They passed churches and fine houses, parks and gardens, all as empty and silent and ghostly as the last. No one spoke as they walked.

Ru's blood ran cold with dread.

Eventually, they came to what seemed to be the center of the city, where a great palace — no, a stronghold — rose up before them. A central square led to the palace entrance, perfectly symmetrical.

And in the center of the square knelt a man.

CHAPTER 40

The man was dressed all in black, a cloak flowing out from his shoulders and spreading around him on the flagstones. He was pale, his face gaunt, his long black hair falling lank over his shoulders. And then, just like the city all around them, the figure's image wavered slightly, and the illusion was broken.

The man was part of the projection. As they watched, dumbstruck, the figure pressed his palms to the ground where he knelt. He seemed to mutter something, and as he spoke, a writhing darkness began to rise from his body. Ru had seen something like it before.

It was the same darkness, impenetrable and impossible, that had seeped from the artifact when she first touched it.

She held her breath, watching, enraptured.

And then, like a silent thunderclap, the darkness burst outward from the kneeling figure like an explosion, filling their eyes and noses and mouths with night.

Ru felt panic bubbling up in her and clasped Gwyneth's hand. "Gwyn," she breathed. "Arch?"

But before either of them could reply, the darkness was gone. They were still in the ghostly city, standing in that bizarrely waving square, and... just as before, there knelt the pale black-clad figure.

"It's looping," murmured Ru. *Taryel*, she thought. The figure, the darkness spreading outward from him...

"What is?" said Archie.

"The projection," said Gwyneth, impatient. "But where did it come from? How long has it been doing this?"

"Two days," said a voice behind them, and they all whirled.

It was Fen. Unshaven and more visibly exhausted than Ru had ever seen him. His eyes, usually so clear and bright, were glazed and edged with red, heavy dark circles hung beneath them.

He held the artifact in his bare hands, casually, as if it was nothing. A simple stone.

"Two days I've been watching it," he went on, taking advantage of their stunned silence. "Over and over. I didn't foresee you coming here, I'll admit. I thought certainly you would stay at the Tower, alert the regent, perhaps send out a regiment of King's Guards to seek me out and apprehend me. But you three? Here, in two days?" He shook his head. "If it helps you any, the projection is useless. I've discovered nothing."

Ru stared, refusing to believe what she now suspected, what she knew in her heart to be true. "Is it yours?" she managed. It took everything in her not to turn tail and bolt.

"The projection?" Fen said. "Yes. It's mine."

Gwyneth spluttered. "*Yours*? Is this more magic, then? Why didn't you just *tell* us you could… could…" she waved a hand.

Fen looked at her in the way a teacher looks at a pupil who is so close to understanding a concept but not quite there yet. "Because I would have been on the table right alongside this thing," he said, holding up the artifact.

Goosebumps formed on Ru's skin, and a chill ran up her spine.

"So what's going on here, then?" Archie demanded, finding his voice at last. "You stole the artifact, brought it to this hell hole, just to sit in the middle of a spectrous city and watch a loop of this… whatever this is?"

Just then, the blackness exploded over them again,

oppressive, and just as quickly it was gone. Again, the figure knelt in the center of the square.

"Fen," Ru said, choosing her words carefully. Knowing that any misplaced question, any wrong move, could be disastrous. She asked, though she already suspected she knew the answers now. "Why did you take the artifact? Why did you bring it here?"

He rubbed a hand over his face, the gesture so familiar yet so strange in this place. "The longer I watch, the less sense it makes. I was looking for answers. I thought if I came here, with the artifact, returned it to its place of origin... but watch. *There*. He places his hands flat on the ground. He says the words. And in a minute we'll be consumed with darkness again, and for what? Surely there is something I missed. *Surely* here, with me, the artifact... surely what I felt in *here* the moment it was found, it was for a purpose."

At the word *here* he pressed a hand to his chest briefly, grimacing as he did.

Ru's heart sank further into her gut, upended. With every word he spoke, the more certain she was of the truth.

"Speak clearly," Archie said, just as the darkness enveloped them again. "Ugh, can't you make this horrible illusion stop? It's making me ill."

"Shut *up*, Arch," Ru snapped, never taking her gaze from Fen, even as the darkness choked them. "Are you that thick? It's the Destruction. Taryel, kneeling in the square. And Fen... he's..." her conviction wavered. What if she was wrong? To accuse Fen of something like that, something so terrible, so impossible; she would have to be certain beyond a shadow of a doubt.

Fen stepped toward Ru, eyes shining. He looked almost mad, lost in some labyrinth of the mind. "I know you feel it," he said, his voice low, just for her. "The artifact speaks to you in the same way it speaks to me."

She clenched her fists at her sides, willing herself to remain strong, to breathe. Just the sight of him made her want to melt, to crumble. A harsh sea wind whipped at her, catching at her overcoat, stinging her face. The spectral buildings did nothing to block the chill. "I knew it affected you," she replied, shivering, trying not to show how cold she was, how afraid. "That night in my room. But I thought... I thought I was the conduit."

Fen turned away, watching the cloaked figure perform his strange ritual again.

"There are some things in this world that make sense," he said, loud enough now that Archie and Gwyneth could hear. "That can be explained by science. That are easily quantified, calculated, represented by numbers and facts, and organized into the correct categories. Most things are like that. But this..." he held up the artifact, its blue-black surface shining darkly in the moonlight. "Centuries ago, it was taken from me. Stolen from my body. Wrenched is probably the most accurate term. And only now, only since meeting you, Ru... only since growing close to you, have I been able to discover what it is. Though what it *means*... another matter entirely."

"Stop talking nonsense," spluttered Archie.

He and Gwyneth had huddled close together, arms around each other, as much to protect from the cold as for comfort. She felt painfully alone then, standing between Fen and her friends, the wind whipping at her body like a punishment.

"The artifact isn't yours, Fen," added Gwyneth, just as the darkness spread to engulf them again. "Is it?"

"No," said Ru, and as she spoke her hair slipped from its bun, falling loose around her face as the wind picked up, carrying it aloft. She gazed through the darkness at Fen, daring him to admit it. Daring him to speak the truth. "It's not his. It was dug up here, in the center of the Shattered City, where it had been buried since the Destruction. Isn't that right, *Fen*?"

Let him correct her. Let him speak his true name. Ru knew she was right. *Wrenched*. He had said it had been wrenched from his body. It was some part of him, an extension of his being...

The artifact, Taryel, Festra, Fen... one and the same.

"Exactly as she says," said Fen, unmoved. "The artifact was discovered in the earth, resurrected after centuries lying dormant. I hadn't known it was there, that it even existed. I couldn't have guessed what it was, except that for some reason my mortal form persisted... I thought it was a remnant of my soul, perhaps..." he trailed off, turning away to stare at the kneeling figure in the square.

His mortal form.

He'd given himself away. The one question that had lingered in her mind, one doubt — Taryel was centuries old, a figment of legend. Fen appeared to be young. But Fen had no home to go to, much of his life a mystery to Ru. His accent was strange, impossible to place. Fen's wisdom was that of a long-lived man, his eyes far older than his supposed twenty-six years.

"I know it's you," she said. Her words cut through the wailing wind, piercing their target.

Fen spun, eyes locked with hers. The truth was written on his face so plainly that her knees weakened, and she had to fight to stay standing. A smile tugged at the edge of his lovely mouth as if daring her to say it.

"You're Taryel." She spoke louder this time, the truth falling into place as heavily as a crumbling castle wall.

Archie and Gwyneth stared at Ru and Fen, their expressions warped in twin horror.

"He what?" Archie said at last.

"Don't be insane," said Gwyneth in an accusatory tone, as if Ru was making some kind of sick joke.

"She's perfectly sane," said Fen, thumbing the artifact with a familiarity that made Ru shiver. "You were right, Ru. Fen Verrill isn't my name. I suppose you understand why I would change it." Then he snapped a finger, and with it, the spectral Taryel vanished, though the projection of the city remained.

"The artifact kept you young," said Ru, shaking — with cold or fear, she couldn't tell. "But I can't seem to make up my mind about what it is. Your soul? Or simply a stone that you've cursed with your magic, tethered to your life in some ungodly way?"

He laughed, and the sound was utterly mirthless, devoid of joy. "Ungodly? On the contrary, the gods have everything to do with it. One god in particular." He moved toward her then, closing the distance in a few long-legged strides. "I'm over five hundred years old," he murmured, the wind carrying his voice away across the ghostly city as he spoke. "The artifact's doing, as you guessed." His face softened. "No... as you meticulously calculated, using every piece of evidence to come to a statistically accurate conclusion."

She stared icily up at him, hating him as much as she was drowning in relief just to be near him again. The way he spoke should have sounded like mockery, if his words had not been laced with an unending sadness.

She pushed windswept hair from her eyes, refusing to stand down, to cower. "Tell me what the artifact is."

He held it up to the moonlight and they gazed at it together, that strange misshapen stone. They had been through so much, the three of them.

Fen sighed, and his shoulders slumped almost imperceptibly. "It took me a while to understand. Far longer than it took you. Ever since that day, the day I became the Destroyer..." His mouth curved bitterly as he spoke the name. "I survived it. Just like you, I woke up blind, naked, in the center of a desolate crater. Even this rotten thing, beating away." His hand pressed to his chest, his heart. "But from that day onward, I simply didn't age. I never died. There was no explanation, no reason for it. I just... persisted, endlessly. It was a punishment. And all the while, I felt distinctly empty, as if something in me was missing, like something had been stolen from me in the moment of my cursed rebirth."

"It's more than you deserve," said Ru, but her resolve had faltered. *Just like you, I woke up...* she pulled the collar of her coat up, her fingers shaking as she fastened it beneath her chin, blocking out some of the wind.

He turned to fix his dark gaze on her, those gray eyes that had once been so dear to her. "It is far more than I deserve," he said. "But what punishment would be adequate for the Destroyer? What penance would you place upon me?"

She faltered. What penance would she place upon him, and, by extension, on herself? She had ended lives here, at this very spot. Living, breathing souls whose bright lights should not have been extinguished that day. The memory alone had been a punishment for Ru, an unending horror that laced her thoughts, sleeping and waking. But had it been enough?

Would it ever be enough?

Just like you.

"Whatever punishment you deserve," she said finally, "is the same that should fall on me."

Fen's expression softened, and at that moment he looked almost like himself again. But Fen didn't exist. He was Taryel, madman, Destroyer.

"I am your punishment," he murmured. "In learning who I am, you've met yourself. And I ask you — why were we not destroyed along with the souls we cut down? Why should *we* have survived when the laws of nature and morality would have sent me, sent you, to an eternity in the fiery abyss? Your actions were unplanned, a mistake, and yet... should that make a difference?" Once again that immortal sheen fell over his eyes, a wall between them. "In my loneliest hours," he said, "I often thought, *this* is hell. I've been here all along."

Hot tears grazed down Ru's cheeks, almost burning her frozen skin as they fell. He spoke of her as if she were like him, a monster, a murderer. She wanted to fight it, to believe that she was different. To remind him that her destruction had been a mistake, the artifact had called to her. *His* artifact had compelled her.

But she knew in her heart that it didn't matter. The intent was irrelevant — they were the same.

As if reading her mind, he moved toward her, gaze sharp. He lifted a hand as if to touch her face, then let it drop. Fen would have dried her tears, would have embraced her. But he was Taryel now, distant and centuries-old, no longer hiding behind a mortal mask. "You hate me. I understand that. Let me at least solve this mystery for you, Ru. The artifact is my heart. My fossilized, blackened, ruined heart."

His heart.

And while science could do nothing to explain it, while logic and physics held no sway over this revelation — a heart did beat in Fen's chest, blood and muscle — yet there in his hand, shining smooth and black, was Taryel's heart.

"The connection between us," she breathed, clenching her hands at her sides to keep from reaching for the stone. She looked up at Fen, forcing herself to wrench her gaze from the artifact. "Why does the artifact speak to me? What bond do we share?"

He sighed, his gaze locked on Ru, searching. "That, I don't know. We're connected, you and I. Both of us bound to the artifact, my wretched heart. But why — I can't guess. I've been looking for answers, reading every book I could find in the Tower... I'm still in the dark."

"It called me here," she said, her voice almost a whisper, but Fen seemed to hear.

"The stone?"

She nodded. "Before I arrived with the riders, all those weeks ago. I felt it. It wanted me. It *asked* me to touch it."

His face cleared and Fen returned, warmth springing up in those grey eyes. "I felt you, too. *You* called me here. I had no prior knowledge of the dig, only... a feeling. A knowing that I needed to come. And when I saw you there, naked and alone, I knew it was you who had called me."

"Ru?" Gwyneth's voice was muffled, wavering in the icy wind, a question — *are you all right? Do you need us to intervene?*

It was as if Gwyneth's voice snapped Ru back to reality. She glanced over her shoulder at Gwyneth and Archie and shook her head slightly. Turning back to Fen she was struck by a deep chill, so bone-cold that she moved instinctually toward him, toward his body heat.

She shivered violently as a gust of wind rushed past, and Fen swept her toward him with his free hand, holding her close, steadying, just as he had done so many times before. As if it were instinct, a thoughtless gesture of protection.

Ru allowed herself for one brief moment to succumb to him. Fen, who didn't exist. Fen, a man who had left her at the Tower... and had never come back. She closed her eyes against the pain of loss that washed through her, cutting at her like minuscule shards of glass inside her heart.

She melted against him, repeating his name, pressing her face into his shirt. A horrible, irrational desire swept over her. She felt as if her own ribs had been wrenched open to reveal a beating organ, her vulnerability, her own heart, too flimsy in its flesh and blood.

Her breaths and blood quickened, her skin heating as Fen's arms enveloped her.

And somehow, helplessly, she felt that he was the only one who could knit her sinews back together. As if she wasn't whole without him, as if her heart would forever bleed from the cuts he'd inflicted.

At that same moment, it became clear to Ru that these feelings, this yearning, was of her heart's own making. The artifact's pull, its incessant tug against her emotions, had nothing to do with it. What she shared with Fen now was honest, pure, and sharp.

Lifting her chin, she caught his dark gaze, just briefly enough to see her own desire reflected in his eyes. Standing up on her toes, curling cold fingers in his coat, she kissed him. He responded slowly, gently. Almost sweetly.

So she allowed herself to give in, just for a moment. She allowed the need for Fen to overcome all else... just for a moment.

"Ru," he breathed, his words like a prayer. "I'm yours. From the moment I felt you, your bright soul calling to me, I was yours. My ruined heart is yours."

It was almost too easy then, their bodies pressed together like one, as he lowered his head to kiss her, his breath on her skin... it was so easy to slip the artifact from his grasp.

And in that breathless instant, before he collected

himself enough to react, Ru turned and tossed the artifact across the square. By some miracle Gwyneth saw it coming and caught it, shoving the stone inside her jacket with a look of sheer terror.

"Go!" Ru shouted at Gwyneth, pushing Fen away with both arms. He stumbled, never looking away from her.

It didn't matter, in the end, whether he had meant to destroy the city, whether he'd been coerced, whether it was an accident. Ru didn't need to ask, just as he hadn't explained. And Ru... had she meant to destroy Lady Maryn and all those researchers that day? The intent was irrelevant.

They were the same, she and Fen. She and Taryel.

But in one way, they still differed. Ru knew that she would fight the fate that had befallen her. She would use the artifact for something true and good, or she would destroy it. She had no way of knowing what Fen would do, whether he had become warped by the centuries, what uses he might have for his own blackened heart.

He had clearly lost himself, but Ru knew exactly who she was. The artifact would remain with her.

"It seems we've arrived in just the nick of time," a clear voice rang out across the spectral square.

The sound cut through Ru's insides like a blade, just as fear boiled up in her chest, her heart skipping a beat. The timbre of it was so clear, so politely bright and well-formed, that it was impossible to misplace the speaker.

She turned and saw him across the spectral square, mounted on a white horse and flanked by half a dozen figures in billowing robes.

Lord D'Luc smiled.

CHAPTER 41

Frigid wind caught the company's flowing white robes, and in the moonlight they seemed to belong with the ghostly city, to have emerged directly from it like spirits.

"I'll take that, please," said Lord D'Luc, flashing his teeth at Gwyneth across the square. His hair moved in the wind as if underwater, wreathing his face in ethereal strands.

"Take what?" Gwyneth's voice shook. She and Archie held hands, their own overcoats flapping around their legs, feet planted firmly in joint defiance.

Lord D'Luc tutted as if addressing a wayward child. "The artifact, dear girl. Bring it here."

Gwyneth didn't move.

Archie pulled her close and hissed something in her ear, but his words were carried away on the wind. As Ru watched the pair square their shoulders, fixing Lord D'Luc and his company with challenging stares, a swell of affection for her friends rose up in her. They were braver than she was, stronger.

"The artifact isn't what you hope it is," said Fen, turning to Lord D'Luc and addressing him with a resigned air. As if he had expected the man's arrival all along. Any remaining humanity, any mortality, had fled from Fen's eyes. He looked almost like that looping specter of himself, skin pale in the moonlight.

"Ah, so the wandering historian has graced us once again with his presence," sneered Lord D'Luc. "Please, enlighten us."

Fen stared back in response, silent.

Ru realized now that Lord D'Luc hadn't seen the projection of Taryel. He'd arrived too late to draw the connection.

"Very well," Lord D'Luc said, his tone careless as he waved a hand. "Ranto, Nell, ensure that these delicate academics don't wander off into danger. Inda, bring me the artifact." The words rang out clear and cold.

Three of the robed riders dismounted in tandem, like three heads of a mythical serpent. They strode toward Gwyneth, Archie, and Ru, white cloaks flapping behind them.

The Children weren't met with much resistance. The cold had taken its toll, draining Ru and her friends, and leaving them weak and confused. Ru wouldn't have known where to go even if she had wanted to run, to make a mad dash for freedom. When Nell's steely fingers gripped her arms, holding her in place, Ru simply let it happen. She watched helplessly as Inda held Gwyneth tightly with one hand, fishing inside her jacket with the other. A moment later, Inda removed the artifact, wrapping it swiftly in a cloth she produced from inside her cloak.

Ru wanted nothing more than to seek the comfort of the artifact, to press a thought to the thread that stretched between them, but she didn't dare. She knew what it was now, how dangerous it was, and she knew why Lord D'Luc wanted it so badly for himself.

Taryel's heart, parted from his body in the precise moment of the Destruction, had now become a distillation of what Ru and Fen… Ru and Taryel embodied: cataclysmic power. It was a weapon.

Cleansing fire.

Inda swept back to Lord D'Luc, handing him the bundled artifact. He took it, never removing his sapphire-hard gaze from Ru's.

"How did you know we were here?" Ru said finally,

her voice woefully small in that great dark city, in the face of the whipping wind.

Lord D'Luc put on a pitying look as if talking down to a child. "We tracked you, of course. It was exceedingly easy; you may as well have left a trail of breadcrumbs in your wake. Come now, let's return to the Cornelian Tower where it's safe and warm; away from this accursed place. I dare not think what madness drove you here." He held a hand out to Ru, an offer of peace. "You may ride with me, Miss Delara, if you wish."

She turned to Fen on instinct. Nell's unrelenting fingers bit into her arms painfully, even through her overcoat.

"Fen?" she said, a plea, a prayer.

"Ru," he said, and she thought she saw the hint of a smile tug at the corner of his pale lips. Then he closed his eyes for a breath, and the image of the city of Ordellun-by-the-Sea, its ghostly towers and squares, wavered and vanished, curling into the night like smoke until nothing was left but the barren waste. Black earth spread out on all sides, reaching onward for miles.

In the heartbeat of confusion that erupted as they were plunged into the darkness of that empty crater, Fen lifted a hand, tracing shapes in the air.

In the next moment, he was gone.

A sphere of crackling black lightning, of charged energy, and Ru's breaking heart were the only evidence that he had been there at all.

"Interesting," said Lord D'Luc, his voice ringing hollow in the vastness. And Ru heard something else in his voice, something coiling serpentine, something greedy.

~

MIDDAY SUN BEAT down on Ru's bare head. The sound of low voices and chatter surrounded her. A hot wind picked up, rustling the eaves of the forest as they rode toward it, the road becoming narrower and shaded. Her dark hair hung loose, lank around her shoulders. She was sweating now, too hot, body aching. She hadn't bothered to remove her coat since the night before, since Fen had gone.

Archie and Gwyn were quiet, their horses trailing after Ru's, all three of them flanked on every side by the Children. As if they would bolt at any moment, as if they had anywhere to go. It was an insult, an affront. Ru noted each movement of the Children, each stern command, each warning — *stay near us. Don't wander.*

But these sensations were a distant hum, a distraction.

She knew now what she had to do.

"Chin up," Lord D'Luc said, slowing his horse's pace until he was alongside Ru. His profile was chiseled as if carved from marble, his golden hair pulled back and fastened at his nape. Bejeweled hands gripped his reins. He flashed a grin, and Ru wondered how she had ever thought him handsome or charming.

"We have so much to discuss," Lord D'Luc continued, undeterred by Ru's silence. They passed into the forest then, under shade at last. The smell of moss and earth, a cool stillness, filled Ru's senses. " We have so many experiments to try. So many questions to answer. I believe we will take our studies in an entirely new direction, an exciting and progressive one. You will be celebrated, Miss Delara. A pinnacle of discovery, an icon in your own time. At last, magic will find its place in the lexicon of science."

"Magic," she echoed, her voice rough from disuse and exhaustion. "Is that why you poisoned the professors? Pushed me to the point of breaking? Why you worship Festra? Don't condescend to me, Hugon." She spat the name.

His blue eyes flashed, his grin predatory. "Poison? You think me so vulgar as to use poison? Though I suppose... not long ago, it might have crossed my mind." He turned away from Ru, watching the road ahead, his expression thoughtful. "Subterfuge, betrayal. Useful tools when wielded deftly. But I learned my lesson when the attack on your carriage failed. I learned how clumsy I'd been. I needed a guiding hand, a keener mind."

She felt the blood drain from her face as cold realization seeped in. Lord D'Luc had proven himself to be coercive, power-hungry, perhaps even mad, but this... Ru grasped for more meaning in his words, for a clear answer. Whose hand was guiding the Children, if not his?

He softened his expression and shook his head, smiling. A mask of congeniality. "You do like to keep me on my toes, Miss Delara. I relish it. But if you work with me, if you fight that stubborn impulse of yours, we could accomplish so much."

Ru glanced back and saw that the rest of the party had slowed, giving Lord D'Luc space to speak to her alone. Gwyneth and Archie glared. They would have ridden to support her, but the Children held them back. Ru imagined leaping from the saddle, rolling, dashing into the forest. Fleeing this monster, freeing herself. But she couldn't leave her friends. Or Taryel's heart.

"And what of Fen?" she asked, the words slipping out thoughtlessly before she could stop them. She had been turning the question over and over in her mind until it had become a sickness, invading her nerves, making her stomach churn. Because in Lord D'Luc's eyes she had seen that he knew, he had understood in an instant that Fen wielded magic. She was desperate to know how he would inevitably twist that knowledge to serve himself.

Hugon laughed, a lovely empty sound. "What of Fen," he said. "An interesting question. One I'd put to you. What *of* him? Will he come for you?"

"I don't know."

It was an honest answer, but a painful one. Ru stared out at the forest, the steadying green of life, of earth, and the passage of seasons. Sunlight cut through the shadows here and there, illuminating gold-flecked motes in the air. A soft wind rustled through the trees, the ferns.

I don't know.

Lord D'Luc shrugged, his mouth curled in a self-satisfied smile. "We'll see," he said.

But his words passed over Ru like vapor, disappearing into nothing as quickly as they came. She had no use for Lord D'Luc, his goals and his plans. He sought power, Festra's cleansing fire. And she now knew that he would stop at nothing to get what he sought.

Ru would follow him back to the Cornelian Tower. She would study the artifact in whatever way he liked, pretending as she always had; all the while she would be planning, learning, seeking an escape, or a way to fight back. It didn't matter how, or when — all that mattered was that his plans, his twisted ambitions, came to nothing.

Because no matter how he pushed her, no matter the demands he made on her body and mind, Ru promised herself one thing above all else: Lord D'Luc would not gain control of the artifact. She would not let him. Because it had called to her, and she had answered.

Taryel's heart belonged to her.

And she was Ruellian Delara, Destroyer.

ACKNOWLEDGMENTS

Rose! First the dedication, and now top billing in the acknowledgments? Obviously. You are the perfect friend and stand-in sister. Thank you for encouraging my delusion when I was convinced I'd be a 14-year-old prodigy author (in a genuine way, not a humoring-me way). You were my first reader, and everything I write is really for you.

Piper, you know what you did. You went and wrote a successful indie book and made me want to do it too. Our friendship is a constant cycle of love and inspiration, and I'm so glad you slid into my DMs that one time.

To my beautiful friends and family who were subjected to the shitty early drafts (of this and other books) with the intention that you would "encourage me to finish the draft by saying nice things about it" — Mom, Megan, and Nikki, thank you for putting up with me.

Brooke, you have been an unending source of joy, support, and encouragement on this journey. Thank you for your lengthy texts during my breakdowns, but mostly for joining me in Gideon Nav horny jail.

Sydney, my first BookTok friend and the first to read *Destroyer*, thank you for erroneously claiming that it will be big on BookTok. This is exactly the kind of delusion I need in my life.

Matt Thorne, you were my biggest and most credible cheerleader when I needed it most, aka grad school. You made me feel like I could actually, like for real, be an author one day.

Mom and Dad (wait, Mom gets two mentions??), thank you for raising me in an idyllic household of unconditional love and support. Thank you also for the

Nerd Gene. Without it, I would have a career and a 401k instead of this book I wrote.

Dad… fine, you get a second mention too. Thank you for sharing your love of Middle Earth, Narnia, a galaxy far far away, and so many other forms of escapism with me. You are the reason that I am insufferable.

To my wonderful little bubble of BookTok, a haven of mutual support in the midst of a very weird community, y'all are actually the best. You know who you are.

Penultimately here but not in my heart, thank *fuck* for my editor Rachel Wharton. I gave her what amounted to a messy wadded-up piece of napkin with smeared words all over it, and she handed it back to me as a book. That's a form of magic. Rachel, you understood everything about *Destroyer* from the plot to the characters to what words I meant to use (instead of other shittier words). You took the donuts from me but you are forgiven, because the cinnamon roll lives on.

Thank you, finally, to the one person who has suffered the most on this journey, the man who cooked for me and put up with all of my crying and designed the cover of this thing (!!!). I love you, Adam. I'm so sorry that you're about to go through all of this again with book two.

ABOUT THE AUTHOR

Meg Smitherman writes romantic stories about magic and world-ending stakes. Based in Los Angeles, she shares her life with a chihuahua, a cat, and a handsome Englishman.

Follow her journey on megsmitherman.com or TikTok (@megsmitherman)

Milton Keynes UK
Ingram Content Group UK Ltd.
UKHW011306290524
443441UK00025B/200